DARK VOYAGE

DARK VOYAGE

Alan Furst

THORNDIKE
WINDSOR
PARAGON

This Large Print edition is published by Thorndike Press®, Waterville, Maine USA and by BBC Audiobooks, Ltd, Bath, England.

Published in 2004 in the U.S. by arrangement with Random House, Inc.

Published in 2005 in the U.K. by arrangement with The Orion Publishing Group Ltd.

U.S. Hardcover 0-7862-6988-X (Core)
U.K. Hardcover 1-4056-1059-X (Windsor Large Print)
U.K. Softcover 1-4056-2048-X (Paragon Large Print)

Copyright © 2004 by Alan Furst
Map copyright © 2004 by David Lindroth
Additional copyright information on page 456.

The text of this Large Print edition is unabridged.
Other aspects of the book may vary from the original edition.

Set in 16 pt. Plantin by Liana M. Walker.

Printed in the United States on permanent paper.

British Library Cataloguing-in-Publication Data available

Library of Congress Cataloging-in-Publication Data
Furst, Alan.
    Dark voyage : a novel / Alan Furst.
        p. cm.
    ISBN 0-7862-6988-X (lg. print : hc : alk. paper)
    1. World War, 1939–1945 — Secret service — Fiction.
    2. World War, 1939–1945 — Sweden — Fiction.
    3. Merchant mariners — Fiction. 4. Dutch — Sweden —
    Fiction. 5. Tramp shipping — Fiction. 6. Ship captains —
    Fiction. 7. Cargo ships — Fiction. 8. Refugees — Fiction.
    9. Sweden — Fiction. 10. Large type books. I. Title.
    PS3556.U76D373 2004b
    813'.54—dc22   2004054143

DARK VOYAGE

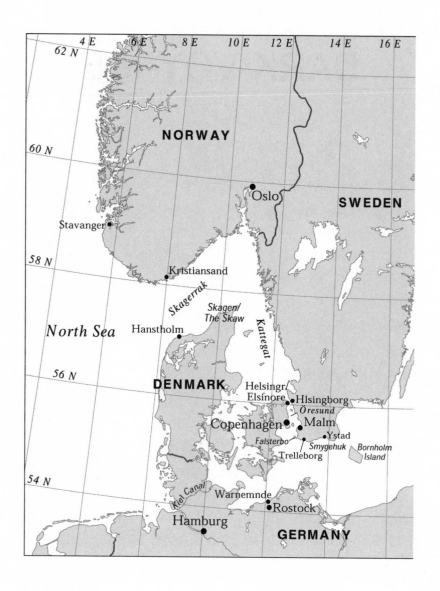

The Baltic
June, 1941

In the first nineteen months of European war, from September, 1939, to March of 1941, the island nation of Britain and her allies lost, to U-boat, air, and sea attack, to mines and maritime disaster, one thousand, five hundred and ninety-six merchant vessels.

It was the job of the Intelligence Division of Royal Navy to stop it, and so, on the last day of April, 1941 . . .

UNDER SPANISH FLAG

In the port of Tangier, on the last day of April, 1941, the fall of the Mediterranean evening was, as always, subtle and slow. Broken cloud, the color of dark fire in the last of the sunset, drifted over the hills above the port, and streetlamps lit the quay that lined the waterfront. A white city, and steep; alleys, souks, and cafés, their patrons gathering for love and business as the light faded away. Out in the harbor, a Spanish destroyer, the *Almirante Cruz*, stood at anchor among the merchant steamers, hulls streaked with rust, angular deck cranes hard silhouettes in the dusk.

On board the tramp freighter *Noordendam*, of the Netherlands Hyperion Line, the radio room was like an oven and the Egyptian radio officer, known as Mr.

Ali, wore only a sleeveless undershirt and baggy silk underdrawers. He sat tilted back in his swivel chair, smoking a cigarette in an ivory holder and reading a slim, filthy novel in beautifully marbled covers. From time to time, he would remove his gold spectacles and wipe his face with a cloth, but he hardly noticed. He was used to the heat, the effect of a full day's sun on the ship's steel plate, and, come to that, used to these ports, hellholes always, Aden or Batavia, Shanghai or Tangier, and he was much absorbed in the noisy pleasures of the people in his novel. On the wireless telegraph before him, a gray wall of switches and dials, the ether crackled with static, his duty watch had less than an hour to run, and he was at peace with the world.

Then, from the static, a signal. On the BAMS frequency — Broadcasting for Allied Merchant Ships — and, he thought, far out at sea. He set the book face down on the work shelf below the radio, put on the headphones, and, with delicate thumb and forefinger, adjusted the dial for the strongest reception.

Q, Q, Q, Q.

For this message he didn't need the BAMS codebook — not since May of 1940 he didn't. It meant *I am being attacked by*

12

an enemy ship and he'd heard it all too often. Here it came again, the operator fast and heavy on the key. And again, and again. *Poor man,* he thought. His fellow radio operator on some battered old merchantman, tapping out his final message, his ship confronted by a surfaced submarine or an E-boat raider, the shot already across her bows or her engine room torn apart by a torpedo.

What Mr. Ali could do, he did. Opened the radio logbook, noted the date and the time, and recorded the anonymous cry for help. DeHaan, captain of the *Noordendam,* would see it when he put the ship to bed for the night — he never failed to check the logbook before going to his cabin. If they had been at sea, Mr. Ali would have notified the captain immediately but now, in port, there was no point. Nothing they could do, nothing anyone could do. It was a big ocean, British sea power concentrated on the convoy routes, there was nobody to challenge the enemy or pick up survivors. The ship would die alone.

The signal went on for a time, fifty seconds by the clock on the radio array, and likely went on longer still, perhaps sending the name of the ship and its coordinates, but the transmission disappeared, lost in the rising and falling howl of a jammed frequency. *Bastards.* Mr. Ali watched the clock; five minutes, six, until the jamming stopped, replaced by empty air. He was taking the headphones off when the signal returned. Once only, and weaker now, the ship's electrical system was almost gone. *Q, Q, Q, Q,* then silence.

DeHaan, at that moment, was ashore — had just left the gangway of the harbor launch and approached a battle-scarred Citroën parked on the pier, TAXI TARZAN painted on its door, its Moorish driver stretched out in the back, hands clasped beneath his head, for his evening nap. DeHaan looked at his watch and decided to walk. The rue Raisuli was supposedly just beyond the Bab el Marsa, Gate of the Port, which he could see in the distance. He had been invited — *ordered,* he thought, that was the honest word — to a dinner given by a man called Hoek. Other than the fact that such things never happened, a perfectly normal request, so, one better go. Put on the shore uniform — double-breasted navy blazer over a soft gray shirt and dark wool trousers, and the tie, blue with a silver spaniel — and go.

He walked purposefully along the quay,

thanking his stars as he passed a Norwegian tanker berthed at the pier and caught the rich aroma of aviation fuel. *Of all the ways he didn't want to die.* DeHaan was tall, seemed tall, and lean, with strength in the arms and shoulders. Regular features: a North Sea face, gray eyes, sometimes cold, sometimes warm, with seafarer's lines webbed at the corners, and rough, fair hair, almost brown, its first gray — he'd just turned forty-one — visible in sunlight. A certain lift to this face; pride, maybe, of profession not position — good as any man, better than none. Thin lips, not far from a smile, that Dutch set of the mouth which found the world a far more eccentric, and finally amusing, place than its German versions to the east. He had big hands, appreciated by women, who'd told him about it. Surprise to DeHaan, that idea, but not unwelcome.

Should he have worn his uniform? The Hyperion Line had one, plain and blue, for their captains, traditional on the first day of a voyage and never seen again, but DeHaan disliked the thing. It wasn't, to him, a real uniform, and a real uniform was what he'd wanted. In May of 1940, when the conquering Germans had stripped out the filing cabinets of the Royal

Dutch Navy administration building in The Hague, they'd surely found, and just as surely refiled for their own purposes, the 1938 application of one *DeHaan, Eric Mathias,* virtually begging for a commission, and service on a destroyer, or a torpedo boat, or anything, really, that shot.

He walked past the railway station and, a few minutes later, entered the narrow streets behind the Bab el Marsa gate — another world. *Fragrant, the Maghreb.* Stronger than he remembered; twenty-five years at sea, he thought, and too many ports. Fresh orange peel on the cobbled street, burning charcoal and — grilled kidney? He rather thought it was, nothing else quite smelled like that. Ancient drains, cumin, incense. And hashish, nothing else quite smelled like *that.* A scent encountered now and again aboard the *Noordendam,* but one mostly ignored it, as long as the men weren't on watch. He was himself, as it happened, not entirely innocent of such things, the stuff had been one of what Arlette called *her vile little pleasures.* One of many. They'd used it one night in her room in the rue Lamartine, balancing tiny morsels on a burning cigarette end in an ashtray and sucking up the smoke through a tightly rolled hundred-drachma note he'd found in his pocket. Then they'd made ferocious and wildly chaotic — *Ah, this! No, this! But what about this?* — love, after which he'd fallen dead asleep for ten hours then woke to make Arlette a colossal Dutch pancake swimming in butter.

In the rue Raisuli, Arab music from a dozen radios, and two Spanish Guardia, in their Napoleonic leather hats, strolling along in a way that told the world they owned the street. Which, officially, they did. Tangier had been since 1906 an International Zone, a free port trading in currency, boys, and espionage. Now Spain had taken control of the city, incorporated into Spanish Morocco, which meant that Casablanca was French, ruled from Vichy, and Tangier Spanish, and neutral, and governed by Madrid. But DeHaan and everybody else knew better. It was, like Paris, one of those cities emphatically owned by the people who lived in it. And how, DeHaan wondered, did Mijnheer Hoek fit into all this? Trader? Emigré? Decadent? All three? Number 18 in the rue Raisuli turned out to be a restaurant, Al Mounia, but not the sort of restaurant where important people gave private dinners.

DeHaan parted the bead curtain, stepped inside, and stood there for a moment, looking lost. *This can't be right,* he thought. Tile floor, bare wooden tables, a few customers, more than one reading a newspaper with dinner. Then a man he took to be the proprietor came gliding up to him, DeHaan said, "Monsieur Hoek?" and that turned out to be the magic phrase. The man clapped his hands twice and a waiter took DeHaan through the restaurant and out the back, into a courtyard bounded by tenements where life went on at full pitch; six stories of white laundry hung on lines strung across the sky, six stories of families eating dinner by open windows. From there, DeHaan was led through a damp tunnel into a second courtyard, an unlit, silent courtyard, then down an alley to a heavy, elaborately carved door. The waiter knocked and went on his way as a voice from within called out, *"Entrez."*

Inside, a small, square room with no windows and, except for a ceiling painted as the night sky — blue background, gold dots for stars, a silver sickle moon on the horizon — there was only fabric. Carpets covered the walls and the floor, a circle of hassocks was gathered around a low table with a brass tray that occupied most of its surface. As DeHaan entered, a man seated in a wheelchair — made entirely of wood except for rubber tires on the spoked wheels — extended his hand and said, "Captain DeHaan, welcome, thank you for coming, I am Marius Hoek." Hoek had a powerful grip. In his fifties, he was pale as a ghost, with sheared fair hair and eyeglasses that went opaque, catching the light of a lamp in the corner, as he looked up at DeHaan.

Rising from their hassocks to greet him, the other dinner guests: a woman in a chalk-stripe suit and a dark shirt, a man in the uniform of a Dutch naval officer, and Wim Terhouven, owner of the Netherlands Hyperion Line — his employer. DeHaan turned to Terhouven, as though for explanation, and found him much amused, all sly grin, at the prospect of the famously composed Captain DeHaan, who couldn't imagine what the hell was going on and showed it. "Hello, Eric," Terhouven said, taking DeHaan's hand in his. "The bad penny always turns up, eh?" He patted DeHaan on the shoulder, *don't worry, m'boy,* and said, "May I present Juffrouw, ah, Wilhelm?"

Formally, DeHaan shook her hand. "Just Wilhelm will do," she said. "Everybody calls me that." She wore no makeup, had fine, delicate features, was about thirty-five years old, he guessed, with thick, honey-gold hair cut very short and parted on the side.

"And," Terhouven said, "this is Commander Hendryk Leiden."

Leiden was broad and bulky, bald halfway back, with a drinker's purplish nose, a sailor's wind-chapped complexion, and a full beard. "Good to meet you, Captain," he said.

"Come sit down," Terhouven said. "Enjoy the walk over here?"

DeHaan nodded. "It's the same restaurant?"

"The private room — who says it has to be upstairs?" He laughed. "And, on the way, a taste of the real Tangier, assassins behind every door."

"Well, that or couscous."

Wilhelm liked the joke. "It's good, Al Mounia, a local favorite."

DeHaan lowered himself onto a hassock as Terhouven poured him a glass of gin from an old-fashioned ceramic jug. "Classic stuff," he said.

"They sell this in Tangier?"

Terhouven snorted. He had a devil's beard and the eyes to go with it. "Not this they don't. This came across on a trawler in May of '40 and flew with me all the way from London, just for your party. Real Geneva, made in Schiedam." He tapped the label, hand-lettered and fired into the glazed surface.

"My friends," Leiden said, "with your permission." He stood, glass held high, and the others, except for Hoek, followed his example. Leiden paused for a long moment, then said, *"De Nederland."* In one voice, they echoed his words, and DeHaan saw that Hoek, knuckles white where his hand gripped the arm of the chair, had raised himself off the seat to honor the toast. They drank next *to victory,* Hoek's offering, and, from Wilhelm, *success in new ventures,* as Terhouven caught DeHaan's eye and gave him a conspiratorial flick of the eyebrows. Then it was up to DeHaan, who'd been desperate for the right words from the moment Leiden lifted his glass. Finally, as the others turned to him in expectation, he said, quietly, "Well then, to absent friends." This was conventional and wellworn but, on that night, with those friends in a Europe held by barbed wire and searchlights, it came back to life.

Terhouven said, "Amen to that," and began to refill the glasses. When he was done he said, "I propose we drink to Captain Eric DeHaan, our guest of honor, who I know you will come to appreciate as I have." DeHaan lowered his eyes, and was more than grateful when the toast had been drunk and the group returned to conversation.

Terhouven told the story of his flight from London, on a Sunderland flying boat, his fellow passengers mostly men with briefcases who were rather pointedly disinclined to make conversation. A nighttime journey, hours of it, "just waiting for the *Luftwaffe*." But then, "the most beautiful dawn sky, somewhere off the coast of Spain, the sea turning blue beneath us."

Hoek glanced at his watch. "Dinner should appear any moment now," he said. "I took the liberty of ordering — I hope you don't mind, it's better if you give them time." A good idea, it seemed, they were happy enough to wait, the table talk wandering here and there. You had to be Dutch, DeHaan thought, to know that the gin was at work. Not much to be seen on the exterior, everyone calm and thoughtful, attentive, in no hurry to take the floor. They were, after all, strangers, for the most part, together for an evening in a foreign city, who shared little more than citizenship in a conquered nation, and its corollary, a certain quiet anger common to those who cannot go home.

"Years since I've been back," Hoek said to Terhouven. "Came out here in, oh, 1927. Looking for opportunity." An unvoiced *naturally* lingered at the end of his sentence — Holland was a trading nation which had, for centuries, used the whole world as its office, so commerce in foreign climes was something of a national commonplace. "And I found a way to buy a small brokerage, in ores and minerals, then built it up over the years. They mine lead and iron, in the south, and there's graphite, cobalt, antimony, asbestos. That's in addition to the phosphates, of course. That pays the rent."

DeHaan knew about the phosphates, Morocco's main export. The *Noordendam*, as it happened, was scheduled to call at Safi, the port serving Marrakesh on the Atlantic coast, to take on a bulk cargo from the Khourigba mines. So, DeHaan thought, it all made sense, didn't it — his boss flying down from exile in London, taking his life in his hands, to bring a jug of Dutch gin to celebrate the loading of one of his freighters. *Well, all will, in time, be explained.* In fact, he had a pretty good idea what was going on, he was simply anxious to hear the details.

"So, your family's here, with you," Terhouven said.

"Oh yes," Hoek said. "Good-size family."

DeHaan thought he saw a flicker of amusement in Wilhelm's eyes, an expression on her face he could only describe as *not smiling*.

Terhouven, making conversation, asked her how long she'd been in Tangier.

"Mmm, not so long, a few years maybe, if you add it all up. I was in Paris, after the war, Juan-les-Pins in the summers, then here, then back to Paris, Istanbul for a while, then back here."

"A restless soul." Terhouven knew her type.

She shrugged. "A change of light. And people, I suppose."

"You're an artist," Terhouven said, it wasn't exactly an accusation.

"After a fashion."

"After nothing," Hoek said firmly. "And nobody. She's shown in Paris and New York, though she won't tell you that."

"In oils?" DeHaan said, meaning *not oils, of course*.

"No. Gouache, principally, though lately I'm back to charcoal pencil." She took a

24

cigarette from a tortoiseshell case with Bacchus and girlfriend on the lid, tapped it twice, and lit it with a steel lighter. "Back to life drawing." She shook her head and smiled ruefully that such an odd thing should be so.

At the door, a firm knock, and three waiters with trays.

The dinner was served in traditional dishes set out on the low table. Bowls of aromatic yellow soup, soft bread still hot from the oven, a grandiose *pastilla* — minced pigeon breast and almonds in pastry leaves, a platter of stewed lamb and vegetables. Once the dishes were set down, glasses packed with crushed mint leaves were filled with boiling water, poured ritually by the chief waiter, who raised and lowered the spout of a silver flagon as the stream curved into the glass. When he was done, the waiter said, "Shall we remain to serve you?"

"Thank you," Hoek said, "but I think we'll manage by ourselves."

This was in French, which DeHaan understood, some of the time, and also spoke, some of the time, and in his own particular way — "the French of a beast," according to Arlette. He had good German and English, like almost everyone in Holland, and, a year earlier, after the invasion, he had added to his forty-book library a Russian grammar. He had no professional, or political, reason for this, it was more akin to chess, or crossword puzzles, a way to occupy the mind in the long hours off-watch, when he needed to distract himself from the captain's eternal obsession: every beat of the engine, every tremor and creak of the ship, his ship, at sea. Thus he found an absorbing if difficult pastime, though in addition to studying the grammar he'd more than once fallen asleep on it, and showered it with ashes, seawater, coffee, and cocoa, but, a Russian book, it endured, and survived.

Terhouven, seated next to him, said, "How was Paramaribo?" He tore himself a length of bread, took a piece of lamb from the platter, studied it, then swished it through the sauce and put it on the bread.

"It's the rainy season — a steambath when it stops." They'd taken a cargo of greenheart and mora wood, used for wharves and docks, from Dutch Guiana up to the Spanish port of La Coruña, then sailed in ballast — mostly water but some scrap iron — for Tangier.

"Lose anybody?"

"Only one, an oiler. A Finn, or so his

book said. Good oiler, but a terrible drunk. Hit people — he was pretty good at that too. I tried to buy him out of jail, but they wouldn't do it."

"In *Paramaribo?* They wouldn't take a bribe?"

"He hit a pimp, a barman, a bouncer, a cop, and a jailer."

"Christ!" A moment later, Terhouven smiled. "In that order?"

DeHaan nodded.

Terhouven finished his lamb and bread, wiped his mouth, then made a face. "Too dumb to live, some people. You replace him?"

"Couldn't be done. So, as of this evening, we're at forty-two."

"You can sail with forty-two."

"We can." *But we need more and you know it.*

"It's the war," Terhouven said.

"Pretty bad, lately, everybody's undermanned, especially in the engine room. On a lot of ships, when they reach port, they have the crew on deck after midnight, waiting for the drunks to come out of the bars. 'Climb aboard, mate, we get bacon twice a day.' "

"Or somebody gets hit on the head, and wakes up at sea."

"Yes, that too."

Terhouven looked over the tray to see if there was anything else worth eating. "Tell me, Eric, how come no uniform?"

"All I knew was 'a dinner,' so . . ."

"Is it wrecked?"

"No, it lives."

"You can have another made here, you know."

Across the table, Wilhelm said to Hoek, "Well, I went to the flower market but he wasn't there."

DeHaan was done with dinner, had had all he wanted and liked it well enough. He'd been everywhere in the world and eaten bravely, but he could never quite forget his last plate of fried potatoes and mayonnaise in a waterfront café in Rotterdam. He took out a packet of small cigars — a Dutch brand called North State, cigarette-shaped but longer, the color of dark chocolate, and offered it to Terhouven, who declined, then lit one for himself, inhaled the brutal smoke, and coughed with pleasure. "Wim," he said, "what is this dinner about?"

Terhouven hesitated, was about to tell all, then didn't. "The Hyperion Line is going to war, Eric, and the first step is taken here, tonight. As for the details, why not wait and see — don't spoil the surprise."

The waiters returned, the first holding the door, the second bearing a tray piled high with mounds of little pastries that glistened with honey, the third carrying two bottles of champagne in buckets of ice. He raised the buckets proudly and grinned at the dinner guests. "Celebration!" he said. "Open both bottles?"

"Please," Hoek said.

When the waiters left, Hoek opened the briefcase by his feet and unfolded a Dutch flag, red, white, and blue in horizontal bars, took it by the corners, and held it above his head. Commander Leiden rose and drew from an inner pocket a sheet of good paper with several typed paragraphs, cleared his throat, and stood at attention. "Captain DeHaan," he said, "would you stand facing me, please?" From somewhere in the neighborhood, the sound of whining Arabic music was faintly audible.

Leiden, in a formal voice, began to read. This was admiralty language, stern and flowery and impressively antique — *hereby*s and *whereas*es and *shall not fail*s, a high wall of words. But plain enough to DeHaan, who blinked once but that was all: Leiden was administering the oath of enlistment in the Royal Dutch Navy. DeHaan raised his right hand, repeated the phrases as directed, and swore his life away. That done, the conclusion was not long in coming. "Therefore, in the name of Her Royal Majesty, Queen Wilhelmina, and by order of the Commissioners of the Admiralty of the Royal Naval Forces of the Netherlands, it is our pleasure to appoint to commission the present *Eric, Mathias, DeHaan,* to the rank of Lieutenant Commander, in the sure and certain knowledge that he shall perform with full honor and endeavor . . ."

It went on for a time, then Leiden shook his hand and said, "You may salute, now," which DeHaan did, and Leiden returned the salute as Terhouven and Wilhelm applauded.

Looking at Terhouven, DeHaan saw a joker's delight, thought, *why no uniform indeed, you sly bastard,* but saw also eyes that shone brighter than they should.

They ate the pastries and drank the champagne and talked about the war. Then, at midnight, the man who worked as Hoek's attendant and chauffeur, a pink-cheeked émigré called Herbert, arrived and Wilhelm and Hoek left them. They could hear the chair bumping along the cobbled alley toward a car parked in a nearby square.

"Quite a character," Leiden said. "Our Mijnheer Hoek."

"A big heart in him," Terhouven said.

"Surely that." Leiden paused to finish the last of his champagne. "He has never married, officially, but it's said that two of his servants are actually his wives, and that the children in the house are his. It's not unknown here. In fact, if he were Mohammedan, he could have four wives."

"Four wives." From his tone of voice, Terhouven was considering the domestic, not the erotic, implications.

"Only two, for Hoek, and it's no more than gossip," Leiden said. "But he does maintain a large household, which he can easily afford."

"Well," DeHaan said, "why not."

"We agree. Whatever their peculiarities, you soon discover, as part of a government in exile, the importance of patriots who have their wealth abroad."

"And want to spend it," Terhouven said.

"Yes, but not only that. What you saw here tonight was the North African station of the Royal Dutch Navy's Bureau of Naval Intelligence."

Terhouven and DeHaan were silent,

then Terhouven said, "May one ask how you found them?"

One may not — but Leiden never said it. Terhouven was himself a patriot of this category and that, by the slimmest of margins, bought him an answer. "They volunteered — at the consul's office in Casablanca. There were others, of course, more than you'd expect, but these two we decided we could trust. If not to be good at it, at least to be quiet. This sort of connection excites people, in the beginning, and they simply must tell, you know, 'just one friend.' " He spoke the last words in the voice of the indiscreet, then turned to DeHaan and said, "You can depend on them, of course, but one of the axioms of this work is that you don't abandon your, ah, best instincts."

DeHaan began to understand the dinner. For a time, he'd thought he might be asked to serve on one of the Dutch warships that had escaped capture in 1940 and gone on to fight alongside the British navy. Now he knew better. Yes, he was newly a Luitenant ter Zee 1ste Klasse, but — and Terhouven's presence confirmed his suspicion — it was the *Noordendam* that was going to war.

"And Wilhelm?" Terhouven said.

"Our wireless/telegraph operator. And, just as important, she knows people — émigrés and Moroccans, plain folk and otherwise. An artist, you see, can turn up anywhere and talk to anyone and nobody cares. Very useful, if you're us. She was among the first to apply, I should add, and her father was a senior officer in the army. So, maybe it's true, blood will tell and all that."

"Are they to give me orders?" DeHaan said, not sounding as neutral as he thought.

"No. They will help you — you will need their help — and they may serve as a re-transmission station for our instructions to you."

"Which are?"

"What we want you to do, and this is the broad answer, is to carry on the war. We, which is to say Section IIIA of the Admiralty General Staff, currently find ourselves crammed into two small rooms in D'Arblay Street, in Soho. Some of us have to share desks, but, frankly, we never had all that much space in The Hague, and we'd learned, over the years, to accept a certain, insignificance. With Holland a neutral state, as she'd been in the Great War, the government had better things to do with its money than to buy intelligence. We had the naval attachés in the embassies, ran a small operation now and again, watched a few ports. Then the roof fell in and we lost the war in four days — the army hadn't fought since 1830, nobody anticipated attacks by parachute and glider, the queen sailed away, and we surrendered. We were humiliated, and, if we didn't believe that, the British found ways to let us know it was true. In their eyes, we stood with the French, the Belgians, and the Danes — not the 'brave but outmanned Greeks.'

"So now, in London, we are left to simmer in the exile stew — de Gaulle demands this, the Belgians want that, the Dutch navy turns the heat down and wears sweaters, because gas is expensive. Thank God, is all I can say, for our tugboat rescue service and for the ships of our merchant fleet, which sail, and are too often lost, in the Atlantic convoys. But Britain needs more — she needs America is what she really needs but they're not ready to fight — and now she has decided, and we may have given her a little help in seeing it, that she needs *us*, D'Arblay Street, thus we need our friend Terhouven here, and we need you. Special missions, Lieutenant Commander DeHaan, at which you shall succeed. Thereby casting some very timely glory on Holland, the Royal Navy, and its beloved Section IIIA. So then, will it be 'yes' or 'no'? 'Maybe,' unfortunately, is at present not available."

DeHaan took a moment to answer. "Is the *Noordendam* to be armed?"

This was not a bad guess. Germany had armed merchant freighters and they'd been more than efficient. Sailing under false flags, with guns cleverly concealed, they approached unsuspecting ships, then showed their true colors, took the crews prisoner, and sank the ships or sent them off to Germany. One such raider had recently captured an entire Norwegian whaling fleet, which mattered because whale oil was converted to glycerine, used for explosives.

But Leiden smiled and shook his head. "Not that we wouldn't like to, but no."

"Well, of course I'll do it, whatever it is," DeHaan said. "What about my crew?"

"What about them? They serve on the *Noordendam*, under your command."

DeHaan nodded, as though that were the answer. In fact, such business as Leiden had in mind was first of all secret, but sailors went ashore, got drunk, and

35

told whores, or anybody in a bar, their life story.

Leiden leaned forward and lowered his voice — *now the truth*. "Look," he said, "the fact is that all Dutch merchant ships that survived the invasion are to come under the control of what's called the Netherlands Ministry of Shipping, and most will then be under the management of British companies, which would put the *Noordendam* in convoy on the Halifax run, or down around the Cape of Good Hope and up the Suez Canal to the British naval base at Alexandria. But that won't happen because the Royal Dutch Navy has chartered her from the Hyperion Line, at a rate of one guilder a year, with a Dutch naval officer in command."

DeHaan saw that Leiden and Terhouven were looking at him, waiting for a reaction. "Well, it seems we've been honored," he said, meaning no irony at all. They truly had been, to be chosen in this way, though he suspected it would be honor bought at a high price.

"You have," Terhouven said. *Now live up to it.*

"It's not final," Leiden said, "but there's a good possibility that your sister ships will be run by British companies."

"Lot of nerve, they have," Terhouven said. "What's the old saying — 'nation of pirates'?"

"Yes," DeHaan said. "Like us."

They all had a laugh out of that. "Well, it's just for the duration," Leiden said.

"No doubt," Terhouven said sourly. The Netherlands Hyperion Line had come into existence in 1918, with Terhouven and his brother first chartering, then buying, at a very good price, a German freighter awarded as part of war reparations to France. Governments and shipowners, over the centuries, forever had their noses in each other's business — bloody noses often the result.

"You've been at this a long time," DeHaan said to Leiden.

"Since 1916, as a young ensign. I tried to get out, once or twice, but they wouldn't let me go."

This was not necessarily good news to DeHaan, who'd taken some comfort in Leiden's being, from the look of him, an old seadog. But now Leiden went on to describe himself as "an old deskdog," waiting a beat for a chuckle that never came.

"Haven't been to sea all that much. Not at all, really," Leiden said. Then smiled in recollection and added, "We never got out of Holland — six of us from the section — until August. Snuck down into Belgium one hot night and stole a little fishing smack, in Knokke-le-Zoute. Hardly any fuel in the damn thing — that's how the Germans keep them on the leash — but there was a sail aboard and we managed to get it rigged. All of us were in uniform, mind you, because we didn't want to get shot as spies if they caught us. We drifted around in the dark for a time — there was a good, heavy sea running that night — while our two amateur sailing enthusiasts had a, *spirited* discussion about which way to go. Then we realized what we looked like, 'bathtub full of admirals' somebody said, and we had to laugh. Office navy, that's us."

DeHaan glanced at Terhouven and saw that they'd both managed polite smiles — Leiden may have been "office navy" but they were not. Terhouven said, "Might as well kill this," and shared out the last of the gin, while DeHaan fired up one of his cigars.

"All right," Leiden said, acknowledging a comment that had not actually been spoken, "maybe we better get down to business."

It was after two in the morning when

they left the little room and walked back down the rue Raisuli, which had grown steeper during dinner. Terhouven and Leiden were staying at a private home near the Mendoubia gardens, while DeHaan was headed for the waterfront. It was a warm night, a spring night, with a breeze off the water and a certain lilt to the air, well known to the town's poets but never named. Anyhow, the cats were out, and the radios turned down — likely out of consideration for the neighbors.

A man in a doorway, the hood of his djellaba up so that it shadowed his face, cleared his throat as they passed by and, when he had their attention, said, *"Bonsoir, messieurs,"* his voice cheerful and inviting. He hesitated a moment, as though they knew who he was and what he was there for, then said, *"Messieurs? Le goût français, ou le goût anglais?"*

It took DeHaan a moment to think that through, while a puzzled Terhouven said, *"Pardon?"*

"Le goût," DeHaan said, "means taste, preference, and *français* means that it is a woman you have a taste for."

"Oh," Terhouven said. "I see. Well, gentlemen, it's on the Hyperion Line, if you care to make a night of it."

"Another time, perhaps," Leiden said.

They came, a few minutes later, to the rue es Seghin, where they would part company. Terhouven said goodby, adding that they might be able to meet the following day. Leiden shook hands with DeHaan and said, "Good luck, then." He held DeHaan's hand a moment longer, said, "We . . ." but did not go on. Finally he said, "Well, good luck," and turned away. He was, as he'd been all night, bluff and brisk, professional, yet just for an instant there'd been an edge of emotion to him, as though he knew he would never see DeHaan again, and Terhouven's glance, over the shoulder as he walked off, confirmed it.

DeHaan headed for the Bab el Marsa and the port. *Le goût hollandais,* he thought. *Drunk and lonely and sent off to die at sea.* But he found that thought offensive and made himself take it back. In the North Atlantic, and everywhere in Europe, all sorts of people had their lives in their hands that night but there was always room for one more, and as to who would see the end of war and who wouldn't, that was up to the stars. When DeHaan was fifteen, his father, captain of the schooner *Helma J.,* had gone copra trading in the

40

Celebes Sea, taking rafts up the jungle rivers, buying at native villages, bringing the copra out in burlap sacks. Then one day he went up the wrong river and was never seen again and, for a horribly awkward half hour, the head of the *Helma J.* syndicate had sat in their parlor in Rotterdam, staring at the floor, mumbling "poor man, poor man, his luck ran out," and leaving an envelope on the hall table. One year later, through floods of his mother's tears, DeHaan had gone to sea.

It was almost three in the morning by the time DeHaan reached the dock. The port launch was long ago tied up for the night but his chief mate had sent the *Noordendam*'s cutter for him, crewed by two ABs, who wished him good evening and started the engine. DeHaan sat silent in the bow as they chugged off through the harbor swell, past dead fish and oil slicks lit by moonlight.

0800 Hrs. 4 May 1941. 35°12′N/6°10′W, course SSW. Low cloud, light NE swell, w/ wves 4/6 feet. No vessels sighted. All well on board. J. Ratter, First Officer.

For the time being, he thought, reading the first officer's entry as he began the forenoon watch, which ran from eight to twelve in the morning. A traditional captain's watch, like the four-to-eight, and the dreaded midwatch. Midnight to four, which called for endless mugs of coffee, as one stared into the night and waited for dawn, but he'd never sailed on a ship where it was any other way. At "the hour of the wolf," when life flickered, and sometimes went out, a captain had to be on his bridge.

He said good morning to the new helmsman — always an AB, able-bodied seaman — at the wheel, and saw that Ratter, his first officer, hadn't gone down to his cabin at the end of his watch but was out on the starboard wing of the bridge, sweeping the horizon with his binoculars. U-boats might well be out hunting, even this close to the British air cover from Gibraltar, and from the open deck of the bridge wing you could see much better than on the enclosed bridge. Not that it mattered, DeHaan thought, they couldn't run and they couldn't fight. They could break radio silence, a hard-and-fast rule for merchant ships since the beginning of the war, but that wouldn't save the *Noordendam*.

Still, despite the war, despite anything,

really, it eased his heart to be back at sea.

The Atlantic on a spring morning, six miles off the coast of Africa. Low cloud bank on the horizon, gray, shifting sky, sea the color of polished lead, stiff breeze from the northeast trades, gulls swooping and crying at the stern as they waited for the breakfast garbage. The real world, to DeHaan, and reassuring after the strange dinner four nights earlier. The blazer was back in his locker, and DeHaan was himself again — faded denim shirt rolled up above the elbows, gray canvas trousers, tie-up leather ankle boots with rubber soles. And a single badge of authority: a captain's hat, a very old and hardworn friend — the gold stitching of the Hyperion Line insignia, twisted rope in the shape of an *H*, faintly green from years of salt air — which he wore with peak tilted slightly over his right eye. A good Swiss watch on a leather strap, and that was that.

Done with his survey of the horizon, Ratter came in off the wing deck and said, "Morning, Cap'n."

"Johannes."

Ratter was in his thirties, with a long, handsome, serious face and dark hair. Three years earlier, he'd lost an eye in a wheat-dust explosion on the *Altmaar*, one of the *Noordendam*'s sister ships. There'd been no glass eye for him at the hospital in Rangoon, so he'd worn a black eye patch on a black band ever since. He was a good officer, conscientious and bright, who had long had his master's papers and should have had his own ship by now, but the financial contractions of the 1930s had made that impossible.

"Service at oh nine hundred?" he said.

"Yes," DeHaan said. It was Sunday morning, and an inviolable shipping tradition called for him to conduct a Divine Service, followed by captain's inspection. He didn't mind the latter so much, though he saw through all the tricks, but the former was a burden. "Compulsory today," DeHaan added. "That means everybody. You already have the bridge, and you can keep the helmsman. Kovacz will take the engine room" — Kovacz, a Pole, was his chief engineer — "and I want everybody else on the foredeck."

"All right," Ratter said. "Full crew."

DeHaan turned to the helmsman. "Come a point to starboard, and signal half speed."

"Aye, sir. Point to starboard, half speed." He turned the wheel — highly polished teak, an elegant survivor of the East India

44

trade — and shifted the lever on the engine-room telegraph to *Half Speed Ahead*. From the engine room, two bells, which confirmed the order.

"I'm going to have to make a speech," DeHaan said, clearly not happy about it.

Ratter looked at him. This never happened.

"We're not going to Safi for phosphates."

"No?"

"We're going to Rio de Oro," DeHaan said, using the official name for the strip of coastal sand known commonly as the Spanish Sahara. "Anchoring off Villa Cisneros — and I don't want to get there much before nightfall, so, save the oil." After a moment he added, "We're changing identities, you might as well know it now."

Ratter nodded. *Very well, whatever you say*. "Liberty for the crew?"

"No, they stay aboard. They all got ashore in Tangier, so they won't take it too hard."

"They won't, and, even if they grumble, it's Mauritania, whatever the Spaniards call it, and you know what they think about that."

DeHaan knew. Sailors' mythology had it that seamen on liberty in the more remote ports of northwestern Africa had been known to disappear. Kidnapped, the stories went, and chained to stepped wooden wheels, treadmills, in the lost villages of the desert interior, where they were worked to death pumping water from deep wells.

"We'll have the local bumboats," DeHaan said. "Crew will have to make do with that. And put the word out that we're due for a long cruise, so, if they need anything . . ."

The mess boy came tramping up the ladderway — metal steps, too steep for a stairway but not quite a ladder — that led to the bridge. Known as Cornelius, he thought he was fifteen years old. He was, if that was true, small for his age, pale and scrawny. He'd grown up, he said, on the island of Texel and had first gone to sea on the herring boats at the age of nine. And running away to sea, according to Cornelius, had greatly improved his lot in life.

"Breakfast, Cap'n," he said, offering a tray.

"Why thank you, Cornelius," DeHaan said. Ratter had to turn away to keep from laughing. DeHaan's breakfast was a mug of strong coffee and a slab of mealy gray bread spread thickly with margarine, which bore, at its edge, the deep imprint of a small thumb.

DeHaan chewed away at the bread and sipped the coffee and stared out at the low cloud on the horizon. In a moment, he'd go back to his cabin, read through the Divine Service — from a stapled booklet, dated Sunday to Sunday, provided by the Hyperion Line — and jot down what to say to the assembled crew. But, for the time being, with bread and coffee, Ratter's silent presence, and fair weather, it was a pleasure to do nothing. The bridge was his true home on the ship — or, really, anywhere in the world. A sacred space, no clutter allowed. Only the helm, engine-room telegraph, brass speaking tube to the engine room with a tin whistle on a chain around its neck, compass mounted in a brass binnacle — a waist-high stand, signal flags in wooden compartments that climbed the port bulkhead, and an arc of grand, square windows in mahogany frames. Access was by doorways that led to the bridge wings, and a ladderway to the deck below — to the chartroom, captain's and officers' quarters, wardroom, and officers' mess.

DeHaan permitted himself time for half

his coffee, then said, "Well, I guess I have to go to work. Just keep it nice and slow, south-southwest at one-ninety degrees, and stay six-off-the-coast." The phrase meant *beyond the five-mile limit,* international waters. "We're running west of Morocco for the next few hours but, technically anyhow, that's Vichy France."

Ratter confirmed the order.

DeHaan took one last sip of coffee, then another, but he couldn't leave. "I just want you to know," he said, "that we're really *in* it now, and it's me who put us there. Maybe something had to happen, sooner or later, but it's going to be sooner, and somebody's going to get hurt."

Ratter shrugged. "That's the war, Eric, you can't get away from it." He was silent for a time, the only sound on the bridge the distant beat of the engine. "Anyhow, whatever it is," he said, "we'll come through."

The wind blew hard on the forward deck, waves breaking at the bow, sun in and out of a troubled sky. The crew stood in ranks for the Divine Service, their heads uncovered, hats held in both hands. Kees, the *Noordendam*'s second mate, a stolid, pipe-smoking classic of the merchant service, counted heads, counted again, and went off to retrieve a couple of convinced atheists skulking in the crew's quarters.

Divine Service was meant to be vague and ecumenical: for Lascar and Malay crews from the East Indies, Moslems — as Mr. Ali was thought to be though in fact he was a Coptic Christian — for Catholics, for everybody; a few simple words addressed to an understanding and comprehensive God. But DeHaan knew the services to have been written by the Terhouven family pastor, a Dutch Reformed minister in Rotterdam with a pronounced taste for Protestant gloom. Thus that day's service was based on the words of Martin Luther: "Everyone must do his own believing, as he will have to do his own dying." Given the speech that DeHaan would be making after the service, the worst possible choice, but this was not the moment to improvise.

Belief mattered, went the homily, one had to have faith in the ways of the Lord, one had to be compassionate, to express this faith by charity toward one's fellow man. A reading of Psalms 93 and 96 came next, followed by a recitation of the reverend's chief work, *The Seaman's Prayer* — a stormy, nightbound opus that made at

49

least some of the men flinch. The word *storm* was not to be said at sea, lest there be one about, which, on hearing the mention of its name, came to see who was calling. After a minute of silent prayer, as most of the men bowed their heads, the service was over.

"Men," DeHaan said, "before you are dismissed for captain's inspection, I must say a few words to you." DeHaan cleared his throat, consulted his notes, then held them behind his back. "We all know that half the world is at war, that we face a powerful and determined enemy. Over the next few weeks, the *Noordendam* and its crew will take part in this struggle by participating in a secret mission. *Secret* — I emphasize the word. It may be dangerous, you may be called on to take up duties which are not usual to you, but I know you will do what has to be done. I know you are capable, I know you are brave, and now you may be called on to prove it. During this time, you will remain aboard ship. Your officers and I will do everything we can to make life easier for you, but you are to expect the unexpected, and meet whatever happens with all your experience and skill.

"We will be anchoring off Rio de Oro

later today, and the bumboat men will be coming to the ship, as usual. For those who may need a little extra money to buy the necessaries, you may call on Mr. Ratter, for the deckhands, or Mr. Kovacz, for the engine-room crew. I would like to end this talk by saying 'if you have questions, ask me,' but I would not be able to answer. I have always been proud of *Noordendam* and her crew, and I know you won't disappoint me. What we do, we do for those at home, in Holland, in Europe, wherever they are." He let them think it over for a moment, then said, "Those of you on watch can return to duty, the captain's inspection will begin at ten hundred hours."

Thank God that's over. He wondered what they'd thought about it. Some of the men had met his eyes — *you can count on me.* Perhaps they'd lost friends or family in the Rotterdam bombing — when Holland had virtually lost the war — an object lesson from stern Papa Germany. Some of the men had stared at their shoes, while one or two seemed angry: at the enemy, at their captain, at life; there was no way to know.

Maybe a third of them had no idea what he'd said, because they didn't speak Dutch, but their mates would find a way to explain it to them. The language of the merchant service was pidgin English, some three hundred words that got seamen through their daily duties and life below deck. A number of them couldn't read or write, particularly the oilers and firemen in the engine-room crew. Former stokers, most of them, from the days before steamships had converted to oil, their hands seamed with black lines where cuts and blisters had healed over coal dust. There were a few communists, some secret, some not, supposedly on Hitler's side since the pact of 1939, and a few who didn't think the Nazi doctrines were all that wrong. But, in the end, they were all sailors, who couldn't leave the life of the ships because they were — and they would say it just this way — married to the sea. A hard life, seen from the shore, brutal and dangerous and, often enough, mortal. Even so, it was in their blood, and it was the only life they wanted to live.

Kees stood by DeHaan's side as the men broke ranks and headed for their inspection stations. Taciturn and reflective by nature, he made no comment, but for a single interrogatory puff of pipe smoke whipped away by the wind.

"There'll be an officers' meeting in the wardroom, before lunch," DeHaan said, answering the puff.

Kees nodded. *Just not enough trouble for some people in this world, they have to go looking for more.* He didn't say it out loud but he didn't need to — DeHaan understood him perfectly.

1830 hours, Villa Cisneros.

DeHaan had anchored *Noordendam* well out in the bay. She could have tied up at the deepwater pier but her master chose, perhaps, not to pay the dockage fee — penny-pinching always a credible motive in the world of tramp steamers.

"Ever been here?" DeHaan asked the AB steering the ship's cutter. There was a chill in the desert air as night came on, and he pulled his leather jacket, sheepskin-lined, around him and held it closed.

"Can't say as I have, sir."

"Seems quiet," the other AB offered.

Benighted, maybe, or, better, godforsaken. But seamen tended toward diplomacy with officers present. A thousand souls in the town, according to one of DeHaan's almanacs. Well, maybe there were, hidden away in a maze of bleached walls and shadows, but, from just off the pier, the place was deserted. *Not much of anything, in Rio de Oro.* Four hundred coastal miles of sand and low hills, and abundant salt, which they sometimes exported — a last tattered shred of the Spanish Empire. But, a neutral shred, and that made it useful.

They tied up to a bollard on the pier and, as DeHaan climbed the stone stairway to the street, a desert wind, smelling of ancient dust, blew in his face. Eight months earlier, on a street in Liverpool, he'd discovered the same smell, had puzzled over it until he realized that it rose from the foundations of old buildings, newly excavated and blown into the air by *Luftwaffe* bombs.

It was only a minute's walk to the Grand Hotel Cisneros — Leiden had told him where to find it — which turned out to be three stories high and two windows wide, a stucco building that had been white at the turn of the century. The lobby seemed vast — a high ceiling with a fan, black-and-white tile floor, dead palm tree in a yellow planter. The clerk, an elderly Spaniard with the face of a mole and a wing collar, stared at him hopefully as he came through the door. In one corner, Wilhelm, in Barbour field jacket and whipcord trousers, was reading a book.

He greeted her, his words echoing in the empty lobby. From Wilhelm, a crooked grin — clearly they couldn't talk here. She rose and said, "My car's just out the back."

DeHaan didn't envy much in this world but he envied Wilhelm her car. It was parked in a small square behind the hotel, between a 1920s moving-company truck and a Renault sedan, a flock guarded by a mustached shepherd in a sheepskin vest and hat, with a rifle slung diagonally across his back. Wilhelm handed him a few dirhams, which he tucked away as he inclined his head by way of saying thank you.

"It's wonderful," DeHaan said. A low, open sports car, weathered by sand and wind to the color of chromatic dust — probably green if you thought about it, with a tiny windscreen, a leather strap across the hood, bug-eyed headlights, and the steering wheel on the right. In British movies, the hero vaulted into cars like this but DeHaan took the traditional approach, snaking his way inside and settling into the leather seat.

"Yes," Wilhelm said. "Mostly." The shepherd stared thoughtfully as Wilhelm tried the ignition, which coughed and died. "Now, now," she said. On the fourth try there was an ill-tempered snort, then, on the fifth, a string of explosions — full power. The shepherd broke into a huge smile, and Wilhelm laughed and waved to him as they went bumping off down the street.

"What is it?" DeHaan said.

"What?"

"What is it?"

"Oh, it's a Morgan. There's more to it, I think, letters or numbers, something."

They were out of town and on a dirt road almost immediately. Past a field of green shoots and a blindfolded ox, harnessed to a wooden bar and walking in a circle around the stone rim of a well.

"It used to belong to a friend of mine," Wilhelm said. "An American. He liked to say that back in the States he'd had all the Morgans — the horse, the car, and the girl."

The dirt track began to narrow and it was almost dark. Then, suddenly, they climbed to the crest of a hill and the ocean appeared on the left. Wilhelm braked to a stop. "There you are," she said.

Down below, the *Noordendam* at anchor, lights shimmering in the haze, a thin stream of smoke from the funnel as one boiler was kept running to serve the electrical system.

"Did you see that old truck? In the square?" Wilhelm said.

"Yes."

"That's your paint," she said. "In metal drums."

"Is somebody watching it?"

"The guard, of course, as you saw. And the driver isn't far away."

"How much do you have?"

"Two hundred gallons. They said at the ship chandler you need gamboge and indigo, and burnt sienna — they wrote the proportions on the drums — to make dark green. And white, for the striping. Of course it needs to be thinned, thinned way down, so there's white spirit."

Wilhelm handed him a sheet of paper with a description printed out in pencil, DeHaan could just barely read it in the failing light. "*Funnel:* black with green band. *Hull:* Black with broad green band between narrow white bands."

"Is that correct?" Wilhelm said.

"That's the description in *Lloyd's Register*. No boot-topping, thank God." Merchant-company colors were often used for the latter — the space that showed when the ship was high in the water, without cargo.

"Then *Santa Rosa,* on the side," Wilhelm said.

"On the bow, yes. And at the stern."

The *Noordendam* was to become the *Santa Rosa*, of the Compañía Naviera Cardenas Sociedad Anónima, with offices on the Gran Via in Valencia. As a ship steaming under a Spanish, a neutral, flag, she could go anywhere. In theory. According to Leiden, the real *Santa Rosa* was in drydock, with a serious engine problem that would require a new casting, in the Mexican port of Campeche.

Leiden, and Section IIIA, presumed that with the wartime suspension of the "Movements and Casualties" page of the maritime journal *Lloyd's List* — daily intelligence on the world of six thousand merchant ships — hostile personnel, at sea or in port, would have at hand only the annual *Lloyd's Register*, and the false *Santa Rosa* would conform to the description found in the section on Spain. That is, if they even bothered to look. It was further presumed that the newly *confidential* — limited-distribution — version of the shipping pages would not be available to enemy observers. On these presumptions, Section IIIA was betting forty-two lives and a ship.

Still, not such a wild bet. The *Noordendam* and the *Santa Rosa* were, if not twins, at least sisters. They were typical tramp freighters, picking up cargo anywhere and taking it to designated ports, as opposed to liners, which made scheduled trips between two cities. They'd both been built around 1920, five thousand gross tons, some four hundred feet long and fifty-eight wide, draft of twenty-five feet, single funnel, derricks fore and aft, blunt in the bow, round in the stern, carrying nine thousand tons of cargo — enough to fill three hundred boxcars — with a top speed of eleven knots. On a fair day with a decent sea. They were similar to the eye, and not unlike a thousand others.

"Are there ship's papers — for the *Santa Rosa*?" DeHaan said.

"No point. You could only use them if you're boarded and, if you are, the game is over. A merchant crew wouldn't survive interrogation, and there's too much on the ship that would give it away, under close inspection. However" — she reached behind the driver's seat and retrieved a soft package wrapped in brown paper and tied with string — "here is my contribution."

She untied the string, turned the paper back, and handed DeHaan a ship's flag — the heavy cotton fabric softened and faded by service in ocean weather. A Spanish flag, the monarchist version reintroduced by Franco in 1939. Two horizontal red bars — blood-red, and not subtle about it — held a wide band of yellow with a coat of arms: between columns, beneath a flowing pennant with motto, an eagle in profile is protected by a checkered shield. DeHaan, from northern Europe, the land of forthright stripes, had always thought it looked like a medieval war banner.

"Seems well used," he said.

"It is."

"Did you buy it?"

"Tried. But, in the end, we stole it. There was a message from Leiden, back in April, 'Obtain a used Spanish maritime flag.' Well, it wasn't to be found in the local souks so we — me and a friend, a trusted friend — took the ferry over to Algeciras for a day. Not much you can't find there, since the war ended — a single boot, sacred paintings marked with a hammer and sickle, old pistols — but they were fresh out of used flags. So we came back to Tangier, went to the chandler, and bought one. New and crisp, sharp, bright, and wrong.

"I tried everything I could think of — washed it in lye, soaked it in seawater, left it in the sun for days — but this flag had its pride and it wouldn't age. Finally my friend said to soak it in bath salts and bake it dry, which led to an amusing fire in the oven and a visit with the firemen. By the time they left, the flag was a little *too* used — which is to say, black.

"Now Leiden had used the word *obtain*, which left us a certain, latitude, so my friend had a bright idea: yachts. Plenty of them stranded in Tangier and Casablanca, at the yacht clubs, and of course the people who own them, some of them anyhow, give parties. Well, we found the flag we wanted — on a huge motor yacht that belonged to the count of Zamora, known in Tangier as 'Cookie,' and pure Groucho Marx. Likely raised some hell in his day but it was probably nineteenth-century hell, because Count Cookie is an extremely old man and doesn't give parties. But we did get ourselves invited to a *cocktail Américain*, at a nearby slip, on a yacht called the *Néréide*, owned by some Italian aristocrat. This grew into a real party, by the way; caviar in the piano, ice cubes down the cleavage, fan dancing with the drapes — a *very* sporty crowd and they didn't miss a trick.

"So, after midnight, I went up on deck for a breath of air, walked back to the pier, went three docks over, and out to the last slip. Only problem was, I had this idiot who'd followed me around all night and now he follows me out to the motor yacht. Definitely a *Mitteleuropa* type, but naïve, or maybe just stubborn, because I'm the girl of his dreams. 'Mademoiselle Wilhelm,' he says, 'you are lovely in moonlight.'

"We're standing at the foot of the gangway, at this point, and I flirt with him and tell him I want that flag. Must have it. Crazy Dutch artist, he thinks, drunk, sexy, has to have a Spanish flag. Well, why not. So we tiptoe across the gangplank and onto the deck, and lower the flag. And, lo and behold, it's an antique — the old bastard must have had it from before the civil war. And, of course, he hears us, or someone in the crew does, because just about the time we get it unclipped, somebody yells in Spanish and we run like hell, laughing all the way.

"Now this is a big flag, and, even folded, it can't go back to the party, so we run to his car, a Lagonda, of course, put it in the trunk and he drives me back to my studio, an old garage, where I have a headache and get rid of him. An hour later my friend shows up, worried sick, thought I was in jail, but we drove right past the guard at the gate of the club."

It was dark on the hilltop and very quiet, a lean slice of waning moon had risen just above the horizon. *New moon on the twelfth,* DeHaan thought. Which was why the operation was planned for that night, and, if it didn't go, would have to wait for June. "We shouldn't stay here too long," he said.

"No, you're right." She set about starting the car.

"I'll send a boat for the paint," he said. "Tomorrow morning."

"I'm in Room Eight."

DeHaan folded the paper back over the flag and retied the string as the engine started. "Thank you for this," he said.

"My pleasure," she said. "Fly it, ah, proudly?"

"I suppose," DeHaan said. "Might as well."

0920 hours. Rio de Oro Bay, off Villa Cisneros.

DeHaan used the chartroom as his office. A bank of teak cabinets filled one wall, with wide drawers that held charts for the seas of the world. Such seas might fold, in the right storm, but not the charts. There was desk space atop the cabinetry, with calipers, pencils, chronometer — all the paraphernalia of navigation. One door led to DeHaan's cabin, the other to the deck.

The AB Amado, prompt to the minute, knocked politely, two diffident taps on the door. "Yes?" DeHaan said.

"Able Seaman Amado, sir." This in English.

"Come in."

He was a shaggy man in his late thirties, with a mustache and a slight limp. There were three Spaniards aboard the *Noordendam* — one was a fireman, and barely verbal, a second, eighteen years old, served as cook's assistant and messroom boy. The third was Amado, formerly a ship's carpenter on a Spanish tramp, who'd signed on as an AB in Hamburg in 1937. Which meant less status, and less pay, but this was a rescue and Amado was happy to be alive.

"Please sit down, Amado," DeHaan said, indicating the other high stool pulled up to the cabinets. "A cigarette?"

"Please, sir." Amado was sitting at attention.

DeHaan gave him a Caporal and lit it, then lit one of his little brown North State cigars. DeHaan had boxes of them, but he could only hope they would outlast the war.

"The speech yesterday," DeHaan said. "It's been explained to you?"

"Yes, sir."

"And that's all right?"

Amado nodded. He took a deep drag of the Caporal and let the smoke out slowly, turning one hand to an angle that meant he wanted to say much more than his English would allow. "Yes," he said. "Very much." DeHaan saw that he was one of those men whose fire had been banked to an ember, but that ember was carefully tended.

Amado now told his story. DeHaan already knew most of it — from the bosun, who served as petty officer and father confessor to the deck crew — which was just as well, because the conversation was hard work for both of them, though the story was simple enough. When civil war came to Spain, it also, in time, came to Amado's ship, a Spanish ore-carrier hauling chromite, from Beira, in Portuguese East Africa, to Hamburg. As they neared the German coast, somebody called somebody a name and a fistfight started, which grew quickly into a brawl between Republican and Falangist crewmen — red and black neckerchiefs appearing like magic — then spread to the officers, except for the captain, who locked himself in his cabin with a loaded shotgun and a demijohn of rum.

In a matter of minutes, the weapons came out. "First knifes, later, ah, *fusiles.*"

"Guns."

"Yes. So this." Amado pulled up his pant leg and revealed the pucker scar.

The Falangists held the radio room, the wardroom, and the officers' mess, the Republicans had the bridge, the engine room, and the crew's quarters, there were wounded on both sides, two seamen fatally stabbed, an officer shot dead. As night fell, the fighting subsided to a standoff — shouted insults answered by wild gunfire, then, at dawn, the Falangists sent out a distress call, which produced, a few hours later, two *Kriegsmarine* patrol boats. When Amado, who fought on the Republican side, saw the swastika flags, he knew he was finished.

But he wasn't. Not quite.

Officers and crew were taken under guard, the wounded patched up, the ship herded into Hamburg harbor. The Falangists, as fellow fascists, were released immediately, while the Republicans — "Bolsheviks, they call us" — were held at the port. German officials then wired the owner of the ship, who wired back an hour later and objected to the arrests: where, he asked, was he to find a replacement crew? Thus, after a day of questioning and a couple of broken noses, they let most of the Republicans go. "But three," Amado said, "not come back."

What the Germans wanted, in fact, was not a few new inmates for their prisons, what they really wanted was the chromite ore, used to harden steel in various war machines — the cargo in the hold of the Spanish ship, and more in the future, all they could get.

But Amado — maybe a ringleader and maybe not, DeHaan wasn't sure — was not going to board that ship ever again. Which sailed without him, while Amado stayed at a seamen's hostel in the Altstadt district, where, two months later, DeHaan found him. "Very bad, Hamburg," Amado said, his face hardening at the memory of it.

From DeHaan, a sympathetic nod, then, "Amado, our ship will be a Spanish ship, for a time."

Amado looked lost.

DeHaan went to his cabin and returned with the paper parcel. He opened it, and when he showed Amado what it held, the man stared for a time, then his eyes lit up with understanding. "Ah!" he said. "I know this . . ."

Amado didn't have much English, DeHaan thought, but he certainly knew deception when he saw it. "That's right," DeHaan said. "And you" — he pointed for emphasis — "the captain." He took off his cap and placed it on Amado's head. "On the radio, yes? Or, or, when we need you."

Amado returned the cap with a rueful smile. *Not for the likes of me.*

"Can you do it?"

"Yes, sir," Amado said. *"Con gusto."* With pleasure.

The bumboat men arrived at dusk, pulling up to the ship's side in an assortment of feluccas with striped awnings, and announcing their wares as they climbed up the steep gangway along the hull. Waiting for them on deck, Van Dyck, the bosun, and AB Scheldt, with folded arms and policeman's clubs carried in loops on web belts.

The bumboat men carried suitcases full of tobacco, matches, cigarette papers, French postcards, fruit, chocolate, chewing gum, buttons, thread, needles, writing paper, and stamps, which they spread out on blankets, everything just so. Then they squatted on their haunches and called out the great virtues, and demeaning prices, of their merchandise — these were not, and God was their witness, merely *stamps*. Business was brisk, DeHaan's offer of money for small necessities had been enthusiastically taken up, and DeHaan himself, standing with Ratter and watching the show, felt compelled to buy a few things he didn't need. He'd always liked Levantine bazaars — there was one in Alexandria where the stone corner at the base of a fountain had been worn to perfect roundness, over the centuries, by the brush of robes.

When a young man with three women appeared on deck, Ratter said, "Never fails, does it." One of the women was young, the other two ageless, all were unveiled, eyes dramatized with kohl, mouths painted carmine. "Tell him no, right? Back to the boat."

DeHaan shook his head. "Might as well get them laid."

"*You*," Ratter said in his brutal French. "Come over here."

The pimp wore a sharp green suit. He hurried over to Ratter and DeHaan and said, "Sirs?"

"Are the girls clean?" Ratter said. "Not sick?"

"They are perfect, sir. They have seen the doctor on Monday. Dr. *Stein*."

Ratter stared at him with a cold blue eye. "God help you if you're lying."

"I swear it, sir. Sir?"

"Yes?"

"May one beg permission for use of your lifeboats? Under the tarpaulins?"

"Go ahead," DeHaan said.

A crowd gathered, the girls smiled, blew kisses, fluttered their eyelashes.

The twilight was long gone by the time the last two bumboats arrived. The early merchants had returned to shore, and most of the crew was on the mess deck, eating dinner, with oranges, the Hyperion Line's contribution from the bumboat market, for dessert.

The bosun and AB Scheldt had gone below, and DeHaan and Ratter waited as the men in djellabas struggled up the gangway. Twenty of them, at least, some carrying wooden crates with rope handles, and breathing hard by the time they reached the deck. One of them laid his crate down, then unbent, coming slowly upright with a shake of the head and a *why me?* grimace on his dark face.

"Quite a long way, up here," DeHaan

said, sympathetically.

The bumboat man stared for a moment, then nodded in agreement. "Like to broke me fookin' balls," he said.

Commandos everywhere.

Five in the first officer's cabin, Ratter and Kees crammed in with the chief engineer on three-high bunk beds, a few more in the wardroom, sleeping on the floor and on the L-shaped banquette where the officers ate, the rest stashed here and there, with Mr. Ali moving to the radio room to free up the cabin he shared with his assistant. Once upon a time, in that prosperous and hopeful year 1919, at the Van Sluyt shipyards in Dordrecht, the *Noordendam* had been designed to carry four first-class passengers — wandering souls or colonial administrators — which was common for merchant ships of the day. She had, it was rumored, actually carried one, but nobody could say who it was or where he went, and in the end all it came to was mahogany trim and a bit more space for the ship's officers who occupied the cabins.

Major Sims, the unit commander, stood the midwatch, midnight-to-four, with DeHaan. Short and trim and, DeHaan sensed, taut with suppressed excitement, he was one of those men with skin too tight for his face and slightly protruding eyes, so that he seemed either irritated or astonished by life, an effect heightened, at that moment, by a deep-brown coat of camouflage cream. "It *will* wash off," he said. "With soap and water." By nature not particularly forthcoming, he did tell DeHaan, in the confidential darkness of the bridge, that he and his men were from "a good regiment, one you'd know," and that he'd "been asking for a special operation for a long time." Well, DeHaan thought, now you have it.

A heavy sea, as they headed north, *Noordendam* rolling and pitching her way through the swells. DeHaan stood at ease by the helmsman, hands clasped behind his back in instinctive mariner's balance, a posture that Sims soon enough discovered for himself. Some of the commandos would surely be feeling queasy by now, DeHaan thought, with worse to come, but Major Sims seemed, anyhow, to be a good sailor. The mess boy appeared on the bridge and DeHaan ordered two mugs of coffee brought up.

"No change in the ETA, is there?" Sims asked.

"Monday a week, the twelfth, off Tunisia — Cap Bon, just after dark. The estimate has us passing the French airbase, at Bizerta, an hour earlier. Of course, that *is* an estimate."

"Quite. When do we go through the Strait?"

"After dusk, on Saturday."

Sims said "Hm," in a way that meant he was pleased. "Better after dark, off Gibraltar, with the German coast watch."

DeHaan agreed.

"When will you become the *Santa Rosa*?"

"We'll start rigging at oh-three-thirty, an hour before dawn, then anchor off a stretch of coast called Angra de los Ruivos, paint with the rising sun, and be on our way by ten hundred hours."

"What's there?"

"There is, Major, truly nothing there. A dry riverbed, Wadi Assaq, and that's it."

They stood silent for a time, the throb of the engine hypnotic. "Five and a half hours, did you say, for painting?"

"We think so. We're painting directly over Hyperion Line colors, so no chipping or sanding. We're using scaffolds and bosun's chairs, hung over the side, and all our best hands — the whole crew will be

73

involved in this — and we've got plenty of rope, cans, brushes, everything."

DeHaan had made a point of that, planning logistics, with the bosun before they left the chandlers in Tangier. He had once, in some forgotten port, watched sailors in the Soviet navy as they smeared paint on with their hands.

"We have only an hour for drying," DeHaan went on, "and we'll have to spray water on the stack to cool it down, and thin the paint so it seems faded. It will look awful, but, that's no bad thing."

Sims's silence implied satisfaction. The helmsman kept steady on 320 degrees, slightly west of north, and the quarter moon was fully risen, its light broken on the rough surface of the sea.

"Our ETA," Sims said, back again to what was really on his mind. "How close do you think we can come?"

DeHaan's voice was tolerant. "Seventeen hundred nautical miles to Cap Bon, Major, past Morocco and Algeria and much of Tunisia. We're rated at eleven knots an hour, and we're actually doing about that, so, by simple mathematics, it's six and a half days. The weather forecast is fair, for the Atlantic, but once we enter the Strait of Gibraltar, we're in the Mediterranean, where storms, you know, 'come up out of nowhere.' Well, they do, and there's tons of Greek bones on that seafloor to prove it. But, the way we think in the trampship business, if not Monday, then Tuesday. All we can ever promise is not to be early."

"We have three nights," Sims said. "For our little man to show a little light. Still, one is, understandably, concerned."

One is, terrified. Not of dying, DeHaan thought. Of being late. *Rule Britannia.*

0420. Off Rio de Oro.

Refuge. This hour in his cabin as the sun came up was DeHaan's night, but he rarely used it for sleep. That came beyond dawn, for three hours, before he went back to the bridge for his eight-to-twelve. He was used to it — sleeping again in the afternoon — and he'd somehow found a way to like it, which, according to the way he'd been raised anyhow, was pretty much the secret of life. He shifted for new comfort on the narrow bunk and stared at the dark porthole at the other end of the cabin.

Not far. The refuge, in steel painted gray, was ten by twelve: a bunk with drawers beneath it, a wardrobe with small desk attached, chair bolted to the floor, sink and toilet in a small alcove behind a curtain. There was a two-shelf bookcase fixed to the bulkhead, the wall, above the desk, which held his forty-book library, his wind-up Victrola, and an album of records in thick paper envelopes. Beyond that, the *Noordendam*: the ceaseless hum and rattle of the ventilator fans, the creak of the ship as it rose from a trough, the pacing of the watch officer on the bridge above his cabin, bells on the half hour, and the engine, drumming away beneath him — let it catch its breath for one heartbeat and his blood raced before he even knew what he'd heard. And, beyond the *Noordendam*, the sound of the wind and the sea.

This presence, this perpetual music, in all its moods, was not to be resisted, and sent him wandering through his own life, or those in the forty-book library. The read, the unread, and the oft read. A few Dutch classics — Multatuli's *Max Havelaar* and Louis Couperus — and some not so classic — a trio of military biographies and a flock of fat historical novels, which were good friends when he was too tired for anything but his native language. A Dutch translation of Shakespeare's plays was better to look at on the shelf than to read, though he had worked through *Henry V* more than once, because it felt like fiction.

Conrad, of course. In whom a Polish sea captain fought a losing battle with a London literary émigré. He had *The Mirror of the Sea*, bought in expectation of philosophy but soon abandoned, guiltily, with a promise to return and do better. The ghastly *Nostromo*, magnificently written but so evil and miserable in its story that it was not to be read, *Heart of Darkness*, which he liked, also *The Secret Sharer* — could that actually *happen*, a cabin shared? — and *Lord Jim*, a real sea story and a good one. One of his mother's brothers had virtually lived the same life, except that, threatened by fire in a cargo of jute in the Malacca Straits, he *hadn't* jumped, and his ship *did* sink, taking Uncle Theo with it.

Conrad shaded off, as DeHaan saw it, to what he really liked, adventure stories with intellectual heroes. These were not so common, but what there was he returned to again and again. *The Seven Pillars of Wisdom*, the story of a military intelligence officer, T. E. Lawrence, sent to stir up Arab rebellion against the Turks during the Great War, when Turkey fought alongside Germany. In the same way, Malraux, *Man's Fate* and *Man's Hope*, in English, and even Stendhal, *The Red and the Black* and *The Charterhouse of Parma*, by "the Hussar of Romanticism," who'd fought, an officer under Napoleon, in all the desperate battles of the Russian campaign and lived to write novels. Those he had in Dutch, along with *War and Peace*, which could be read at the bleakest moments of life at sea and still provide, somehow, almost magically, consolation, a world away from the world.

DeHaan looked at his watch, it was almost four-thirty in the morning. He lit a cigar, and watched the drifting smoke as it rose in the air. They were running at *Dead Slow* now, had been for an hour, as Ratter and the bosun supervised the preparation for painting. He heard the squeak of block and tackle, shouted commands, a curse, a laugh — work under way sounded like nothing else. The porthole remained black but the edge of dawn was out there somewhere, and soon the engines would stop and he would hear the steam winches on deck and the slow, grating slide of the anchor chain as it was run out.

DeHaan ran his eye across the shelves, along the row of faded covers — books did not fare well in sea air — past the nautical almanacs, his Bowditch, *The American Practical Navigator*, Nicholl's *Deviation*

Questions and Law of Storms, past his dictionaries, to the end of the middle shelf, to the Baedeker for France, and a few novels in French. *My Mother's House*, *The Vagabond*, *Claudine in Paris*, and *Claudine at School*.

Colette.

He was a slow reader in French, very slow, but there was a simplicity in these books, a joyous shimmer, in the words and beyond, that coaxed him along. And more. It wasn't just the schoolgirls, kissing and petting and scheming against the headmistress — erotic in a hundred ways but nothing wrong with that — it was also the garden. The *rue*. The cat and the sky. It was, as DeHaan put it to himself, the perfect compass south to his north — to the cruelly practical life he had to live outside this cabin. A dream world, the winding road and its plane trees, the *auberge* with its rusty garden chairs on the gravel beyond the French doors.

These were not illusions. He had been there. And at the end of that road, in a lumpy bed in that *auberge*, Arlette had wondered why he chose to leave it. To make his money, she supposed, one had to do that. And, she said, with a melancholy twitch and wriggle to make her point, so went the sorry world. Not two years ago, he realized, the last spring before the war. He'd met her in a café in Amsterdam — she was there with a girlfriend who knew a fellow captain — and, *Noordendam* in drydock in Rotterdam, they'd gone off to Paris, and then to the countryside.

His life with women had always been a victim of his life at sea — brief affairs recollected at length. Occasionally close to mercenary — gifts, whatnot — and sometimes passionate, but typically on the great plain that lay between. The last time, after parting with Arlette that spring — forever, she'd said — had been the previous October, in Liverpool, with a woman he'd met at a rather refined club for naval officers. She was an ambulance driver, a WREN, young and pink and immaculate and talkative, and so fiercely intent on pleasing him he suspected she never felt a thing. A sad evening, for him, after Arlette.

A flaming redheaded Breton, fire goddess, with a floating walk and a hot temper, a hot everything. At a crucial moment on their first night together, what his hand found pulsed, and the heat of it surprised, then inspired him. "It's my skin," she said later, during a brief repose, a Gauloise hanging from her heavy lips. Very white, and *thin,* she said, so the touch of a hand set her alight. Always? No, not always. But now. "I knew it would be like this," she pouted, accusing him of exciting her. Of course she was flattering him, enticing him, making him her own — he knew it, and was flattered, and enticed. Still, she wasn't lying, her skin *was* pale, and delicate, her grandiose behind, after lovemaking, flushed and mottled in the light of the night-table lamp.

She was, he thought, a couple of years older than he was. She worked in the shops, she said, first this job, then that, it was all the same. And she had come to Amsterdam, she more or less told him, for an adventure, bored with those men she could have met in Paris. What, he wondered, would become of her, now that the Germans occupied the city? This vision worried him; she was not a woman who would avert her eyes, was not someone who could disappear into the scenery.

The light in his porthole had turned to dawn, and when DeHaan felt the ship lose way and the anchor was let down he rose from his bed and went to take a look. They were a mile off the coast; low hills, gray sand, a light surf that broke against a cliff. He took off his shoes and sighed with pleasure, shed his shirt and trousers, and slid beneath the blanket on his bunk. He finished the cigar, tapped it out in a metal ashtray, and closed his eyes.

They'd spent two days in Paris, after the countryside, then he had to take the early train back to Holland and went alone to the station, past a market, a church, streetsweepers with a water truck. Very soft, the light in Paris, at that time of day.

As DeHaan went up to the bridge for his eight-to-twelve, the painting was fully under way, scaffolds slung over the side, ABs handling the tackle that operated the bosun's chairs. Back at the stern, a loud splash was followed by sarcastic hoots of "Man overboard!" followed by some ripe curses from Ratter and the order to "haul that sonofabitch back on board, goddamnit!" Beneath a bright sky, his funnel now wore half a stripe of Spanish green — so he'd named the color — and he could see the bosun dangling up there, peering nearsightedly at the blistered iron, each stroke of the brush applied with concentrated finesse. "Fucking Rembrandt himself," Ratter said, when DeHaan joined him.

"Not so bad." It had been one thing to

scheme about the deception, something else to actually do it. Ratter felt the same way, he guessed, but neither of them would say it. Yet. "Looks like we're on schedule," DeHaan added, determinedly cheerful.

He took a turn around the ship, then went down to the lower deck, where Sims had his men caring for their weapons — stripping and oiling Sten guns and two lethal-looking Brens, machine guns with small tripods on the barrel, whetstoning knives with rubber handles, loading ammunition belts. Most of the men had their shirts off, and chatted amiably as they worked. They would likely have preferred to be on the top deck, in the sunlight, but a German air patrol was always a possibility and Sims well knew it. DeHaan wished them all a good morning, then returned to the bridge, where Cornelius was waiting with his breakfast. Thickly cut bacon, almost warm, between two slabs of bread, and strong coffee. Fresh bread was produced daily on all merchant ships, and the conventional wisdom said that one got either good cooking or good baking, but the Noordendam's cook had clearly been left out of that equation. DeHaan chewed away at his sandwich, dense and rubbery, and stared out at the empty sea.

When he was done, he strolled onto the bridge wing, coffee in one hand, and swept his binoculars along the shore. Ratter was below him, at the foot of the ladderway, and DeHaan called out, "Anything stirring, this morning?"

"One of the lookouts saw a truck, about oh-six-thirty."

"There's a road, up there?"

"Not on any map we have — maybe a goat track. The road goes inland."

"What sort of truck?"

"All I saw was a dust cloud, moving north."

DeHaan looked again, slow and careful, but there was nothing.

They were under steam by 1020. There was a cloud bank on the far horizon, but a long way west, and rain rarely came to this coast, so DeHaan felt reasonably safe. The *Noordendam* was no more, her name chipped and sanded off; she was now the *Santa Rosa*, on the bow and stern, with *Valencia*, her home port, added beneath the latter. It was Van Dyck's job to change the name on the ship's life preservers, and he would repaint them later that morning.

As they moved north, into the open sea, DeHaan had Ratter take the bridge. One final job remained — he could have ordered it done, normal practice, but, for whatever reason, he felt he had to do it himself. He went to the stern, unfolded the Spanish flag, and ran it up the low-angled mast. He'd had a look at the ship's copy of *Lloyd's Register* and he knew her checkered history. She was the *ex-Kavakos–Piraeus* — built at the Athenides yards in 1921 — *ex-Maria Vlasos–Larnaca*, *ex-Huittinen–Helsinki*, then, at last, in 1937, *Santa Rosa–Valencia*, now owned by the Cardenas Steamship Company SA.

A new life, DeHaan thought, as the flag snapped and fluttered in the breeze. *Ghost Ship, Section IIIA — London*. Making, according to her faked manifest, for the Turkish port of Izmir, to take on a cargo of hides, baled tobacco, and hazelnuts.

9 May. Hamburg.
S. Kolb.
So he was called, on his latest passport — Mr. Nobody from the state of Nowhere. He was bald, with a fringe of dark hair, eyeglasses, a sparse mustache — a short, inconsequential man in a tired suit. He lay on a bed on the top floor of a rooming house in the Zeilerstrasse, not far from the docks, a narrow room with a

window at one end. It was a warmish night, and still, and the curtains hung limp in the dead air. Outside, the city was silent, with only the intermittent call of a foghorn from the sea beyond the harbor.

S. Kolb had been in this room for ten days, most of his time spent lying on the bed, reading newspapers. This was, in general, the way he spent his life, except when he had to work, and that was only now and then, for an hour, sometimes, or twenty minutes. But he hadn't worked at all in Hamburg, this was simply the place from which he was to go to another place. He'd worked in Düsseldorf, where he'd committed murder, and in Karlsruhe, where he'd collected a sheet of paper.

The paper, specifications for a machine, was hidden in plain sight, in a file with similar papers, in his briefcase. Nothing unusual, for a salesman of industrial machinery, supposedly working for a company in Zurich. No border guard, not even an SS officer on a Monday morning, would know that it mattered. And it actually might, he thought, though he was one of those men who had always suspected that, in the end, nothing mattered, and he'd more or less built his life on that principle.

What certainly did matter, at that moment, was a message from an Englishman called Brown. A decent, dog-and-garden sort of a name, he thought, euphonious, that implied a euphonious sort of a life — the odd revolver and lockpick aside. Of course Brown was no more his real name than S. Kolb was his, and if there was any distinction to be made, it lay in certain filing cabinets, where Brown was designated a *workname,* and S. Kolb an *alias.* Mr. Brown, a fattish, placid fellow, who hid from the world behind pipe and sweater, was just then responsible for getting S. Kolb out of Hamburg, and S. Kolb found himself wondering, for the hundredth time, just how the hell he was going to manage it.

Six days earlier, the steamship *Von Scherzen* had not appeared in Hamburg harbor, and while the men at the port office wouldn't exactly say what had become of her, their faces hardened a certain way when he inquired, which suggested that she was at the bottom of the sea. But she would not, at any rate, be part of the escorted convoy of German ships which had been scheduled to sail to Lisbon. He would, they told him, have to wait for a berth on a different ship, and they deeply regretted the inconvenience.

So did he. This was difficult work, equal parts danger, discretion, and waiting, a mixture that was, to say the least, hard on the nerves. Its traditional palliatives were alcohol and sex — yet more danger and discretion required here, but one had to do *something.* One could go mad reading newspapers. But newspapers were, at least, safe; women were not. Of course he knew that the port of Hamburg virtually swarmed with prostitutes, one could have anything one could pay for, but many of the men who sought them out were known to be traveling alone, far from home, and such men were, especially under the present regime, of interest to the police. It was caution and discipline that had kept S. Kolb alive all these years but now he sighed miserably as he felt their chains tighten around his chest. *No,* he told himself, *this is not for you.*

Or was he, perhaps, being too hard on himself? He was, as it happened, waiting for a woman — this was the third night he had waited — and there was a bottle of apricot brandy hidden, from himself as much as anyone else, at the back of the top shelf of the room's armoire. This woman, known only as Fräulein Lena, was his single contact in Hamburg and he had gotten in touch with her when the *Von Scherzen* didn't appear. She had somehow, and one could meditate at length on that *somehow*, signaled his predicament to Mr. Brown, and it was now her job to bring him news of a revised set of travel plans, which would reach Hamburg by means of a clandestine W/T set.

No secret radio could transmit from Germany — the Gestapo listened to all frequencies and would have a position fix on it soon enough — but coded messages could be received. This situation echoed that of ships at sea, naval and civilian, which could listen to transmissions but had, otherwise, to maintain radio silence. Some irony in this, Kolb thought, the governments of the warring nations had thereby attained a certain ideal level of supervision: one could only be instructed, one could not ask questions, one could not talk back.

So, by necessity a good soldier, he waited for orders. But he did allow himself some measure of speculation, to wit: if Fräulein Lena were to come to his room with instructions for his exfiltration from this wretched city, could she not also, perchance, provide an hour of tender oblivion? Kolb closed his eyes and set his newspaper on the floor. All hail to caution, yes, but with Lena he shared a secret life — would she perhaps be amenable to a secret tryst? Did he dare to ask? She was colorless and plain, somewhere in the middle of her life, quite heavy, and thoroughly bound in corsets, her iron bulk, in his imagination, tumbling free, prodigiously sweet and plentiful, as they were — only God knew how — dismantled.

No, he did not dare. Life had taught him one lesson: trust nobody. If only he had learned that in time, he would not be in this city, in this woeful room with curtains where green knights rode across a yellow field. In the Austrian city of Linz, his father had worked as a clerk in a bank, and the young S. Kolb, on finishing secondary school, had been installed as a junior clerk in that same bank. Where he was, a year later, found to be embezzling money, moving a small portion of the funds into an account in his own name. He was confronted, humiliated, discharged, and threatened with prosecution. His family, with terrible effort, had managed to make good on the missing money, and the police were never notified.

He had, however, not stolen the money. Someone else — he suspected a senior officer of the bank — had done it, and left a trail that led to him. This he told his parents, and they wanted to believe him, but, in their hearts, they couldn't. Thus he learned the brutal lesson: life was governed by deceit, and by power. Not the Golden Rule, the Iron Rule. Kolb had to leave his hometown but managed, by persistence, to find a job as a clerk in one of the government ministries in Vienna. The armaments ministry, it so happened. And soon enough, in a café on the elegant Kärntner Strasse, he met a genial young woman who, in time, introduced him to a rather less genial foreign gentleman, who taught him a clever method by which he could supplement his meager salary.

That was many foreign gentlemen ago, he thought, nostalgic for his youth, those long-gone days of Mr. Hall and Mr. Harris and Mr. Hicks — tubby old Brown was a recent incumbent, having materialized, the way they did, only last January. Pleasant and mean, all of them really, explaining nothing but what was required.

In the long hallway that led past his room, Kolb heard footsteps, a heavy tread, but they passed by his door and receded down the corridor. Kolb looked at his watch and saw that it was after midnight.

Not that it mattered — women came to men's rooms in these places, at any time of the day or night. *Fräulein Lena, meine Schatze, meine kleine Edelweiss, where are you?* Perhaps he'd been abandoned, simply left to fend for himself. For a time, he dozed, then woke, startled, to three discreet taps at the door.

9 May. Off Kenitra, French Morocco.

The dog watch, four to eight in the evening, was traditionally split in two, so everybody could eat dinner. DeHaan stood the first half, on the ninth, and, in fine rain and mist, squinted through droplets on the windows as *Noordendam* butted north, beam on to a short, steep sea, with the northern trade blowing spray over the bow. Out on the wings, the lookouts' oilskins ran streams of water. Major Sims came up to the bridge and said, "Filthy weather, out there."

DeHaan looked for a tactful answer — Sims had obviously not been at sea in filthy weather, because this was far from it. "Well, tomorrow we'll be going east," he said. "In the Mediterranean."

Sims was clearly pleased with the answer, and nodded emphatically. "One tries, of course, to keep one's people occupied," he said. "But, you know how it is, the way they feel now, the sooner the better."

They stood in silence for a time, then DeHaan said, "There's one thing about this, mission, Major, that I really don't understand."

"Only one?"

"Isn't a commando operation usually done with a submarine?"

"Ideally, it is. And it started out that way, I believe, but we only have so many, and they're mostly up north. In fact, we were damned close to canceling the thing, then somebody came up with the idea of a merchant ship. A neutral."

Noordendam was laboring too hard, DeHaan thought, and had the helmsman come a few points west.

"Truth is," Sims said, "where we're going, it's not healthy for submarines. Our side has the east and west ends of the Med, with Gibraltar, and the fleet at Alexandria, but, in the middle, that's another story. There are French airbases at Algiers and Bizerta, Italian planes across the Sicilian Channel at Cagliari, and they have a naval base at Trapani, and, since January, the *Luftwaffe* is operating from an airfield in Taormina, in Sicily. Submarines don't like airplanes, Captain, as I'm sure you know, and add the destroyers, which fly seaplanes from their decks, and you stand a rather good chance of losing your submarine."

"And a commando unit."

"That's not really the thinking, I'm afraid. It's the Andrew, the Royal Navy, wanting to keep what it has. You can replace commandos."

And tramp freighters. "I suppose you can," DeHaan said. "Anyhow, we're proud to do our part."

"Your crew? I'm sure your officers are."

"Hard to tell, with the crew. They always do what needs to be done, that's just life in the merchant marine. I think the men with families in Holland like the idea of a raid. As for the rest, it's probably different for each of them. We had six German crewmen in August of '39, then, in September, after war was declared, four of them asked to sign off, including our second engineer, and we put them ashore in Valparaiso. But the other two stayed on. There was a time when we didn't think about these things — nation of the sea and all that — but then the politics started, in 1933, and everything changed. Our chief engineer, Kovacz, was an officer in the Polish navy. He came aboard in January of 1940, in Marseilles. He'd been in port, up in Gdansk, when the Germans attacked.

His ship blew up in the harbor."

"Bombed?"

"Sabotage, he says."

"Bloody war."

"We had to sign him on as a fireman, but we lost our chief engineer a few months later and Kovacz was right there in the engine room. We're lucky to have him."

"And your two Germans? Still aboard?" He meant the question to sound like ordinary conversation, but there was an edge in his voice.

"Yes, and they're good seamen. One's an anarchist, the other didn't want to die for Hitler. He's young, nineteen maybe. They've had a few bad moments, fights in the crew quarters. Officially, I don't know about it, and the men sorted it out among themselves."

"It's no different with us," Sims said. "An officer can only do so much."

Sympathy, DeHaan thought, *as commanders we all face the same problems,* and decided to take advantage of it. "What are you after, Major, on Cap Bon? I know I shouldn't ask but I'm responsible for this ship, and for the lives of my crew, and on that basis maybe I have a right to know."

Sims didn't like it. Went silent as a stone, and, for a long minute, it was very quiet on the bridge. Then he walked over to the bulkhead, away from the helmsman. DeHaan let him stand there for a while before he followed.

"For you only, Captain DeHaan. May I have your word on that?"

"You have it."

"Commando operations are meant to do many things: they upset the enemy, they help public morale — if they're reported, they destroy strategic facilities. Communications networks, power stations, dry-docks."

Sims was just talking so DeHaan waited, and was rewarded.

"Also," Sims said, "coastal observation points."

"Like Cap Bon."

"Yes, like Cap Bon. They seem to be able to watch our ships, even at night, in dense fog. We must get convoys through, Captain, to our bases on Malta and Crete, because the Germans are going to attack them. Must. Without these bases, as points of interception, our forces in Libya, all our operations in North Africa, are in peril."

"At night? In fog?"

"Yes."

"Can that actually be done?"

"Apparently it can. We suspect they're

using infrared searchlights, which can 'see' the heat of ship engines."

DeHaan knew the span of nautical technology — there was hardly any aboard the *Noordendam* but it was still his job to know what there was. Even so, he had never heard the expression *infrared*. "What kind of searchlights, did you say?"

"Infrared. An invisible barrier, like a curtain, projected from both shores. Bolometers, Captain." Sims almost smiled. "Sorry you asked?"

"I know about radio waves, radars, but, after that . . ."

"Goes back to the Great War, in Germany, they've been playing with it for a long time. But, now that I've told you, here's my end of the bargain. If we manage to get technical equipment back to your ship, and something happens, to me, and my lieutenant, be a good fellow and make damn sure the thing finds its way to a British base. Will you do that?"

DeHaan said he would.

"There," Sims said. "You see? All you needed was something more to think about."

On the tenth of May, in the early evening, they passed through the Strait of Gibraltar. The mist and rain continued, but they steamed with running lights on, as a devil-may-care neutral ship would, and DeHaan could feel the telescopes and binoculars of the shore watch, British and German, French and Spanish, as they entered the Mediterranean.

DeHaan did not remain on the bridge for his midnight watch, instead, after a look at the charts, he left the helmsman to work alone and met with Ratter, Kees, and Kovacz in the wardroom. Ratter had the assistant cook produce coffee and a can of condensed milk, which he poured liberally into his mug while repeating the time-honored quatrain "No shit to pitch / No tits to twitch / Just punch a hole / In the sonofabitch," then stirred it in with the end of a pencil.

"It looks like we're going to be on time," DeHaan said. "The twelfth, just before midnight. Sometime after that, the commandos go ashore. We'll run them in as close as we dare, then drop anchor about two miles out, ship dark, and there we wait. The signal for return is two flashes of a green light, so we'll have deckhands standing by to lower scramble nets."

"And the gangway?"

"Might as well."

"What if they don't show up?" Kees said.

"We wait. For three days."

For a moment, no one spoke. Then Ratter said, "Three days? Anchored off Tunisia?"

"We'll be boarded," Kees said.

DeHaan nodded.

Finally Kees said, "What about the weather?"

"Last report from Mr. Ali, the meteorological forecast for allied shipping, says that this system has settled in all over southern Europe, and is likely to continue." The forecast came in code — the weather-report war one more small war within the big war.

"We want that, right?" Ratter said.

"I suppose we do. Anyhow, we'll need to rework the watch list, so we have the best people at the helm, and on deck."

"Vandermeer at the helm?" Kees said.

"No, on watch. Young eyes are better."

"Schoener, then," Ratter said.

"A German, for this?" Kees said.

"He's right," DeHaan said. "Use Ruysdal. He's older, and steady."

"Mr. Ali in the radio room?"

"As usual. But I want a good signalman, maybe Froemming, on deck with the Aldis lamp." He meant the hand-operated, shut-tered light that flashed messages.

DeHaan turned to Kovacz. As with many Poles, Kovacz's second language was German, sufficiently fluent so that Dutch, the nautical part of the language at any rate, came easily to him. He was a little older than DeHaan, stooped and bearlike, with thinning curly hair and sunken, red-rimmed eyes. His speech, always delib-erate, came in a deep, gravelly bass thick-ened by a heavy accent.

"Stas," DeHaan said. "You take the en-gine room, with your best oiler and fireman."

Kovacz nodded. "Boilers up full?"

"Yes, ready to run for it."

"Run like hell," Kovacz said with a grin. "Screw down the safety valve."

"Well, be ready to do it if you have to. Everything working?"

From Kovacz, an eloquent shrug. "It works."

"Lifeboats in good shape?" DeHaan asked Ratter.

"I'll make sure of the water tanks. The chocolate ration's missing, of course."

"Replace it. Davits, lines, blocks?"

"I replaced a rotten line. Otherwise, all good."

The assistant cook knocked at the ward-room door, then entered. He was an Alsa-tian, short and plump, with a classic mustache, who looked, to DeHaan, like the dining-car steward he'd once been. "Patapouf," DeHaan said, the word was French slang for *fatty*. "More coffee, please. Any dessert left from dinner?"

"Some pudding, Captain." A thick, po-tato-starch concoction with dried dates.

"Anybody joining me?"

There were no takers. "Just for me, then, Patapouf."

"Aye, Captain," he said, and waddled off.

The meeting lasted another twenty min-utes, then DeHaan went back up to the bridge for a quiet watch. At 0400, when he returned to his cabin, he cranked the handle of his Victrola and put on his rec-ord of Mozart string quartets. He opened one of the drawers built into his bunk and, from beneath a sweater, withdrew a belt and holster, well spotted with mildew, which held a Browning GP35 automatic, made in Belgium. Firing a 9-millimeter Parabellum round, it was the standard-issue sidearm for the Dutch military, and served as the captain's weapon, always to be found on a merchant ship. Three years earlier, when it had replaced an ancient revolver, DeHaan had thrown an empty tomato-sauce can off the stern and banged away at it until, evidently unharmed, it disappeared beneath the waves.

He took a box of ammunition from the drawer, disengaged the magazine, and began pressing the oily bullets into the clip. Ratter had the other weapon on board — that he knew of, at any rate — a .303 Enfield rifle, which was kept in a locker in his cabin. When attacked by an enemy vessel, a freighter had only one tactic — to turn stern to, where it could accept the most damage without sinking, and try to run away. That, and the pistol and the rifle, completed the ship's defensive array. Some British merchantmen were being outfitted with antiaircraft guns and small cannon but such martial measures were not for the likes of the *Noordendam*, and most certainly not for *Santa Rosa*. The Mozart, however, was scratchy but pleasant against the sound of the sea, and DeHaan found himself calm and contemplative as he armed for war.

11 May, 2300 hours. Off Mostaganem, Algeria.

DeHaan was sound asleep when somebody pounded on his door.

"Yes? What?"

A lookout opened the door and said, "Mr. Kees says for you to come to the bridge, sir. Right away, sir."

DeHaan managed to get his shirt and pants on, and went barefoot up to the bridge, the ladderway cold and wet as he climbed. Kees was waiting for him on the wing.

"There's some damn thing out there," Kees said.

DeHaan stared out into the rain and darkness, saw nothing. But, somewhere out to port, just astern, was the low rumble of an engine.

"Smell it?" Kees said. "Diesel fumes, and no outline I can see."

A ship low to the water, with big engines that ran on diesel. DeHaan swore to himself — that could only be a submarine. Which could hide and fight beneath the sea but by preference attacked at night, at speed, on the surface, where it could run at sixteen knots instead of the underwater five. Kees and DeHaan walked to the stern and peered out into the gloom.

"He's stalking us," Kees said.

"We're a neutral ship."

"He may not care, DeHaan, or maybe he knows better."

"Then he'll demand surrender, and, if we try to run, he won't waste a torpedo, he'll sink us with his gun."

"What can we do?" Kees's voice was unsteady, and querulous.

"We can refuse," DeHaan said. "And do our best with what comes next." He'd played this moment out in his mind a thousand times but now he realized he would not surrender. The presence of a British commando unit gave him an excuse, but that's all it was. *Final orders*, he thought. *Firefighting crew, distress call, lower boats, abandon ship.*

It was a fine rain, almost a mist, but he was soaked, water running down his face. A minute went by, and another, long minutes, then Kees said, "My God," as a dim shape, gray and low, emerged from the darkness beyond the *Noordendam*'s lights. A moment later, a hatch opened at the top of the conning tower and a man's upper body, in silhouette, appeared above it. A searchlight came on, the beam swept back and forth across the deck. Then, amplified by a loud-hailer, a challenge, an Italian version of the standard "What ship?" An Italian submarine, then. Perhaps, DeHaan thought, the *Leonardo da Vinci* — fine job of naming there — infamous for attacks on British convoys. The challenge was repeated, the officer, likely the captain himself, clearly growing impatient.

DeHaan held his open hands on either side of his mouth and shouted, *"Santa Rosa, Santa Rosa!"* He was blinded by the light shining in his face. It moved to Kees, who shielded his eyes with his hand, then it shifted forward to the bridge. Turning to Kees, he said, "Go get Amado. Do it yourself." He saw that several crewmen had come aft, and were milling about in small groups. "And get those people *below*," he said. Then he called out, *"Momentito, per piacere, capitán vene, capitán vene!"* Which was pretty much the extent of his Spanish, or Italian, or whatever he'd said. Maybe some Latin in there, in case they were monks. The captain's hat he'd always imagined Amado wearing was in his cabin, on a peg behind the door.

The figure with the loud-hailer climbed down the conning tower and walked up to the bow. DeHaan was suddenly conscious of his bare feet — but maybe that wasn't so bad. Here on this rusty old whore of a Spanish tramp. DeHaan tried for an ingratiating smile, said *"Momentito,"* and raised

105

helpless hands. The figure, in full naval uniform, stared at him as though he were a bug.

Now both of them stood there, watching each other, until DeHaan heard footsteps on the deck and Kees appeared, with his arm around Amado's waist. In an undertone, Kees said, "Oh Christ," and half-carried Amado to the edge of the deck where, DeHaan could see, he dared not let him go. Amado, roused from his bunk in the crew's quarters, was shirtless and, a loopy half smile on his face, drunk as a lord. "You're the captain of the *Santa Rosa*, remember?"

Amado nodded fervently, *ah yes, of course*. He closed one conspiratorial eye.

The officer shouted in Italian, angrier by the minute, and Amado shouted back in Spanish, the words *Santa Rosa* repeated several times.

Another question.

From Amado, *"Cómo?"*

Tried again.

Kees said something to Amado, who yelled, his words well slurred, some sentence that included the words *Izmir* and *tobacco*.

Another figure appeared next to the officer, a big, burly fellow with full beard and black turtleneck, a submachine gun carried carelessly at his side. The officer asked another question, Amado tilted his head — what's he saying?

"Tell him 'Valencia,' " DeHaan said. Better, he thought, to answer *some* question.

Amado did it, then stumbled and, but for Kees, would have pitched into the water. Kees, out of the side of his mouth, said, "I think he's going to be sick."

The man with the beard began to laugh, and, a moment later, the officer joined in. *And the captain was dead drunk!*

The officer shook his head, then dismissed the whole stupid business with a cavalier wave of his hand. The two returned to the conning tower and disappeared, the engine rose in pitch, and, with its exhaust vents pumping clouds of black smoke, the submarine rumbled away into the night.

DeHaan wanted a drink, he had a personal bottle of cognac in his cabin. He left Kees to deal with Amado, who'd fallen to his knees, and headed back toward the bridge. There was, on the way, a ventilating fan built into a louvered housing, some four feet high. As DeHaan went past, he saw that Sims and one of his men were kneeling in its shadow. The soldier held a rifle with a sniper scope, the weapon's strap circled tight on his upper arm to keep the gun steady, a practice common to the target shooter, and the sniper.

DeHaan raised his eyebrows as he went past, and Sims gave him a smile in return, and a brisk little salute.

12 May, 1830 hours. Off Bizerta.

Twice that day they'd been looked over. First by a reconnaissance flying boat, flat-bottomed cabin suspended below wings with pontoons, French roundels on wings and fuselage. Sims guessed it might be a Breguet 730, but admitted he'd only seen photographs. He was sure, however, of the one that showed up in the late afternoon, an Italian Savoia-Marchetti in desert camouflage with a white cross on its tail, called the *Gobbo,* "the Hunchback," Sims said, for the bulbous shape of its cabin.

Both planes came down to five hundred feet and circled for a good look. Behavior anticipated by DeHaan who had his full cast on deck — the cook and his assistant, in their usual dirty aprons, peeling vats of potatoes, and three deckhands sitting in a circle on the hatch cover of the forward hold, playing cards. He'd had a laundry line strung between two cargo booms, with shirts and drawers flapping in the wind, and, according to instructions, all the men on deck looked up at the planes and waved. The French pilot waved back. Toward dusk, a column of smoke was sighted on the horizon but the ship, whoever she was, showed no interest in the *Noordendam*.

As night came on, DeHaan called for *Dead Slow* from the engine room. They were not far, he thought, from Cap Bon. Finding it would not have been a problem, in better days, when every point and cape, harbor and river delta on the merchant shipping routes showed identification lights, described in the almanacs, but war had turned the coasts to low, dark shapes at the edge of the sea — once again the sea of Homer. Ratter had taken bright-star sights the night before, and shot the sun at midday. He had the navigator's gift, a mathematician by birth, and was formidably better than DeHaan, or anyone on board, at celestial dead reckoning. And, when a soft glow lit the landward sky, he said it was Bizerta.

On this night, the ship's lights were never turned on, and they steamed along slowly, on calm waters, edging toward the coastal desert. At 2010, a flight of aircraft was heard above, headed due east. "Could be ours," Sims said. They flew high above the *Noordendam*, a distant, steady drone, and their passage lasted thirty seconds. The ship was now at the geographical center of the Mediterranean war: Sardinia and Sicily to the north, British bases at Malta less than two hundred miles to the east, Wavell's desert divisions, fighting in the Italian colony of Libya, another few hundred miles south, German-occupied Greece and British forces on Crete maybe eight hundred miles due east. Just after nine in the evening, DeHaan went down to the radio room to join Mr. Ali for the BBC news.

DeHaan enjoyed his visits with Ali, a sophisticated Cairene — cigarette in ivory holder and gold spectacles — highly educated and proud of it, who spoke British English, learned in colonial schools, and had been heard, more than once, to use the expression *old boy.* A good wireless operator, he spoke parts of many languages, and, by tuning in hourly to BBC broadcasts, had become the ship's newspaper.

DeHaan had missed the first part of the broadcast, so Mr. Ali brought him up-to-date. The lead story reported fighting in Iraq, where British troops had occupied

Basra and the southern oilfields. The Rashid Ali government was allied with the Axis powers, and sought German intervention, but, the broadcast said, nothing could stop the British advance on Baghdad.

"And then," Mr. Ali said, "there has been the most terrible bombing of poor London. The British *Museum*, which I have visited, and Westminster *Abbey*." This over the announcer's voice reporting the flight of Rudolf Hess, third-highest official in the Reich, to Scotland, where he'd parachuted to earth and was "presently being questioned by government officials." The announcer left the story rather abruptly, suggesting that neither the BBC nor anyone else knew what was really going on, and proceeded to the "Personal Messages," coded communications to clandestine operatives all over Europe and North Africa:

"Mr. Johnson's class, at the Preston School, is visiting the zoo. Mr. Johnson's class, at the Preston School, is visiting the zoo.

"Gabriel, cousin Amelia has a bouquet. Gabriel, cousin Amelia has a bouquet."

And on, and on, as DeHaan and Mr. Ali sat transfixed by words that had, to them, no meaning at all, except as poetry.

★ ★ ★

12 May, 2030 hours. Off Cap Bon.

"We're turning around," DeHaan told the helmsman. "Come hard left rudder to two seventy degrees."

Ruysdal, at the helm, repeated the order, and they began the wide sweep that would send them back the way they'd come — the equivalent, for this five-thousand-ton monster, of pacing back and forth. They'd been cruising at slow speed since dusk, the atmosphere on the ship tight as a drum, with half the crew on deck, squinting out toward land, in search of Sims's "little man with a little green light." But life sometimes went wrong for such little men, and DeHaan wondered what Sims would do if he never turned up.

He wondered also about the possibility that the ship was "visible," as Sims put it, to an observation point on shore. Thus their reappearance, after a twelve-mile run to the east, coming back the other way, would hopefully register as a second vessel, the two ships passing in the night, as it were, though for all DeHaan knew the people on Cap Bon with the demonic apparatus could figure out exactly what was going on and a largish artillery round was

112

just now on its way to the bridge.

Waiting.

The commandos were assembled on deck amid their gear, faces blackened, their cigarettes red dots in the darkness. The bosun, with a crew standing by, ready to assist, paced the deck where the scramble nets had been slung over the side. DeHaan occupied himself by watching the sea, which stayed calm, only a light chop, fortuitous for men who had to paddle more than a mile in rubber boats. The northeast winds, for the time being, were off doing something else, but that, DeHaan knew, wouldn't last.

Ratter was up in the bow, where an AB was casting a lead line — the *Noordendam* was in as close as DeHaan dared take her, with visibility, light rain, new moon, down to a mile or less. As for Sims, he was everywhere, sometimes on the bridge, the privilege of command allowing him the luxury of not sitting still.

2130. 2230. Maybe it *wasn't* Cap Bon. On the bridge, Sims muttered under his breath, peered at the coastline, took five steps this way, five steps back. DeHaan wanted to help, to provide some distraction, but there was nothing to be done. *Been in London lately? What did you do before the war?* No, that was worse than silence. He looked at his watch, again, and saw that it was still 10:45, then thought about noting the change of course in the log, but clearly he couldn't. He would falsify the day's entry, though logs were sacred books and it went against deep instinct to write lies in them. His mind wandered here and there, Arlette, the girl in Liverpool. And what became, these days, of captains who lost their ships and survived? Join somebody's navy, at best. Or take another merchant ship, to lead another lamb to another slaughter.

Then, hurried footsteps up the ladder to the bridge — one of Sims's men, breathing hard with excitement. "Major Sims, sir, Smythe says he seen a light, and one of the sailors too."

Sims cleared his throat and, perfectly calm for all the world to see, said, "Very well."

"Good luck, Major," DeHaan said. "See you in a while."

Sims looked at him for a moment, then said, "Thank you," turned, and followed the commando out the door.

Forward of the bridge, there was muted commotion, shadows moving about, something clattered to the deck, then the boats were lowered to the water and the commandos climbed down the nets and paddled away into the night. "Come right to three fifty, Ruysdal," DeHaan said. Then, to the lookout on the wing, "Have Van Dyck prepare to drop anchor. In ten minutes or so."

DeHaan went out to the wing facing the shore. Shapes in the darkness, almost the entire crew was ranged along the edge of the deck, watching the boats as they pulled away.

0115 hours. Off Cap Bon.

Noordendam swung slowly at the end of her anchor chain, DeHaan and Ratter had stationed themselves on the bridge wing and, sleep being out of the question, most of the crew remained on deck. From anchor, a mile or so out, Cap Bon was a span of gray beach that climbed to an empty horizon. Lifeless, it seemed to DeHaan, dead still. With the engines shut down, there was only the lap of the sea against the hull, rain dripping on iron, and the slow creak of the cargo booms. In the distance, a faint rattle, muffled by the weather, which stopped, then, an afterthought, reappeared for a brief encore. "They're fighting," Ratter said. Instinctively, they both raised their binoculars and focused on the horizon.

"See anything?"

"No." Then, "I see that."

A flare burst red against the sky, sputtered as it floated toward the earth on its parachute. A second followed, both well east of where DeHaan thought they'd be. On deck, the crewmen called out to one another in low voices. The second flare was almost gone when there was an orange flash, with a low *crump* that came rolling out over the water seconds later. Then another. Ratter counted out loud, as though calculating the distance of a storm by the interval between lightning and thunder.

"They're really at it, now," DeHaan said, listening hard. He heard the fight as a series of brief stutters, whispery and dry, the volume climbing and falling. Joined by a louder version, deeper, not so fast, which went on for a long time, then ended with another flash. *So much for silent assault.* DeHaan had seen the knives, and assumed their use would lead to a quiet conclusion, but it hadn't. The heavy machine gun returned, and this time it continued, and, through the binoculars, he could see what looked like lines of flying sparks. DeHaan glanced at his watch, where seconds turned into minutes. And, at eleven minutes, more or less, the battle ended.

0305. Kees had joined them, they were all in oilskins now, with hoods up, as much against the wind as the rain. No whitecaps yet, but the waves were slapping hard against the hull and the rain blew sideways.

"Back any time now," DeHaan said. The planning said three hours, then they would return to the shore and show a signal light.

"An hour overdue," Kees said. "And soon enough it'll be dawn, and we'll be sitting out here. For no particular reason."

"If somebody shows up," DeHaan said, "we're repairing a valve."

"Or the J-40," Ratter said. This was meant as a joke. The *J-40 Adaptor* was an old navy story: a small steel box with a handle, nobody knew what it was for, eventually a cook put a carrot in it and cranked the handle and it came out the other end shaped like a tulip.

"You think they know what's going on, at Bizerta?" Kees said.

"They'd be here if they did," Ratter said.

"They could've seen the flares, or maybe had word on a telephone, or a radio."

"So, where are they?"

"Well, with the French, you never know."

It was 0335 before they saw the light.

DeHaan breathed a sigh of relief. "Finally," he said.

After a moment, Ratter said, "What's he doing?"

They stared through their binoculars. The light was yellow, with a powerful beam blurred by the haze, on and off, on and off. Ratter said, "That's no recognition signal, that's *Morse*."

"Three short, three long, three short," Kees said. "Where I come from that's an *S*, an *O*, and another *S*, and, the way I learned it, it means *save our souls*."

"I'll want the rifle," DeHaan said to Ratter. And, to Kees, "Boat Four — get the crew up here and prepare to launch."

"You shouldn't be the one to go," Ratter said.

DeHaan knew he was right, and pretended to think it over. "No, it's for me, Johannes. And right away. Get the signalman to make back *Confirmed. Help coming.*"

DeHaan went quickly to his cabin, snatched the Browning in its holster and worked on buckling the belt, beneath his oilskin, as he ran back up the ladderway. On deck, organized confusion. The number four lifeboat — *Santa Rosa* painted on its bow, for which he silently thanked Van Dyck — was swung out on its davits, ready to lower. Of the three-man crew, the AB Scheldt was already aboard, settling the oars in the oarlocks, and AB Vandermeer was trotting from the forecastle. The signalman was standing by the boat, working the shutter on the Aldis lamp, and Ratter was just emerging from below, Enfield in hand. "It's loaded," he told DeHaan. "Eight rounds on the clip." He handed DeHaan extra clips, which he stuffed in the pocket of his oilskin. Meanwhile, Patapouf, the assistant cook, was running toward the boat. *What now? Cocoa?*

DeHaan grabbed Ratter by the sleeve, pulled him close and said, voice low and tense, "What the hell is he doing here?"

Kees, standing by the winch a few feet away, saw what was going on. "Braun's got a sprained ankle," he said in an undertone. "Patapouf's the listed replacement." DeHaan grimaced, nothing to be done about it, and climbed into the boat.

The boat swayed as Patapouf struggled over the gunwale, then settled himself on the bench, chin held high with bruised French dignity. He'd seen the officers squabbling and knew that it was about him. Turning to DeHaan he said, "I served in the army, Captain."

Rifle in hand, heading for God only knew what on the beach, DeHaan was embarrassed, and nodded that he understood. Ratter put a flashlight on the seat next to DeHaan. "If you need help, two short, one long."

"Lower away," Kees said, as the winch engine produced a squirt of steam and began to grind.

At the oars, Scheldt and Vandermeer worked against the heavy sea as the boat rode up the waves and smacked down in the trough, and, even with DeHaan and Patapouf bailing away, the water rose to their ankles. When they were halfway to shore, the man on the beach started signaling again, which gave them a position fix, a few hundred yards east of where the tide was driving them.

"Signal back, Cap'n?" Vandermeer said. He was a tough kid, short and skinny, with fighting scars on his face, who'd been hired off the dock in Shanghai.

"No," DeHaan said. "We don't know who else is out there."

A fast ride in, once they hit the shoreline, and they vaulted over the side and ran the boat up the gravel shingle, then dragged it higher, into the dune grass, safe from the tide. It was raining harder now, and their oilskins snapped in the wind. DeHaan took the flashlight, and handed the Enfield to Patapouf. "Know how to use it?"

"Yes, sir. I think so."

"What'd you do, in the army?"

"Cook, sir, during the war, but they taught us how to shoot."

DeHaan handed him the extra clips.

They headed east, footsteps crunching on the shell litter. Ten minutes, fifteen, twenty. Then, an English voice, somewhere above them, almost lost in the rumble and crash of the surf. "Who are you, then?"

"From the boat," DeHaan said. "Captain DeHaan."

They saw him as he rose, silhouetted against the sky, Sten gun pointed at them, then swung aside. "Glad you came. It's a fucking horror up there."

"Where?"

"Few hundred yards inland." He joined them, looping the Sten's strap over his shoulder. "I'll take you," he said. "If I can find it — should've left fucking breadcrumbs." Was it Sims's sergeant major? DeHaan wasn't sure, the man's watch cap was pulled down over his forehead, and he was limping. "Stepped in a hole," he said.

"Who are you?" DeHaan said.

"Aldrich. Sergeant Aldrich."

They set off along the beach. After a few minutes, DeHaan said, "What happened?"

"Christ — what didn't!" They crunched along for a time. "We left one guard and our Arab with the boats — ahh, skyline here, gents." He bent low to the ground, scurried up the dune, over the top, and down the other side, to a twisting, stony path flanked by broken boulders. "Bloody fucking thieving bastard, turned out. He ran off with them. Or someone did. Or who fucking knows. Anyway, we couldn't find Wilkins and we couldn't find him."

"And Major Sims?"

"Couldn't find him either."

They trudged on in silence, the path turned to dreamscape — low canyons of splintered rock shining wet in the rain, scrub trees and brush, terrain that forced a tack every few yards, over ground which rose and fell so that, with a blank horizon, it seemed as though the land had closed behind them. "He took two men," the sergeant said, "and they went to circle round the flank, and that was that. When we finally got those bastards to give up, we went looking for him, but . . ." DeHaan felt his foot slide, tried to catch himself, then fell flat on his back. "Careful, there," the sergeant said — a comic line, now that it was too late to be careful. "The whole bloody mess was more than we bargained for," he went on, as DeHaan got to his feet. "You'll see." When they were again on their way he said, "We called out to them, whistled, flashed a light, but they were just, well, gone. It ain't all that rare y'know, I was with the expeditionary force, May of '40, up by the Dyle River in Belgium, and it happened all the time."

A rock wall appeared from the darkness, the sergeant stopped and said, "Ahh, this bugger." He stood still, looked to one side and the other, then said, "It goes to the right here, doesn't it. Yes, right." Down a narrow defile into a valley of rocks, then up a steep slope, some kind of flint, where DeHaan tried to use his hands but it was like broken glass. *Lost in this place,* he thought, *you would give up.* A few minutes later they came to a wadi with a foot of fast water rushing through it — so fast they had to fight to keep balance as they crossed. The sergeant worked at climbing the bank on the far side, sand crumbling away as he tried to get a foothold, then hauled himself up on the third try and extended a hand to help the rest, saying, "Come on now, Mabel."

"Do you think they were taken?" DeHaan said.

"Taken," the sergeant said. "Something took 'em, yes, that's about it, isn't it."

At last, a gulley, where mounds of gray rags lay amid tangled wire in a few inches of water. The survivors of *the whole bloody mess,* DeHaan realized, soaked and exhausted, with a manned Bren at either end. At the middle of it, the lieutenant struggled to sit upright. "Well, damned glad to see *you,*" he said, a smile on his dead-white face. One pant leg had been sheared off and his hand was pressed against a bandage wrapped around his thigh. "We *will* need a lift," he said, apologizing for the inconvenience. Silently, DeHaan counted the men in the gulley — eleven — and realized they could manage with one boat. The lieutenant saw what he was doing and said, "Four dead, five missing, including the major, I'm afraid, and two so badly wounded we had to leave them."

DeHaan knew there'd been twenty, plus Sims, and thought he'd miscounted, until he discovered a German officer in with the rest, lying on his side with his hands tied behind his back. Sitting next to him, his guard, one of those teenaged soldiers who looked thirteen — a pinched face, out of some Victorian slum, spattered with blood. On the floor of the gulley, broken aerials, steel boxes with dials and gauges, each of them trailing snarls of copper wire, and two concave disks — one a parabolic mirror with a cracked face — about three feet wide. Some or all of it bolometers, DeHaan thought.

"Looks like you got what you came for," he said.

The lieutenant nodded. "And a Jerry. Technician, from the insignia on him." DeHaan could just make out the pinion wheel of an engineering officer on the man's sleeve. "So a good raid, if we make it back. Could've been cleaner, of course, but they had a little protective force, French officers and Tunisian troops, and they just had to make a fight of it. Didn't last long, but . . ." In the sky, a distant whine, and all the men looked up as it grew louder, then faded into the distance.

"Fucker's back," one of the men said.

"He knows we're down here," the lieutenant said. "We cut their telephone lines but we didn't get the radio, not right away.

And one of the officers shot off a couple of flares."

"Last thing he did," the sergeant said.

"We don't know who he was signaling," the lieutenant said, "but we took fire from a second unit as we left. So, they're out there, somewhere."

DeHaan looked at his watch. Maybe an hour until daybreak, he thought. Using his Sten as a cane, the lieutenant got to his feet. DeHaan and his crew took a share of the captured apparatus, DeHaan carrying two of the metal boxes. One of them had been smashed in the middle, as though someone had tried to disable it with a rifle butt, and the glass in the gauges was shattered. On top of the control panel was a brass plate with a trademark, Zeiss, and, below that, WÄRMEPEILGERÄT 60.

The trek back to the beach was slow, hard work; the lieutenant, and one of his men, needed help in order to walk and DeHaan, near the head of the column, looked at his watch more than once. The magic boxes were light at first but grew heavier over time, while the wind strengthened with the approach of dawn and the chill left his hands and feet numb and settled deep inside him. When they heard the plane they stopped, the sergeant, moving ahead of the column as scout, holding up a hand until it passed. Would the pilot see the darkened *Noordendam*, anchored off the coast? DeHaan couldn't find a way to believe he wouldn't. But, so far, no explosions from that direction. Surely, he thought, that would happen at daybreak, when the real fighter planes would be up and hunting.

A silent march, except for the men who swore as they fell, and it took forever to cross the wadi, where the water was now well above their knees. At one point, after circling the cliff, they found themselves in a strange corridor between narrowing sandstone walls, and the sergeant had them turn around and go back.

DeHaan was watching him, about fifty feet ahead, when one of the men, who must have gone the wrong way when they doubled back, stepped between them. A man he didn't recall seeing, all those days on the ship, which was very odd, because he certainly had his own, rather flamboyant, style. But, after all, commandos, a special breed. This one wore a heavy beard, had a cloth attached to the back of a kepi and a long rifle slung on his shoulder.

The man looked up, saw DeHaan, and, for a moment, they both stared.

Suddenly, from behind, a loud whisper, "Get *down* you fucking cheesehead." What? A name stuck to Dutchmen, so it must be him. He started to turn around, then flinched as a Sten fired off and something whizzed past his ear. Now he went down, fumbling beneath the oilskin for the Browning. Somebody else fired as DeHaan turned back to look for the bearded man but he'd vanished. *Kepi, French Foreign Legion.* He managed to get the pistol free and worked the slide to arm it as men ran past him and somebody yelled, "Get him, Jimmy." Another burst, where he couldn't see, and another, which produced an indignant roar, as though somebody'd had his foot stepped on. Indignation ended abruptly by a third, very short, burst.

"They're over there."

They were. Stuttering flashes and French shouts and a thousand bees. DeHaan pointed the Browning toward the gunfire and pulled the trigger, shells ejecting past his cheek until they stopped. A few seconds later, silence. Then the metallic snap of magazines being replaced and the voice of the sergeant. "Right, then. Hop it." One of those wizards with a mystical sense of direction, DeHaan thought, hoped, he now led them off down some new path.

A bizarre procession. The lieutenant hobbling along with his Sten-gun cane, his helper pulling him by the elbow, the German prisoner — a balding clerk, squinting as though he'd lost his glasses — hurried along by a commando at his side, behind them a man with a Bren in one hand while the other dragged the parabolic mirror, which bounced along the slippery rock as he ran low to the ground. DeHaan followed, trying to free the empty clip from the Browning with one hand as he trotted past Patapouf, who lay on his back, arms flung wide, staring up at the rain. DeHaan knelt by his side, reached for the pulse in his neck with two fingers. The commando behind him took a handful of DeHaan's oilskin and hauled him to his feet. "Gone to God, sir. Leave him be."

"Patapouf," DeHaan said. *Fatso.* The immense stupidity of it clouded his vision.

"I know, sir. Can't be helped." A thick accent, high-pitched voice, the teenager with the pinched face. "He stood up to fire, see, and you oughtn't to do that."

DeHaan picked up the Enfield and the boxes.

Then, reluctantly, he began to run.

IN
ADMIRALTY
SERVICE

20 May. Alexandria.

Room 38 in the Hotel Cecil, on the Ras el Tin seafront.

Demetria. She was, she said, Levantine, of Greek origin, and, hair, eyes, and spirit, dark in every way. By day, the headmistress of a school for young women, "very prim and decorous, with uniforms." But — she'd looked at him a certain way — she wasn't really like that. The look deepened. Not at all.

True. Freed of her daily life, and a stiff linen suit, her underwear buried somewhere in the tumbled sheets of the hotel bed, she lay back in her flesh, luxuriant, legs comfortably apart — the color the

French called *rose de dessous* casually revealed — and smoked with great pleasure. Black, oval cigarettes with gold rims, and heavy perfume. Idly, she played with the smoke — let it drift from her mouth, then, with little puffs, sent white whorls rolling up to the plaster medallion on the ceiling. "It shames me to say it," she said, "but I smoke only in secret."

Something shamed her? DeHaan lay at her feet, across the bed, propped on an elbow. "I won't tell," he said.

Her smile was tender. "I was truly proper, you know, once upon a time. Then, my husband went and died on me, poor soul, when I was thirty-eight." She shrugged, exhaled, puffed at the smoke. "These Greek communities, Odessa, Beirut, Cairo, are very straitlaced, if you are of a certain class. So, wickedness is a problem. Which is strange in this city — it's very free here, for certain people, but not for someone like me. I did have a few, suitors, for a time, even a matchmaker. Oh Demetria, for you this gentleman of decent means, completely respectable, la-la-la. No, no, not for me."

"No," he said, "not for you."

"It's better with the war, God forgive me for saying it, live tonight for tomorrow you die, but, even so, *chéri,* that moment just now was my first *petit mort* in a long while." She sighed, and stubbed the cigarette out in an ashtray on the night table.

It was quiet in the room, the wash of the sea on the wall of the Corniche very faint and distant. She lay back on the pillow and raised her heels, inviting him into the parlor. DeHaan slid himself up the bed until he was close to her. From here, a better view, one that proved to be of heightened interest as the seconds ticked by. So, closer still.

"*Yassou,*" she said.

What? No matter, he couldn't answer.

Gently, she wove her fingers into the hair on the back of his head. "Oh my dear" — meant to be insouciant but her breath caught on the word — "there too."

He stared up at the medallion on the ceiling as she snored beside him, one heavy leg thrown over his. *Nymphs up there, two, three — five!* Should he turn off the lamp? No, darkness woke people up. And he was content to lie still, pleasantly sore, and a little light-headed, as though cured of a malady he didn't know he'd had. *Petit mort,* she'd said, *the little death,* a polite French euphemism for it. Yes, well. A few days earlier, steaming away from Cap Bon, he'd been close to the *grand mort,* not at all polite.

Headed for the British naval base at Alexandria, over a thousand nautical miles to the east, a four-day voyage, with luck; they would move from the air shadow of the Axis bases to that of the RAF, so the greatest danger lay in the first forty-eight hours. But it was only an hour after daybreak, as he was beginning to think that maybe they'd gotten away with it, that the French showed up. Late, but with panache. A patrol boat, sleek and steely, a handsome bow wave telling the world how fast she was.

A long way from help, they did what they could. The lieutenant had Mr. Ali send a cluster of ciphered numbers, while the commandos, with two Brens and a scoped rifle, waited just below deck. Vain hopes, DeHaan knew, a sea battle didn't work like that. Amado was readied, sober as could be and scared witless, but the French were in no mood for dithering. Coming up astern of the *Noordendam,* they ran up the signal flag SN — international code for "Stop immediately. Do not scuttle. Do not lower boats. Do not use the wireless. If you disobey I shall open fire on you."

Well, that was clear. "Ignore them," he told the lookouts.

The engines stayed on *Full — Ahead* while the lookouts swept the forward horizon, but such petulance was not to be taken seriously. There was a snarl from the French loud-hailer, thirty seconds allowed for compliance, then the slow, heavy drumming of a big machine gun and an arc of red tracer that curved gracefully a foot over the bridge. *Ça va?*

"Stop engines."

The patrol boat, bristling with aerials, carrying a cannon on the foredeck and paired machine guns, moved cautiously to come up beside them. "To port, Cap'n." The lookout sounded puzzled. "At ten o'clock. Some kind of . . . it's a seaplane."

DeHaan used his binoculars. It was big and ungainly in the gray sky, cabin hung below a broad wing with fat pontoons, the whine of its engine rising above the bass rumble of the freighter. Friend or foe? An AB came charging up the ladderway onto the bridge. "The lieutenant wants to start shooting."

"Tell him 'not yet.' "

As the AB ran off, the patrol boat accelerated to full power, and DeHaan turned to see it making a wide sweep, heeled over with the speed of its turn and, plainly, running away. From what? Not a French plane, a British Sea Otter, a graceless workhorse but armed with .303 machine guns, and more than a match for the patrol boat, now seen as a white wake in the distance. The Sea Otter did not pursue — shooting up the patrol boat would have produced fighter planes from Bizerta, and that was a battle no one, at least that morning, wanted. *So then, let us agree to disagree.*

Instead, the Sea Otter circled above the *Noordendam* and, clumsy as it was, tilted itself left and right, which at least suggested, to the waving crew below, a jubilant waggle of the wings. As it left, flying due north, DeHaan understood that it could only have come from a destroyer, watching them on radar from over the horizon, and receiving their radio signal. A poor man's aircraft carrier — lowering its seaplane to the water for takeoff, then hauling it back up after a landing at sea. DeHaan ran his binoculars across the northern horizon. Empty, nothing to be seen. Still, they were out there somewhere, the Royal Navy, themselves in dangerous waters, keeping watch on their boxes and wires.

She woke, slightly damp, and sent him to open the window. A warm night, the sea dead calm, some cloud, some stars, and the silence of a darkened city in time of war.

"What time is it?" she said.

He went to look at his watch on top of the bureau, said "Ten after three," and returned to the window, conscious of her eyes following him as he walked across the room.

"How lovely, I was afraid I'd slept too long." She leaned over and turned off the lamp, got out of bed and came up behind him, skin lightly touching his, and reached around his waist.

"In front of the window?"

"Why not? Nobody can see me."

Everywhere, her touch was light as air, and he closed his eyes. "I don't think you mind being teased," she whispered. "No, I don't think you do. Of course, if you do, you must tell me. Or, even, if you don't mind, you may tell me that. May say, 'Demetria, I like you to do this to me,' or maybe there are other things, you need only say them, I am a very understanding sort of person."

★ ★ ★

Later, back in bed, he asked, "What did it mean — the Greek word you said?"

"*Yassou?*"

"Yes."

"Means 'hello.' "

"Oh."

They were quiet for a time, then she said, "Are you married, Eric?"

"I'm not," he said. "I almost was, when I was twenty, just out of the naval college. I was engaged, to a nice girl, very pretty. We were in love, most of the way, anyhow, enough, and she was willing to be the wife of a sailor — never at home, but . . . I didn't."

He'd grown up amid the families of merchant officers, the wives eternally alone, raising children, knitting miles of sweaters. He was often in their homes — perfectly kept, the air thick with the smells of wax and cooking, and thick also with sacrifice, absence, clocks ticking in every room. And, in the end, though he couldn't say what else he wanted, he knew it wasn't that.

"And your family?"

"In Holland, my mother and sister. I can only hope they are surviving the occupation. I can't contact them."

"Can't?"

"Mustn't. The Germans read everything, and they don't like families with relatives in the free forces. Better, especially for someone like me, not to remind them you exist. They are vengeful, you know, will bring people in for questioning, lower their rations, force them to move."

"Still, at least they are in Holland. The Dutch are decent people, I think, with sensible politics."

"Most, but not all. We have our Nazis."

"Everyone has *some*, *chéri*, like cockroaches, you see them only at night. And, if they come out in daylight, then you know you have to do something about it."

"More than some. There is a Dutch Nazi party. Its symbol is a wolf trap."

She thought about it, then said, "How utterly horrible."

He nodded.

"And you? Perhaps a bit to the left?"

"Not much of anything, I'm afraid." This was no time to talk about the unions, the Comintern, the brutality — the knives and iron pipes — of politics on the docks. "I believe in kindness," he said. "Compassion. We don't have a party."

"You're a Christian?" she said. "You

138

seem to, ah, like the bed a little too much for that."

"Small *c* perhaps. Actually, as master of a ship, I have to give a sermon on Sunday morning. Pure agony, for me, telling people what to do. Be good, you evil bastards, or you'll fry in hell."

"You actually say such things?"

"I'd rather not, but it's in the book we use. So, I mumble."

"You have a good heart," she said, "God help you." She put a hand on his face, turned it toward her and kissed him, a warm kiss for being who he was, and for what would become of him.

He wondered, later on, about this conversation. Was it just conversation, or something more? Interrogation? Of a sort? Bare-assed, perhaps, but, even so, revealing. His life, his politics, who he was. That did hurt him, that idea, since for a time, while she was asleep, his heart ached because dawn would turn them into pumpkins. Why could not this be his usual life? People did live such lives, why was his fate different? Because it was, period. And not so bad; there was, at least, the occasional *amour*, the chance encounter. But was it chance? *Stop*, he told himself, *you*

139

think too much. Lovers ask questions, nothing new there. But meeting her was, well, fortuitous, and he had come to understand, after only a few weeks and the barest touch of experience, that a clandestine world was corrosive in just that way. It made you wonder.

And it was certainly true that, only an hour after he docked at the port of Alexandria, they were after him. First a staff intelligence officer, a captain, sweating in a little office. Thanking him for what he'd done, then asking him to write out a description of what had happened, a report. This was conventional, the captain said, and, if he didn't mind, he could do the bloody thing right now and they'd chat about it and that would be that.

But that wasn't that. Because just as they finished, there appeared a sort of Victorian apparition, a phantom materialized from the halcyon days of the British Empire. Heavy and red-faced, with china-blue eyes and an enormous, white, handlebar mustache, and even a hyphenated name — Something-Somethington — followed by "Call me Dickie, everybody does!"

Dickie had heard all about the *Noordendam* mission — "But must say *Santa Rosa,* eh?" — and wanted to shake

DeHaan's hand, which, heartily, he did. Then insisted on drinks, and more drinks, at a rather sinister bar buried in the backstreets behind the waterfront, then "a damned nuisance of a tea," at the khedivial yacht club, founded, he told DeHaan, when the Turkish viceroys ruled the city. The tea was offered by the British overseas arts council, or something like that — so very many drinks — where he was introduced to Demetria. Who stood close to him, with lavish glances, and put a hand on his arm while they talked and, eventually, mentioned supper. So it was off to a restaurant, where nobody ate much, and then, soon enough, the dear old Cecil, DeHaan feeling, somewhere in his astrology, the pull of exceptional stars. Or, put another way, too good to be true.

But so good he didn't care if it was true. And, he reasoned, she could have done what she needed to do in the little Greek restaurant — table chat would've sufficed, it didn't really need to be pillow chat.

Did it?

The daylight *Noordendam*, when night finally had to end in Room 38, was not easy on DeHaan. To technicolor memories and a head throbbing with Dickie's drinks, the freighter added its scent of burnt oil and boiled steam, fresh paint cooking in the sun, fierce clanging and shouting, gray ducts and bulkheads, and the whole thing, topped off by a plate of canned herring in cold tomato mush, pretty well did him in. "I'm going to my cabin," he told Ratter. "If the ship sinks, don't call me."

Ratter didn't, but Mr. Ali did. With a discreet but persistent tapping at DeHaan's door. *Go to hell,* DeHaan thought, rolling off his bunk. *And whatever it is, take it with you.*

"Forgive me, please," Mr. Ali said. "But a most urgent message for you, Captain. Most urgent."

He handed DeHaan a W/T message in plain text, which required his presence at a certain room in Building D-9, "this a.m., at 0900 hours." DeHaan swore, dressed, and set off down the gangway to find Building D-9. Everywhere in the harbor was the British Mediterranean fleet, countless ships of every sort, all of them, that morning, doing work that needed jackhammers. The sun blazed down, DeHaan wandered among a forest of low buildings and quonset huts, where nobody seemed to have heard of D-9 until a Royal Marine guarding a barracks said, "Are you looking for the registry people?"

"D-9, is all I know."

"They're in Scovill Hall, some of them anyhow, temporarily. It's the Old Stables building."

"Stables? For horses?"

"Well, fifty years ago, maybe."

"Where is it?"

"Quite a way, sir. Down this road a quarter mile, then turn left at the machine shop. Then, ah, then you'd best ask. For Scovill Hall, sir, or the Old Stables."

"Thank you," DeHaan said.

"Good luck, sir."

It took a half hour, by which time his head ached miserably and his shirt was soaked through, to find Scovill Hall, and several false trails before he reached the right room where, in the outer office, three WRENs were talking on telephones. One of them put a hand over the mouthpiece and said, "Sorry, rotten morning, you'll have to wait." He sat next to an officer from the Royal Greek Navy, based in Alexandria, along with the government in exile, since the fall of Greece at the end of April. "Very hot, today," DeHaan said to the officer.

Who raised his hands helplessly, smiled, and said, "No speak."

They waited together while the phones rang relentlessly — came back to life almost immediately after the receiver was put back in the cradle. A messenger hurried in, then another, cursing under his breath. "Be nice, Harry," one of the WRENs said.

For forty minutes, it never slowed.

"Sorry, he can't come to the phone."

"He'll call you back, sir."

"Yes, we've heard."

"No, their number is six forty, we're six fifty . . . No, it's another building, sir . . . Sorry, sir, I can't. I'm sure they'll answer when they can."

"Captain DeHaan?"

"What? Oh, yes, that's me."

"He'll see you now, Captain, that door to the left . . . No, that's the loo. There you are, Captain, that's him, just go right in."

Behind a gray metal desk, a naval lieutenant: university face and white tropical uniform — open collar, knee-length shorts, and high socks. Not yet thirty, DeHaan thought. The lieutenant, trying to finish up a phone call, pointed to a chair without missing a beat. "We really don't know much over here, it's coming in a little at a time. Total confusion, since yesterday. . . . I certainly will. . . . Yes, absolutely. Must ring off, Edwin, try me after lunch, will you? Count on it, goodby."

When he hung up, the phone rang again but he just shook his head and looked at DeHaan. "Not going well," he said.

"No?"

"Surely you've heard. They're on Crete, since yesterday, an air assault. Thousands and thousands of them, by parachute and glider. We got a lot of them before they hit the ground but still, they're holding. Extraordinary, you know, never been done before. Anyhow, you are?"

"Captain DeHaan, of the Dutch freighter *Noordendam*."

"Oh? Well, congratulations then."

He went to an open safe, and began to page through a sheaf of papers. Didn't find what he was looking for, and tried again. "Right," he said, relieved, "here you are." He had DeHaan sign his name in a book, with the date and time, then handed him a single sheet of yellow tele-printer paper.

MOST SECRET

FOR THE PERSONAL USE OF THE ADDRESSEE ONLY

NID   JJP/JJPL/0447

145

OAMT/95-0447 R 01 296 3B - 1600/18/5/41

From: Deputy Director/OAMT
To: E. M. DeHaan
           Master/NV Noordendam

MOST IMMEDIATE

Subj: Hyperion-Lijn NV Noordendam
           Amendment to status:
           All cargos, routes and ports of call
           to be directed henceforth,
           as of the date above, by this office

0047/1400/21/5/41+++DD/OAMT

"All clear?" the lieutenant said. The phone rang, then stopped.

"The message, yes. The rest" — DeHaan shrugged. "Who, exactly, is telling me this?"

"Well, NID is Naval Intelligence Division."

"And OAMT?"

"OAMT. Yes, certainly, that's an easy one." He pulled out the extendable shelf below the edge of the desk and ran a finger up one side of a list. "That is" — he hunted — "why that's the good old Office of Allied Marine Transport, that is. Fine chaps, over there."

This was very dry, and DeHaan, despite everything, almost laughed. "Who?"

"Can't say more. Now logically, Captain, you'd belong to the Ministry of War Transport, the convoy people, but logic's taken a hell of a beating since '39, so you'll just have to make do with those OAMT rascals."

"Ah, any particular rascal, that you know about?"

"I suspect there is, and I'm sure he'll be in touch with you. Meanwhile, anything you need, I'd suggest the people at the port office."

He came around the desk, DeHaan stood, they shook hands, and the lieutenant said, "Well, success, they say, always brings change, right? So, all for the best. Right?"

22 May. Campeche, Mexico.

A quiet port, on the northern coast of the Yucatán peninsula, looking out over the Gulf of Campeche. Not much happened here — now and then the local revolutionaries shot up the bank, and the occasional freighter called, but there was never very much money in the bank, and a high sandbar and the *temporales,* autumn

147

storms, sent much of the merchant trade elsewhere, to Mérida or Veracruz. Otherwise, the region was known for fearsome vampire bats and tasty bananas, and that was about it.

But there was some considerable excitement on the night of the twenty-second, which drew a crowd to the waterfront, which in turn drew a mariachi band, so the evening, despite the disaster, was festive. And the presence of a certain couple, vaguely middle-aged and well dressed, of obscure European origin, was noted, but not much discussed. They sat at an outdoor table at the Cantina Las Flores, on the leafy square that opened to the quay, the man tall and distinguished, with silvered temples beneath a straw hat, the woman in a colorful skirt and gold hoop earrings. They were from Mexico City, somebody said, and had made their way to the town by train and taxi, arriving two days before the excitement, before the Spanish freighter, called the *Santa Rosa*, caught fire at the end of the pier.

The *Santa Rosa*, having delivered drums of chemicals and crates of bicycles and sewing machines at Veracruz, had taken on a cargo of henequen — sisal hemp, raw cotton, and bananas, bound for Spain, then broken down, one day out of port, and put in to Campeche for repairs. This was nothing new to Campeche, everything broke down here, why not a freighter? The ship had docked in early April, which became May as the crew worked below deck and at a small machine shop ashore to repair the engine, while they waited, and waited, for parts. And — once again the local fate behaving as it usually did — the job was very nearly done when a cargo hold filled with henequen caught fire. The crew did what it could, the local firemen were called out, but the fire made steady progress, something blew up, and the crew left the ship and stood around on the dock, hands in pockets, wondering what came next.

At the foot of the pier, people drank beer and talked and listened to the band as night fell, bright yellow flames danced above the deck and the air was fragrant with the aroma of roasting bananas. It was a patient crowd, watching as the ship listed slowly to port, and waiting for it to roll over and disappear so they could go home.

The couple watched with them. Plenty of Europeans in Mexico City, what with war and politics in Europe, but one rarely saw them here. Actually, there'd been two more, a pair of young men, explosives experts generally employed by the Communist party in Mexico City, though at times willing to provide services on a freelance basis if the money was right. They were not, however, in Campeche that night, were on their way somewhere else by the time the fire drew a crowd. That left the couple, drinking red wine at the Cantina Las Flores.

"Really," the man said, "I only spent ten minutes with her."

"More like twenty," the woman said.

"Well, a party, you know, one talks to people."

"Oh don't be so innocent, *please*. She looks at you a certain way, people notice."

"She does not, *mi querida,* appeal to me. All those teeth."

At the end of the pier there was a soft *whump* as a gust of yellow flame flared high above the ship and the crowd said "Ahh."

The woman looked at her watch. "How long must we stay here?"

"Until it sinks."

"It's finished. Anyone can see that."

"Oh you never know — a sudden miracle."

"Unlikely, I would say. And I'm tired."

"You can go back to the hotel, you know."

"No, I'll stay here," she said, resigned. "The boys are gone?"

"Hours ago."

"So, should there be a miracle, as you say, what could you do?"

"I could, attend it."

She laughed. He was, had always been, a lovable bastard. "You," she said, shaking her head.

22 May. Port of Alexandria.

DeHaan was called to the port office at noon and told what the *Noordendam* had to do — preparation to begin immediately. "This is an emergency," the officer, a captain, told him. "So it's you, the *Maud McDowell*, from Canada, and two Greek ships, *Triton* and the tanker *Evdokia*. We need you, laddie," the captain said. "You're volunteering, right? I mean, you know what's involved — they're running out of everything. And it's only three hundred and seventy miles to Crete, maybe a day and a half. You make eleven knots, don't you?"

"We try."

"*Triton* may be a bit slower, but you'll be escorted, two destroyers, anyhow, and maybe some air cover. Good company. After that, you can go back to doing whatever it is, but we need everybody we can put our hands on, right away. So?"

"We'll go, of course. You can start loading whenever you want."

"We've already started, as it happens, trucks on the dock. And, something extra, we're going to repaint you, so you're back to being the *Noordendam*."

DeHaan nodded. He wasn't surprised — this was a full-scale invasion, and resupply was everything.

"We'll get it done," the captain said. DeHaan thought he might be a naval reserve officer, a merchant captain drafted into the Royal Navy, which made him, for some reason, feel better. "So, the best of British luck to you. And" — a mischievous smile — "no smoking."

DeHaan asked to use the telephone in the port office and called the number Dickie had given him. A woman with an Oriental accent answered, took his number and, fifteen minutes later, Dickie called him back. "Good to hear from you, DeHaan," he said, but his normal bluster was undercut by a worried note — what the hell does *he* want?

DeHaan told him about the orders from the port office.

From Dickie, a brief silence, only an airy hiss on the line. "Hm. Damned inconvenient, I'd say. But . . ."

Did he know?

"It would appear," he said, gaining momentum, "that the war has interrupted our war, but, nothing to be done, eh?" Meaning *surely you aren't asking me to get you out of this.*

But DeHaan was himself at war — they could do with him what they wanted, but he would, in return, have what he needed. Or else. "There is one condition."

"Oh?"

"The *Noordendam* must have a medical officer, a doctor. We won't sail without one."

More hissing. "Really." He didn't care for DeHaan's tone.

Too bad. "Yes, really."

"Well, I see your point."

"I'll be aboard, third slip, Pier Nine, all day, likely two or three days. Sailing time is secret, of course, but it isn't far off."

"Right, then, I'll have a go. Best I can do, I'm afraid."

"Find him, Dickie."

"Right."

DeHaan hung up. The curse of the trampship captain was that he had to serve as shipboard doctor, a medical manual provided for his use. And every time a seaman reported sick with a bellyache, DeHaan, reaching for the epsom salts, could think only one thing — *appendicitis*. Freighter captains had performed appendectomies at sea, the manual showed you how to do it, and, sometimes, given the extraordinary constitutions of merchant sailors, the patient actually recovered. To date, DeHaan had set broken bones, stitched up gashes, and treated burns, but the idea of surgery made him shudder.

Then, a few days earlier, he had determined that his doctoring days were over. It was daylight when they reached the ship off Cap Bon, and DeHaan realized that the sergeant who'd led them back to the beach, who'd explained his limp by saying he'd stepped in a hole, had lied. Walking across the deck, he left a bloody footprint with every step. Apparently, one of the surviving commandos served as corpsman, because DeHaan heard no more about it, but he believed that the sergeant had been shot, and had sworn to himself that he would not again take men into danger without a medical person to treat the wounded.

As he hung up on Dickie, none too gently, he thought, *"Right,"* yes, *right is what*

154

you are; hardheaded, stubborn Dutchman, better give him what he wants.

No smoking. Well, he guessed not. DeHaan returned to his ship to find a very hardworking crew, a very *quiet* crew. Cargo hatches off, winches grinding and steaming, booms swinging left and right, Van Dyck in charge. In the Egyptian heat the bosun had taken his shirt off, his torso thick and smooth, not a muscle to be seen. Van Dyck was the strongest man he'd ever known — DeHaan had seen him, on a bet, tear a deck of cards in half. But strength didn't matter that afternoon, Van Dyck was working with a delicacy worthy of a jeweler, not a bump, not a brush, not a hitch, as the cargo was lowered slowly, slowly, into the hold. First the crates, with stenciled markings: land mines, 75-millimeter tank shells, .303 ammunition, then the bombs, 250- and 500-pounders, stacked laterally all the way to the top of the hold. Five thousand tons of it, and more to be carried on deck. Along with four tanks, lashed down forward of the bridge and, up at the bow, two Hurricane fighter planes.

"Christ," Ratter said quietly, when DeHaan joined him on the bridge. "Anything happens, we won't come down for days."

They were at it all night, the piers floodlit despite the possibility of German air raids. Alexandria had been bombed, and would be again, but the convoy had to be loaded, and that meant working straight through until the job was done. On the *Noordendam*, they worked twelve-hour shifts with four hours' sleep and sandwiches for every meal. DeHaan was on deck, kneeling next to Van Dyck — who wore gloves to handle the hot steel — as he replaced a broken gear, when his doctor showed up.

He hadn't really known what to expect. Retired medical officer maybe, living with his wife in cheap and exotic Alexandria. But no such person stood at the foot of the gangway, where a Royal Marine guard shouted up, "Says he's here to see the captain."

"Send him up."

The man, a hesitant smile on his face, climbed the gangway slowly, carefully, hand white on the rope that served as a railing, lest he go flying off into the water and be swallowed by a sea monster.

"Are you Captain DeHaan?" he said,

consulting a scrap of paper. "Am I on the right boat?"

And what language was this? Not Dutch, and not quite German. Yiddish, then, and DeHaan saw exactly what Dickie had done and, despite himself, felt a surge of admiration.

The man was in his twenties, wore a baggy black suit, a narrow black tie, a white shirt — now gray, from months of washing in hotel sinks — and a black hat, perhaps a size too large. He had a high forehead, and anxious, inquisitive eyes — a hopeful face, prepared for disappointment, with shoulders already hunched in the anticipation of it. "My name is Shtern," he said.

Working around the open cargo holds, the crew was too attentive to the visitor for DeHaan's taste, so he took him off to the chartroom, where they sat on stools by the sloping map table.

"Dr. Shtern, welcome to the *Noordendam*," DeHaan said in German, "though she is called the *Santa Rosa* just now."

"Doctor? Well, almost."

"You're not a doctor?"

"Formerly a medical student, sir, for three years, in Heidelberg."

"You are German?"

"Not really anything now, sir. We came from the Ukraine, originally, a small place."

"Three years," DeHaan said. "But you can do everything a doctor does, no?"

"On cadavers, I have worked extensively. Unfortunately, they made us leave Germany, so I could not continue."

"You came to Alexandria, from Germany?"

"Well, first to Antwerp, for a time, until we tried to go to Palestine. We saw it, from the boat, but the English arrested us and we were put in a camp, on Cyprus. Then, after a few months, they let us come here."

"What we need on this ship, Herr Shtern, is a doctor, so from now on you'll be Dr. Shtern, if you don't mind."

"Anything, sir, as long as money can be sent to my wife — it's been very hard for us. We are Jews, sir. Refugees."

"We?"

"My wife, and three children, little ones." Proudly, he smiled.

"Merchant crews are usually paid off at the end of a voyage, whenever that is, but if you'll give us the particulars, we can arrange for the money to be wired to your wife."

"You have a dispensary, sir? Instruments?"

"We'll get you whatever you need. Today, Dr. Shtern."

"And, sir, may I ask, about the money?"

"As an officer, you'll earn thirty British pounds a month — about a hundred and fifty dollars."

Shtern's face lit up. "Thank you, sir," he said. "Thank you so much."

"You can thank me, Dr. Shtern, but what we do here is dangerous," DeHaan said, thinking of the *little ones*. "Especially now. I hope you understand that."

"Yes, I know," he said quietly. "I read the papers. But I must find something to do."

"I'm going to send you off with my first officer, he'll make sure you get everything you want — we have some medicines, take a look at them, but our inventory is primitive. Also, we'll buy you clothes, so you don't have to worry about that."

Shtern nodded. "It will all be new for me," he said, "but I will do my best, sir, you will see."

It was after eleven that night when DeHaan finally got around to doing what he'd been putting off for days. He sat at the table in the wardroom, drinking coffee, and working on a wireless message to Terhouven. Outside, the loading continued, a symphony of whistles, bells, and drumming machinery, but DeHaan, concentrating hard, barely heard it. The commercial code used by the Hyperion Line was likely no mystery to the British — or anybody else, he assumed, so he had to write as elliptically as he could, and trust that Terhouven would read between the lines.

The first part was easy, a monthly salary to be paid, to a bank in Alexandria, for a recently hired medical officer. Next — now it grew difficult — the new cargo, "designated by local authorities for a Mediterranean port." And if Terhouven, following the war in the London papers and knowing the origin of the transmission, thought that meant a load of figs to Marseilles, then so be it. For the last, the hardest, part, the best DeHaan could do, after a number of false starts, was "You will be aware of changes in our administrative status." This puzzle Terhouven could work out, if he didn't know already: so much for Section IIIA of the Dutch Admiralty's General Staff and Commander Leiden, they were now under new ownership. And, as to who exactly that might be, well, it was those people to whom one referred elliptically.

Not that Terhouven could do anything about it but, far away in the land of paper, life did go on — with war-risk insurance held by so-called "clubs" of shipping lines, money changing hands, lawyers, and, in general, all the byzantine apparatus of vessel ownership. Did their change in status affect any of this? DeHaan didn't know — maybe all it meant was that Terhouven could now worry in new and interesting ways.

Ratter entered the wardroom, collapsed onto the banquette, took his hat off, and ran his fingers through his hair.

"Johannes."

"Eric."

"Coffee?"

"Something."

"Go get a bottle from the chartroom, if you like."

"I will, in a minute. For now, I'll just bother you."

"No bother, I'm just finishing up a wire for Terhouven."

"Ah, if he could only see us now. He'd shit."

"I expect he would. How's the work?"

"Miserable. We broke a cable, dropped

ten bombs down on top of everything else."

"They go off?"

"Seem not to have. Give 'em time, though. And, the midnight-watch crew was short two men."

"You look for them?"

"I did, and gone they are."

DeHaan swore.

"One of the Spaniards, and AB Vandermeer."

"No, Vandermeer?"

"Tough little guy was not so tough, turns out. By now, he's getting himself screwed cross-eyed, and means to stay alive. Will you turn them in?"

DeHaan thought about it. "No. Let them live with themselves. What about our doctor?"

"Hard at work, and very eager. Bandages, Mercurochrome, splinted up a crushed finger. Glad to be rid of that, Eric?"

"Maybe a little."

"One of the men called him 'the rabbi.'"

"To his face?"

"No."

"You stop it?"

"I said, 'You can call him that when he sews up your worthless hide, but until then, shut your fucking mouth.' I think he got the idea. What are you telling Terhouven?"

"We're now in British hands — the dark side of the navy."

"Not this convoy."

"No, but if we don't blow up, we will go places and do things."

Ratter shook his head. "Stranger and stranger, isn't it."

DeHaan read back through the wire, and printed *EMD* at the bottom.

"But," Ratter said, "now that I think about it, the last time I went to a Gypsy, she said something about mysteries. Shadows? Darkness? Something."

"Did you, really?"

"You know, I actually did. In Macao, years ago. She was Russian, a redhead."

"And?"

"She told my fortune. I thought maybe there would be more, but there wasn't."

DeHaan folded the paper in half. They would have to keep radio silence, once they were under way, so Mr. Ali would send it before they sailed. "We're due to refuel, in a few hours," he said. "Food and supplies, everything."

"Until then, did you say something about a bottle?"

"Left-hand cabinet, third drawer down. Bring it in here, I'll join you."

23 May, 0300 hours. Port Administration Building.

In a small room in the basement, a briefing by the captain of the HMS *Ellery*, the destroyer that would lead the convoy. The masters of the four merchant ships took notes — key signals to be made by Aldis lamp or flag, zigzag course to make life harder for enemy submarines, meteorological report. The captain paced back and forth, sometimes pausing to scribble a number or a diagram on a blackboard, bits and pieces of chalk flying off as he wrote. Now and then, the two Greek captains looked at each other — what did he say? The first time it happened, the Canadian master of the *Maud McDowell*, a fat, white-haired old rogue, glanced over at DeHaan and cocked an eyebrow.

"The situation on Crete," the destroyer captain said, "turns on the battle for the airfields, Maleme, Heraklion, and Retimo. The Germans have taken Maleme, and paid dearly for it, and continue to do so, under counterattack by a New Zealand division. We hold the port of Sphakia, on the south side of the island. It's been a very hard fight, we've lost ships, and aircraft, but we've sunk one of their troop convoys — five thousand men — so the thing's a long way from being over, and this convoy could make all the difference. Understood?"

The captains nodded.

"So then, to conclude, let me remind you again that the important thing is to keep your station — if you lag behind, we can't help you. Understood?"

They understood.

"Very well, H-hour is oh-four-hundred, and off we go. Last chance for questions — anybody?"

No questions.

The captain laid down his chalk, picked up an eraser, and began to clean the board. When he was done, he turned and, for a moment, looked at them. "Thank you, gentlemen," he said.

0520 hours. At sea.

They sailed in a diamond pattern: the *Ellery* protected the left flank, the two Greek ships led, side by side, followed by *Maud McDowell* and *Noordendam*, the destroyer HMS *Covington* on the right. With Kees at the helm, DeHaan stood below the bridge and watched the *Covington* as she maneuvered.

She was, to DeHaan's eye, a handsome thing. Long and gray, in the gray light of dawn, trailing white gulls as she slid through a gray sea studded with whitecaps. The canvas covers were off her guns and, from time to time, he could hear the sharp bark of an announcement over the Tannoy speakers. Restless, she altered course, angled a point or two east of the convoy, then, a minute later, swung back to the west. This in response, he supposed, to the ASDIC system, pinging away, searching for the echoes of submarines beneath the water. With thirty-four knots of speed to their eight, she was not unlike a border collie, patrolling back and forth, guarding her four fat sheep.

DeHaan was, that morning, particularly tuned to his engine, its pitch, its vibration in the deck beneath his feet. Now, even at eight knots, a speed dictated by the ancient *Triton*, it was laboring. Because *Noordendam* was clearly overloaded — holds full to the hatch covers with bombs and mines, the foredeck carrying the four tanks and the Hurricane fighter planes, the wind sighing, a strange, ghostly hum, as it blew across their wings.

Then, suddenly, the engine slowed. DeHaan froze for an instant, then ran up the ladder to the bridge, where Kees was already shouting down the voice tube. "What are you doing?" DeHaan said, taking the tube from Kees. Before he could answer, DeHaan heard Kovacz say, " . . . get it done as soon as we can." He didn't wait to hear more, handed the device back to Kees, and headed for the engine room, four decks below.

He skidded down the ladderways, as various crewmen turned to look at him, eventually reaching the grilled platform at the top of the final ladder, thirty feet above the engine room. From there, he peered down through a haze of oily smoke, tinted red by the engine-room light. Below, a forest of pipes, three giant boilers, auxiliary engines, condensers, generators, pumps, and, its giant brass pistons now rising and falling at slow speed, the engine itself. It hurt to breathe down here, there was no air, only fumes — steam, singed rags, burning oil, scorched iron. Hot as hell, and louder, the noise of running machinery swelling to fill the huge iron vault and echoing back off the hull.

As his eyes became accustomed to the darkness, he saw the firemen and oilers gathered around the number three boiler, with Kovacz at the center, wielding a four-foot wrench. As DeHaan watched, Kovacz set the wrench on a thick pipe, a fireman grabbed the handle beside him, and together they hauled, trying to break the pipe loose from an elbow joint. DeHaan ran down the ladder.

Kovacz's denim shirt was black with sweat, and a bright red scald mark ran up the inside of his forearm from wrist to elbow. In order to be heard, DeHaan had to shout. "Stas, how bad is it?"

Kovacz nodded toward the pipe and said, "Blew a fitting, so number three is shut down." From a crack in the elbow joint, a plume of steam spurted ten feet in the air.

"Can we make eight knots?"

"Better not — we'll have hell to pay with the other two."

"How long, Stas?"

Kovacz didn't bother to answer. Using a wet rag, which steamed as he grabbed the wheel on the head of the wrench, he tried to force it tighter on the pipe, then took hold of the handle. "On three," he told the fireman, counted, and growled with effort as he thrust his weight downward. For a moment, his feet left the deck. *Psia krew,* he said in Polish. *Dog's blood.*

An oiler appeared with a steel mallet and looked inquiringly at Kovacz. "Yes, try it." The oiler swung the hammer back, paused, then banged it hard on the elbow fitting, trying to break the rust in the threads. Kovacz and the fireman tried again, but the pipe wouldn't give. Kovacz left the wrench in place, put his hands on his knees and lowered his head. "All right," he said, voice just rising above the din, "somebody go and get me the goddamn saw." He stood back up, wiped some of the sweat off his face, and met DeHaan's eyes. *Sorry.*

"Polish navy was never like this," DeHaan said.

"The fuck it wasn't."

On deck, the AB serving as signalman was waiting for him. The rest of the convoy had moved away, but the *Covington* was standing close off their beam. From the wing of the destroyer's bridge, an expertly operated Aldis lamp was flickering at them. "They want to know what's wrong," the signalman said.

"Make back, 'Mechanical problem.' "

The signalman began to work the shutter on the lamp. When he was done, the *Covington*'s signaller responded. "He says, 'How long?' sir."

"I wish I knew," DeHaan said.

" 'Unknown,' sir?"

"Yes."

As the message was completed, the *Covington* abruptly changed course and circled away from *Noordendam*, gaining speed as she moved.

The signalman said, "What's she doing, sir?"

DeHaan wasn't sure. Thirty seconds passed, the *Covington* now heading due east, then her bow came over hard in a very sharp change of course. Now DeHaan knew exactly, and took great care that the AB saw no sign of what went on inside him.

From the *Covington*, a double bleat on its Klaxon. A slow count to six, then the hull of the *Noordendam* rang, a brief, dull note, as though it had been hit with a giant rubber hammer. And, a few seconds later, twice more.

The AB's eyes were wide.

"Depth charges," DeHaan said.

0700. The *Covington* sailed away, and *Noordendam* was alone on the sea.

The destroyer's attack had lasted twenty minutes, the ship quartering above the suspected submarine and, as the freighter crew watched, deploying its barrel-shaped depth charges in groups: three rolled over rails at the stern, two fired outward by deck mortars — a traditional pattern called the *five of clubs*. Years earlier, when DeHaan was still serving as a second mate in the Dutch East Indies trade, his first officer had explained the principle of depth charges in a way he never forgot: water had its own physics, especially where explosions were concerned. "If you've decided to end it all," he'd said, "and you want to make sure, fill your mouth with water and put the muzzle of the gun in there — you'll blow the back of your head off."

The *Covington*'s attack had evidently not succeeded — assuming it was a submarine in the first place, ASDIC was known to discover phantoms of its very own — because no oil, no debris, rose to the surface. And no giant bubbles, though German subs could, and did, send up *Pillenwerfers,* false bubbles meant to deceive their attackers. Therefore, likely having lost contact, the destroyer could not stay long as nursemaid to the *Noordendam*, so wished her well and disappeared over the horizon. The freighter was kept just under way, as Kovacz and his crew struggled in the engine room, and everyone else waited for the torpedo.

Still, the day turned out to be nice.

Not too warm, thanks to a sharpening breeze, and mostly sunny, except for some heavy cumulonimbus clouds in the southern sky. Pretty ones — thick and gray at the bottom, white and sharply curved as they rose, and wispy on top against a rich blue sky. Oh, Kees kept grumbling about a falling barometer, but trust him to see the dark side. "It's going to blow seven bells of shit all the way up to Genoa" was the way he put it to DeHaan. But not much the captain could do about that, was there, and the *Noordendam* lay low and heavy in the sea, certainly a plus when iffy weather was expected.

For DeHaan, there wasn't much to do. He wandered here and there, at one point stopping by the radio room to see if Mr. Ali had heard anything new on the BBC. As DeHaan opened the door, Ali was bent over his table and very concentrated, one hand holding a headphone to his ear, the other teasing the dial. When he saw DeHaan, he offered him the headset, saying, "We're getting somebody's radio — on the high-frequency band."

Noise was all it was, initially, a transmission well beyond its calculated range, though signals were known to wander great distances if they reached the open sea. After a moment, DeHaan realized the noise was a heavy drone — interference? No, it changed octaves, then fell back, faded away to silence, but returned. With a voice, which called out ". . . south of you!" and sounded as though the speaker had been running. Then the signal broke up.

DeHaan started to take the headset off but Ali held up a hand, *wait.* He was right, the drone came back, for a moment perfectly clear. *Airplane engine.* "Nine-forty! Nine-forty! He's . . ." Lost. A sharp burst of static, maybe static, or something in the plane. Then, seconds later, "Oh bloody hell," said quietly, to himself. Again, the signal broke into snips of noise, then faded out. DeHaan held the headset away from his ears and said, "Where is it coming from?"

"On Crete, I think. An airplane. Working with armor perhaps, nine-forty the number on a tank."

"Can't really hear much," DeHaan said. In fact he could, but didn't like doing it, and handed the headset back to Ali. "You'll try for the BBC?"

Ali glanced at the clock on his panel. "A

few minutes yet, Captain," he said.

By 0850, Kovacz had the engine back up to full steam. DeHaan calculated that the convoy had gained, in three and a half hours, twenty-one miles, which the *Noordendam* could make up — eleven knots to the convoy's eight — in seven hours. For that time, they would sail alone. An inviting target, for anybody who happened to be in the neighborhood, but if they hadn't been attacked by now, DeHaan guessed, they were probably safe. Either *Covington*'s ASDIC sounding had been a false contact — a sunken ship, perhaps — or the submarine had been driven off. Meanwhile, the storm was gaining on them; heavy clouds turned the morning dark, and a curtain of rain spanned the southern sky where dazzling forks of lightning fired off two and three at a time, with distant claps of thunder. The wind was rising, but they had also a following current, which added speed as they chased the convoy.

DeHaan, unable to fight Germans or weather, and running as fast as he could, had to do *something*, so turned his attention to morale. They'd taken on fresh beef at Alexandria, and he ordered it served for lunch, with mustard sauce — the cook's one good trick — and potatoes, a double beer ration, and fresh pineapple for dessert. Then he had the officers rounded up for coffee.

Kees had to remain on forenoon watch, as did the Danish fireman, Poulsen, now serving as apprentice second engineer, but Ratter, Kovacz, Ali, and Shtern — the creases still evident in his work shirt and trousers, a blue officer's cap set squarely on his head — all gathered in the wardroom.

When they were settled, DeHaan announced that by 1600 hours they should be rejoining the convoy.

"Didn't you tell me," Ratter said, "that we would have air cover?"

"I did. But, as you see . . ."

"They're in trouble," Kovacz said. "We're lucky to have anything."

"True," Mr. Ali said. "The eight o'clock BBC had that certain sound to it."

"What sound?" Shtern said.

"The sound of losing. 'Enemy attacks in great strength.' 'British forces making a stand.' What they said about France in '40."

"What if they lose Sphakia?" Ratter said.

"They'll let us know," DeHaan said.

Ratter's grin meant *are you sure?*

"Better be ready for it," Kovacz said. "What they have on Crete are British and Greek troops evacuated from the Peloponnesus, three weeks ago. Some of them ran all the way from Albania, and you know what retreat is, it's chaos, lost weapons, missing officers, busted vehicles — this isn't a *stand* on Crete, it's a *last* stand."

"You saw it, Mr. Kovacz, in '39?" Shtern said.

"Some of it, yes. All I wanted."

"They might hang on," DeHaan said. "*They* don't think they're finished. More coffee, Dr. Shtern?"

"Yes, thank you."

"There's cream and sugar — better enjoy it while it lasts."

Shtern took a spoonful of sugar. DeHaan asked Ratter how Cornelius was coming along — the mess boy had replaced Patapouf as assistant cook.

"Can't say. The cook mumbles to himself all day, but then, he always did. Food's the same."

"This cook," Shtern said, then wasn't quite sure how to put it.

Mr. Ali laughed. "May I smoke?" he said.

"Below deck, certainly," DeHaan said.

Ali fitted a cigarette into his holder. "Life at sea, Dr. Shtern, you'll get used to it."

A knock at the wardroom door produced one of the AB lookouts, binoculars around his neck. "Mr. Kees wants you, Captain."

The AB was badly shaken, and everyone looked at DeHaan. Who wanted to sigh, but couldn't, so said, "I'll be back," and put his saucer on top of his cup. Rising, he checked his watch — life had returned to something like normal for one hour, no more.

On deck, a dozen crewmen stared silently out to sea, where a tower of black smoke rose two hundred feet in the darkened sky, thick smoke, stronger than the wind, driven by heavy orange flame that boiled and rolled at its base. DeHaan held out his hand and the AB gave him the binoculars. It was the Greek tanker *Evdokia*, down at the stern.

When he reached the bridge, Kees said, "That was our torpedo, you know. I've been wondering where it was."

"Any survivors?"

"Haven't seen any. Navy would've picked up what was left."

Fourteen thousand tons of oil, aviation gas,

whatever they had. The sea around *Evdokia* was covered with burning oil.

"They'll always take a tanker, if they can get one," Kees said.

That was true. DeHaan had heard of convoys where a tanker was literally roped between two destroyers. He raised the binoculars and swept them across the burning sea, but all he found was an upside-down rubber raft, its fabric stained with age.

He gave the binoculars back to the AB. "There might still be someone in the water," he said.

"Aye-aye, sir," the AB said. He swallowed once, then turned to keep watch.

DeHaan headed for the wardroom.

Later, he took the four-to-eight, and worked *Noordendam* through the storm. She rode like a pig, with all her weight, wallowing in the valleys, nosing up the oncoming wave and hauling herself over. As Ratter came up to relieve him they sighted the *Ellery*, a mile or so behind the convoy, and the destroyer changed course in order to guide them in. As they fell into line behind the *Maud McDowell*, they saw her hit by lightning, and, for an instant, a ball of blue fire danced on the lightning rod at the masthead. Which worked, apparently, guiding the charge down to the sea, and not into the holds. Had that happened, they would have known.

As the storm passed over them, DeHaan returned to his cabin, where he tried to sleep. He was desperately tired, down to nothing — the other sense of *exhausted,* and various parts of him throbbed and ached. *So, sleep,* he told himself. But he couldn't. In fact, insomnia was nothing new. As a child, he'd nightly tricked himself to sleep by imagining that he was on a train, the last car of a train, which was filled with beds, where everybody he knew lay safe and asleep, where it was up to him to close the door at the back of the car, and, making sure it was closed, he could then climb into the last bed, and go to sleep.

But that was a long time ago.

So he turned on the lamp and stood before the forty-book library. *Who wants a job?* France, war, the travails of the Van Hoogendams, dog-eared at page 148. A legacy, a sinister uncle, the beauteous Emma, and, then, oblivion.

25 May, 1830 hours. Port of Sphakia.

It had been lovely here, once upon a time. A Mediterranean fishing village, with

179

tall, narrow houses jammed together in a circle around the port, their peeling, sun-bleached walls ochre or Venetian red, apricot or pastel green, nets hung to dry over rough cobbles, fishing boats bobbing in cerulean water. You can only get fish — the travelers would say, returning to a cold summer in Rotterdam — bread and figs and goat cheese and wonderful bad wine, and the mail comes once a week if it comes at all but the sun shines and the sky is blue.

Now, one of the houses had lost its front wall, you could see old wallpaper and un-made beds, while its neighbors were missing the glass in their windows, and the one over the *taverna* had a charcoal-col-ored blast pattern on the third floor.

At the western end of the little bay they'd handled cargo. One tall derrick was bent in the middle, and from another came showers of blue sparks as the welders worked in the dusk. But it was, at least, deep. Enough so that the freighters could tie up to the pier, as camouflage-painted trucks arrived to take the cargo away. DeHaan counted four cranes that looked like they still worked, and a tender was at-tempting to fix a line to a small trawler, floating hull up where the wooden timbers of the dock had burned for a time before they were extinguished. Out in the bay, the *Ellery* and the *Covington* joined a heavy cruiser, and various corvettes and mine-sweepers, all of them guarding what DeHaan suspected might be the last usable port on Crete.

Moments after they tied up, a naval warrant officer, who looked like he'd been awake for days, came aboard and found DeHaan. "We'll unload the Greek ship first," he said, "except for your planes, we'll want those right away."

"Are we under fire here?" DeHaan asked him.

"Now and then," the officer said. "It's been, in general, pretty thick."

From the mountains behind the port, DeHaan could hear artillery exchanges, the echoes bouncing off the slopes before they reached the harbor.

When the planes came, a few minutes later, it turned out that the town of Sphakia was the proud owner of a siren. It wasn't much of a siren, some tired old thing the mayor bought, that climbed up and down in a bass voice, cracked and hoarse, and got the dogs barking. The alarms from the warships in the bay were far more convincing, Klaxons sounding a series of shrill bleats as the sailors ran for their battle stations.

DeHaan had, at that moment, walked the warrant officer to the gangplank and waited courteously until he reached the dock. He was a fair-skinned man with reddish hair, not placid but steady, and surely hardened to mishap, and he seemed, as he turned and searched the sky, more than anything else, annoyed. Not frightened, not furious, it was simply that what was coming his way would cause him work and irritation, was the last straw, and he pressed his lips together and slowly shook his head, then strolled off down the dock toward the *Maud McDowell*.

The planes were Junkers 87s — Stukas, single-engine dive-bombers with fixed wheels in curved wells on wide struts. Three of them, coming in from the north, from Maleme, maybe twenty miles away, skimming over the treetops at five hundred feet and clearly headed for the port. By then, the navy had been radioed by British troops on the front lines so, from the cruiser, from both destroyers and the smaller ships, came a blizzard of antiaircraft gunnery. Oerlikon guns, firing at a rate of five hundred rounds a minute —

eight-second bursts from sixty-round drums, changed quickly by the loader — and Bofors guns, a hundred and twenty rounds a minute, but with heavier shells. Every fifth round, on both weapons, was a tracer, so the fireworks were spectacular, dozens of long red streams flowing over the *Noordendam*, then tracking downward as the planes dove. DeHaan stood transfixed, tracer whizzing above his head, lower, and lower.

The bombers attacked three abreast, and the one in the middle blew up right away, the second crashed into the forest on the lower slopes, setting the resinous pine trees ablaze, while the third pilot veered, too much fire in his face, got rid of his bomb — which blew up a stable behind the town — slanted over the water to the east of the ships, trailed smoke for a moment, and cartwheeled into the sea.

The second wave did better. Following the curve of the mountain, then turning sharply over the port. One bomb raised a giant waterspout between the *Triton* and *Maud McDowell*, a second, hit by gunfire, blew up its plane a hundred feet above the *Noordendam*, showering the deck with burning metal, and the third — well, nobody saw what happened to the third.

Where's the RAF? Not here. Except for the two Hurricanes on the *Noordendam,* tied down with steel wire. Otherwise, only a new set of Stukas. But the navy was doing well, the hammering and drumming was frantic, and constant, though some of it hit the houses in the port, white puffs of plaster blowing off the walls.

DeHaan scrambled up the ladderway to the bridge, where Kees and an AB were watching the show. Then he was on his back, the AB lying across his legs, both of them covered with glass, while outside it was raining iron, first a light patter, then a heavy downpour. As DeHaan tried to free himself, he realized he'd gone deaf in one ear and shook his head like a dog, but it didn't help. Then Kees appeared, blood running from his nose and flowing down either side of his mouth, and, once he managed to get DeHaan stood upright, he cupped a hand beneath his chin and spit out the stub of his pipe.

Looking around, DeHaan realized that there was no glass in the windows, which made it easier to see flames, up by the bow, and, as he watched, a bright yellow flash. So, they were on fire. *And that's that.* He tried to run, but he was very wobbly, and staggered like a drunk out onto the bridge wing. Somebody had set off the fire siren, and he could make out dark figures dragging a hose toward the bow. Going forward, he met Van Dyck, who led one of the firefighting crews, hanging on to a high-pressure hose, which sent a thick stream of water onto one of the tanks, which was burning, and periodically firing a shell into the sky from a hole in its front deck.

"*Maud McDowell*," Van Dyck shouted.

DeHaan looked for it but he couldn't see it. He saw the *Triton*, but not the *Maud McDowell*, because it wasn't there. It wasn't burning, it wasn't sinking. It wasn't.

30 May. Port of Tangier.

Wilhelm made tea with a flourish, raising and lowering the kettle as the stream of water splashed onto the mint leaves packed in the bottom of a glass. "My tea ritual," she said. "This time every day."

The sun was setting in the window of her studio. Lying back on a divan, her model, wearing only a blanket with tiny silver mirrors hanging from threads, smoked a cigarette and watched like a cat.

"Right, Leila?" Wilhelm said in French. "Time for tea."

"Is it always poured like that?" DeHaan said.

"It cools the water," Leila said. "So you don't break the glass." She was beautiful, strangely so, and though she'd covered herself modestly with the blanket, Wilhelm's easel revealed what lay beneath it. In heavy pencil shaded with scribbles, her hip curved as she reached for an orange in a bowl beside the divan. DeHaan looked for the bowl, but there was only a stack of books.

"We wondered when we would see you again," Wilhelm said, now in Dutch. DeHaan turned his head as she spoke — only some of his hearing had returned on one side.

"You almost didn't see me at all," he said. "She doesn't understand Dutch, does she?"

"No." The idea was faintly amusing. "I wouldn't think so." She finished pouring the tea and left it to steep, an oily cloud rising from the leaves in each glass. From the pocket of her faded cotton shirt she took a cigarette. "Care for one?"

It was a Gauloise — what British seamen called a *golliwog* — and DeHaan lit it with particular pleasure. "And life here?" he said.

"We are, how to say, *fully engaged* — is that the military term?"

"Yes."

"Leila dear," Wilhelm said, "I think there's hot water now."

Leila put out her cigarette, gave Wilhelm a complicit smile — *very well, I'll leave you alone with him* — and padded off into the other room. A moment later, the sound of a shower.

"Anyhow, it's good to see you," Wilhelm said.

"I had to get away from that damn ship," DeHaan said. "We're ordered to anchor here, for the moment, but I expect we'll be off again soon enough."

"Was it terrible?"

DeHaan was surprised, but apparently it showed. "We were in the war," he said. "A few close calls. Other people had it much worse, but it was bad enough. We had a tank, deck cargo, catch fire — we weren't sure how that happened, maybe an antiaircraft round — and we had two hoses on it, a lot of water, but every time we stopped it glowed red. The people in Alexandria had loaded it fully armed, a crazy thing to do, and the ammunition kept going off. It should've gone over the side, but we couldn't get near it, and

187

it was too heavy anyhow. The deck got very hot, and we had bombs under there."

"Was anybody hurt?"

"Earlier, we lost a man."

"I'm sorry, Eric."

"Yes, I am too, but we were lucky not to lose more." He believed in the modern idea that it was good to talk about bad experiences but now he saw that it wasn't really so, not for him. "What do you mean, 'fully engaged'?"

"Oh, something big's going on here, we're only a small part of it, but we've bribed half the clerks at the electric company." She paused, then said "Who knows" in a dark, ironic voice, as though she were telling a ghost story.

"This is coming from Leiden's office?"

"No, it's the British now. We've either been promoted, or demoted, or maybe just under new management, it's hard to know. Whatever it is, it's *grown*, and they ask all the time, in that crusty way they have, if we can get help. Which isn't so easy, but we've tried. And been turned down, more than once, which makes poor Hoek furious."

"Can I do something?"

"I doubt they'd like that. Maybe lucky

for you, because the police have been around. Someone's not happy."

"Moroccan police?"

"Spanish. Anyhow, they say they're police, show you a badge, but . . ."

"What do they want?"

"They ask about so-and-so, who you've never heard of. I get the feeling they just want to get in the house and have a look, and maybe scare you a little."

"Does it work?"

"Of course it does, these men in their suits, very serious, it makes you wonder what they know." She shrugged.

In the other room, the shower was turned off. "So, then," Wilhelm said, "the price of cheese."

30 May. Baden-Baden.

For S. Kolb, the nightmare continued.

Now in a nightmare spa town, amid crowds of SS officers dripping hideous insignia — skulls, axes, god-awful stuff — chins held high, girlfriends hanging on their arms. Their left arms — the right was reserved for saluting, for heilhitlering each other, every thirty seconds. *Nazi heaven*, he thought.

Three weeks earlier, he'd been marooned in Hamburg, waiting for his case officer, the Englishman who called himself *Mr. Brown*, to find him a way out of nightmare Germany, as the ship he was to take to Lisbon had been inconveniently sunk. There he'd moldered, in a sad room on a sad street near the docks, waiting for the agent *Fräulein Lena* to return, and, alone for days with only newspapers for company, had been overwhelmed by fantasies about this woman — stern, middle-aged, corset-bound, but more wildly desirable lonely hour by lonely hour. She only *seemed* to be a stuffy doughmaiden of the *Mittelbourgeoisie*, he decided. Beneath that whalebone-clad exterior, banked fires smoldered, secret depravities lurked.

And, lo and behold, they did!

Dangling helplessly between caution and lust, he'd broken to the latter, and, when Fräulein Lena finally knocked at his door, long after midnight, he had invited her to share his bottle of apricot brandy. So thick, so sweet, so lethal. And, she agreed. It was quite some time before anything happened, but, when they reached the last quarter of the bottle, a polite conversation between strangers was ended by a big apricot kiss. God, she was as lonely as he was, soon enough strutting around the room in those very corsets — pink, however, not black — that had set his imagination alight. And, he did not have to dismantle them, as he'd feared, she did that herself and took her sweet time doing it as he watched with hungry eyes. And, soon enough, he was to learn that secret depravities did lurk — the same ones shared by humanity the world over but never mind, they were new and pink that night, and slowly but thoroughly explored. Even, at last, that final depravity, the most secret of them all, which lay hidden beneath *the seventh veil,* so-called, which is archetypically never dropped.

Well, she dropped it.

And betrayed him.

She'd met him, a few days after their night together, in a tearoom — bright yellow, with doilies and frilly curtains and everything too small, and she'd brought good news from Brown. This involved former Comintern operatives on a Latvian fishing trawler that would make an unscheduled call at the city on the twenty-seventh. He was to be spirited away by these men, ethnic Russians from the Latvian minority, and left at an Italian port — Nice, formerly French, lately Italian, and reputedly flexible for suspicious passengers, coming or going, who traveled with money. And, she was eager to report, she had a fresh, new identity for him, that old *S. Kolb* was getting a little shopworn, *nicht wahr?* These papers she would present to him, *in his room.* And this would take place *tomorrow afternoon.* At which time, her look said it all, unspeakable delights awaited him.

And, then, he knew. She'd sold him, or was about to, or was thinking about it. What, exactly, was he reading? Her eyes? Voice? Soul? He couldn't say, but his antennae blazed, and that was all it took. And, an experienced operative, he'd learned that in the matter of flight sooner was always better. So he took her hand above the bundt cake, told her he could barely wait, might they go somewhere right away, and be, together? It took a fraction of a second before she reacted, and in that instant he shivered as though the Gestapo had stepped on his grave. "Tomorrow, my sweet," she said.

He said he would be right back, then it was off to the toilet, lock the door, out the window, and up the alley. Maybe they were waiting for him but he didn't think so. They would be at the hotel, *tomorrow afternoon,* or when he got back. *Why?* But he had no time for that — he scuttled up the street and ducked into an office building, where he hid in the office of an insurance brokerage — a potential client concerned that his heirs should not suffer penury. Thirty minutes later he was on his way out of town, possessions easily abandoned, as they had been in countless other hotels. In his profession, one didn't keep things.

But really, why? He didn't know. Maybe she'd been theirs from the beginning, maybe it was just that day, maybe because of the weather, maybe because he'd led her into sin. Poor, helpless Fräulein Lena, tempted, and seduced. He'd certainly been told and told, don't *ever* do that. Well, he had, too bad, and now began a new nightmare, the nightmare of the local trains. All aboard for Buchholz, Tostedt, Rotenburg. Always locals — trolleys, if he could get them — never an express, never first-class, these were subject to constant passport controls. He slept standing up, or sitting in the corridor, packed into crowds of sweaty bodies, soldiers, workmen, housewives, Germans who, despite war and bombs and Adolf Hitler, had to go to Buchholz, or Tostedt, or Rotenburg.

Was he on a list? What had she done? Hard to betray him without betraying herself, so it had to be managed anonymously. "I think the man who calls himself S. Kolb is a spy. He stays at this address." Well, if that was the case, he wasn't on an *important* list — these we want — he was perhaps on a *long* list — these we want to talk to. A sea of denunciations in a state like Germany, Fräulein Lena's would be one more. Still, he couldn't register at a hotel, he couldn't cross a border, so he had to live on the trains. And, in time, if he were lucky, he would arrive at Stuttgart, his last-chance city.

His arm's-length contact, for emergencies only, please. He'd memorized the wording, which had to be exact, and the procedure, which had to be scrupulously observed. So, reaching Stuttgart at last, he began:

For sale: a woman's bicycle and a man's bicycle, one is red, one is green, 80 reichsmarks for both. Goetz, Bernstrasse 22.

The day the listing appeared, he was to go to the local art museum, climb to the third floor and there, at twenty minutes past two in the afternoon, contemplate Ebendorfer's *Huldigung der Naxos* — *Homage to Naxos*, a hideous, romantic rendering of a Greek shepherd, who sat cross-legged before a broken column, played his pipe, and gazed at the snowcapped mountains in the distance.

Spend ten minutes, no more, no less. Did they know, he wondered, how long ten minutes, in the company of Ebendorfer, could be? In the event, no spies came. Only two well-dressed women, who glanced at him and spoke briefly, commenting, no doubt, on his execrable taste. Poor S. Kolb; filthy, smelly, hungry, frightened, and, now, ridiculed. By three, he was on the sweet little train that chuffed its way to Tübingen.

He paid homage to Naxos again, the following day, and, once more, as a museum guard terrified him with a friendly nod, the day after that. Then, just as he was about to abandon the shepherd, a well-dressed gent appeared at his side.

"Do you admire Ebendorfer?"

"Well, I know the one in Heidelberg."

Rescued! The two-part protocol completed. Then his savior said, "Wretched thing," stood for a moment in perverse admiration and added, "It really is perfect, you know."

The next day they took him to Baden-

Baden, where he slept on a cot at the back of a shop. Forty-eight hours, he spent there, listening to the little bell that rang every time the door opened, to the chatter between customer and clerk, to the assertive ring of the cash register. Finally, the man from the art museum reappeared, wheeling a bicycle, and told S. Kolb he would be riding to the village of Kehl, where he was to visit a certain house near the bridge over the Rhine, and someone would take him out of Germany.

Thus, Baden-Baden. A bald little man with a fringe of hair, glasses, a sparse mustache, a tired suit, walking a bicycle through the immaculate streets — surely he did not belong in the same world with these splendid SS gods. Could he be, um, a *Jew?* A few irritated looks suggested precisely that but nobody said anything. Baden-Baden was for health, for vitality, for cleanliness of body and mind, by day, and gymnastics at night — *Yah!* — so nobody wanted to bother with scruffy S. Kolb. As long as he didn't enter a hotel or a restaurant, he could be allowed to walk his bicycle down the street. One of them waved him along, *hurry up.*

This made him so nervous he climbed on the bicycle and tried to ride it. But the seat was too low and his knees stuck out, and he veered right, then left, as they laughed at him — big, hearty SS laughs. Of course he would kill most of them, in time, by means of one paper or another, but this was obviously not the moment to remind them of that. He fell only twice on the road to Kehl, where a surprise awaited him.

An eighty-year-old woman, at least that, who dressed him in the uniform of a zoo guard, hat and all, put his suit in a small valise, gave him some papers with passport photographs — close enough — then took him across the bridge into Strasbourg. She could barely walk, held on to him with one hand while the other gripped a cane, and was so bent over he had to lean down to hear her when she spoke. "They don't bother me at the border, and they won't bother you." And they didn't, as he helped mother cross into France. Still, his heart fluttered as they waited on line, the old woman knew it, and squeezed his arm. "Oh calm down," she said.

Once past the control — very casual, for them, she said she would take the train back, and he tried to thank her for what she'd done but she wasn't interested in gratitude. "The bastards killed my son," she said, "and this is my way of thanking *them*." He saw her off on the train to Kehl, then went looking for his sort of hotel.

It was different here, he always noticed it right away, it smelled different. Because, here in Strasbourg, it was still France — despite the decrees that followed the surrender of 1940, the province of Alsace returned to German statehood. Still France — despite occupation, despite Vichy, despite its own police, who could be as bad as the Gestapo and worse. Still France — where escape was always possible. That's what made it France.

31 May. Algeciras, Spain.

It took three hours to cross the Strait of Gibraltar, Tangier to the port of Algeciras. The current was stiff here, running through the narrow passage into the Mediterranean — submarines, once in, could not get out unless they surfaced — and this, at times, made for a memorable crossing. But not that day; the sun sparkled on the water, the Arab and Moroccan passengers sheltered beneath the canvas awning, while DeHaan managed to get off by himself, found a private length of railing, and watched the African coast as it fell astern.

He'd been directed to this meeting by a second wireless message from the NID, deciphered and handed to him by Wilhelm. It was much like the earlier one, arcane ranks of numbers and letters embracing a brief message, dry as a bone, in fact an order, with no room for discussion or dissent. "They seem to want you in Spain," Wilhelm said, in her studio.

Ice cold, but, at least, efficient. A plain Citroën picked him up at the Plaza de la Victoria — Franco's victory, that year — on the Algeciras waterfront and took him out a white, dusty road, very nearly a car width wide, through pasture occupied by long-horned red cattle, then an endless forest of cork oak. Someone's *estancia*, the naval intelligence people apparently lived well, or had friends who did, and that turned out to be the case.

A servant in a white jacket waited at the door of a vast Edwardian house — a triumphantly English presence, with its battery of chimneys, in the Andalusian landscape — and led him through a grand entry hall — DeHaan looked for the suit of armor but it wasn't there — through a library and a red plush parlor to a tile-floored conservatory on a garden, with a view of shrubs and parterre which could survive the arid climate only with the attention of a platoon of gardeners. The house and grounds seemed untouched by the *guerra civil,* which implied considerable political skill on the part of the owners, who'd had to deal, in the midst of war and chaos, first with the Republicans and their communists, then with the Nationalists and their fascists. And not a brick out of place.

"Commander Hallowes," said a tall man, rising to meet him as the servant faded away. "I am pleased you could come."

He had a smooth, youngish face and prematurely white hair, wore a coffee-colored linen suit and a striped tie, which likely indicated membership in something or other, and DeHaan sensed there was more to the name — a title, honorific initials — so much a part of him they did not require mention. He stood easily, relaxed, before a wall of cacti in glazed urns, gestured toward a pair of cane chairs and said, "Shall we sit here?" Next to DeHaan's chair was a table where a drink awaited him, along with a dish of almonds.

"I'm over from Gibraltar," Hallowes said as they settled themselves. "I'd have had you come there but it's a difficult place to meet, anyone going in or out from the mainland is carefully watched, openly by the Spaniards, covertly by the Germans — they like to believe, so my friends allow me the use of their house."

"One could do worse," DeHaan said.

"Yes, quite."

DeHaan had a sip of his drink, some kind of golden aperitif that tasted of herbs and secret recipes — the taste elusive, but very good.

"So," Hallowes said. "Were you banged up on Crete?"

"Not too badly. Some damage to the hull, lost all our glass, but nothing we can't fix. We had one AB knocked cold, two seamen deserted in Alexandria, when they saw the cargo, and our assistant cook was shot during the raid."

"Morale good, even so?"

"Yes, even so."

"Ready for more, then."

"I'd say we are. Is it all over now, Crete?"

"Yes, all over. We evacuated everybody we could, but more than ten thousand were taken prisoner. However, they lost seven thousand men, so it was quite expensive for them. They took a chance, because they feared we'd use the airbases to raid the Roumanian oilfields, and they got what they wanted, but they did pay dearly. We hope that means they won't try the same thing on Malta, because we really must have it — if we can't disrupt their supply lines, there'll be hell to pay in North Africa."

Outside, a gardener in a straw hat began to sprinkle water on a potted geranium.

"Speaking of airbases," DeHaan said, "we thought we'd have air cover, in Crete."

"Yes, well, that's the problem — the Mediterranean problem. It was difficult on Crete, but, frankly, it's worse on Malta. All they had there, the first year, were three Gloster Gladiators, little biplanes, and much cherished, called *Faith*, *Hope*, and *Charity*. They'd been discovered in crates, in the hold of an aircraft carrier, and they were valiant. Unfortunately, only *Faith* survives."

"Can you get a convoy in?"

"We've tried, and will again, but the rate of loss is fifty percent. In any event, that's not where you're going — we have bigger things in mind for you. To begin with, we plan to turn you back into the *Santa Rosa*. At the stroke of midnight, you know, abracadabra."

It wasn't much of a joke, but DeHaan managed a smile. "Isn't somebody going to *notice,* one of these days? That there are two of us?"

"Oh, I shouldn't concern myself about that," Hallowes said. "Anyhow, this will be the *Santa Rosa's* final voyage, and, when it's over, well, then we'll see. What comes next."

Hallowes waited, but DeHaan just finished his drink. He had, for a moment, a whiff of déjà vu, as though this had happened before, perhaps the Dutch captain of a seventy-four-gun ship-of-the-line meeting with a British admiral, as they laid plans to fight Germany, Spain, France, whoever it was that year. Finally DeHaan said, "This voyage, in the Mediterranean?"

"Baltic."

"Up there."

"Yes, that's right. Part of our scheme of high-frequency direction finding, HF/DF, we say, or Huff-Duff, like the Americans. Silly sounding but very real, and crucial now, for my people. We can destroy them, if we can find them, and we've got to get better at that, and right away. The numbers are 'most secret' — that's always the way with numbers isn't it — but I don't mind telling you that we've lost over sixteen hundred merchant ships since 1939, half to submarines, and if we can't get our fixes, on their planes, U-boats, warships, faster and better, we'll starve as the guns go silent."

Hallowes finished his drink and called out, "Escobar?"

DeHaan could hear him, shuffling through the adjoining rooms. Hallowes ordered two more aperitifs. "I mean, why not, right?"

When the servant had left, DeHaan said, "And the details?"

"Being made final, as we sit here. To be transmitted by courier — no W/T for this operation, so expect him. Meanwhile, make sure you're well fitted out: oil, water, food, everything. And if the Tangier chandlers can't help you, let us know about it."

"We can top off. We will have to, for the Baltic, that's thirty-five hundred miles, but they took good care of us in Alexandria, your people saw to that, Dickie, and so forth."

"I'm sure they did," he said, pleased. Then, "And so forth?"

"Well, the people at the base."

"Oh."

"Out of curiosity, why are you using a freighter? Isn't this sort of thing done by airdrop?"

"What we're moving is too big, Captain.

Antenna masts, forty feet high, specially fitted trucks, and the reception equipment itself is delicate, and heavy, the worst of all combinations, so it can't be trusted to parachutes. And, there is a lot of it — we want a coastal observation station, fully mounted. That means they'll listen to all the frequencies, not only HF, but VHF, UHF — produced by sparks from spark plugs jumping to magnetos in aircraft engines, and the low end as well, because some German ships, disguised merchant raiders, are using Hagenuk radio, an ultra-shortwave system with a range of only a hundred miles, and, with our present stations, we can't hear them. Anyhow, even at night, it would be difficult for intrusion aircraft. Big German radars, up in that part of the world, so what we need is the rusty old tramp, rusty old *neutral* tramp, helpless and slow, wandering the seven seas to make a few pesetas for the owner."

DeHaan was silent for a moment, then said, "All right, the Baltic. Not a big sea, as they go, but it takes in quite a few countries."

"It does, and all of them difficult, at the present moment."

Yes, DeHaan thought, *that's the word.*

The USSR, and Finland, a German ally, just defeated in a war with the Russians, who'd occupied Lithuania, Latvia, and Estonia a year earlier, Sweden neutral, Denmark occupied, and Germany itself. *Difficult.*

"But it's wiser just now," Hallowes went on, "not to give out coordinates. If I were you, I'd expect the courier in a week or so, then you'll know. You may even be, surprised."

And far enough away so that if I yell you won't hear it.

The servant arrived with the drinks, and Hallowes said, "You'll stay for lunch?"

"*Espadon,* they call it."

DeHaan took a second helping — a sweet, white-fleshed fish. "Best I've had in a long time," he said. "Though, when it's fresh caught, there isn't much in the Mediterranean that isn't good."

"No, not much. Do you care for sea bream?"

"It can be strong."

"That's polite, Captain. A woman friend of mine calls it 'Neptune's terrible secret.' "

"Well, after a couple of months of canned herring . . ."

They went on, from this to that, luncheon talk, until they'd made their way through the second glass of wine and started on the third, then DeHaan said, "When I was in Alexandria, in fact with your man there, I happened to meet a woman." He paused, waited for Hallowes.

Whose "Yes?" — when it finally arrived — was a little ragged at the edges.

"Ah, nobody you know, I suppose. Know about."

Hallowes was relieved, the subject was espionage, not, not God-only-knew-what. "No, Captain, not our style, but not a bad idea to wonder, the way the world goes these days."

"Well, I did wonder."

"Not German, was she? Russian? Hungarian?"

"Local, I believe."

"Mm. Still . . ."

The ferry wasn't in when DeHaan was driven back to Algeciras, so Hallowes's driver left him at the Reina Cristina, the city's good hotel, where he could wait in the bar. DeHaan would have liked to walk around, but the infamous Andalusian wind was swirling dust in the streets and the city was poor and grim and vaguely sinister, so, the barman promising to let him know when the ferry made port, he sat at the bar, ordered a beer, and lit up a North State.

It had been foolish to ask Hallowes about Demetria, he realized, on two counts. First of all, Hallowes could easily have lied, maybe had lied, and second of all, she was lost, no matter who she was or what he felt. Still, he would have liked to know, because the night they'd spent together had stirred him and he wanted more.

But she was in the past, now, would remain a memory. When they'd told him at Sphakia that he'd be in convoy back to Tangier, not Alexandria, he'd understood that he would never see her again. He might have found a way to get a letter to her, if he'd been clever and had eight weeks, but what would he have said? Book passage on a local destroyer and come see me in Tangier? No, their morning coffee in the room at the Hotel Cecil, when at last they'd had to admit to themselves that they'd made all the love they could, had been a last meal.

Like the one with Arlette. Late April of 1940, tragedy on the way, only a few weeks left but nobody knew that. "Our last night," she'd said. "You will take me to dinner." She chose the restaurant, the Brasserie Heininger, down by the Place Bastille, and DeHaan had known it was a mistake the moment they entered. It was much too splendid, white marble and red banquettes and gold mirrors, lavishly mustached waiters rushing past with platters of *langouste* and *saucisson,* the tables jammed with smart Parisians, laughing and shouting and flirting and calling for more wine, all of them wildly overheated with war-is-coming fever.

Not for us, he'd thought. She'd asked him to wear his uniform, hat and all, and he had, while she'd squeezed into an emerald dress from some earlier, leaner time. And, there they stood, behind a velvet rope, a rueful DeHaan now too well aware that they were meant for the bistro, not the brasserie. While they waited, a handsome couple swept in the door, said something clever to the maître d', and seated themselves. The maître d's look was apologetic, but these were people who did what they liked. DeHaan, battered captain's hat hidden, he hoped, beneath his arm, just tried to look like he didn't care.

Then the *propriétaire* showed up. He could have been no one else, short and harassed, waiting uneasily for whatever would go wrong next. But this — this he could fix. "I am Papa Heininger," he told them. He never said a word about it, but DeHaan knew it was the uniform, even a merchant captain's uniform, which, to him, meant something. "Table Fourteen, André," he said to the maître d', shooing him off. Then, to DeHaan, "Our best, Captain, for you and madame."

And so it was. Every eye followed the procession to the holy table — who are *they?* With a flourish, the maître d' whipped away the *réservé* card, then seated Arlette with dramatic care, clasped his hands maestro-style and said, "To begin, I think, *les Kirs Royales?* And champagne to follow, of course, yes?"

Yes, of course, what else. And, after that, the perfection of excess. *Choucroute,* sauerkraut with bacon, pork, and sausage, again *Royale,* which meant more champagne, poured over the sauerkraut — the Roederer he'd ordered just wasn't enough. And, when the old lady who sold flowers in the street came walking among the tables, he bought Arlette a gardenia. She put it in her hair, snuffled a little, kissed him, was laughing again a moment later, excited, happy, *triste,* drunk on champagne, all the things she liked best and all at once.

As they waited for their coffee, DeHaan nodded at the mirrored wall above the banquette. "I might very well be wrong," he said, "but that hole in the corner looks as though it was made by a bullet."

"It was," she said.

"Wouldn't they, repair it?"

"Never! It's famous."

Well, he thought, in the dim light of the Reina Cristina bar, *there would be more.*

He looked at his watch, where was the ferry? The barman brought him another beer. At a nearby table, two men were talking German. He could see them in the mirror; hard-faced types, smoking hard, coarse and loud and serious. A strange conversation, how some people got in *over their heads,* in *hot water,* didn't know *what was good for them.* Almost as though it were a scene played for his benefit — they talked to each other, but they were really talking to him. One of them met his eyes in the mirror, lingered, then looked away. No, he thought, it's nothing. Just this damned city, its harsh wind and shadowed streets, which had overheated his imagination.

Arlette, the brasserie. "Now, home," she'd whispered to him as *l'addition* arrived on its silver tray. A particularly Gallic twist to this bill, in DeHaan's eyes, because it was much too low, the *Kirs Royales* and champagne nowhere to be found. They had been, it seemed, honored guests, but not *too* honored — one didn't eat for free, that wasn't honor, that was decadence.

By then it was very late, the tables mostly deserted, and the *propriétaire* opened the door for them as they left, letting in the cool April night. DeHaan thanked him, the *propriétaire* shook his hand and said, *"Au revoir, à bientôt."*

Goodby, we'll see you soon.

1 June. Rue de la Marine, Tangier.

DeHaan found the office in a fine old building off the Petit Socco. A cage elevator moaned softly as it climbed, one slow foot at a time, to the third, the top floor where, down a long hallway of trading companies and shipping brokerages, a glass door said M. J. HOEK and, below a black line, COMMERCE D'EXPORTATION. Hoek's secretary, a Frenchwoman in her forties, knew exactly who he was. "Ah, here you are — he's been waiting for you." She led him briskly down a corridor, trailing a strong scent of sweat and perfume. "Captain DeHaan," she announced, opening the door to an inner office. A large room, lit by grand, cloudy windows that looked across the street to the Compagnie Belge de Transports Maritimes building, its name carved across the limestone cornice.

Hoek's kingdom was crowded but comfortable — wooden filing cabinets topped by stacks of unfiled correspondence, a black monster of a nineteenth-century safe, commercial journals and directories packed together on shelves that rose to the ceiling, where an immense fan turned slowly, with a gentle squeak on every revolution. All of this ruled from a massive desk between the windows, where Marius Hoek sat in a swivel chair. His face lit up when the door opened and he wheeled himself around the desk to greet DeHaan. "Best office furniture they ever invented," he said. The wheelchair, DeHaan saw, had been pushed into a corner.

"So," Hoek said, moving back behind the desk, "the sailor home from the sea. Shall I send out for coffee? Pastry?"

"No, thank you," DeHaan said, taking the chair on the other side of the desk.

They were silent for a time. It had been a long month, for both of them, since they'd met for dinner, and that was acknowledged without a word being spoken. Finally, Hoek said, "They wired us that you'd be coming, something to do with a courier."

"Yes — plans for his reception. Though it could be 'her,' now that I think about it."

Hoek nodded — *always the unseen possibility.* "Details, details," he said, almost a sigh. "You know, DeHaan, I had no idea . . ." He took off his glasses and rubbed the dents on the bridge of his nose. "Well," he said, putting the glasses back on, "let's just say it's more work than I imagined."

DeHaan was sympathetic. "And complicated."

"Hah! You don't know. Well, maybe you do. Anyhow, I barely have time to earn a living." After a moment he added, "Supposing that I could — because the business has gone to hell all by itself, never mind this other nonsense."

"No customers?" DeHaan said, incredulous.

"Oh, plenty of customers, customers crawling up the walls. The whole world wants the minerals, now more than ever, and they bought like crazy in the thirties, what with all the rearmament. 'Strategic materials,' that's the gospel, and they'll take whatever you have. Cobalt and anti-mony. Phosphates. Asbestos. Lead and iron ores. Turns out that anything you can dig from the earth either blows up or keeps you from being blown up, starts fires or stops them. So, there isn't much you can't sell, but just try shipping it. And, if you can, it's torpedoed, or bombed, or hits a mine, or just disappears. Peace was a much better arrangement — for me, anyhow. But not for everybody, I'll tell you that. They're getting rich in Switzerland, the greedy bastards, because they're buying for Germany."

"And you won't ship to Germany."

"I never would have, believe me. But now I do, sometimes. Never direct, always to a third country, a neutral, but it's no secret, no matter what the manifest says. I do it because I've been *told* to, by our imperious friends, in order to seem neutral. It makes me sick, but who cares."

"They're not wrong, you know," DeHaan said.

"Maybe not, but, if that weren't bad enough, suddenly I'm fighting for the *British!* Bless their valorous hearts and all that, but I signed up to fight for Holland."

"We both did."

"And now, it's the same with you."

"It is, and they didn't ask. What happened to Leiden?"

"Shoved aside, I assume. 'There's a war on, sonny.'" Hoek spread his hands — *the way of the world*. "So now, they're in charge of my life, as well as all the others who've joined up, though I can't tell *them* that."

"Still you've managed, to recruit."

"I've tried. Too often — made a total ass of myself in the expatriate community. Which is small, and incestuous, and lives on gossip. I'm very indirect, but in the end you have to ask, and some of them are horrified. 'Keep it to yourself,' I tell them, but they won't, not for long."

"But, surely, a few . . ."

"Yes, a few. I had nine, two weeks ago, now I'm down to eight. One poor old bastard, that I used to play chess with, was run down by a truck as he was crossing the street. Either he was drunk, as he usually was, or he was murdered — how am I supposed to know? I'm an amateur, DeHaan, and this profession isn't for amateurs. How long this war is going to last I don't know, but I doubt I'll see the end of it."

"I think you will, Mijnheer Hoek, you are a very resourceful man. Which is why you were asked in the first place."

"*I* certainly thought I was, now I'm not

so sure. Though we have made some progress. Mostly through the efforts of Wilhelm, who is magnificent, and three more women, two Dutch housewives and a Canadian nurse, all of them fearless."

"What are they doing — if you can tell me that."

"Why not? We spies can at least talk to each other, no? Here we're in the real estate business — villas, coastal villas. We try to contact the owners, the agents, the servants, even the plumbers. Anybody who might know what goes on with the tenants. Who are sometimes German operatives, using the villas to keep watch on the Strait. They've got all sorts of infernal devices in these places, electronics, whatnot, telescopes that see at night. The trick is to get inside and look around, but it's very difficult. These aren't nice people, and they are suspicious — Mevrouw Doorn, the dentist's wife, knocked on a door to ask for directions and got bitten by a guard dog. Still, they do have to leave, one can't stay home forever, and, when they do, we watch them. Some of them wear Spanish uniforms, and they have Spanish friends. One thing I have learned is that old Franco isn't as neutral as he likes to pretend."

"And, once you know something?"

"We wire our friends, then it's up to them. Last Wednesday, for example, the Chalet Mirador, out by the Cap Spartel lighthouse, just blew up — the whole thing went into the sea, and took a piece of the bluff with it." Hoek paused, then said, "Probably not a kitchen fire."

"No," DeHaan said, "probably not."

Hoek drummed his fingers on the desk blotter and turned his chair sideways so that he faced his wall of journals. "The things I never thought I'd do," he said.

When he didn't continue, DeHaan said, "You aren't the only one, you know."

Hoek turned his chair back to face DeHaan. "Yes," he said, "I know."

"There is something I need to do here," DeHaan said. "What with the raid and the convoy, I've lost three people, so I have to hire crew in Tangier. And my way of being indirect, as you put it, will be to sign them on for a normal voyage and explain later, out at sea."

"Cuts down on refusals."

"That's the theory."

"Even so, it can't be easy to hire people, these days."

"It is not, but I have to try. Some of my crewmen are serving double watches, and that can't go on indefinitely. Now as it happens, we may already have one replacement, because a day out of Sphakia we discovered we had a stowaway. He'd managed to sneak aboard, somehow, while we were unloading cargo, and hid in the paint locker, where a couple of my ABs found him. He tried to run away — where he thought he was going I can't imagine — but they ran him down and tied him up with a rope."

"A sailor?"

"Soldier. A Greek soldier. Somehow he got separated from his unit, or they were all killed — we're really not sure what happened. He's just a poor little man, half-starved. We can barely talk to him, because nobody speaks the language, but my engineering officer's a good soul and he says he can make him an oiler. Otherwise, we'd have to turn him over to the police and there isn't much to be gained, doing that."

"A deserter," Hoek said.

"Not everybody can face it," DeHaan said. "He couldn't. Anyhow, if I keep him, I need two more. At least that — I'd like five, but that's not reality."

Hoek thought for a moment, then said, "I might have somebody who can help you. He's a young Moroccan, very sharp and ambitious. I suspect he's mixed up with

Istiqlal, but that might not be so bad, if you think it through."

"What's Istiqlal?"

"Our local Independence movement — out with the Spaniards and the French, then a free Moroccan state. His name is Yacoub." He spelled it, then said, "Do I need to write it down?"

"No, I'll remember. Yacoub is his first name?"

"Last. Say it anywhere on the waterfront and they'll know who you mean. He works down at the Port of Tangier office, a clerk of some sort, but he knows everybody and gets things done. There are surely merchant sailors in Tangier — maybe they aren't at the hiring hall — but if they can be found, Yacoub will find them. He's a gold mine, and, according to the British, he can be trusted."

"Thank you," DeHaan said. "Now, about our courier."

"Yes, the courier. He's to be here for forty-eight hours — don't ask me why because I don't know — so he, or she, will need a hotel. Probably best not to be secretive — the local people seem to know everything, and that will only sharpen their interest — so, someplace busy, lots of coming and going, where they don't think about the clientele too much as long as they overpay. In that case, it's not a hard choice: the Grand Hôtel Villa de France, to give it its full name, which is that gaudy old whore up on the rue de Hollande. You know it?"

"I don't."

"Well you will. Probably you should take a room there, the night he arrives, because he can't go anywhere near the ship — in fact, you can't be seen together. Do ship captains do that? Take hotel rooms?"

"Sometimes, for a long stay in port."

"That's what I would do. Now I'll take care of the reservation, once they wire me a name and a date, and then I'll get the information to you."

"By wireless?"

"No, by hand."

DeHaan thought back over the details, then said, "All right, it sounds like it will work."

"Yes, doesn't it. It always does, until something goes wrong," Hoek said, clearly amused by all the things that went, unforeseeably, wrong. "And now, Captain DeHaan, I must insist you take a coffee with me."

"Well, I'd like some," DeHaan said.

Work on the *Noordendam* would go on without him, for the time being, and he'd never liked being on ships in port.

After Hoek sent his secretary out for coffee, DeHaan asked for news of home.

Hoek opened a drawer and handed him a long sheet of paper. At the top it said, in heavy black letters, *Je Maintiendrai*, "I will maintain," the motto of the Dutch royal family. DeHaan knew what it was — a resistance newspaper. Printers had always flourished in Holland, so that aspect of the resistance, at least, was widespread and well rooted. "May I keep it?"

"Pass it along, when you're done."

"How did you get it?"

Hoek looked smug. "Oh, it just found its way," he said. "They give the best news they can, which isn't much. We're not getting it like the Poles — the Germans want a quiet occupation, for their Aryan brethren, so sheep's clothing is still the uniform of the day, but they are methodically destroying the country. All the food goes east, and, the way the Germans have things fixed, the money goes with it. Their attitude, when they win wars, has never changed — *vae victis*, they say, *woe to the conquered*."

"I fear for my family," DeHaan said.

"It's very hard to know about it, and to know there's nothing you can do to help."

"Yes, but 'nothing' is not quite what you're doing, is it." He leaned forward, and lowered his voice. "I have to tell you, Captain, that you should be careful, in this city. Because I believe they are in the early stages of knowing about us. Perhaps just bits and pieces, at the moment, a few papers on a desk somewhere and there are, no doubt, more pressing papers on that desk, but someone is working on it, and, when he's satisfied, something will be done, and done quickly, and there won't be time for discussion."

"Months?"

"Maybe."

"But not weeks. Or days."

Hoek shrugged. *How would I know?*

2 June. Office of the Port Administration, Tangier.

DeHaan knew who Yacoub was the moment he saw him. He belonged to a certain tribe, native to the port cities, to Penang and Salonika, to Havana and Dar es Salaam. It was a tribe of young men, young men of humble origin who, with only their wits to help them, meant to rise in the world, and, to that end, had obtained a suit.

They wore it all day, every day, and, because they were rarely the original owner, worked hard to keep it looking the best it could. Next, with help from an old book or an old man, they taught themselves a foreign language, maybe two or three, and practiced at every opportunity. Then, at last, to go with the suit and the language, they learned to smile. How glad they were to see you! What did you need? Where did you want to go?

In the port office, hidden away in a maze of piers and drydocks, Yacoub's suit was gray, his smile encouraging, his English good, his French better. He looked at the clock, and hoped DeHaan would not mind waiting for him at the small souk just off the corniche for, say, twenty minutes? Not too long? His apologies, but he did have some work that had to be finished.

A small souk, but crowded — stalls packed together in a narrow alley, where a thin stream of black water ran down a drain in the pavement, and the smell, aging goat hide and rotten fruit, was almost visible. A good place for the ancient flywhisk, DeHaan thought, brushing at his face, and a good place for recalling the time-honored clichés about the eyes of veiled women. He bought an orange, and enjoyed it almost as much as the act of dropping the peels in the street, according to local custom. When he finished it, and found the water pipe and rinsed his hands, Yacoub fought free of the crowd.

He led DeHaan from stall to stall, from camel saddle to copper pot, as though he were a guide and DeHaan a tourist. They spent a minute on the weather, then DeHaan asked about hiring crew. Yacoub was not optimistic. "They have vanished, sir. The war has taken them."

"And the hiring hall?"

"You may visit, and see for yourself." What he would see, according to Yacoub, were a few murderers and thieves, and a one-legged drunk with one eye — "Formerly a Lebanese pirate, some say" — if he hadn't already shipped out.

This was highly embroidered, but DeHaan got the point. "There must be a few," he said. "Not quite murderers and thieves. War or no war, men leave ships."

"Not many, these days. And often enough they don't go back to sea. This is, after all, Tangier; here you can hide from the war, find a woman, find a way to make a little money — sailors are good at many things, as you know — in a city that doesn't care what you do."

"But, surely not *all* of them stay ashore."

"Never all. But, of those few who leave, fewer still wish to change ships, and they don't last long. The blackboard at the hiring hall is covered with jobs, Captain, top to bottom."

DeHaan declined to offer on a wellworn prayer rug. The merchant looked up to heaven and lowered the price, then Yacoub hissed a few words under his breath and the man went away.

"I will ask my friends," Yacoub said. "My friends who know things, but there is perhaps one other possibility. Tangier has many sailors' bars, all sorts, the famous Chez Rudi, for example, and various others, some of them dangerous. But there is one, in a small street in the medina called rue el Jdid, that is known as l'Ange Bleu, the Blue Angel, though it has no sign. Sometimes sailors go there to look for old friends, if they see their ship in port, and sometimes they go to look for a new berth. Quietly. And if the master of a ship were to offer good money, it's said, the man might be interested. And, even if he's not, he will tell his friends about it."

They walked out of the shadowed souk

and onto the corniche. A fine morning in June, the wind soft and suggestive, legions of strollers out to *faire le promenade*. For that moment, at least, the romantic soul who'd called the city "the white dove on the shoulder of Africa" had got it right. And Yacoub, inspired by the day, now began a discourse on the local gossip — rich Englishmen and Americans, lovers in love with the lovers of their lovers, poets and lunatics, intrigues at the sultan's court. And scheming pashas, who conspired with foreigners in their reach for power.

"Always foreigners," Yacoub said. "Perhaps we deserve our history, but heaven only knows the blood we've spilled, trying to stop them from coming here. Spanish armies, French legions, German agents, British diplomats — since the turn of the century, fighting us and each other. And then, at last, that special curse all its own, French bureaucrats, so in love with power they made rules for snake charmers."

"It is their nature," DeHaan said. "Nobody really knows why."

"I believe that Holland, also, is a colonial nation."

"Yes, in the East Indies, we are."

"And South America as well, no?"

"There too — in Suriname, Dutch Guiana."

"Do you think it just, Captain?"

"It began a long time ago, when the world was a different place, but it can't go on forever."

"So we believe, and some of us hope that Britain will help us, if we help them to win this war."

"Nobody can see the future," DeHaan said, "but promises are sometimes kept, even by governments."

"Yes, now and then," Yacoub said.

Politics, DeHaan thought. Too often the destiny of Yacoub's tribe. Because, with the suit, and the language, and the smile, they had turned themselves, unwittingly, into perfect agents. Knowing everyone, going everywhere, they were recruited for this scheme or that, for national independence or foreign ambition, given money, made to feel important, and then, all too often, sacrificed.

Yacoub was silent for a time, as they walked past the *Club Nautique* and the ship chandlers' warehouses, headed for the pier that led to the Port Administration building. When they paused at the foot of the pier, he said, "If you would care to accompany me to the office, Captain, I believe there is mail being held for you."

On the harbor launch that took him out to the *Noordendam*, at anchor a mile offshore, DeHaan had time to read, and consider, two letters. The first was a copy of a bank draft, sent to him from the Tangier branch of Barclay's Bank, received by wire from their office in London. The draft, from the Hyperion Line, with a London address, could be read as a response to his earlier wire to Terhouven, informing him of the ship's change of administration. A substantial amount, a number familiar to DeHaan, it was sufficient for refueling and stores, as well as the paying off of the crew. Crews were traditionally paid off at the end of a voyage — formerly that meant Rotterdam but those days were gone — so Terhouven had chosen a call at a Moroccan port as a substitute. What else did it mean? He wondered. His next destination was an unnamed port in the Baltic, pending the arrival of the courier, but it seemed he would be going north in ballast — except for the secret apparatus — so, logically, he would be taking on cargo in the Baltic, then heading he knew not where.

But, now that the crew was to be paid, it

would not be their new home port —
which he assumed was London, maybe
Liverpool, or Glasgow. They had to be
going *somewhere,* once their mission was
completed, but Hallowes had not been
specific, saying only that it would be the
final voyage as the *Santa Rosa.* He hadn't
meant that it was to be the *Noordendam*'s
final voyage, had he? *No, they would never
do that.* Britain, desperate in the grip of the
U-boat blockade, needed every merchantman afloat. So DeHaan told himself.

The second envelope bore no stamp. It
was addressed to *Captain E. M. DeHaan,
NV Noordendam,* with *By Hand* written in
a lower corner. This was in typescript, produced, it appeared, by an old portable machine that lived a hard life — the ribbon
had not much ink left to it, the top of the *a*
was broken, and the *t* had lost its bottom
curl. Inside, a sheet of cheap lined paper,
not folded but very carefully torn off,
saving the other half for later use. The language was English — the Russian version.

1 June, 1941

Captain DeHaan: As you are in port,
could you grant me interview? I talked
with you in Rotterdam, in 1938, for

newspaper article. Thank you, I am at Hotel Alhadar.

Best wishes,

Then, signed in pencil, *Maria Bromen*.

He remembered her well enough, a Russian maritime journalist who wrote for *Na Vakhte*, *On Watch*, a shipping newspaper published in Odessa, as well as for *Ogonyok*, the illustrated weekly, sometimes for *Pravda*, and occasionally for the European communist dailies. This was not conventionally a job for a woman, and Bromen was young, in her thirties, but she was, it turned out, determined and serious and knowledgeable about the shipping trade. DeHaan, too well aware of the Comintern — the agency in charge of subversion in the seamen's unions, probably would not have met with her, but she'd found some way to get at Terhouven and he'd asked DeHaan to go ahead with it. "Tell her Hyperion is an enlightened employer," he'd said. "We don't ignore the welfare of our crews." DeHaan had done his best. And, formal and rigorous at first, she'd relaxed as the interview proceeded, was, he realized, simply intent on doing her job, and not at all the Soviet sourpuss he'd expected. In the end, DeHaan was honest with her and, though he never saw the article, Terhouven had, and declared it "not so bad."

DeHaan looked up from the letter and saw the rust-streaked hull of his ship, looming above the launch. Hallowes, he thought, the Germans at the Reina Cristina bar, his conversations with Hoek and Yacoub, now this. *Why don't you all go to hell and let me sail the seas.*

The launch sounded two blasts on its horn and, eventually, the *Noordendam*'s gangway was lowered a few feet, froze, was taken back up, then lowered again.

Over the next three days, business as usual. The crew was paid off and, after dire warnings from the officers to keep their yaps shut, went ashore and raised the usual hell, found the offerings on Tangier's sexual bourse more than equal to their imaginations, then drifted back to the ship in twos and threes, pale and placid and hungover. At least they all came back, and DeHaan and Ratter were spared visits to the local jails. Shtern diagnosed an oiler's fever as malaria, patched up two ABs after a fight in a bar, and treated their Greek soldier, Xanos, after he managed, while tending the lone active boiler, to have his shoe catch fire. "Don't ask me," Kovacz growled, "because I don't know." DeHaan granted himself leave, stayed in his cabin, read his books, played his records, and tried to keep the world on the other side of the door.

Where it stayed until the afternoon of the fifth, when Yacoub appeared with the news that Hoek wished to see him, and was waiting at his office. DeHaan knew what that meant, allowed himself one deep breath, then dog-eared the page in his book. Since the launch was already waiting, they returned to Tangier together.

In Hoek's office, the windows rattled as the *chergui*, the local wind, blew hard from the east. After polite conversation, Hoek said, "Well, he's here. Checked into the Villa de France last night. In Room Thirteen."

DeHaan and Hoek exchanged a glance, but let it lie.

"Tonight, then," DeHaan said.

"Yes. He'll be waiting. According to my source at the hotel, he's young, English, and carries only a briefcase. In short, he looks like a courier."

"I guess they know what they're doing."

Hoek's expression meant *they'd better.*

"As long as I'm here," DeHaan said, "what do you think of this?" He handed Hoek the note from the Russian journalist.

"Christ, just what we needed," Hoek said. "Russians."

"Any chance it's innocent?"

"Hardly. What's she doing here?"

"They're everywhere, in the ports. Just keeping up with the maritime news, is the way they put it."

"In other words, spies."

"Yes. What's your opinion? I'm inclined to do nothing."

Hoek thought it over, then said, "I'd see her."

"You would?"

"To find out what it's about, yes. If she's trying to confirm something she'll have to ask you — maybe over the river and through the woods, but she'll get there."

"Well," DeHaan said. *Why court trouble?*

"Not responding is a kind of answer, you know."

DeHaan nodded, still reluctant.

"It's up to you," Hoek said, "but if you see her, could you send a note with Yacoub?"

DeHaan said he would.

"Has he been any help?"

"He suggested a sailors' bar — l'Ange Bleu. Maybe I'll try it."

"Might as well," Hoek said. From the outer office came the sound of a teleprinter, tapping out a long message with a chime at the end of every line. Hoek looked at his watch. "So then," he said, "you'll be sailing right away."

"In a few days, unless they've called it off."

"They haven't."

DeHaan stood, and said, "I'd better walk over to the hotel. While they still have rooms."

"Oh, it's a big hotel," Hoek said. "Of course, you know," he paused, then said, "we may not see each other again."

DeHaan didn't answer, then said, "Not for a while."

"No, not for a while."

"Maybe when the war is over, I'll be back. We'll have another dinner," DeHaan said. "With champagne."

"Yes, a victory dinner."

"Let's hope so."

"Oh, I expect we'll win, sooner or later."

"A lot to do, in the meantime."

From Hoek, a very eloquent shrug, and the smile that went with it.

Then they said goodby.

At three in the afternoon, DeHaan checked into the Grand Hôtel Villa de France. It was, as Hoek had put it, a gaudy old whore — green marble lobby, bright rosy fabric on the furniture, gilt torchères on the walls by paintings of desert caravans. But it was also, unexpectedly, a quiet old whore. In the vast lobby there was only a single guest, an Arab in robe and burnoose, rattling his newspaper. And in the courtyard, when DeHaan got to his room and opened the French door, there was that curious hush of provincial hotels in the afternoon, broken only by twittering sparrows.

DeHaan tipped the bellboy, who'd carried his small canvas bag, waited a few minutes, then took the staircase to the floor below, and, down a long carpeted hallway, found Room 13. He knocked, discreetly, then, after a minute, knocked again. No answer. He returned to his room, hung his jacket in the closet, lay on the bed, and stared at the ceiling. Four o'clock, five. Tried again. No response. Was this the right room? He looked around, saw only closed doors up and down the silent corridor. Maybe the courier had other business in Tangier. DeHaan went back to the room.

By seven, the hotel had come to life. A piano, downstairs in the tearoom, began playing what sounded like songs of the Parisian *boites,* bouncy, almost marchlike. In the courtyard, doors opened and closed, somebody coughed, lights went on behind the drawn curtains. DeHaan, meanwhile, despite his status as clandestine operative, wanted dinner. But he had no intention of appearing in the dining room, so tried Room 13 once more, and, after listening at the door and hearing only silence, set off to find l'Ange Bleu. A more productive way to spend his time, he thought, than waiting in his room.

He had to ask directions but, in the heart of the medina, he eventually discovered the rue el Jdid, a street of wide steps, and, near the top, a bar with no sign. He entered, sat on a wooden stool and waited for the Moroccan barman, busy with a couple of patrons on the neighboring stools. The barman glanced at him, raised a finger, *back in a minute,* and came over to DeHaan, who ordered a beer and asked if there was anything to eat. No, nothing to eat, but the beer, a Spanish brand called Estrella de Levante, was dark and filling.

The barman returned to his other customers — sailors, DeHaan thought, one of whom resumed the telling, in English, American English, of what seemed to be a long and complicated story. "Now nobody on the ship knew what the cushmaker did," he said, "but they didn't want to let on, so they asked him what he needed, and he said he needed a metal shop and a lot of tin. Well they had that so they gave it to him and he seemed happy enough. Worked away in there day after day, welding that tin together. If anybody asked about it, they said 'Oh, he's just the cushmaker,' but day after day they wondered, what's he doing? Weeks went by, the whole ship waited. Finally, they saw he'd built a big ball of tin, all the seams welded real good, flat, you know? So next thing the cushmaker goes to the captain and says, 'Captain, now I need a derrick and a blowtorch.' Captain says okay, and, next morning, the cushmaker gets a couple of guys to help him and they roll that tin ball, it's big, maybe ten feet around, out of the shop and onto the main deck, where the derrick is. Next he hitches the ball to the derrick cables, and has it swung out just where he can reach it, but it's over the water."

The barman looked around, checking on

his other customers, then leaned his elbow on the bar. The story had apparently been going on for quite a while. "Over the water, see?" the man continued. "Then he takes this blowtorch and he begins to heat the ball, it's big, like I said, but he doesn't quit, just keeps that blowtorch going. By now, the whole ship is watching — guys up from the engine room, guys who just happen to have something to do on deck, everybody. Finally, the tin ball begins to glow, a little bit at first, then bright red. The cushmaker stands back and rubs his chin, like this. Is it hot enough? Is it ready? Yeah, he thinks, it's just right. He puts the blowtorch down and he signals the guy on the derrick, let go! The derrick man pulls the release lever, and the ball drops right into the sea."

The barman waited. Then said, "And?"

"And it went *cushhhhh*."

Both sailors grinned, and, after a moment, the barman managed a laugh.

"Cushhh, yes, it's funny," he said, and went off to see another customer.

The storyteller turned to DeHaan. "I don't think he got it."

"No," DeHaan said. "He thought you were making fun of him."

"Jeez," the man said.

"It ain't a Moroccan joke," his friend said.

"I'm Whitey," the storyteller said. "And this is Moose."

The nicknames were a good fit, DeHaan thought. Whitey had long, pale hair, combed straight back, and Moose was broad and thick. "My name is DeHaan," he said. "Captain of a ship out there." He nodded toward the bay.

"Oh yeah? Which one?"

"*Noordendam*. Netherlands Hyperion Line."

"Dutch."

"That's right."

"What do you do?"

"Dry cargo tramping."

Whitey nodded. "You in to bunker?" That was the old term, for the bunkers loaded with coal, still used for refueling with oil.

DeHaan said he was.

"We're off the *Esso Savannah*, so maybe it's our oil."

"Could be. Actually, I'm in here to hire ABs."

"Oh yeah? Well, that's us, but we're happy where we are." He turned to his friend. "We like Standard Oil, right?"

"Yeah sure, we love it," Moose said.

"No, really, it's okay," Whitey said. "Some guys always think it's better somewhere else, but it's all about the same. In the U.S., anyhow."

"You'd be surprised, what we pay," DeHaan said.

"On a Dutch tramp?"

"When we're short crew, yes."

"Well," Moose said, "we won't be on the *Savannah* too much longer."

"No?"

"What he means," Whitey said, "is that as soon as old Rosenfeld gets us into this war, we're gonna go regular navy."

"Are you sure they'll let you?"

"Sure, why wouldn't they?"

"Because, if the U.S. gets in, they'll need every tanker they can get."

A brief silence. The two sailors would be, in DeHaan's version of the future, at sea in an enemy tanker, no longer protected by American neutrality. Finally Whitey said, "Yeah, may-be." Then he downed the last of his beer and said, "Have one on us, Captain — boilermaker, shot'n-a-beer, okay?"

DeHaan would have preferred to stay with beer alone, but Whitey was too quick for him, and called out, "Hey, Hassan, three more down here."

The shot was rye, sticky sweet, and bottled in Canada, according to the label. But DeHaan was too well aware that imported whiskey was an iffy proposition in foreign ports, and he could only hope that it hadn't been brewed up in some garage in Marrakesh. Still, no matter what it was it worked, and, by the third round, DeHaan knew he would stagger when he got off the stool. Good for comradeship, though. Whitey and Moose let him know in no uncertain terms how sorry they felt for the people locked up in occupied Europe, and how they were itching to get a crack at the Nazis. They'd seen British tankers ablaze off the beaches of Miami, where the local citizens, excited by the idea of U-boats *right out there,* came down to the water to watch the show.

By eight-thirty, the bar was crowded and noisy, and DeHaan, despite the boilermaker fog, knew he had to go find his courier. "Gentlemen," he said, "I believe it's time I was on my way."

"Nah, not *now.* You ain't hired anyone yet."

DeHaan looked around. A barful of drunken sailors, likely the most he'd manage was to get his nose broken. "I'll try another night," he said, swaying as he stood up. He reached in his pocket for money, but Whitey peeled a few dollar bills off a roll and tossed them on the bar. "That's too much," Moose said, as DeHaan said, "No, let me."

Whitey waved them off. "Make it up to Hassan," he said. "Cushhh."

DeHaan laughed. He couldn't wait to tell this joke — maybe the courier would like it. Moose looked dubious, but said, "Well, okay, I guess." Then, to DeHaan, "Where you headed, pal? Down the port?"

"No, no. You fellows stay."

"What? You gotta be kiddin'," Whitey said. "Let you go out there alone? Us?" He shook his head, *some people*.

And he wasn't wrong. They came out of the bar into a warm night, carefully descending the steps of the rue el Jdid. And Whitey, in a mellow tenor, was just getting started on his repertoire, having reached "Finally I found one, she was tall and thin/ Goddamn, sonofabitch, I couldn't get it in," when two men stepped out of an alley. Hard to know who they were. They wore dark shirts and trousers and straw hats with the brims down over their eyes. Spaniards? Moroccans?

The two sailors didn't like it. They turned around and stood still, while the two men took a few steps, then stopped, ten feet above them.

"You want something from us?" Whitey said.

DeHaan sensed they didn't speak English. One of them put a hand in his pocket.

"He's mine," Moose said. "You take the other one."

Whitey put his index and pinky fingers into his mouth and gave a sharp, two-note whistle. This produced a few silhouettes from the doorway of l'Ange Bleu at the top of the street, and a shout, "Somebody need help?" For a long moment, a stalemate, then, from the doorway of the bar, the sound of a bottle broken off at the neck.

That did it. The two men walked slowly down the steps, past DeHaan and the sailors. They were leaving, not running away. One of them looked DeHaan in the eye, then angled his head sideways, down and back, an appraisal. *If it was just you.* "And fuck you too," Moose said, taking a juke step toward the men. One of them said something, the other laughed. They continued down the steps, fading into the darkness, their footsteps audible until they turned a corner at the bottom of the street.

5 June, 2105 hours. Room 13, Grand Hôtel Villa de France.

DeHaan caught the smell of burning while he was still out in the corridor, and it was strong in the room. "You're DeHaan?" the courier said, closing the door.

"That's right."

"Where've you been?" He'd hung his jacket over the back of a chair and loosened his tie. A briefcase, straps unbuckled, lay on the bed by a few stapled booklets with green manila covers, an address book, and a service revolver.

"I did try earlier," DeHaan said.

The courier was as Hoek's man at the hotel had described him — young, and English. In fact, very young, and very tense, his face pinched and white. "Well, I had other business," he said. He looked DeHaan over for a time, then said, "I believe you met a friend of mine the other day, over in Cadiz."

DeHaan's mind was not working at full speed, but eventually he realized what was going on and said, "No, not Cadiz. Algeciras."

That satisfied the courier. "All right, then," he said. "Been out celebrating, have you?"

"I had business in a bar. So, a bar." Where he'd drunk a fair amount of beer. "Excuse me a minute," he said.

The burning smell, he discovered, was coming from the bathroom. When he came out, he looked quizzically at the courier and said, "What the *hell* did you do in there?"

"What do you mean?"

"You know what I mean."

The courier's face reddened. "One's told to destroy papers by flushing them, or burning them. I thought to burn first, then flush. Both, you see, to make sure."

"And set the toilet seat on fire."

"Yes. You won't tell Hallowes, will you?"

"No, I won't tell anybody." He covered his face with his hands, as though tired.

"I know," the courier said.

"I'm sorry," DeHaan said. He had to wipe his eyes.

The courier turned away and began to sort through his papers. Finally he found what he wanted and handed DeHaan a yellow slip with numbers on it, three groups of three, and a megahertz frequency.

"You'll keep radio silence, of course, but we'll find ways to contact you, if we need to. You must under no circumstances attempt to contact us — with one exception. The line of code I've given you should be sent to that frequency, any time of day or night, and sent twice, if your ship is attacked or boarded, or if you believe the operation is going to be exposed. We would always help you, if we could, but it isn't really *for* that, you see. It's for *other* people, put in harm's way if you are compromised. Quite clear, Captain?"

"Yes."

"Then here are your orders." He handed DeHaan a brown envelope. "I will wait while you read them."

DeHaan took a single sheet of paper from the envelope and read it over, knowing he couldn't really absorb the information until he'd had a chance to spend time on it. When he looked up, the courier was holding the address book open with one hand, and had a pen in the other. "You'll sign for the codes and the orders, Captain."

DeHaan signed. "What if I have questions?"

"I don't answer questions," the courier said. "I only place the documents in your hands."

"I see," DeHaan said.

"And there shouldn't be questions," the

courier said. "It's all quite specific."

He went upstairs to his room and opened the door on the courtyard. Had he closed it, when he left? He didn't remember, evidently he had. Down in the tearoom, the piano had become a quartet, with a saxophone. They were playing, with more enthusiasm than grace, a song he knew, a Glenn Miller song, "Moonlight Serenade." Across the courtyard, a woman was sitting at a table and putting on makeup. DeHaan took off his jacket and shoes, lay down on the bed, and slid the sheet of paper out of the envelope.

MOST SECRET

For The Personal Use Of The Addressee Only

NID   JJP/JJPL/0626
OAMT/95-0626 R 34 296   3B - 0900/2/6/41

From: Deputy Director/OAMT
To: E. M. DeHaan
                 Master/NV Noordendam

MOST IMMEDIATE

Subj: Hyperion-Lijn NV Noordendam
      To sail 0400 hrs 7/6/41 port Tangier to

anchor at pos. 38°32′N/9°11′W to convert to steamship Santa Rosa. Thence to port Lisbon, 4.3 miles up river Tagus to wharf at foot rua do Faro marked F3. Contact shipping agent Penha, rua do Comercio 24, to load special cargo and receive manifest for cooking oil, tinned sardines and cork oak bound port Malmo. Sail port Lisbon 0200 10/6/41 for pos. 55°20′N/13°20′E one mile off Swedish coastal region Smygehuk. At 0300 21/6/41 await two green flashes, confirm two green flashes, for boarding of ARCHER to direct offload special cargo. Sail Smygehuk by 1800 21/6/41 to port Malmo pier 17 for cargo sawn pineboard bound port Galway. Sail port Malmo 27/6/41. While at sea, receive further instruction.

0626/1900/5/6/41+++DD/OAMT

PORTS
OF
CALL

The secret life of the Spanish freighter *Santa Rosa* had been betrayed on the twenty-eighth of May, in a brief conversation a thousand miles from Tangier.

It happened at the Baltic Exchange, on a street called St. Mary Axe, amid ancient merchant banks and assurance companies, in the commercial heart of London known as the City. There, beneath marble pillars and glass domes, the shipping and cargo brokers of London met every working day, from noon until two, to have a drink, to trade intelligence about the maritime world, and to fix dry-charter contracts. It needed only a handshake, and a cargo of coal or grain or timber was on its way.

Born as a coffeehouse in 1744, the Baltic had seen great and tumultuous times — the Napoleonic Wars, the Danish trade war, the frantic speculation in tallow of 1873, when cow fat lit the streetlamps of London and half the Continent. But no more. The grandeur remained — a liveried servant still stood at a pulpit and called out the names of brokers, but, these days, some did not answer. With so many ships under national supervision, with the oil people keeping to their offices and teleprinters, with American brokerage now done in New York, at the bar of the Downtown Athletic Club, it was lately a sparse crowd that gathered for the noon fixing.

Still, it continued; for Asian ports, for South America, for the European neutrals, cargos had to be transported, "lifted" in the local slang, and the brokers, men like Barnes and Burton, were grateful for whatever came their way. After all, this was what they did, had done, every day of their working lives, though Barnes and Burton, cargo broker and shipping broker, would have been horrified had they ever discovered what they did on the afternoon of the twenty-eighth. Because they were the staunchest of patriots, Barnes and Burton, maybe too old for military service, but they served as best they could — Barnes a London air-raid warden by night, Burton drilling every weekend with his Home Guard unit down in Sussex, where the Burtons had always had a house.

It was almost two when they met at the Baltic. Burton represented several of the smaller Spanish shipping lines, Barnes was that day brokering a cargo of Turkish salt, but finding an available tramp was proving difficult. "What about the *Santa Rosa*," Barnes said. "I've heard she's in the Mediterranean."

"Wish she were," Burton said.

"Where is she?"

"Done for, I'm afraid."

"Really."

"Yes, burned to the waterline, in Campeche."

"You're sure?"

" 'Fraid so."

"You don't say."

"Mm. A few days ago. And just about to sail, after repair."

"Campeche?"

"That's right. If you can hold on for two weeks, I might have the *Almería*."

"It will have to do, I suppose."

This was very odd indeed, Barnes thought. He paid great attention to shipping intelligence, and he'd heard, on the exchange floor, that the *Santa Rosa* had called at Alexandria. And that word had come from on high, from one of the magnificent old lions of the Baltic, a grizzled, fully bearded Scot, decorated twice in the last war, a man whose sources were everywhere, east and west, a man who had never been wrong. But he said nothing of this to Burton, the floor was not the place to contradict one's colleagues.

Still, he fretted about it on his way back to the office. Walking along St. Mary Axe, where the Widows and Orphans Assurance Society was now a bombed-out shell, he was sharply reminded that it was 1941, and the days of the ghost ship were long gone. Only in boys' books now, *Strange Tales of the Sea*, the old clipper ship seen entering a fog bank and never coming out — until ten years later. No, someone was simply mistaken, badly mistaken. Who?

Back at the office, he told the story to his secretary. "Doesn't make sense," he said. "Burton certainly seemed to know what he was talking about."

"Maybe there are two of them," she said. "Anyhow, why don't you ask somebody else?"

By God he would! And, that very afternoon, sent a wireless message to an old
friend, who ran a trading company in Alexandria.

He had an answer the next day. His
friend had asked around, in the port, and
the Spanish freighter *Santa Rosa* had, in
fact, called there, one week earlier. His
man at the ship chandler's recalled the
colors, and they'd had a look at *Brown's
Flags and Funnels* so, no doubt, *Santa Rosa*.

Just about there, Barnes began to suspect what was going on. Monkey business.
Something to do with insurance, maybe —
the shipping world had more than its share
of rogues — or, even, government monkey
business. Really, why not? *Damned inge-
nious*, he thought, and let the matter drop.
As to which government, friend or foe or
in between, he couldn't say, but, at the end
of the day, he was a cargo man, not a shipping man, and best not to pursue these
sorts of things.

And nothing would have come of it,
even though the listeners at the German
B-Dienst transcribed the cable, which was
in clear, and filed a report. A report of
little interest — who cared that the British
had chartered a Spanish tramp? No one
would have bothered with it, but for the

fact that the German NID man in Alexandria reported that the *Santa Rosa* had come into port. And hadn't come out. Now that *was* interesting. So then, where was she? Or, better, who was she?

DeHaan woke at dawn on the morning of the sixth. The sparrows were back, down in the courtyard, otherwise the hotel was pleasantly silent. By then, he'd virtually memorized the NID order, had taken it apart — the dates, the locations, the nautical miles from one port to the next, and found it tight, but possible. Everything would work as they'd directed — as long as everything worked. True, they'd left him a little time for breakdown or weather, but very damn little — it was Royal Navy time, not merchant marine time. Still, Kovacz and the sea gods willing, they could do it.

Would have to.

Because they did not have the traditional three-day opportunity for contact — that was timed to the hour. Which it had to be, because this was a bold, a brazen, operation. The southern coast of Sweden, particularly the barren beaches of the Smygehuk, were a hundred miles from the German naval bases at Kiel and Rostock, and he could expect patrols, by air and sea, so it was no place for *Noordendam* — as *Santa Rosa* or what-you-like — to be steaming back and forth. *Dear God,* he thought, *let there be fog.*

He looked at his watch on the night table, 5:10. So he'd be sailing in less than twenty-four hours. Better that way, less time to tie himself in knots. As for *Noordendam,* she was ready as she'd ever be — well bunkered and victualed, freshwater tanks topped up, new medical officer, and, now that they'd been shot at and survived, a veteran crew aboard.

So, down to the port, take the launch out to the ship, and farewell Tangier, native maidens waving from the shore. One maiden who would not be waving was the Russian journalist, and for that he was thankful. Because he had been wondering about her. Something wrong with that letter, he thought. What's she doing here, really? Of course he did have *some* time, maybe the morning, to do whatever he wanted — rare pleasure, for him. But no time for *that,* surely. *That* meaning the typical Soviet nonsense. What do you think about the world situation? Would you work for peace and justice? Maybe you'll talk to us now and again. Need money? No, with all the details he had to think about, he didn't need to subject himself to that. Though if he were honest with himself he would have to admit she'd been perfectly correct the last time they'd met. Straight as a stick, she was. Slavic and serious. What else?

6 June, 0820 hours. Hotel Alhadar.

Hard to find, in an alley off an alley, grim and dirty and cheap. The desk clerk sat behind a wire cage, worry beads in one hand, a cigarette in the other, and, beneath his tasseled fez, a mean eye — *who the hell are you?* "She is not here," he said.

DeHaan retreated, feeling foolish and betrayed and annoyed with himself. Then she appeared, as if by magic, catching up to him as he hurried down the alley. "Captain DeHaan," she said, out of breath. "I saw you go into hotel."

"Oh," he said. "Well, good morning."

"We go in here," she said. A few steps led down to a tiny coffee shop, dark and deserted. DeHaan hesitated, he didn't like it.

"Please," she said. "I must get off street."

What? He followed her in, they sat down, a young boy came to the table, and DeHaan ordered two coffees. "I hoped you would come," she said. It wasn't courtesy, she meant it.

Across the little table, she was much as he remembered her, though now he realized she was older than she was in his memory. No one would ever call her pretty, he thought. But you would look at her. A broad, determined forehead, high cheekbones, eyes a severe shade of green, almost harsh, a small mouth, down-curved, ready for anger or disappointment, thick hair, a dulled shade of brown, like brown smoke, swept across her forehead and pinned up in back. She wore a pale gray suit and a dark gray shirt with a wide collar — shapeless and lax, as though worn for a long time — and carried a heavy leather purse on a shoulder strap. But the detail that stood out, above everything else, was the presence of some inexpensive and very powerful scent, the sort of thing to use if you were unable to bathe.

He took out his packet of North States and offered her one. "Yes, thank you," she said. Even in the cellar gloom of the coffee shop he could see shadows beneath her eyes, and, when she held the small cigar to his match, her hand trembled.

"Is there to be an interview?" he said.

"If you like." For a moment she pressed

her lips together, then turned her face away.

"Miss Bromen," he said.

"A moment, please."

She concentrated for a few seconds, then pushed the hair back off her forehead. "I read your ship was in Tangier, and I remembered it. I remembered you."

"Yes? From Rotterdam."

"Yes, Rotterdam."

He waited for more, but she inhaled her North State and said, "It's hard, not to have cigarettes."

Silence. Finally, DeHaan said, "You're writing stories, in Tangier?"

Slowly, she shook her head.

"Then . . ."

The coffee arrived, thick and black, in tiny cups, with a bowl of brown, crystalline sugar in broken lumps. She put one in her cup and stirred it as it fell apart, started to take a second, then didn't. "I am running away," she said, her voice casual, without melodrama. "It is not easy. Have you ever done it?"

"No," he said. Then, with a smile, "Not yet."

"Better you don't."

"I'm sure of that."

"You must take me away from here,

Captain, on your ship."

"Yes," he said. When her face changed, he hurried to add, "I mean, I understand. Of course there's no possibility of my doing that."

She nodded — she knew that perfectly well.

"You do understand," he said.

"Yes, I know." She paused, then lowered her voice and said, "Is there some thing, some thing I could do? I don't care what."

"Well . . ."

"I will work. They have women, who work, on Russian ships."

"And sometimes in Holland as well, on the tugboats and barges. But *Noordendam* is a freighter, Miss Bromen."

She began to answer him, to argue, then gave up, he saw it happen. After a moment she said, "Is there food here, maybe?"

That he could do. He signaled to the boy and asked him for something to eat.

"Beignets?" the boy said. "There is a bakery nearby."

As DeHaan reached into his pocket for money, he wondered how much he had. Quite a lot, actually, and of course he would give it to her. When the boy left, he said, "Miss Bromen, what happened to you? Can you tell me?"

"I am running from *Organyi*," she said, with a sour smile — *what else?* The Russian word meant the organs of state security, secret police. "It's a game you must play, in my work. They want to use you because you are a journalist, and journalists talk to foreigners."

"You worked for them?"

"No, not completely. They asked me to do things, I said I would, but I did not do well, was not — clever. I did not defy them, you cannot, but I was stupid, clumsy — any Russian will understand this. And I never became important, never spoke to important people, because, *then* . . . And was better to be a woman, weak, though they wanted me to go with men. Then I would say I was virgin, would almost cry. But they never went away, until purge of 1938, then one was gone, another came, then he was gone.

"But, it did not last and, one day, in Barcelona, here comes the wrong one, for me. He did not believe I was stupid, did not believe tears, or anything. He said, 'You will do this,' and he said what would happen if I did not do it. With him, one and one made two. So then I ran. Left everything I had, got on train to Madrid. Maybe France was better idea, but I was not thinking. I was frightened — you know how that is? I had come to the end of my courage."

She paused, remembering it, and drank the last of her coffee. "But they did not chase me, not right away. I think maybe the bad one in Barcelona did not want to say, to report, what happened, but later he had to, probably because there was someone above him who also knew how one and one makes two. Then, one day in Madrid, I saw them, and the one friend I had did not want to talk to me anymore. It was then second week in May, and again I ran. To Albacete. By then, I had very little money. I had sold watch, pen, Cyrillic typewriter. I learned from refugees, from Jews, how to do it. It was strange, how I found them. When you are running away you go to the city, and then to a district where you feel safe, and there they are, they have done the same thing, found the same place. Not with rich, with poor, but not too poor so that you don't belong. Then, in the markets, in the cafés, you see them. Ghosts. And you, also, are a ghost, because the self you had is gone. So it is recognition, and you approach them, and they will help you, if they can. But I think you know all this, Captain, no?"

"It is on my ship," DeHaan said. "Any ship — we are part of the world, after all. So most of my crewmen can't go home. Maybe never again in their lives."

"Can you?"

"No. Not while the war goes on."

The boy returned from the bakery with a plate of fried twists of dough sprinkled with powdered sugar. He placed it on the table and DeHaan gave him a few more dirhams — too many, evidently, the boy's eyes widened, and he said thank you in the most elaborate way he knew.

The *beignets* were freshly made, still warm, and smelled very good. Bromen said, "I see these every morning — they carry them through the streets on a palm leaf." She ate carefully, leaning over the table.

"They're good?"

She nodded with enthusiasm. He tried one, she was right. "Excuse me," she said, licking the sugar off her fingers.

"So," DeHaan said, "you came to Tangier."

"A dream to the refugees, North Africa. You can go anywhere, from here, if you have a lot of money. You can even work. It's hard in Spain, after the war they had, people are poor, very poor, and police are terrible. So I came here, my last hope, one week ago. No money, nothing left to sell, only passport. I stole, sometimes, little things — some of the refugees have the gift, but I don't."

"I will help you, Miss Bromen. Let me do that, at least."

"You are kind," she said. "This I knew in Rotterdam, but I fear it is too late now, for that."

"Why too late?"

"I have been seen, found. Not conveniently, for them. On the avenue that comes out of Grand Socco, they were in car going the other way, and by the time they stopped, I had run away down a little street and I hid in a building."

"How could you be sure it was them?"

"It was them. Once you know them, you can recognize."

DeHaan found himself thinking about the Germans at the Reina Cristina.

"They saw me, Captain DeHaan, they stopped their car. Right where it was, they stopped. That was all I saw, I didn't wait, so maybe I *was* wrong. But next time may be when I don't see them. And then, well, you know. What will happen to people like me."

"Yes, I know."

"Do you? They will not kill me, not that minute," she said. There was more, but she hesitated, perhaps unwilling to use the words she used with herself, then did it anyhow, her voice barely above a whisper. "They will degrade me," she said.

They will not. DeHaan leaned forward and said, "Let me tell you about money, Miss Bromen, sea captains and money. They have it, but, other than giving it to their families, they have no way to spend it. Only in port. Where you can spend like a drunken sailor — certainly I have spent like a drunken sailor — but those pleasures just aren't that expensive. All this to tell you that I will buy your freedom, you can tell me what it costs, and it will be my pleasure to buy it for you. A new passport, ship passage, we'll take a piece of paper and add it up."

"Will cost *time*," she said. "I know, I have seen them, the richest ones, waiting, and waiting. For months. All the money in the world, can bribe, can buy gifts, but still they wait. If you don't believe, ask the refugees, I will introduce you."

"And so?"

"So must be a ship at night. To a neutral port. No passport control going out, no passport control getting off. *Disappearance.*

With no tracks to sniff."

From DeHaan, a sour smile. "Is that all."

"I know ports, Captain. I know how they work."

She was right, and DeHaan knew it.

"No other way can work," she said. "I am sorry, but is true."

Then they were silent for a long time, because there was nothing more to be said, and all that remained for him was to stand up and walk away. And he told himself to do precisely that, but it didn't take. Instead, he made a wry face and muttered angrily to himself. What he said was in Dutch, and not at all nice, but she knew what it meant, and rubbed her eyes with her fingers. Keeping a promise to herself, he suspected.

6 June, 2105 hours. Bay of Tangier.

He'd enlisted, for this brief mission, his best, the bosun Van Dyck, who sat in the stern and steered the ship's cutter. It was choppy on the bay that evening and DeHaan braced himself against the gunwale as they neared the lights of the city. In his pocket, a rough map, penciled on a scrap of paper. Simple enough, she'd said, there was a small, unused pier at the foot of the rue el Khatib, and a street that led to an old section of the port, where, in time, he would find a row of large sheds that faced an abandoned canal, the fourth one down occupied by a Jewish refugee who managed to exist by adjusting compasses aboard merchant vessels. DeHaan had only to knock on the wooden shutter and someone would open it.

He'd asked her, more told her, to leave with him then and there, for safety's sake, and go immediately to the ship, but she wouldn't hear of it. Almost pleading, she said there were a few small things to be retrieved from the hotel but, most of all, she had to tell people, people who had cared for her, that she was leaving. When he tried once more, she offered to take the port launch, but he couldn't let her do that — the Spanish police had a passport control at the dock. No, he would pick her up in the ship's cutter. Back on board at noon, he'd looked up the rue el Khatib in *Brown's Ports and Harbors*, where, on the map of Tangier, it lay at the very edge of the page, on the ragged eastern border of the port — no longer a port at all, really, long ago deserted by commerce and left to crumble away. The map had a small street coming in from the west, while the street leading away from the port, on her map, was not shown.

Van Dyck slowed the engine as the pier came into view. By now, the lights of the main port were well west of them, but, by dead reckoning based on the flashing Le Charf beacon, they'd found the foot of the rue el Khatib. He hoped. This was not the most sensible thing he'd ever done, and Van Dyck didn't like it, had been particularly uncommunicative since they'd left the ship. Ratter didn't like the idea either — a woman passenger on board — but it was only for two days, DeHaan explained, until they reached Lisbon. From Ratter, at that point, a quizzical, one-eyed glare — *why are you doing this?*

No choice, he thought, as they neared the shore. And, really, what did it matter, one more lost soul? Kovacz, Amado and his mates, Shtern, Xanos the Greek soldier, his German communists, all of them really, fugitives in one way or another, set to wandering the world. *Always room for one more on the good ship* Noordendam.

Van Dyck cut the engine and used the boat's momentum to glide alongside the dock. DeHaan stood, ran a rope around a cleat, and tied them off. It wasn't long for the world, this pier — the boards rotten and sprung, one side sagging toward the water, the corner post nowhere to be seen.

"Is this it?" Van Dyck said.

"Yes, it should be."

"Will you want me to come along?"

"No, you stay with the boat."

"Safe enough to leave it, Cap'n."

"I know, but no point in both of us going."

Van Dyck held the cutter against the pier as DeHaan stepped off. "Want me to hold on to that?" he said, pointing to DeHaan's head.

DeHaan took off his captain's hat and tossed it to the bosun. Who was right, he thought — alone at night on the docks, it was better to be just a common sailor.

At the end of the pier, a lone streetlamp cast a circle of yellow light. DeHaan paused beneath it, a swarm of night moths attacking the bare bulb above him, squinted at the map, put it in his pocket, and set off down a silent street of closed shops. No lights here, no radios, only a few stray cats. The street stopped dead at a high wall, but the map told him to turn left, and he found an alleyway, just wide enough to walk through, between the wall and the last building. The end of the alleyway disappeared into shadow, and he hesitated briefly, then went ahead, running his hand along the wall as he walked. At the far end, a dirt path bordered by underbrush led to a sandy field, then passed beneath an immense tank that had once been used for oil storage. Here the path widened to a dirt road, then turned sharply and ran beside an ancient brick warehouse with black broken windows.

Which went on forever, it seemed. He kept walking, past boarded-up entries and loading platforms, another wall now on his right. *Penned in,* he thought. Likely there was a road on the opposite side of the building that went down to the bay, but there was no sense of water here, only night, and deep silence, but for a few cicadas beating away in the darkness. At last, he reached the end of the warehouse and found a railroad track, weeds grown up between the ties, a faint odor of creosote still lingering in the air. *As it used to.* When he was twelve, in the port of Rotterdam, brave with his friends, amid rusting machinery and alleys that led nowhere. He stopped for a moment, took the map from his pocket, and lit a match. Yes, that carefully drawn ladder meant a railroad track, with crosshatched lines showing three canals beyond it. Where were they?

He reached the first one a few minutes later. Dead fish, dead water, an Arab dhow half sunk at the far end. Again he lit a match to look at the map, then, just as he shook it out he heard, thought he heard, a voice. Just for an instant, a high voice, one or two notes, like singing. But, as he tried to figure out where it was coming from, it stopped, and the silence returned — a complete hush now, the cicadas gone.

At the end of the canal, he found a tributary, a second canal, with a cinder path beside it and a long row of sheds that disappeared into the darkness. It was the fourth in line that he wanted — she'd put an *X* in a box on the map. He counted four, and stood before a heavy wooden shutter. Could there be people inside? He heard nothing. He put a tentative hand on the shutter, then knocked. The shutter moved. He stepped back and stared at it. On one side of the shutter, an iron ring that took a padlock had been pried free, leaving three screwholes in a patch of yellow, splintered wood, freshly gouged, while the metal hasp, with closed lock still on the ring, had been bent back on itself. He knocked again, waited, then took the bottom of the shutter in both hands and rolled it up, to reveal a doorway.

"Hello?" He said it in a whisper, then again, louder.

Nothing, and the door stood ajar.

He pushed it open, and counted to ten. *Go back to the pier. You do not want to see what is inside this shed.* But he had to, and stepped through the door to find a square room with plaster walls, the air heavy with mildew. There was a straw mattress with a blanket on it, and a row of books at the foot of the wall, held up by rocks used as bookends. On the opposite wall, on a rough pine table, a lantern lay on its side in a puddle of kerosene, which had wicked up into a sheaf of papers and half a bread. On the floor, a few more papers.

"Is anyone here?"

He said it just to say it, first in German, then again in French, knowing there was no point, knowing there would be no answer. And knowing, also, that whoever had been here was not coming back.

Sick at heart, shaken, and very angry, he left the shed and walked away. Maybe someone was watching him, maybe not, he almost didn't care. And he was a fool, he knew, for being without the Browning pistol, lying peacefully beneath his sweater, but he'd never thought to bring it. Well, he would fix that — if he lived through the night, if he ever saw his ship again, and if he were, ever again, tempted to leave it. He walked at full speed, almost a trot, but it was after ten by the time he reached the alleyway, the street of closed shops, and, at last, the pier. As he approached the cutter, Van Dyck said, "What happened?"

"Not there," DeHaan said. He stepped heavily into the boat, whipped the rope free of its cleat, and sat in the bow.

Silently, Van Dyck handed him his hat, then went to start the engine, which chose that moment to balk. Both of them swore as Van Dyck fiddled with the choke, then tried again. "We'll row the goddamn thing if we have to," DeHaan said.

"Take it easy, Cap'n. It's just flooded."

DeHaan could smell that perfectly well, and settled in to wait. "Where'd she go?" Van Dyck said.

"I don't know. Maybe somebody took her."

Van Dyck was silent, but his face closed in a certain way — the world had grown more evil than he ever thought it would. Again he tried the engine, which coughed a few times, then started with a belch of black smoke. "That's better," Van Dyck told it, opening the throttle. He put the engine in gear, and, with a wide, sweeping turn, headed the cutter back toward the bay.

They were a minute or two out when a car came roaring down the road from the port and, tires screeching, skidded to a stop at the edge of the pier. "Oh Christ," DeHaan said. "Now we're going to be shot."

"What?" Van Dyck said.

DeHaan knelt on the floorboards and gestured for Van Dyck to do the same. But the shots never came. Instead, a man and a woman leapt from the car and ran to the end of the pier. He was an old man, and he could barely run, but he did his best, waving his arms, yelling words they couldn't hear.

"Cap'n?" Van Dyck said.

"Better turn around."

0800 Hrs. 7 June, 1941. 35°50′N/6°20′W, course NW 275°. Fog and heavy SE following sea. Departed port of Tangier at 0340 hrs., w/ 41 crew aboard. Two eastbound vessels sighted. All well on board. E. M. DeHaan, Master.

With his log entry completed, and Ratter taking the forenoon watch, DeHaan stood on the bridge wing with the AB lookout, who peered dutifully out into the gray mist through his binoculars, though he couldn't see much of anything. DeHaan found his heart much eased, that morning — back at sea, back where he belonged, swaying with the roll of the ship, staring down at the foamy bow wave in gray Atlantic water. He didn't mind the fog, which had its own smell, salty and damp — God's own perfect air out here in the breeze. On the ocean liners, a few hours from landfall at the end of a voyage, passengers could always be counted on to ask the nearest steward about a certain unpleasant scent, decay perhaps, as the temperature climbed. "That's land, sir," the steward would say. "You can smell it long before you see it."

From somewhere north of them, the low moan of a foghorn. On the other side of the bridge door, Ratter reached up and pulled the cord above his head and their own foghorn, just aft of the bridgehouse, gurgled for a moment, sent a steaming spurt of water onto the roof, then produced a great shuddering bellow that rattled the glass in the windows. DeHaan looked at his watch — a wardroom meeting, at nine, so he could stay on his bridge. The morning log entry was true enough, all *was* well on board as *Noordendam*, steady and determined, steamed west through the fog, easily making her knots with a following sea.

Maria Bromen was settled in Ratter's cabin, next to his own, while his first officer had moved in with Kees. She'd taken a long shower the night before, DeHaan had listened to it through the bulkhead as he lay on his bunk and tried to read. A complicated story from Bromen, once she'd been seated in the cutter. She said that she and her refugee friend had returned to the shed just before eight o'clock, saw that someone had pried up the lock, and, without going inside, left in a hurry, going to the room of another refugee. There followed a nightmare — someone who had the use of a car would take her to the pier, but that someone, always at a certain café, was not there, couldn't be found, until it got so late he *had* to be found, and, finally, was, at last, though almost not in time.

But all's well that ends well. In a few hours they would anchor for repainting, then, as *Santa Rosa*, dock at Lisbon on the evening of the ninth. For Bromen, a chance to slip away into the night. After leaving her at the coffee shop, the day before, he'd stopped at

Barclay's Bank and obtained a substantial packet of American dollars, so she would disembark with money to spend, and DeHaan could at least hope she would find a way to survive. It was possible, he thought. As Spain was technically neutral but slanted toward Germany, Portugal was neutral but a quiet ally of Britain, an alliance that went back to the fourteenth century. So Portuguese officials might look the other way, might not be so eager to please their German friends. Thus, with false papers and a little luck, she could wait out the war in Lisbon. As long as the *Organyi* didn't find her. There he couldn't be sure, because they were, it was said, everywhere, and relentless. Still, a chance. And maybe, with very good false papers and a great deal of luck, she might even get across the ocean. To a much safer place.

At 0900, a wardroom meeting. DeHaan presiding, with Ratter, Kees, Kovacz, Ali, Shtern, and Poulsen, the Danish fireman now serving as Kovacz's provisional second engineer. Cornelius served coffee, it was almost like old times. Not like old times: a call at Lisbon for secret cargo — masts, lattice aerials, and three trucks, bound for Smygehuk, on the bare coast of southern Sweden.

"Past the German bases on the Norwegian coast?" Kees said. "Then the Skagerrak and the Kattegat? The Danish pinchpoint? Shit oh dear. Minefields and E-boats every inch of the way. Very well, let's have a betting pool. I'm putting ten guilders we never see six-east longitude. Ratter? In?"

"Remember, we're a Spanish freighter," Ratter said bravely.

"And I'm Sinbad the Sailor."

"It worked once."

"By God's grace and luck's good hand, it worked. With Italians."

"Please," Shtern said, "what is the Kattegat?"

"The channel between Denmark and Sweden," Kees said. "Kattegat means the cat's hole — it's very narrow."

Under his breath, Ratter said, "And you would know."

"Who's waiting for us?" Kovacz said.

DeHaan shrugged. "A codename is all they gave me — could be anybody."

"So the Swedes don't know about it, right? Otherwise, we'd be hauling the stuff into Malmö."

"That's how I read it," DeHaan said.

"Or do they, perhaps, choose not to know," Ali said.

"Neutral politics, Mr. Ali. Anything is possible."

"When do we have to be off Sweden?" Kovacz said.

"Before dawn on the twenty-first."

There was a pause while they calculated.

"We'll just make it," Kovacz said. "If we can get out of Lisbon by the eleventh."

"It should be fast," DeHaan said. "We're supposed to pick up a manifest, for cork oak and whatnot, going up to Malmö, but we don't actually load anything."

"After Sweden, what then?" Ratter said.

"Then we do go to Malmö, for sawn pine boards headed down to Galway."

After a moment, Ratter said, "Irish Free State, so, neutral to neutral, on a neutral vessel."

"That's the idea. But we get further instructions at sea — I would bet that means a British port."

"And the end of the *Santa Rosa*," Kees said. "And then — convoys?"

DeHaan nodded. Bad, but no worse than what they'd been doing.

"Will we go down the Swedish side of the Kattegat?" Poulsen said.

"Of course," DeHaan said. "I'm not sure it matters, but we'll try."

Kovacz said, "I can tell you it *doesn't*

matter. Not up in the Baltic — the Germans do whatever they like, and the Swedes don't get in their way. Don't dare. Otherwise, it's blitzkrieg for them and they know it."

Mr. Ali tapped his cigarette holder so that an ash fell into the ashtray. "He's right." *And I can prove it.* Clearly, from his expression, Mr. Ali had a story to tell, and they waited to hear it. "For instance," he said, "just yesterday morning, there was a French ship, wiring back to the owner in Marseilles. In clear, this was — the two of them going back and forth. And, from what I could make out, they were taking wolframite ore up to Leningrad, but a patrol ran them into port and now they're stuck there. Not allowed to leave."

"Of course," Ratter said. "That's tungsten — armor plating, armor-piercing shells, very hard to get hold of, these days, so the Germans want it for themselves."

"No doubt," Kees said. "But the Soviets are supposed to be their allies."

"Did the French ship give a reason?" DeHaan said.

"The owner asked, then the Germans cut them off. Jammed the frequency, and, when the French radioman moved up to another, they jammed him there."

"That's very strange," DeHaan said. "If you think about it."

"Not so strange," Kovacz said. "They're getting tired of each other."

"Anything else on the radio?" DeHaan said. "BBC?"

"Not much new. The fighting in North Africa, and the death of the Kaiser, in Holland, after twenty-three years of exile."

"Bravo," Ratter said. "And may he roast in hell."

"He never liked Hitler, you know," Kees said.

"Said he didn't. But his son's an SS general — I'm sure he liked him."

"Anything else, Mr. Ali?" DeHaan asked.

"Only the usual — Germans strengthening units at the Polish frontier."

Kovacz and DeHaan exchanged a glance. "Here it comes," Kovacz said.

5 June. Hotel Rialto, Tarragona.

S. Kolb lay on the tired old bed and tried to read the newspaper. A knowledge of French didn't really help, with a Spanish paper, and the one he'd been given at the cinema was dense and difficult, just his rotten luck, with only a few photographs and no comics. Spain's version of *Le*

Monde, maybe, with long, thoughtful articles. He preferred being unable to read brief, sensational articles, in the working-class tabloids.

This might not have been such a bad hotel, he thought, once upon a time. Down on the nicer part of the waterfront, view of the Mediterranean, six stories high — the sort of place that might have been used by British travelers on a budget. But no longer. An artillery shell had hit the upper corner, during the war, so a few windows were boarded up, there was a black burn pattern on the wall above them, and, everywhere in the hotel, the evil smell of old fire.

No matter, he wouldn't be here long. In Stuttgart, he'd come back under Mr. Brown's control, and damned thankful for it, at the time. Saved his worthless hide, no doubt. Truth was, if you had to live the clandestine life, you'd better do it in a clandestine system — you'd live longer, as a rule, because going it alone was almost impossible. Still, there'd come a moment, standing in front of that wretched painting in the museum, when he'd been tempted to disappear, to live some other way. *Not now,* he'd thought, not in the middle of a war, when everybody had to fight, on some side. But later on. Maybe.

Such ingratitude! After all, they'd taken great pains to protect him. Like grandma's precious china bowl — ugly thing, you hated it, but you took care not to break it. They'd slid him carefully out of Strasbourg, into the Unoccupied Zone, Vichy, and down the length of France, in an ambulance, a truck, even a horse-drawn vegetable wagon — Kolb with a smelly old farmer's beret pulled over his ears. Handsome living, if you lived that way. Sharing the local food, whatever poor stuff they had. Once a pretty girl to sit with on a train. And, finally, into Port Bou — the Pyrenees border crossing — in a hearse. An assistant undertaker, thank God, the coffin they'd carried had been heavy and elaborate, lined with black satin, it didn't look like there'd be all that much air to breathe in there. And who wanted to die in a coffin?

Of course, when they spent time and money on you, they weren't trying to save your life, rather trying to find some way you could lose it working for them. So, he thought, they had something in mind.

In Lisbon, apparently. Earlier that evening, he'd seen their little man, come down from the consular office in Barcelona, he supposed, an hour north of Tarragona. Well, he hadn't really seen him — it was dark in the cinema, a Spanish knight up on the screen bashing a few Saracen heads before breakfast — but he was a familiar presence. Rather heavy, with an asthmatic wheeze, and clearly regarding the man *eight rows down one seat in from the aisle* as little more than a package. Other than a brief protocol — "I trust this seat's not taken, can you tell me?" "An old lady was there, but she's gone away" — he'd only sat beside him for the requisite half hour before vanishing, the newspaper left behind on the seat.

Would it have cost him so dearly to add a few words? A whispered *Good luck*, or something like it? Something human? No, not him, not even a comment about the moronic movie, just labored breathing, and a difficult newspaper with hand-lettered instructions on the inside of the back page — as always. Which added up to the night train to Lisbon, and then, no doubt, his next hotel, likely somewhere near the docks. The docks, the docks, always the docks, crowded with spies. There were some in his profession, he knew, who didn't live that way at all — who traveled first class, who strolled through casinos with a woman on each arm, but that wasn't his legend. Damn his genes anyhow. Born to a clerk, looked like a clerk, they'd made him a clerk. It was all a great clanking machine, wasn't it, that went round and round with little puffs of steam and never stopped.

Damn, he was hungry, his stomach gnawed at him. Didn't help his mood much either. But the food in the seedy restaurants got worse as you moved south. At least in the north they fed on potatoes, here it was oil and beans, beans and oil, all of it laced with garlic, the sacrament of the poor, which didn't agree with Kolb. *And the same damn story in Lisbon, no doubt.*

The night train to Lisbon — more poetry than fact, that description. After a local up to Barcelona, S. Kolb spent the better part of two days on a broken wicker seat in a third-class carriage, in with the sausage eaters and the cranky infants, a few obvious refugees, and an endless parade of tired soldiers. The cast changed, but Kolb remained, as they puffed slowly across the Spanish countryside, standing in this station or that, or marooned far out in the middle of nowhere.

It was after midnight when he finally arrived at Lisbon's Estacão do Rossio and found the *woman in the green scarf* waiting for him on the platform. She drove him not to a hotel on the docks, but to what he took to be a rooming house, up in the Alfama district, below the Moorish citadel. No, not quite a rooming house, he was told, a hideaway for various agents, headed here or there, and best not to see the others, or let them see you. He did hear them, though they were quiet in their rooms, and broke the rule only inadvertently, opening his door at the same moment his neighbor did. A tall, spindly fellow, professorial, who stared at him for a moment, then stepped back inside and closed the door. A surprise to Kolb, the way he looked. Kolb had heard him, on the other side of the wall, moaning in his sleep, and had imagined a very different sort of man. Still, not so bad in the hideaway — at least they fed him — his beans in oil brought up on a tray, with a tiny chop that might have been goat. Stingy, the British Secret Intelligence Service.

He saw Mr. Brown the following morning. Plump and placid, pipe clenched between his teeth, so you had to work like hell to understand his clenched words. But Kolb did, in fact, understand all too well.

After hearing of his travels, while making notes on a pad, Brown said, "We're sending you up to Sweden." Kolb nodded, secretly very pleased. A neutral country, clean and sensible with large, accommodating women — a bit of Kolb Heaven, after all the hell he'd been through. "You don't speak the language, do you?" Beyond *Skoal!* not a word, but *Skoal!* might be perfectly adequate.

"How do I get there?" Kolb said.

"We're sending you up on a freighter. Dutch merchantman disguised as a Spanish tramp. They'll let you off in Malmö. Ever been there?"

"Never."

"It's quiet."

"Good."

"Then, perhaps, to Denmark."

Occupied. But politely occupied.

"Of course from Denmark, one can easily travel to Germany."

"They may know who I am — I suspect Fräulein Lena denounced me."

"We're not sure she did, and she's with the Valkyries now. Anyhow, you'll have new papers."

"All right," Kolb said. As if it mattered whether he agreed or not. Still, there was a glimmer of hope — Sweden, where, if they caught him, he would be interned. If they caught him? Oh they would catch him all right, he'd make damn sure of that.

"Don't mind?" Brown said, eyes narrowing for a moment.

"A war to be won," Kolb said.

Brown may have sneered, he wasn't sure, there was only a puff of smoke, rising from the bowl of his pipe. Could that have been a sneer? "Indeed," Brown said, and told him he'd be leaving after midnight on the tenth. "You'll be taken to the dock," he said. "Can't have you wandering around Lisbon, can we."

8 June, 1600 hours. At sea.

DeHaan came to the bridge for the first half of the split dog watch. The repainting was still in progress, but getting toward the end. The crew, he thought, had never worked this hard. It had been decided, at the wardroom meeting, that they would be told only that the ship was headed north, its destination secret, with a call at Lisbon and no liberty. Was it the idea of a secret mission that inspired them? Something clearly had, because they put their backs in it, every single one of them, the full crew toiling away on the scaffolds, and working fast. And, this one time at least, the weather held. The idea that an important operation could be ruined by a few showers of ocean rain seemed almost absurd, but the history of war said otherwise and DeHaan knew it.

Ratter came loping up the ladderway with a burlap sack in one hand and a glint in his eye. "Care to see what I bought in Tangier?"

He reached into the sack and brought forth a round tin canister with hand-lettered marking at the center. FUTLIHT PARED, 1933, it said, then, JAMS CAGNI/ JONE BLONDL.

"Ten reels," Ratter said. "Probably all of it, or there's another movie in there somewhere."

"Where'd you get it?"

"Thieves market."

Strange things wandered through the world of ports, DeHaan thought, living lives of their own. Had this walked away from a Tangier cinema? A passenger liner? A complicated journey of some sort, anyhow, to arrive on the *Noordendam*.

"I thought," Ratter said, "we might show it as a reward, after the painting."

"I can repay you, from the mess fund."

"No, no. It's my gift, to the ship."

"Do we still have the projector?"

"It took some searching, but we found it in the hawser locker."

"Of course, where else? Does it work?"

"Don't know what will happen if we put film in it, but I hooked it up and it ran. There were rats living in the speaker, they'd eaten the wires, but Kovacz put it back together."

The projector had been on the *Noordendam* before DeHaan came on as captain, nobody had any idea where it came from. "Movie at twenty-one hundred hours," he said. "Have the bosun rig up a canvas screen on the foredeck."

A lovely night for a movie; a great white sweep of stars spread across the black sky, a light headwind that snapped and billowed the canvas screen, so that James Cagney sometimes swelled, sometimes jerked violently, to great cheers from the audience. The projector worked, after the necessary ten minutes of fooling around, though it ran slightly fast, so that the actors appeared to be in a bit of a hurry. The sound, however, from the rewired speaker, was not so good, the voices muffled, as though the characters were eating bread, and sometimes the music swam, odd and otherwordly — *Footlight Parade*, the supernatural version.

None of it mattered. The officers and crew sat on a hatch cover and had a fine time — some of them couldn't understand a word of it, but that didn't matter either. It was a Busby Berkeley movie, so there was plenty to look at; crowds of girls in skimpy costumes and, soon enough, in bathing suits, forming and re-forming in a water ballet that ended in a grand climax, a fountain of swimmers, sleek and sinuous, waving their arms like graceful birds.

Ratter ran the projector and DeHaan sat by his feet. Looking out over the seated crew, it struck him how few they were, only a handful of men, really, on the vast reach of the deck, beneath an ocean sky. A few minutes into the movie, Maria Bromen appeared on deck, a little hesitant, uncertain where to sit. DeHaan waved her over and made space by his side. Evidently she'd washed her clothing and hung it up to dry, because someone had found her a pair of dungarees and a sweater, and she wore a scarf over her head, knotted beneath her chin. "Do you always have movies?" she said.

"Never. But the first mate found this in Tangier."

After a moment, she said, "The English is difficult, for me."

"James Cagney has trouble with his wife, but Joan Blondell, his secretary, is secretly in love with him."

"Ah, of course."

Then, a little later, "What happens now? He's a sailor?"

"Plays a sailor, in the production number."

"So. He fights!"

"Well, sailors in a bar."

After the fight, a song:

> *Here's to the gal who loves a sailor.*
> *It's looking like she always will.*
> *She's every sailor's pal.*
> *She's anybody's gal.*
> *Drink a gun to Shanghai Lil.*

10 June, 0300 hours. Port of Lisbon.

They had to have a pilot, entering the Tagus River, picked up off the town of Cascais, in order to cross the sandbars that built up at the mouth of the river. Pilots tended to be outgoing and talkative, seemed to enjoy that part of the job, and this one was no different. To DeHaan, he spoke English. "War has slowed down," he said. "Except for Libya, and that goes nowhere. Advance, retreat, advance."

DeHaan agreed. From the last newspaper he'd seen, and Ali's reports of the BBC, it certainly seemed that way.

"It may be the time for diplomats, now," the pilot said. "Hitler has what he has, and the British and Americans will find a way, with Japan. Is this how you see it?"

"One could say that." DeHaan was being polite. "But the occupation is a hard thing, for Europe."

"For some, yes. But it was not good before the war, with the communists, and men who could not find work." He paused, then said, "You are not Spanish, are you."

"Dutch."

"I thought you could be German. How does it happen that you are captain of a Spanish ship?"

"The last captain quit, without notice, and I was what they could find. Likely it won't last, though."

"Crew is Spanish?"

"Some. You know how it is with the merchant tramps, everyone from everywhere."

"Truly. And there is a lesson for the world, no?"

DeHaan agreed, and busied himself with the log, then spoke back and forth with the engine room. When they were safely in the

Tagus, made fast to two tugboats, and the pilot boat came alongside, DeHaan wasn't sorry to see him go.

Four in the morning, DeHaan on the bridge. With the tugs fore and aft, the *Noordendam* made slow way upriver, past pier after pier, while the city beyond lay still and silent, the final hour of its darkness broken only by streetlamps and a few lights dotted across the hills. Always, a part of him came sharply alive at these moments. To be awake while the world slept was a kind of honor, as though command of the imaginary night watch fell, for just that moment, to him.

By 0530 they had, as promised by the tugboat captain, tied up to the pier at the foot of the rua do Faro, a white *F3* painted on the side of the cargo shed. DeHaan, in normal times, would have left the bridge for his cabin, but these were not normal times, and he stayed where he was. As the first light of dawn settled on the city, the waterfront came to life: stevedores, lunch boxes in hand, heading for a shape-up on the neighboring wharf, the night's last whore going slowly home on her bicycle, the local seagulls coming to work, a sun-bleached black Fiat pulling up in front of the cargo shed, an army truck arriving next, a few yawning soldiers, lighting cigarettes and chatting among themselves, forming a ragged line at the foot of the pier, followed by an elderly couple with a suitcase, who stood back from the soldiers and settled in to wait. As DeHaan watched, more civilians arrived, until he'd counted forty or so, then stopped counting as the crowd grew.

At 0750, Kees showed up for the forenoon watch. "What goes on, out there?"

"I'm not sure. A crowd of refugees, it looks like."

"I thought this was all a secret."

"Well, keep an eye on it," DeHaan said, heading for his cabin, anxious for a few hours of dead sleep.

But this was not to be, not right away. In the corridor that led to his cabin, the chartroom door stood open and Maria Bromen was seated on a stool. She stood when she saw him. "I came to say goodby."

She had repaired herself as best she could — her suit and shirt pressed, sensible shoes polished, hair pinned up. "They loaned me the iron," she said. "It looks right?"

"Oh yes, looks perfect. But I thought you

would leave at night."

"Don't you sail today?"

"We'll try — we're a few hours late, but there are things that have to be done, so it will be after midnight."

"Still, I will go now, and I wanted to thank you. There is more I want to say, but I think you know. So, thank you, and I wish you safety, and happiness."

"There's some kind of commotion out there," DeHaan said. "Maybe you'd better wait for a while."

"Yes, refugees, I saw them. They want to get on your ship, to leave this city, but the army won't let them. It has nothing to do with me."

"They have no idea where we're going."

"They don't care. There will be rumors — South America, Canada — and they will offer money, jewelry, anything."

After a moment he said, "Well, good luck, and be careful. Is there anything you need?"

"I have everything, because of you. I will be richest Russian girl in Lisbon."

DeHaan nodded and met her eyes, he wanted to keep her. "So then, goodby." He extended his hand and she shook it, formally, Russian-style. Her hand was ice cold.

"Perhaps we will meet again," she said.

"I would like that."

"One never knows."

"No." Then, "You will be careful."

"I must be, but, now that I am this far, I think it will turn out well. I know it will."

"You don't want to wait for night."

She didn't.

Stubborn. But it had kept her alive, waiting for luck. "At least let me take you past all that on the dock."

"Alone is better. I will go right by the soldiers, they won't care, their job is only people who want to leave."

"Yes, you're right," DeHaan said.

They shook hands once more and she left. Halfway down the corridor she turned toward him, walked backward for a step or two, her face closed, without expression, then turned again and walked away.

DeHaan left the ship at 1030, headed for the rua do Comércio, the office of the customs broker. At the end of the pier, the soldiers made a path for him through the crowd of refugees, shooing people aside, barring their rifles and pushing when they had to. They were not brutal, only doing what they'd been ordered to do, and there was a certain practiced feel to the way they went about it. It took no time at all, his passage, but long enough. Voices called out to him, in this language or that, someone offering a thousand dollars, someone else holding a diamond ring above the heads of the crowd. *I can't take you.* Maybe he could, after a battle with the port officers, but he secretly agreed with Kees, that they'd never see longitude six-east, so where he would take them, more than likely, was to the bottom of the sea, or into a German camp.

"Is something wrong?" Penha, the customs broker, asked when he arrived. So, it showed.

DeHaan just shook his head.

Penha was short and dark, well dressed, and very nervous. "I've been waiting for you," he said. "I was here very late, last night."

"We lost time," DeHaan said. Their ship's log instrument — a line run from a gauge in the chartroom into the water that calculated miles gained — had showed them losing way to strong current on the voyage to Lisbon.

"Your cargo is in the shed on the wharf. I'm supposed to let you in, and to give you this." He had the false manifest on his desk, and gave it to DeHaan immediately, glad to be rid of the thing. "You are not what I expected," he said.

"What did you expect?"

Penha shrugged. "Buccaneer — of some sort." He used the French word, *boucanier,* oddly romantic, the way DeHaan heard it.

"Captain of a Dutch freighter, that's all."

Penha lit a cigarette. "This is not what I do, ordinarily."

"No, I'm sure it isn't," DeHaan said. "And a month ago I would've said the same thing. And a year ago, my country just went about its life, but everything changed."

Insufficient reason, from the look on Penha's face. "This is a business where honor matters — trust, personal trust, is all there is. That is my signature, on that piece of paper in your hand."

Shall I apologize? Penha was not acting out of conviction, he realized, had apparently been forced to do this. "There's no plan to show this to anyone, Senhor Penha," he said. "It's a form of insurance — and likely will remain a secret."

"A secret. Are you sure?"

"Yes, I would say I am."

"Because I'm not so sure."

After a moment, DeHaan said, "Why not?"

A long silence. Only sounds of the street

outside the quiet office as Penha tried to decide what to do, went back and forth — tell, don't tell — then caution won out. Finally he said, "There are reasons."

DeHaan gave him time to change his mind, time to say more, but the battle was over. "I should be getting back to my ship," he said, as he rose to leave.

"You will have to load tonight," Penha said. "And I'm supposed to be there." *Unless you say otherwise.*

"Is nine too early?"

"It will do."

"I have to sail, as soon as possible."

"Yes," Penha said. "You should."

It was a fifteen-minute walk, back to the pier at the rua do Faro. An unremarkable walk, through the commercial district behind the port, on the way there, but different on the way back. For whatever ailed Penha, DeHaan discovered, turned out to be contagious. For instance, the man idling in front of a shop window on the corner of the rua do Comércio. Or the couple looking out over the river, who glanced at him as he passed. And, on the street side of the cargo shed, the Peugeot sedan, parked by the road that allowed trucks to drive down the pier. Behind the wheel, a plump, middle-aged man, smoking a pipe and reading a newspaper, spread out across the steering wheel. To DeHaan he seemed particularly content, perfectly at peace with the world, as though this was the best, really the only, way to read a newspaper, parked in one's car by a cargo shed. As DeHaan came even with the car, the man looked up, stared at DeHaan for a few seconds, then rolled his window down. "Captain DeHaan?"

"Yes?"

The man leaned across the seat and opened the passenger door, then said, "Can you join me for a minute?"

What was this? When DeHaan hesitated, the man added "Please?" Not the polite version of the word, something less. The man put the pipe back in his teeth and waited patiently. Finally, DeHaan went around the front and climbed in the passenger side. Sweetish smoke filled the car, which had a fancy interior, with soft leather seats. "Much appreciated," the man said. "If I say the name Hallowes — does that help?"

"Yes, I suppose."

"My name is Brown," the man said. "I'm at the embassy, here in Lisbon."

"The naval attaché office?"

"Mmm, no, not really. But what I do isn't so different from your friend Hallowes. Same church, different pew, eh?"

"He asked you to speak with me?"

"Oh no, he didn't do that. But we're all on the same side, in the end, aren't we. You understand?"

After a moment, DeHaan nodded.

"Good, best to have that out of the way. Now Captain, I'm here because I have a small problem, and I need your help."

DeHaan waited. Inside, rising apprehension.

"The, ah, *Santa Rosa* sails tonight, I believe, for Sweden. Do I have that right?"

"For Malmö, yes."

"Of course, the official version. And very discreet, to put it that way."

"Mr. Brown, what do you want?" This was blunt and direct and had no effect whatsoever.

"A friend of mine needs passage, up to Sweden. I was hoping you might do me the favor of taking him along."

"I don't recall that being in my orders, from the NID."

"Oh, the *NID*," Brown said, deeply unimpressed. "No, probably it wasn't. Nonetheless, it's what I'm asking you to do, and

302

the NID needn't know about it, if that's what concerns you. He's just a meager little man, you won't even know he's aboard."

"And if I say no?"

"Is that what you're saying? Because I wouldn't do that, if I were you."

"Why not?"

"Why not," Brown said, as though to himself. "Have you noticed a Fiat automobile, parked on the pier?"

"Yes, I saw it."

"Inside the car are two Portuguese men. Plain enough, nothing special about them, except that they are important. Powerful, that's the better word. They can, for example, impound your ship and intern your crew, but neither of us would want that, would we, what with the war effort and all. You really must go to Sweden, but one extra soul on board will make no difference, certainly there's room for him."

Certainly there was. But if he did what Brown wanted, once, he had a feeling it might be twice, and that it wouldn't end there. And Brown wouldn't dare to impound his ship, his job wouldn't survive doing something like that. *All right then, get out of the car.*

"You aren't averse to taking a passenger, are you?"

The current running beneath his words had stiffened — this was barely a question, almost a statement, and DeHaan realized it was a reference to Maria Bromen.

"And I expect the welfare of, um, any passenger, would mean something to you, no?" *And, in Lisbon, because I can do it, I will, friend.*

"Yes, it would," DeHaan said.

"Ah then, we have no problem at all."

It took DeHaan a moment longer, then he said, "No."

Brown nodded — *this always works.* "You are helping to win the war, Captain. Even if very little is explained, even if you don't care for the way things are done in my part of the world, you are. We must all lend a hand, if we're to prevail, isn't that so?"

"When does he arrive?"

"Oh, that's up to you, Captain. When do you want him?"

"Before nine, we'll be busy after that."

"I'll have him here. And we're both very grateful, believe me. And, I should add, any difficulties here in Lisbon, you need only get in touch." He reached into the pocket of his jacket and handed DeHaan a blank card with a telephone number written on it. "That's the British Embassy — they'll know how to contact me."

It occurred to DeHaan, as it was meant to, that he was now owed a favor, and he wondered if it could be used to help Maria Bromen — it might even get her to Britain. But he sensed that would open a certain door, in her life, to what Brown called *his world,* a door that didn't open from the other side. DeHaan put the card in his pocket and got out of the car.

"Goodby, Captain," Mr. Brown said. "And thanks again."

2035 hours.
A pair of headlights turned the corner of the cargo shed, then went off as the car drove slowly to the end of the pier.

2130 hours.
The cargo shed was vast, seen from the inside, its ceiling thirty feet high. DeHaan, accompanied by Kees and Kovacz, followed Senhor Penha past mountains of stacked drums and bales until he found their consignment — an island of raw wood crates circled by a wire with a metal seal. Without ceremony, Penha took a wire cutter from a leather case and snipped off the seal. "Now it's yours," he said. He pro-

duced a paper for DeHaan to sign — *cork oak, sardines, cooking oil* — and departed, his hurrying footsteps receding down the length of the shed, followed by the emphatic slam of a door.

"Not much, is it," Kees said, squatting to inspect one of the crates. By freighter standards, hardly anything at all. The twenty-footers were no doubt sections of tower, the lattice aerials flat, and ten feet across. There were also a dozen square crates, eight by eight, and three flatbed trucks, painted matte black.

"We'll have to manhandle this stuff to the end of the dock," DeHaan said. "Our crane will get it aboard from there."

"The trucks, for the twenty-footers," Kees said. "The one on the end facing backwards, and driving in reverse. We'll need crew to get them on there." He put a hand on one of the eight-foot squares. "What's in here?"

"No idea," DeHaan said. "Supplies, maybe."

Kees took a prybar from his belt, the nails squeaked as a board came free and a hard-edged shape in oiled paper bulged through the opening. "Smell the cosmoline?" he said. He opened a clasp knife, slit the paper and peeled it back, revealing gray steel shining with lubricant. "This will be a submachine gun, I think, if you can find the magazine."

"I'm sure it's packed, in there somewhere," DeHaan said.

"That's what my wife used to say," Kovacz said.

"Go get help," DeHaan said to Kees, as he hammered the board back on.

As Kees left, Kovacz climbed into the nearest truck. "I wonder if they drained the tank," he said. He felt around for the ignition switch, then the engine came to life with a huge hammering roar that echoed off the high ceiling. "Christ, what's *in* here?" he shouted over the noise. He shifted into first gear, there was a loud metallic bang as it engaged, then the truck crept forward, a slow foot at a time. "That's all of it. I bet it'll do fifteen, downhill."

"Regeared," DeHaan yelled back. "All torque, no speed."

Kovacz drove a few feet more, then stopped and turned the engine off. "My uncle Dice has a farm in Leszno, he'd love this thing."

"He'll have to wait," DeHaan said.

When Kees returned, he had half the crew with him. Together they heaved and cursed until the first section of a tower rolled onto the truck bed. DeHaan, driving the backward-facing truck, didn't get reverse on his first try, which caused a mass shout of alarm until he stamped on the brake. He got it right the second time and the two trucks crept through the broad doors at the end of the shed and moved slowly down the pier.

When he climbed down from the cab, Ratter was waiting for him. "Awake, O Lisbon," he said, grinning.

"Can't be helped," DeHaan said.

"We'll have police," Ratter said. Then he peered into the darkness, nudged DeHaan with an elbow, and nodded back toward the cargo shed, where a lone figure stood in the shadows. "If that's who I think it is," he said, "you better go back there."

It was loud and busy at the cargo shed, so DeHaan led her away, to the dark edge of the pier where the river current lapped at the pilings. "Forgive me," she said. She was very tired, her voice soft with regret. "Maybe if I had waited for the night . . ."

"What happened?"

She took a deep breath, tried to steady herself. "They arrested me." *Of course, what else.* "I never even got to street. Two men, in a car. Not the regular police, some other kind, the political kind, I think."

"And?"

"And they took me to an office, and told me that I did not have visa for Portugal, so, if I choose to stay, I will be interned. They were polite, not angry — it is just the way their law is."

"What does that mean, exactly? Did they explain it to you?"

"A camp, it means. Somewhere east of the city — they said the name but I forgot it. It isn't like Germany, they said, but I would have to stay there until I could go somewhere else."

"Where would you go?" DeHaan said.

"Back to Russia, they said. Or back to Tangier, if the Spanish would let me. Or wherever I could get permission to go. I could write letters, they said. All the internees write letters, although the mail is irregular."

"But they let you come back here."

"Yes, in time. They kept me in the office all day, brought me a sandwich, then they told me I could come back here — it would be as though I never entered the country, they said, if I returned to the ship."

Was this, DeHaan wondered, Mr. Brown at work? He tried to figure it out, if this, then that, but it was a tangle of possibilities — including the possibility that he knew nothing about it. "Miss Bromen," he said. "Maria. What we are going to do is very dangerous. You were on the ship when we repainted, and you know what that means."

"Yes, I know."

"Then you know it may not succeed, it may end in a bad way. If we're caught, we'll be taken under guard to a German port. Or sunk. So it's possible that life in a Portuguese internment camp would be better, much better, than what can happen if you are aboard my ship. You would be alive, and then there is always hope. And they can't keep you there forever. This war will end, sooner or later, they all do, and, even if the British capitulate, there would be some kind of settlement, treaties, arrangements."

"I don't think I can live in a camp," she said, shaking her head slowly. "But that's what you think I should do, isn't it."

"I don't want you hurt, or dead. I don't want you in a German prison."

She shrugged and said, "I don't care. If there is a chance to escape, to find a place

310

where they will leave me alone, I will take it. There's no time to explain, but I grew up in a country that was a prison, and it happened that I was one of the ones who couldn't bear it. So I managed, with my work, to get away. Not far enough, but almost." She looked at him. "Almost, right?"

"Yes, almost." It surprised him, how angry he was. He wouldn't let her see it, but to be this close, the lights of the evening city just beyond the wharf, made him angry. What difference would it make, if she were there?

"I know it is inconvenient," she said. "To take me — wherever you are going. You can say no, I won't argue. They are waiting for me, the two men in their car, out on the street. They expect me to return, that's what they told me."

"No," he said. "I won't send you back. But you may not thank me, later on, for taking you away."

She raised a hand, as though to touch him, then didn't. "Then I'll thank you now," she said. "Before anything happens."

They walked back down the pier, toward the *Noordendam*, past the slow, rumbling trucks with a few sailors sitting on a long crate. At the ship, the bosun was directing the attachment of steel cables that hung down from the crane, and, as DeHaan and Maria Bromen went up the gangway, the first section of a tower rose slowly into the air.

11 June, 0240 hours. At sea.

"Steady on course three one zero."

"Aye-aye, sir."

"We'll bear northwest for an hour or so. And make full speed."

The helmsman shoved the arrow to *Full — Ahead,* two bells sounded and, a moment later, the answering bells came back from the engine room. Behind them, the pilot boat, returning to port, and the fading lights of the coast. Cornelius came to the bridge with a mug of coffee and a can of condensed milk. DeHaan drank off some of the coffee, added the thick milk, and stirred it with the end of a pencil. "How's everything below deck?" he said.

"We're glad to be away, Cap'n."

"Yes, me too," DeHaan said.

Cornelius stood by his side for a time, watching the sea ahead of them. When he turned to go, DeHaan said, "Coffee's good today, tell the cook I said so."

Cornelius said he would, and left the bridge. DeHaan looked aft, at the Spanish flag flapping in the wind, and their wake, phosphorescent in the moonlight. An eight-day voyage lay ahead of him. According to *Brown's Almanac*, Lisbon to a point due west of Glasgow was eleven hundred nautical miles, a hundred hours, four days at their speed of eleven knots. There were two routes to choose from, after that, Elsinore–by–Kiel Canal — Elsinore the British, rather Shakespearian form of the Danish port Helsingör, while the Kiel Canal ran through the northern heart of Germany. But that idea was beyond brazen. Instead, they would take Elsinore-by-Skaw, which meant the port of Skagen on the northern tip of Denmark. There was a shorter route, by way of what were called "the belts" — channels through the Danish islands — but the curve around to the Baltic would've swung them too close to the German coast. Going further east, down the three-mile pinchpoint between Helsingör and the Swedish coast, it was less than a day to Malmö, and only a few hours east to the Smygehuk.

Back up to Malmö for the sawn boards, he thought. And Kolb's departure, then on to Ireland, in theory, and Maria Bromen's departure. Another week, if they got there. So then, for two weeks, she would be in Ratter's cabin.

1900 hours, dinner in the officers' mess. All the officers, except for Kees on dog watch. Maria Bromen, back in dungarees, black sweater, and canvas deck shoes; and their traveling spy, Mr. Brown's "meager little man." He was certainly that — short and seedy, bald, with a fringe of dark hair, eyeglasses, and sparse mustache. And very diffident. He was, DeHaan observed, rather adept at diffidence. As everyone gathered for dinner, Kolb waited to see who went where, waited cleverly, shifting about, until all the others were seated, then took the remaining place. DeHaan said, "Miss Bromen has rejoined us for the voyage north, and we have one more passenger, Herr Kolb." DeHaan went around the table with names, and Kolb nodded and mumbled, "Pleased to meet you, sir," in heavily accented English.

"From where do you come, Herr Kolb?" Mr. Ali said.

"From Czechoslovakia," Kolb said. "Up in Bohemia, where it's German and Czech."

"You are German, by birth?"

"Some part," Kolb said. "It's all very mixed, up there."

"And your work?" Kovacz said.

"I am a traveler in industrial machinery," Kolb said. "For a company in Zurich."

"Business goes on," Ratter said. "War or no war."

"It does seem to," Kolb said, not quite reluctantly — it wasn't his fault. "War or no war."

Cornelius served the dinner: barley soup, black sausage and rice, and Moroccan oranges. Maria Bromen, using a thumbnail, deftly carved the skin off her orange, then ate it in sections.

When dinner was over, and DeHaan headed for his cabin, Ratter caught up with him in the passageway. "Who is he, Eric?"

"A favor for the British, he's going to Malmö."

"Is he dangerous?"

"Why do you say that?"

"I don't know. Is he?"

"He's just a passenger. I didn't really want to take him, but they insisted, so here he is."

"Everybody's been wondering, since yesterday."

"Let them wonder," DeHaan said. "One more unknown, leave it at that."

"You're aware that he toured the ship, this morning? He went everywhere, down to the engine room, crew's quarters."

"I didn't know, but so what? What's he going to do? Put it down to curiosity and forget it, we have more important things to worry about."

12 June, 0510 hours. Off Vigo.

A hundred miles east of them, in the dawn mist. DeHaan had always liked the port — a huge bay, easy docking, a town that welcomed sailors. A Dutch fleet had taken Vigo, during one of the eighteenth-century wars, fighting alongside a British squadron. The instructor at the naval college had shown them an old map, drawn in the odd perspective of the period, a line of big ships riding little semicircle waves. Then, during the Napoleonic Wars, it had played some role, what? The British? The French fleet?

There was a knock on the port window of the bridge. Ruysdal, the lookout, was motioning for him to come out on the wing.

"Over there, Cap'n."

Rising and falling on the low swell, a cluster of drifting shapes. DeHaan squinted through his binoculars. "Put a light on it," he said.

Ruysdal worked the searchlight, and a

yellow beam settled on the cluster. Bodies. Maybe twenty of them. Some of them in dark clothing, others wearing skivvy shorts — they'd been asleep when it happened, a few wore life jackets, and two of the men had roped themselves together at the wrist. DeHaan looked for insignia, for some identification, but, even with the searchlight, the gray dawn hid it from him. "Can you see the name of a ship? Anything?"

"No, sir."

There was more; debris, pieces of wood, a strip of canvas, a white life preserver — but if there was a name on it, it floated face down.

"Stop the ship, sir? Put out the cutter?"

DeHaan watched, looking for a sign of life as the bodies lifted and turned in the ship's bow wash and slipped away astern. "No," he said. "There's nothing we can do."

Ruysdal kept the light focused on the bodies until they disappeared from the edge of the beam. "Damn shame, sir, whoever they are."

"I'll note it in the log," DeHaan said, returning to the bridge.

13 June, 1920 hours. Off Brest.

The dinner conversation was in English, mostly, but sometimes German, for Kovacz and Poulsen. They managed — everybody helped their neighbor, it was better than silence, and better, come to that, than the smoked fish and beans.

"Where are we tonight, Captain?" Kolb said.

"Off Brest, approximately. Well off, about two hundred miles."

"The minefields," Ratter explained.

"Yes," Kovacz said. "Big naval base at Brest."

"And submarines," Mr. Ali said.

"They come out of La Rochelle, I think," Ratter said. "Not that it makes any difference, they're all watching us."

"Easy prey," Kolb said. "But why bother?"

"They've sunk neutral ships, both sides have," Ratter said. "Maybe somebody just wants to put another mark on their score, so they push a button."

"Or, a bad mood," Mr. Ali said.

"Yes," Ratter said. "Why not?"

Nobody had a reason why not — such things did happen, and always would.

"It is vile, this war," Maria Bromen said. "All of them."

"It will end," DeHaan said. "Some day."

"War?" Kolb said.

"This war."

"Have you heard the one about Hitler and the end of the war?" Kolb said. "He's in his office and he's looking at his portrait, and he says to it, 'Well, they're trying to get rid of me, but you're still hanging there. What will become of us, when the war is over?' And the portrait says, 'That's easy, Adolf — they'll get rid of me and hang you.'"

A translation followed, with a few laughs. Mr. Ali gave a BBC report, and comment on that held out until dessert. More oranges, gratefully received, then Ratter went to the bridge to relieve Kees and the rest returned to their cabins. DeHaan and Maria Bromen were the last ones in the passageway, standing in front of their doors.

"So then, good night," he said.

"Yes," she said. "Sleep well."

Claudine in Paris? DeHaan stood musing in front of his library and tried a paragraph. Long Atlantic rollers now, below him, the ship taking her time on the way up, engine at work, then down into the trough.

14 June, 0645 hours.

RAF skies, today. They'd crossed 50°N latitude at dawn, if they were on schedule. The ship log seemed to think so, though he wouldn't feel certain until Ratter shot the noon sunsights. Something of a border, fifty-north, France falling away to the south, the English Channel off the starboard beam as *Noordendam* swung away from the minefields that guarded the Western Approaches. Swung away, as well, from the lights of neutral Ireland, a safe haven. Better that they couldn't see them, he thought — he'd certainly considered putting Bromen ashore there, before they curved over Britain into enemy waters, but they had no time to make port, couldn't abandon her alone in the cutter, and, come to that, couldn't afford to abandon the cutter either.

So she had to stay aboard. His passenger. Of course he'd hoped for more, but that hope had climbed some interior hill, then tumbled down the other side — the midnight knock at the midnight door to remain locked away in his imagination. Because she would say no. Say it tenderly, no doubt, but he very much didn't want to hear her say it. And having her so near him made it much worse. *Proximity.* One of Desire's great inventions, wasn't it. Office partition, apartment wall, bulkhead — one would not, in fact, become a spirit and float through to the other side, but the thought was there.

A turn around the deck. He told the helmsman to stay on course and left the bridge. The sea had grown stronger overnight, *Noordendam*'s prow nosing through heavy swells as spray flew high above the bow and sent up little puffs of steam as it hit the deck. DeHaan stood dead still. This couldn't be what he knew it was. He trotted forward and knelt down, the salt spray stinging his eyes, and pressed a hand against the iron surface. Then he ran for the bridge.

The siren's wail produced both fire crews, sprinting for their hoses, and Ratter and Kees. Shouting over the siren, he told them where it was. Ratter got there first, wrapped his hand in his shirttail and spun the wheel that opened the hatch to the number one hold. When he threw the hatch cover back, gray smoke poured up from below. "Get a hose over here!" Kees yelled. An AB poked a nozzle into the opening and DeHaan had to grab him as he pulled the lever back and the high-pressure stream whipped the hose and almost sent him into the hold. "Give me that,"

DeHaan said and Kees handed him a flashlight. But, lying on his stomach and peering down into the darkness, he could see only a shifting cloud of smoke.

"What the hell is it?" Ratter said.

No answer. Hold fires were caused by spontaneous explosions, from dust, or slow combustion in damp fibers. "There's ammunition in those crates," Kees said. "Or worse. It'll blow us open."

Ratter put a foot on the first of the perilous steps, iron rungs, that descended into the hold. It was thirty feet, three stories, to the keel, sailors died when they fell down there, and the rungs extended only six inches — the shipyards didn't sacrifice space needed for cargo. Ratter coughed as he climbed down and, as DeHaan followed, said, "I'll thank you not to step on my fucking hands, Eric."

"Sorry."

Kees slithered backward off the deck and DeHaan watched his foot turn sideways, probing for purchase on a slippery rung. Above them, the AB adjusted the hose so that the white stream of water hissed past their heads — one slip of the hand and all three of them were finished. Someone on deck, maybe Kovacz, growled, "You're too close."

Some intelligent soul now turned on the lights — which meant the electrical system hadn't burned, and revealed one of the trucks, with its hood and cab in flames. "Turn off the hose and hand it down," Kees yelled.

"Don't try it," DeHaan shouted.

"Don't worry about that," Kees shouted back.

The light helped them go faster. Too fast, DeHaan's foot skidded off a rung and he grabbed the one above him with both hands, the flashlight clattering as it landed below.

By the time they reached the bottom, all three were breathing through handfuls of shirt. Kees turned the hose on and played the stream over the burning truck. The fire in the cab went out immediately, but burning gasoline in the engine kept coming back to life. They moved forward, sloshing through an inch of brown water, finally lying down in it and sending the stream up into the engine from below. That did it. "Should I hit the crates?" Kees said.

"No, better not," DeHaan said.

Standing in front of the charred, smoking hood, Ratter said, "Trucks catch fire by themselves. Happens all the time."

"You didn't drain the tank?" DeHaan said to Kees.

"I thought they'd need to drive it right away."

DeHaan walked over to the crate nearest the truck, one of the eight-by-eights, and felt for heat. The wood was smoke-blackened and warm to the touch, but no more than that. "Would've caught, in time," he said.

"Sabotage," Ratter said.

"Maybe."

"That little German."

Like a graceful bear, Kovacz clambered quickly down the rungs, a rag tied bandit-style over his nose and mouth, then stood with them and stared at the burnt truck. "It catches fire? All by itself?" he said, taking a pair of fireman's gloves from his back pocket and putting them on. He walked over to the truck, waving the smoke away from his face, and yanked the door open. "Ignition switch is on," he called out. "Maybe the wires heated up."

"Too much time since we loaded," Ratter said. "Battery wouldn't last that long."

"Ever hear of it?" DeHaan said.

After a moment, Kees said, "Once. On

the *Karen Marie,* some kind of big touring car."

"So it can happen," DeHaan said. Then called out to Kovacz, "Anything in there that doesn't belong?"

"Not that I can see."

"Get rid of him," Ratter said, meaning Kolb.

"How would I do that?" DeHaan said. "Hang him from a crane? With the crew assembled?"

"You can, you know," Kees said. "And quietly, if you have to."

"That's crazy," DeHaan said. But Kees wasn't entirely wrong. DeHaan was, according to the Dutch Articles, "Master next to God," and that meant he could do pretty much anything he wanted.

Kovacz backed out of the cab, then opened the hood. All four of them peered at the engine, the smell of burned rubber hose heavy in the air. "Nothing," Ratter said. "How the hell did he do it?"

"Wait a minute," Kovacz said. He reached below the engine and peeled a black scrap of fabric off the metal. "Oily rag?"

Silence. They stared at each other, all of them with tear streaks running through the soot below their eyes. Kees coughed and said, "Maybe the woman did it."

"Or somebody in the crew," DeHaan said. "Or maybe it was in there when we loaded it."

"Ignition switch on?" Kovacz said.

"If it stalled on the dock, and nobody checked . . . ," DeHaan said. Stranger things had happened, they all knew that, and hold fires were often mysterious. "Anyhow, they have two more," he said. "Let's hope that's enough. Johannes, I want you to take a walk around the ship — paint locker, places like that, you know what I mean."

Ratter nodded. "What do we tell the crew?"

"Oily rags," DeHaan said.

2010 hours. Off the Irish coast.

True Atlantic weather, now, barometer falling, maybe a storm system up north. Kolb didn't show up for dinner, but in this kind of sea the ship's pitch and roll could keep passengers in their cabins. "Feeling all right?" DeHaan asked Maria Bromen as they left the table.

"It doesn't bother me."

"Go up on deck and watch the horizon, if you have to."

"I will do that," she said. Then, "Could you tell me, maybe, where we are?"

When they reached the chartroom, he unlocked the door, turned on the light, and spread a chart out on the slanted top of the cabinet. She stood close to him, he could smell soap. Nice soap, nothing they had on the ship. "We're about here," he said, pointing with the calipers.

"So tomorrow, here?"

"Sea's against us. We'll be lucky to be off Donegal Bay."

"Do you have, a certain time, to be somewhere?"

"Yes, but in this business you give yourself an extra day. Always, if you can."

"And you mustn't tell me where we're going."

"I shouldn't," DeHaan said, feeling slightly silly.

"Who I would tell? A whale?"

DeHaan smiled and slid the chart back in its drawer. "Don't you like surprises?"

"Oh, some, yes. This one, I don't know."

He turned the light off and held the door for her. Once again, they stood by their cabin doors and said good night. DeHaan's was halfway closed when she said, "It's possible . . ."

He came back out. "Yes?"

"You have a book, I could read?"

"Come and see if there's something you like."

He closed the door behind her, started to sit on the bunk, then leaned against the bulkhead as she looked over the library.

"Dutch, French, more Dutch," she said, disappointed.

"There's some in English — don't you read it?"

"Hard work, for me, with dictionary. What's this?"

"What?"

"This."

He walked over to the bookshelf. She had her finger on a Dutch history of eighteenth-century naval warfare. "I don't think . . ." he said.

When she turned around, her face was close to his and her eyes were almost shut. *That sullen mouth.* Dry, but warm and extravagant, and very soft. And delicate — they barely touched. She drew away and ran her tongue over her lips. Not so dry, now. For a time they stood apart, arms by their sides, then he settled his hands on her hips and she moved toward him, just enough so that he could feel the tips of her breasts beneath the sweater. By his ear, her breath caught as she whispered, "Turn off the light."

He crossed the cabin and pulled the little chain on the lamp. It took only a few seconds but when it was done she'd become a white shape in the darkness, wearing only underpants, long and roomy, almost bloomers. She stood still, waiting while he undressed, then said, "Take them down for me." He did it as slowly as he could, finally kneeling on the floor and lifting each foot to get them off. She liked him down there and hugged him for a moment, a strong hug, arms around his neck, then let him go and ran for the bed.

Where it was all rather forthright, to begin with, but that didn't last.

The *Noordendam* creaked and groaned in the night sea. *Much better than a room,* he thought, the rough blanket wound tight around them, the two of them wound tight around each other.

"They brought it aboard in Rangoon," he said. "The last item in the shipment, a big wooden barrel. Some poor Englishman, they said, colonial administrator, going home to his family burial ground in England. They'd filled the barrel with brandy, you could smell it, to preserve the body. So we put it down in the hold but we had a bad storm, in the South China Sea, and it got stove in and began to leak. Well, we couldn't leave it like that, not in high summer, so we opened it up and there he was, in his white tropical suit, along with some watertight metal boxes, packed with opium."

"What did you *do* with it?"

"Overboard."

"And him?"

"Got him a new barrel, an old paint drum, and filled it with turpentine."

"I grew up in Sevastopol," she said. "So I am Ukrainian, Marya Bromenko. 'Maria Bromen' came later. I thought, for Western journals, maybe better. Such ambition I had. My parents had great hopes for me — my father kept a little store in the port; tobacco, stamps, whatnot. For me he wanted education, not so easy but we managed. We managed, we managed — better than most. Always we had something on the table — potatoes, in the bad times, potato pancakes, in the good, as you can see."

"See what?"

"I am big down below, not so much on top, a potato."

He ran his fingers down her back. "Mm, not much like a potato."

"I know you think so. I knew the first

time I saw you, how you felt."

"It showed?"

"To a woman, we know. But still, I was as I was, never to be a ballerina, and I hated the idea of becoming one more teacher. So, a journalist. I went to the university, in Moscow, for a year, but 1919, you know, the civil war, sometimes no class, or you had to march. And you had to say the right thing, because they would ask you about the other students, who's a spy, and you had always provocation — 'Don't you hate that bastard Lenin?' — and I got tired of it, weary, and afraid, and I thought, maybe better, go home to Sevastopol. I think I had, even then, a premonition, that I would get in trouble with these people.

"But my dear father wouldn't give up — he got me a job, with a little journal we had there, news of the port and the ships. I worked hard, and eventually I found a good story, about the *Lieutenant Borri*, a French minesweeper that brought troops to Odessa, and her captain, one of those French adventurers who write novels. Claude Farrère, he was called, a villain, but interesting. It was this story that got me hired at *N'a Vakhte*, where, to begin with, I wrote from the woman's view. What do you eat, on board your ship? Do you miss your sweetheart, at sea? Small stories, soft at the edge. Like Babel, though not so good, more like, maybe, Serebin. They are called *feuilletons,* leaves, that's the technical name. You always had to put in a little communism — the food is better than under the czar, I miss my sweetheart but I am working to build socialism. We all did that, you learned how to do it, to keep the commissars quiet." She yawned, then stretched.

"It's getting late," she said. "You have to work soon, no?"

"Not until midnight."

"Must make you tired, to sleep in two parts."

"You get used to it."

"Still, I should let you sleep."

"I have my whole life to sleep."

When they were quiet, they could hear the wind sighing at the porthole and the rain beating down on the deck. "It's a storm outside," she said.

"Not too bad, just ocean weather."

She yawned again, then moved around until she was comfortable. "Would you like to touch me a little?"

"Yes."

15 June, 1810 hours. Off Glasgow.

DeHaan was in the chartroom when he heard the plane, the whine of a small engine passing above them, which faded away, then returned. He hurried up to the bridge wing, where a small biplane was circling back toward them in a cloudy sky. A two-seater, some kind of reconnaissance aircraft he didn't recognize, with British insignia on the fuselage. Kees opened the bridge door and said, "He's been signaling to us."

"How?"

"Waving out the window, pointing to the foredeck."

The plane passed over the bridge, flying so slowly that DeHaan wondered it didn't stall. The pilot held something out the window, swooped low over the foredeck, dropped it on the hatch cover, then waved again as he flew away.

DeHaan and the watch AB went forward and recovered a zippered canvas bag. Inside, a chunk of kapok, that would have kept the bag afloat had it landed in the sea, and a sheaf of papers in a plastic envelope.

DeHaan took it back to the bridge. "What is it?" Kees said.

He wasn't sure. Typed instructions, with courses and positions underlined, and routes between fields of tiny crosses marked out in red pencil. Finally he said,

"Minefields. In the Skagerrak. It's very precise."

"Up-to-date," Kees said.

"Looks like it."

"So top secret — not even for the radio."

"No, I don't imagine they'd want anybody to know they have this."

Kees studied the maps, then, with a tight smile, said, "You know, I just might lose my bet."

"I think you might," DeHaan said. "This gets us well beyond six-east."

"Well, I won't pay off just yet."

"No, I wouldn't, just yet."

DeHaan called a senior officers' meeting at eight, and Ratter, Kees, and Kovacz joined him in the wardroom. He chased Cornelius, cleaning up after dinner in the mess area, then laid out the minefield maps and routes on the table.

"What I wonder," Ratter said, "is how we would do this if we were a real Spanish freighter."

"By radio, once we were in the North Sea. That's a guess, but I don't think the *Kriegsmarine* gives out maps — not to neutrals."

"Not many of them," Kees said. "Only a few blockade runners. They aren't led through, are they?"

"I don't think so. There's quite a lot of traffic up there, once you get past the Norwegian coast — Swedes down to Germany with iron ore, Norwegians and Danes, hauling all sorts of cargo. And however they do it, we'll be in among them, just one more freighter."

"Recognition signals?" Kovacz said.

"God I hope not. The British would've warned us, if there were. Could they do that? Every Argentine and Portuguese tramp going into the Baltic?"

Kovacz shrugged. "Hardly any go, like Kees said. British blockade maybe works better against Germany — they have to depend on Sweden, Russia, the Balkans."

"That's what Adolf always carried on about," Ratter said. "Geography."

"Nazi lies, Johannes," Kovacz said. "It was always about *Wehrwille* and it still is." It meant the will, the desire, to make war.

Leaning on his elbows and looking down at the maps, Ratter said, "They need this cargo, don't they. Really need it."

"I hope so," DeHaan said.

"They need it all right," Kovacz said. "For U-boats. For, ah, what's the word, *signatures*. The British have direction-finding antennas everywhere — Iceland,

335

Newfoundland, Gibraltar, Cape Town, other places, just look at a map and think it through. So they get all the signals, and plot positions on charts, and maybe make a kill, but this station, in Sweden, is for U-boats. Built in Kiel and Rostock, then tested, worked up, in the Baltic. Each radio operator is different, has his own signature, the way he uses the transmission key, so, once you recognize him, you can figure out which U-boat is where. What the NID wants to do is write the life story of each submarine, find out its number, maybe even the name of its commander. They want to watch it from its birth, at the Baltic yards, to its death. Because if U-123 is in the Indian Ocean, it isn't on the Atlantic convoy routes."

Ratter lit a cigarette and shook out the match. "Stas, how do you know all this?"

"When I was in the navy, in Poland, we had people at work on these things. The earth is four-fifths water, that's a lot of room to hide, so the great trick of naval warfare has always been to find the enemy before he finds you. You're finished, if you can't do that, and all the courage and sacrifice in the world simply adds up to a lost war."

North, and north. Into the heart of the

storm on the evening of the sixteenth, where the wind shrieked and thirty-foot waves came crashing over the deck and sheets of driven rain sluiced down the bridge-house windows. It was DeHaan who took the storm watch, but Ratter and Kees were on and off the bridge all night long, everybody in oilskins, including the helmsman, hands white on the wheel, who stood a two-hour shift before DeHaan sent him below and had a fresh one take over. The force of the storm blew out of the west, and DeHaan kept giving up a grudging point at a time, fighting for his course, because *Noordendam* couldn't take it full on the beam. Finally Kees said, "Turn into the goddamn thing for Christ's sake," and DeHaan gave the order, swinging due west and heading up into the wind. Mr. Ali came up, now and again, blinking as he wiped his glasses with a handkerchief, to report distress calls coming in on the radio — the North Atlantic taking hold of the war that night and trying to break it in half. Then a savage gust of wind snapped the aerial and Ali appeared no more.

It backed off, the morning of the seventeenth, with a violent red-streaked dawn, and DeHaan staggered down to his cabin, stripped off his clothes, and crawled into bed. He woke, some time later, to find something soft and warm in there with him, and spent a few seconds being exceptionally happy about that before he fell back asleep. Woke again, alone this time, he thought, until he came up from under the blanket and saw her standing at the porthole and gazing out. He watched her till she felt it and turned around, wiping her eyes. "You are looking at me," she said.

"I am."

"Well then," she said. And came back to join him.

They were a day and a half late, steaming up past the Hebrides and swinging around the Orkney Islands into the North Sea, but there was still time to reach the Smygehuk by the twenty-first, as long as the weather held fair. Which it did, but for a series of line squalls in the wake of the storm that neither DeHaan nor the *Noordendam* took very seriously. These had been busy sea-lanes before the war, but no longer — only a few fishing boats, a British destroyer in the distance, a corvette that came up on their starboard beam and stayed with them for twenty minutes, then found something better to do. They were alone after that, in choppy gray waters, cold and grim, running south-southeast between Britain and Norway, with the Skagerrak, portal to the German Empire, lying some twelve hours to the east.

At dusk, DeHaan took a commander's tour around the ship — a campfire-to-campfire, night-before-the-battle tour. Slow and easy, with all the time in the world, he stopped to smoke a North State with some off-watch ABs, had a salt-beef sandwich and cold tea in the crew's mess, sat on a bench in the workshop that adjoined the engine room and chatted with the oilers and firemen. He grew prouder of his crew as the evening wore on — there was none of the usual griping and bitching, no tales of thievery or fistfights. Nothing quite like danger, he thought, to cure the bullshit of daily life.

He took Amado aside and told him he might be on stage once more, in the coming days. He asked Van Dyck if he could rig a communication line from the bridge to the radio room, and Van Dyck said he could, using spares kept on hand for the bridge/engine-room system. "It'll look like hell," the bosun said. "Tube running down the helm and across the deck."

"Do it anyhow," DeHaan told him.

He visited with Shtern, in a former storage locker, heavily whitewashed and made over into an infirmary, a red cross painted on the door, and finally with S. Kolb, found reading in the wardroom.

"Good book, Herr Kolb?"

Kolb held the spine up for DeHaan to see. H. Kretschmayr, *Geschichte von Venedig*. "A history of Venice," he said. "I found it at my hotel in Lisbon."

"Wars and trading fleets?"

"Doges."

In those hats.

"It goes only to 1895," Kolb said. "But maybe that's not so bad."

"We will be entering German waters, tonight," DeHaan said. "I thought I'd let you know."

"Am I to be assigned — an action station?"

DeHaan was diplomatic. "We don't expect to be doing very much fighting, Herr Kolb, but, if something happens, we know where to find you."

"I can work a radio, sir."

I bet you can. "Oh? Well, we'll keep that in mind."

Ratter shot starsights at 2100 hours, and calculated they would cross a line parallel to Stavanger, Norway — six degrees east longitude — not long after midnight. "Their front door," he said.

"Yes, if we're going to be stopped, it will happen there."

"Ship dark? In midstream?"

"No, all lit up, and six off the Norwegian coast."

At 0018 hours, on 20 June, 1941, the NV *Noordendam* entered German-occupied Europe, curving around a welcoming minefield that served, on this sea border, as barbed wire. DeHaan noted it in the log with particular care, because he sensed they would not be coming out. A dark shore, to the north. Blacked out. No lighthouses, no lightships, no bells or horns or signal buoys — none of the navigational apparatus that had helped mariners find their way for centuries. Still, with nothing more than a sickle moon, it should have been like any night sea voyage — ship's bells on the half hour, engine full ahead, wake churning behind them — but it wasn't, because whatever was watching and waiting out there could be felt. *Calm down,* DeHaan told himself, but it didn't help, and Ruysdal, beside him at the helm, wasn't doing much better. "Bearing zero nine five, Cap'n," he said, for absolutely no reason.

"Steady as she goes," DeHaan answered. Like dogs, he thought, barking at the night.

Then all hell broke loose.

From the coast, huge searchlight beams went stabbing into the sky and DeHaan grabbed his binoculars, followed the beams, saw nothing. But a distant hum to the west deepened, as he searched, to a low rumble, then swelled to the full roar of a bomber formation. In answer, antiaircraft cannon: dozens of them drumming together, with pinprick flashes from the shore and flak burst high above — slow, silent puffs turned ash-gray by the searchlights. The first bombs were like sharp thunder, single explosions that broke over the rhythm of the cannon and rolled across the water, then more, and louder, all run together as the main body of the formation came over target. With, clearly, at least some incendiaries, which, whatever they hit, produced great pillars of orange fire as smoke poured up into the sky.

A shadow sliced through the lower edge of a beam and Ruysdal said, "Dive-bomber." Its engine screamed as it fled away, lights chasing it until it banked hard and came howling out over the sea, toward the *Noordendam*, where a crowd of sailors on deck cheered wildly and waved as though the pilot could see them. "Brave sonofabitch." This from Ratter, standing over the green binnacle light, which lit up his face from below as though he were a kid with a flashlight.

DeHaan turned back toward the shore in time to see a second dive-bomber — or the first, back for more — a black flash against the firelight, followed by a beautiful white starburst, with smoke trails that arched high in the air, and one blurred snapshot of what might have been a superstructure. "Ship?" he said.

"Looks like it, sir," Ruysdal said.

"They're after the naval base at Kristiansand," Ratter said.

It continued. Stuttering antiaircraft, the night lit by fire. "I think there's a possibility," Ratter said, "that this is for us."

"They wouldn't do that," DeHaan said.

"Are you sure?"

After a moment he said, "No."

One of the searchlight beams had found a bomber, a thin line of smoke streaming from the fuselage beneath its wing. A second searchlight joined in, then a third. They were very good at it now — they'd pin this bastard against the clouds as long as they liked. Not so long. The plane rolled over, very slowly, then tumbled like a falling leaf, this way and that, until it plunged into the sea and left no more than steam.

BALTIC
HARBORS

They left the Skagerrak minefields on a perfect summer morning.

Coming around the Skaw at 0730, with Ratter and DeHaan working together on the bridge, where they'd been all night, draining mug after mug of coffee and poring over the British maps until they were sure they had it right and only then ordering the course changes. They had also, since midnight, stationed two ABs at the bow, watching the water ahead of the ship, because it never got all that dark up here this time of year — almost Midsummer's Eve, the Scandinavian sky pale and silvery long before the sun rose. Otherwise, it seemed to DeHaan like normal commercial life in the Kattegat — two Norwegian coasters up ahead of them, a coal-burning freighter in the distance, and, the only sign of occupation, a converted trawler, flying the naval swastika, patrolling the Danish shoreline.

For the first time in fourteen hours, DeHaan relaxed, and began to think about his aching feet and the bunk in his cabin. He'd just slipped the maps back in their envelope when one of the lookouts came charging up the ladder and shouted, "Loose mine, Cap'n, off the port bow."

"Come to full stop," he told Ratter, then trotted after the AB, who could really run. They got up to the bow in a hurry but, he realized, he might just as well have taken his time, because the minute he saw it he knew there wasn't a thing in the world he could do about it.

It bobbed thirty feet off the bow, a rusty iron ball, long ago painted orange, with detonator horns sticking out all over and a broken chain trailing down into the water. Not especially warlike or sinister, from the look of it, simply practical; six hundred pounds of amatol, enough to blow up a village.

Transfixed, DeHaan and the ABs stood still for a moment and watched as the thing slid past them. The engine was stopped but that didn't matter, momentum would carry them along for quite a while, as it would despite a hard-rudder change of course. They might have used the rifle on it, DeHaan thought, but it was much too close. No, all he could do was walk back along the deck, keeping it company, waiting to see if fate would send a small wave or a little cat's paw of wind, finally standing at the stern, by happenstance still alive, and watching as it floated away on the sun-dappled water.

The master of the *Noordendam* and one of his passengers were absent from dinner on the night of the twentieth. Some time early the next morning they would be off the southern coast of Sweden, no doubt a busy time for all, so he'd perhaps chosen that evening to rest, sending the mess boy to the kitchen for onion and margarine sandwiches and relieving his personal, chartroom store of two bottles of lambic beer. Rich stuff, thick and deep, brewed by merry friars — one would suppose — in the cellars of the Saint Gerlac abbey in Belgium, the saint's emblem, a hermit in a tree, handsomely rendered on the label. Saint Gerlac came in very large bottles, with ceramic stoppers to reseal the beer if its drinking were perchance interrupted —

by a rain of gold coins or an unexpected birth — and had to be finished later.

By seven-thirty they'd entered the Oresund, channel to the Baltic and the narrowest part of the Danish pinchpoint, with an occupied, blacked-out port of Helsingör on the Danish side, and pretty lights in the Swedish Hälsingborg, three miles across the sound. The *Noordendam* stayed well to the neutral side of the water, so passed close to Hälsingborg.

A long, slow dusk, that time of day. DeHaan's cabin was dark, beer bottles and sandwich plates on the floor, clothes piled neatly on a chair. "Can we go and see it?" she asked, climbing out of bed. DeHaan unlatched the brass fitting on the porthole and opened it wide — a warmish evening, the air felt good on his skin. They were close in to Hälsingborg, close enough to see the wooden buildings in the harbor, all painted the same shade of red, close enough to see a long row of sailboats, and a man who'd walked his dog out to the end of the sailboat dock and waved to the freighter as it went by.

"Would be nice," she said. *To be here together.*

"It would, some day."

"Some day." Which will likely never

come, she meant. "Does something happen tonight?"

"We get where we're going, about two in the morning, we unload a cargo, and then with a little luck we're bound for, well, not home, but somewhere like it."

"Ah," she said. "I thought so."

"You knew?"

"It's in the air, like before a storm."

At the municipal pier, two boys stood waist-deep in the oily water and splashed each other.

"You know how to swim?" he said, only half joking.

"You would let me?"

It took him a slow moment to understand that this was a woman's question, not a fugitive's question, and he put his arms around her and pulled her back against him. It felt so good he didn't speak right away, finally said, "Never," then added, "Also the water's too cold."

"This country is too cold." The municipal dock fell away behind them, replaced by a cluster of tiny houses where the town turned back into an old village. "But what if it should happen that we could go, somewhere?"

"Then we'd go."

"Where?"

"Somewhere in the countryside."

"Which countryside?"

"France, maybe. At the end of a little road."

"Oh? Not by the sea?"

He smiled. "With a view of the sea."

"Like in a book," she said. "You would be on a terrace, with a spyglass." Using circled thumbs and forefingers she made a pretend spyglass, pointed it at the porthole and squinted one eye. " 'Oh the sea, how I miss it.' You would too, my sweet friend."

Now the edge of Hälsingborg was gone, and they steamed past flat, rocky coast in gray light. "It's like this until we get to Copenhagen," he said.

"I was there. I like those people, the Danes, and they have good food. Very good food. Or, anyhow, they used to."

"It's not so bad for them, not so bad as other places."

"Will be bad. You'll see."

They were quiet for a time, not happy that they'd strayed back to real life. "You feel good back there," she said. "So interested."

"Yes?"

"Yes." Gently, she unwrapped his arms and went to the bookshelf where he kept the wind-up Victrola. She took the album of records off the shelf, then chose one. "Is this good?"

It was the Haydn cello quartet. "I like it."

"Can we play it while — we go back to bed?"

"For ten minutes, then it ends."

"Let it end."

"It will go chk-taca, chk-taca."

She made a face, a scowl, annoyed that she couldn't have what she wanted. "Stupid thing," she said.

They passed a darkened Copenhagen, then the lights of Malmö. A Swedish patrol boat shadowed them for a time, a little too close for comfort, then backed off without bothering to challenge. Likely they assumed the *Santa Rosa* was hauling war materials, down to Kiel or Rostock, and were disinclined to irritate their German neighbors, staring at them across the strait. DeHaan was back on the bridge by then, just after midnight, where he thought about her and thought about her, mostly *why now* thoughts, about how the world gave with one hand and took away with the other.

They rounded the Swedish coast soon after that, coming into the Baltic, and, a kind of miracle, on time. *No,* he thought, *not a miracle.* Hard work. Particularly Kovacz, down in the engine room, holding *Noordendam* to her best eleven knots. Fighting his war against a rickety pipe system, mending it at the elbows where the steam liked to break free and see if it could scald somebody, putting his heart's blood into the rise and fall of the great brass piston rods. There should be a medal for them, Kovacz and his firemen and oilers, or a *mention in dispatches.* But there would be nothing like that, of course, because for this kind of work there were no dispatches. Perhaps a muted smile from Hallowes but they'd never see it. There would be one final, arid message from the NID, DeHaan thought, a destination, then silence.

Ratter was out on the bridge wing, shooting his stars, his Gothic Sextant With Artificial Horizon aimed up at the heavens, because they had to hit 55°20′N and the longitude right on the nose. Ratter, too, deserved a medal. *Andromedae, Ceti, Eridani, Arietis, Tauri, Ursae Majoris, Leonis, Crucis,* and *Virginis* — just like Odysseus, patron saint of any captain so mother-dumb he could get lost in the Aegean. Ratter took another reading, then peered at his almanac:

"Corrections for the Moon's Upper and Lower Limbs." At least the stars were visible, with only a few drifting shreds of moonlit cloud. Black night and driving rain would have been welcome, except that they never would have found their position. So they had to be visible, and they were, in this thin summer darkness, and too bad for them.

"Johannes?"

"Yes."

"Getting what you need?"

"Pretty much, I am."

"How are we doing?"

"Good. We're just off Cuba."

21 June, 0250 hours. Off the Smygehuk.

The *Noordendam* ran dark now. And silent — bell system turned off, crew ordered to be quiet, engine rumbling at dead-slow speed on a flat sea. A mile off the port beam, one fishing village, a few dim lights in the haze, then nothing, only night on a deserted coast.

On the bridge, DeHaan and Ratter, the AB Scheldt out on the wing, a green signal lamp held at his side, while Van Dyck waited with a crew at the anchor winch. DeHaan looked at his watch, he had a few minutes to wait, so called down to the radio room, using the newly installed voice tube. "Mr. Ali, everything as usual?"

Ali's voice was excited. "It is not, sir, it is *not*. The whole world is transmitting! Up and down the bandwidth — one stops, another starts."

Ratter could hear the tone but not the words. "What's going on?"

"Heavy wireless traffic," DeHaan said. Then, to Ali, "Anything in clear?"

"A few words in German, maybe harbor boats. But the cipher, dear me! And fast, sir, a lot that must be sent."

"Any idea where it's coming from?"

"How would I know? But they're strong signals, so it could be Germany."

What is this? Something sudden, was all he knew. Invasion? Political upheaval? *The war is over.* "Have you listened to the BBC?" he asked.

"At midnight. But nothing new — fighting in the Lebanon, Mr. Roosevelt speaks. Then music for dancing."

DeHaan thanked him and hung the tube back on its hook. In the faint light of the binnacle lamp, 2:58.

"Any idea why?" Ratter said.

"No."

2:59. 3:00. "What do you make it, Johannes?"

"Oh three hundred."

"Scheldt?"

"Cap'n?"

"Show two, three-second signals."

"Aye-aye, Cap'n."

A count of ten, no more, and the answer. DeHaan turned the engine telegraph to *Full — Stop* and told Ratter to drop anchor. As the chain began to run out, a familiar sound, echoing over the water from the east. Tonk. Tonk. Tonk. A sound he'd heard all his life — a fishing boat with a one-cylinder engine, the voice of its single stroke amplified by a long exhaust pipe run up through the roof of the wheelhouse, very resonant and loud, a Steamboat Willie cartoon honk. "Here she comes, sir," Scheldt called out from the wing.

"Have Mr. Kees get a line on her, and lower the gangway."

Ulla, she was called, maybe the captain's wife or daughter, and when DeHaan climbed down to her deck he saw that she was a classic of the breed — fishy and smelly, nets hung everywhere, her scuppers, the vents that let water run out when she was hosed down, thickly crusted with a generation of dried scales. He counted eight in the crew, fishermen by the look of them, in overalls and boots and heavy beards. The captain, a hefty viking in a home-knitted blue-and-yellow watch cap, stood by the door of the wheelhouse, aloof from all these strange goings-on aboard his boat.

Two of the others were armed fishermen — one with a Sten hung on a leather strap, the other with a big pistol in a shoulder holster. This was the leader, a young British naval officer, a Scot by his accent, who identified himself as the ARCHER of the NID orders, then stood back, obviously very relieved when DeHaan offered to have the *Noordendam* officers manage the cargo handling. DeHaan wasted no time — Van Dyck and a few ABs boarded the *Ulla*, then, with Kees running the cargo crew on the ship, they soon had the first truck lowered to the deck of the fishing boat.

DeHaan and his crew stayed on for the one-mile trip to shore, where the *Ulla* was tied off to a piling and, after a lot of shouting and a few mashed fingers, the truck was pushed onto a ramp, then rolled down into the water sloshing at the tide line, where its engine was started and it was driven a few feet up the sand. "Well I'll be damned," one of the fishermen said to DeHaan. "This begins to look like it might actually work." A rather donnish fisherman, this one, by the tone of his voice, arch, and faintly amused. He was tall and spindly, with thin red hair and beard, and tortoiseshell eyeglasses.

DeHaan looked up into the night sky. "It will take some time," he said. "We won't get it finished by dawn."

"Our patrol comes a little after eight," the man said, following DeHaan's eyes. "He's very regular — eight and ten-thirty and four-thirty. A Blohm and Voss spotter plane, a flying boat."

"Is he ever, ah, early?"

"Never. Very punctual fellow, our German."

"That's useful."

"It is, isn't it. So we can work at night."

"And what do you do?"

"Me? I'm the local boffin."

"Boffin?"

"You know, the science chap."

"Oh, a professor."

"Used to be, but I'm in the navy now. It was the RAF came calling, originally, but they didn't *quite* know what to do with me, so I was sent off to the navy, where they gave me a wee little rank and said, 'Now *you* go to Sweden.'"

The captain reversed his engine, came about, and the *Ulla* tonked back out toward the freighter. "Quite a noise, that," said the professor. "If I had a drill with a metal bit, I could turn it into a calliope, but I don't think Sven would care for it."

"No, I doubt he would. Is that your specialty?"

"Sound, yes. Waves and UHF and whatnot. I spent twenty years in a basement laboratory — I'm not sure the university *actually* knew I was there. Then the war came, and no more pings and toots for me."

As they neared the *Noordendam*, Kees already had the second truck suspended from a crane. "I should tell you there's a third truck," DeHaan said, "but it burned up in the hold."

"However did that happen?"

"We don't know. Can you manage with two?"

"Oh yes, I should think, it only has to haul the towers up. We've got a sort of ramp to climb — you'll see."

"Use the burnt one for parts, maybe."

"We shall. If we last long enough to wear something out."

Along with the second truck, the *Ulla* was loaded with three of the long crates. It

358

was well after four, by then, with summer dawn just getting started. Looking up at the sky, DeHaan saw fading stars and wisps of distant cloud to the west, with darkish, troubled sky beyond. *Rain by midday.* He'd know for certain as soon as he could check the barometer. Not good news, Baltic weather was famously treacherous — bad storms came suddenly, in all seasons.

DeHaan sat in the back of the lead truck, with the professor, Van Dyck, and the front ends of the crates. Behind them, the second truck drove in reverse, the same system they'd used on the Lisbon dock. Their progress over the sand, then through low scrub, was, with the geared-down engines, very slow but very steady. Finally, some two miles inland, the driver signaled back to the second truck, they rolled to a halt, and the engines were turned off.

They'd stopped at the front yard of what looked like an abandoned farmstead. DeHaan got down from the truck, took his hat off, ran his fingers back through his hair. *Somebody's dream,* he thought, *once upon a time.* A burned-out cottage, the sagging remains of an old fence. There was nothing else, only the wind, sighing across empty fields and rustling the weeds of the dead garden.

The British officer and one of the fishermen walked some way beyond the cottage, then rolled back a large camouflage net. DeHaan was impressed, he hadn't seen it at all. "For the spotter planes," the professor said. "What do you think of it?"

"Well done."

"The best film company in England made that."

As they walked toward a squared-off entry to a tunnel, maybe twenty by thirty feet, the professor said, "Had your breakfast?"

"Not yet."

"Good."

DeHaan soon enough understood why. As he entered the tunnel, the smell very nearly made him retch. "Damn, what is it?"

"Never smelled a mushroom cellar, have you."

"No."

"We think this may have been a mine, a long time ago, though what they were mining remains a mystery. Then old somebody came along, built himself a little house, and decided to use the chamber for growing mushrooms. It's the growing medium that smells — mushrooms feed on rot. Now, as to what the medium may have been, that's a topic for discussion, and here we split into three camps: there's the pig-manure faction, the rotten-potatoes crowd, and a compromise party — pig manure *and* rotten potatoes. What are your views?"

"I'll never eat another mushroom."

"Maybe get it from the woods, if you're a fatalist. Come along, then." They walked down the tunnel, then the professor took a lantern from a peg on the wall and lit it by flicking a match with his thumbnail. An immense gallery, like a great ballroom — its sides and ceiling braced with boards, extended far beyond the lamplight.

"You sleep down here?"

"Not in decent weather, but, when winter comes . . ." He shrugged, nothing to be done about it. "We're working on our heraldic crest — a silver dragon rampant, holding his nose with thumb-claw and forefinger, below the scrolled motto, *Phoo!* Anyhow, you see how it works, we keep the towers flat in here, then haul 'em out at night with trucks. Once we get them seated on cement pads and pulled upright, we can listen to Adolf's submarine and ship trans-missions. The whole band, everything, even the medium-wattage stuff, military housekeeping, mostly, but you get quite a lot *en clair*."

"And you have electricity? Out here?"

"Oh no, that's the beauty of it. We have generators, or, rather, you have them. You *do* have them, don't you?"

"Everything they shipped," DeHaan said.

They worked hard as a red sun came over the horizon and lit the sea. Loading the *Ulla* with more and more weight as she sank lower and lower and the captain glared at them through slitted eyes. But she had calm water and only a mile to go and, by 0650 hours, the *Noordendam* had offloaded the last of the cargo. "We're grateful for your help" — a Scottish growl from the commanding officer, and a handshake, then DeHaan climbed back up the gangway. Most of the crew were on deck, watching as the *Ulla* made its final run to the beach. Some of them waved, and the fishermen waved back and made vee signs.

Kees took the bridge and got them quickly under way — they couldn't be seen to be anchored — while DeHaan and Ratter went down to the wardroom. Once they were seated at the table, Cornelius brought up a pot of coffee and what turned out to be toast. "If you have to be in a war," Ratter said, "you might as well do this. Think it will matter?"

DeHaan couldn't say. It might, the NID thought it would, and *Noordendam* wasn't the only freighter in the world that day, unloading God-knew-what cargo on a desolate shore. You had to add it all up, he thought, maybe then it meant something. He leaned back and closed his eyes for a moment, then took a North State from its packet and drew the ashtray to him, lit a match, lit the small cigar, then burned the NID orders.

The Blohm and Voss flying boat appeared at 0810, heading east along the Swedish coast, so passing a few miles north of *Noordendam*. The plane never wavered from its course, the rough drone of its engines loud for a moment, then fading away into silence. And if the observers noticed them at all, they saw no more than an old Spanish freighter, making slow way beneath them, coming from Riga or Tallinn, going about its ordinary business.

By then, DeHaan was in his cabin, sprawled on his bunk and sound asleep. He did not hear the German patrol, he barely — three hours later — heard the alarm clock, which jangled proudly for a time, then wound down to a tinny cough before it died. Normally, he would have reached over and shut the thing off, but he couldn't move his hand. Slowly, the world came back to him, one piece at a time — where he was, what he had to do — and he forced his legs to swing over the edge of the bed, went to the sink, bathed his face with handfuls of warm water, decided not to shave, and shaved.

Then he went looking for Maria Bromen, but she wasn't in her cabin. Eventually he found her on the afterdeck, sitting with back braced against the housing of a steam winch, face raised to the sun. She opened one eye and squinted up at him, then said good morning. "I came to visit, earlier, but you slept like the dead."

"You were there?"

"For a little, yes."

A smile of apology. "I could use some more," he said. "After the noon watch." *If you'd care to join me for a sleep.*

"We'll be then in Malmö?"

"We should be. Waiting to load cargo."

"How long, will we stay there?"

"Two or three days, if they work straight through, but it's different in every port —

some fast, some not. There was one time, when we took on coal in Calcutta, we were loaded by bearers, hundreds of them, men and women, walking up the gangways with baskets of coal on their heads. That took two weeks."

"Swedes don't do that."

"Not for a long time, no."

She was pensive for a moment, and he suspected that she was counting days, the days they had left. Two or three at Malmö, maybe a week more as they steamed to Ireland.

Finally she said, "Still, they might take their time."

Yes, maybe.

Shtern and Kolb appeared, taking a turn around the deck together, hands clasped behind their backs, as though they were passengers on an ocean liner.

"Good morning, Captain," Kolb said. "Pleasant weather, today."

"It is. One should enjoy it."

1220 hours. Off Falsterbo headland.

Course north-northwest, to swing around the peninsula that jutted south and west from the Swedish coast. Sky turning gray, with dark blue patches and low scud to the west. So, soon enough, rain, but not yet. DeHaan rubbed his eyes, smoked, and drank coffee to stay alert. From the lookout on the port wing: "Ship approaching, Cap'n."

"What kind?"

"Small coal-burner, sir, from the smoke. She's about three miles to port, on a course to meet us."

Coming from the Danish coast?

DeHaan got her in his binoculars — black smoke from a stack behind the wheelhouse, aerials on the roof, single cannon mounted on the foredeck, *M* 56 painted on the bow, red and black swastika flying at the masthead. "Come to two twenty-five," he told the helmsman. "Hard rudder left, and smartly."

"South to two twenty-five," the helmsman said, spinning the wheel. They would, if they maintained this course, pass astern of her.

Slowly, the *Noordendam* answered her rudder, swung her bow to port, then steadied as the helmsman brought the wheel back. After thirty seconds, an elated DeHaan thought the tactic had worked but then, punching through the low swell, the prow of *M* 56 shifted south — a sharp turn, that brought her image, in DeHaan's binoculars, to a narrow, dead-on profile.

From the wing, the lookout's voice was tense and sharp. "Changing course, Cap'n. Meeting us."

DeHaan used the whistle to call down to the engine room. When Kovacz answered, DeHaan said, "Come to the bridge, Stas. Right away, please."

In less than a minute he came puffing onto the bridge, breathless from running up ladderways, his denim shirt sweated dark at the armpits and across the belly from the heat of the engine room. "Eric?" he said. "What is it?" DeHaan handed him the binoculars and pointed out to sea. Using his big thumb to adjust the focus, Kovacz tracked the approaching ship for a few seconds, then said, "Shit."

"What is she?"

"Minesweeper, M class. Could be French or Norwegian, originally, an old thing, built just after the war, 1919, maybe 1920. They use them for coast patrol, mostly, but if there's a mine they can take care of it." He handed the binoculars back to DeHaan and said, "And they are going to challenge."

"Doing it now," DeHaan said, looking through the binoculars. A sailor at the rail had an Aldis lamp going, blinking Morse at him, his hand fast and expert on the shutter. *What ship?* DeHaan kept the glasses trained. "But they're not in any hurry," he said, gauging the rate of closure between the two ships.

"The hell they aren't — she's only got ten, maybe twelve knots in her and she's using every bit of it."

"Stay at three-quarter speed," he told Kovacz. "And we'll see what happens." Had they read his course change as evasion? Maybe he'd made a mistake.

Kovacz went to the door, then stopped and turned back to DeHaan. "I won't be taken prisoner, Eric."

DeHaan lowered the binoculars and met Kovacz's eyes. "Easy does it, for now. All right?"

"Just so you understand."

As he left, DeHaan called to the lookout on the starboard wing. "Have Mr. Ratter come to the bridge, and find AB Amado and bring him up here. Fast!" Sliding his hands down the railings, the AB went down the ladderway in three hops. Meanwhile, from the port lookout, "They're signaling again, sir."

"Very well, get the Aldis lamp and make back, '*Santa Rosa*, Valencia,' but take your time."

"Aye-aye, sir. I can't go very fast."

"Good. And get the letters wrong."

"Count on me, sir."

Under a mile now, and closing. DeHaan looked at his watch. 12:48. On the *M 56*, sailors moving around on deck, and an officer, sweeping his binoculars back and forth across the *Noordendam*. Full uniform for the crew — some of them in navy crew caps, almost berets, with ribbon on the back — and the officer, blue jacket and trousers, white shirt, black tie. On this chunky, coal-burning old pot? DeHaan didn't like it. From the speaker tube to the radio room, three clicks from Mr. Ali. DeHaan picked up the tube and said, "Yes?"

"Do I send anything?" Ali said.

"No, stay silent."

As DeHaan returned the speaker tube to its hook, Ratter hurried through the door. He'd apparently been taking a shower; his hair was wet, his shirt was hanging outside his trousers, and he was barefoot. DeHaan found himself looking at the eye patch — was it dry? Did he take it off to shower? Ratter raised his binoculars, focused on the German ship, and swore under his breath. "They've run up a *Stand To* signal," he said.

DeHaan saw that he was right. "Go down to the chartroom, Johannes, and find the minefield maps, in the third drawer in the cabinet to the left, slipped into the chart for the Mozambique Channel."

"If we burn them we'll never get out."

"I know. But put them somewhere — in a ventilator duct, somewhere like that."

"Aren't we in Swedish waters?"

"Would you do it now, please?"

"Make a run for the coast — why not?"

"Now?"

As Ratter left, Kees appeared, followed by the AB and Amado, who looked pale and frightened. DeHaan turned the engine telegraph to *Full — Stop*. "Think he'll challenge?" Kees said.

"He already has. We're waiting for him."

From Kees, the sigh of the man who'd known this would happen. The engine-room telegraph rang, confirming the order to stop, and DeHaan heard the engine shut down. Kees said, "So then, we use Amado."

"Give him some answers — we've got a few minutes yet. We're steaming in ballast from Riga, where we delivered Portuguese cotton and bagged jute. And we're headed up to Malmö for sawn boards."

"Might as well try it," Kees said. "Maybe

we'll be lucky a second time." From his voice, he didn't believe it.

"Maybe we will."

Kees shook his head, looking very sour and dispirited. "Paint and a flag," he said. "Not much."

"No," DeHaan said. "Not much."

With the engine shut down, *Noordendam* began to lose way, rocking gently in the swell. *Paint and a flag.* Of course the NID could've done more, but they hadn't. Because if the *Noordendam* had been caught with the secret cargo, what clandestine apparatus would've made any difference? And, now that they'd completed their mission, it didn't matter what happened to them. They just had to keep quiet. Would they? Forty-one souls, plus Maria Bromen and S. Kolb?

Kees had taken Amado to a corner of the bridge house and was, slowly and carefully, explaining what he should say. Amado's head jerked up and down — yes — he understood — but he was plainly terrified. DeHaan fixed his binoculars on the *M* 56, the officer now stood at the rail. He was young, in his early twenties, chin held at a certain angle, back stiff as a board. As DeHaan watched, he put a hand on either side of his officer's hat and made sure it was on straight.

The *M* 56, engine idling in neutral, stood off their port beam, a sailor now seated behind the iron shield that held a long-barreled machine gun. When the officer stepped to the railing, loud-hailer in hand, DeHaan and Kees walked Amado, now wearing the captain's hat, out to the bridge wing, then down to the deck, where DeHaan handed him their own loud-hailer.

"What is your destination?" The German words boomed out over the water.

Amado said, *"Habla usted español?"* DeHaan barely heard him. Amado looked for the switch, found it, turned the device on, and tried again.

The officer lowered the loud-hailer for a moment, then raised it and repeated the question — slower, and more forcefully. That was the way with foreigners, you had to make them understand you.

It didn't work with Amado, who asked, once again, if the officer spoke Spanish.

The officer took a long look at DeHaan and Kees, then said, "Can your officers speak German?"

What? Amado shook his head and spread his hands.

The officer pointed to Kees, thrusting his finger, three or four times, for emphasis, then called out, *"Officer, officer."*

Kees put out a hand and Amado gave him the loud-hailer. "Bound for Malmö," he said, in German.

"Who are you?"

"Second mate."

"What was your last port?"

"Riga."

"What cargo do you carry?"

"In ballast."

And now we can all be on our way.

The officer held the loud-hailer at his side and took a long, thoughtful look at the freighter, bow to stern and back again. Then he called out, "Remain stood to," and walked back to the bridge house. He was, DeHaan thought, the executive officer of *M 56*, and was going to consult with the captain on the bridge. Could he somehow check their story? DeHaan doubted it — the Russians had occupied Latvia a year earlier, and, despite being the nominal ally of Germany, wouldn't be in a hurry to answer questions. And the *M 56* couldn't just wire to the Port of Riga — that would require a long journey up through the layers of *Kriegsmarine* administration.

"What's he doing?" Kees said.

"Arguing with his captain. He wants to board."

"Why would he?"

DeHaan smiled. "I could start with early days in school and go on from there, but it would all come down to who he is. Has always been."

"We *are* in Swedish waters," Kees said. "You can see Falsterbo. Should we point that out?"

"I don't think they care."

"Bastards."

On the *M 56*, the sailors, most of them not yet out of their teens, stared curiously at the *Santa Rosa,* and the three men on her deck, awaiting the pleasure of their officer.

"How long do we stand here?" Kees said.

"Until he decides what he wants to do."

Finally, an older man in officer's uniform, with a well-kept gray beard, stepped out of the bridge house. *Brought back out of retirement?* Stuck on a minesweeper with a teenaged crew. DeHaan met his eyes, then thought, *merchant captain?* Did he shake his head? Just very subtly? *Can't do a thing with him?* No, probably not, probably just his imagination. The man returned to the bridge and, a moment later, the young officer walked back to the railing, looking proud and pleased with himself, a holstered pistol now worn on a web belt around his waist. He raised the loud-hailer and, speaking slowly, called out, "Stand by and prepare to be boarded."

"Send Amado below," he told Kees. "Then go to the radio room, have Ali send the coded message, twice, and burn the paper. Then, put the BAMS codebook in the weighted bag and dump it off the starboard beam."

"They'll see!"

"Put it under your shirt, on the side away from them."

"What if they figure it out?"

"Then they'll shoot you."

They were, he saw, well drilled, and well practiced. Two of them stayed in their cutter, and he counted eight in the boarding party that climbed the gangway — five armed with infantry rifles, one with a carbine, one a steel submachine gun with box magazine and fold-down shoulder brace. Once on deck they fanned out in pairs — to the radio office, the crew's quarters, the engine room — while the officer marched to the bridge, shadowed by a dark, hulking bully with a heavy brow — *his personal ape,* as DeHaan put it to himself — who carried the submachine gun.

At close range, the officer was tall and fair-skinned, with a pale frizz from sideburn to sideburn that was meant to be a beard. Bright-eyed and eager, mouth set in a permanent, meaningless smile, he was a young man in love with power, with command, with salutes and uniforms, orders and punishments. Facing DeHaan on the bridge, he stood at attention and announced himself as "Leutnant zur See Schumpel. Schumpel." *Remember that name.* Only a sublieutenant, Schumpel, but not for long. All it would take was one success, one lucky moment, and he would be on his way upwards. And today, DeHaan thought, was his day, though he didn't yet know it. "Do you also speak German?" he asked DeHaan.

"I do."

"And you are?"

"DeHaan."

"What rank?"

Not yet. "First officer."

"So you are able to locate the ship's papers, logbook, roster of seamen and officers."

"I am."

"You will bring them to the wardroom."

Well, that was that. The ghost ship was about to lose its sheet, and all DeHaan could do was obey orders. He took the logbook from the bridge, stopped at the chartroom — Schumpel's ape two steps behind him — and collected the rest. Of course he could have handed it over, but that wasn't the form. Better for him to carry his guilt in his own two hands, that was the way Schumpel wanted it.

Once they were seated at the wardroom table, Schumpel said, "Is it you who are the captain of this ship? Or is that your colleague?"

DeHaan didn't answer.

"Sir, be reasonable. That little Spanish man is not the captain of anything. Or perhaps, like the English poem, he is the captain of his soul, but no more than that."

"I'm the captain," DeHaan said.

"Good! Progress. Now, the logbook and ship's papers."

Schumpel, it turned out, was a lively reader. He ran his finger along a line until it stopped, delighted at what it found, and went no further until it received a verbal confirmation — "Mm? Mm" — from its master. Who said, when he looked up from the papers, "The ship I am aboard would appear to be Dutch, and properly called the NV *Noordendam*. Is that correct?"

"It is."

"May one ask, then, why you are painted like a Spanish freighter?"

"Because a Dutch ship cannot enter the Baltic."

"And at whose direction was this done?"

"At the direction of the owner."

"Yes? And what exactly did he have in mind, do you think?"

"Disguise, Leutnant Schumpel."

"It would seem so, but what would he gain, by doing that?"

"Money. More money than he would make from British convoys, much more."

"For doing what? Some sort of secret mission?"

"Oh, that's rather a grand way to put it. Smuggling, that's a better word."

"Smuggling what?"

"Alcohol, what else?"

"Guns, agents."

"Not us. We carried wine and brandy, without tax stamps, first to Denmark, then to Riga."

"To Denmark. You are aware that Denmark is a German ally, currently under our supervision?"

"Drink is drink, Leutnant Schumpel. In

hard times, times of war, say, it helps men to bear up. And they will have it."

"And exactly where, on the Danish coast, did you deliver this wine and brandy?"

"Off Hanstholm, on the west coast. To Danish fishing smacks."

"Called?"

"They did not have names — not that night, they didn't."

"Unlikely, Captain, for Danish fishermen, but we'll let that pass for the moment. More important: I presume, that when my men interrogate your crew, they will tell the same story."

"They will tell you every kind of story — anything but that. They are merchant seamen, a vocation, I'm sure you know, given to sea stories and lies to authority. One will say this, the other that, a third something else."

Schumpel stared at him, DeHaan stared back. "You will of course lose your ship, Captain, and you can look forward to spending some time in prison."

"It's not my ship, Leutnant, and the money we made smuggling is not mine either."

"It belongs to . . ."

"The Netherlands Hyperion Line, formerly of Rotterdam. Owned by the Terhouven family."

"And the idea of prison, does not bother you?"

"Of course it does. I must say, however, it is preferable to the bottom of the sea."

"Perhaps." He took a moment to square up the papers in front of him. "We will collect, from your crew, all the seaman's books. We do discover the most curious people, sometimes, sailing in our territory. Do you, by the way, have weapons aboard this ship?"

"No. I can't vouch for the crew, of course, but nothing that I know about."

"On your honor, Captain? We will search, you know."

"On my honor."

"You don't have passengers, do you? Not listed on this roster?"

"We have two. A Swiss businessman, the traveling representative of industrial firms in Zurich, and a woman, a Russian journalist."

"A woman? A Russian journalist?"

"She is traveling with me, Leutnant Schumpel."

DeHaan waited for a complicit smile, but it didn't come. Instead, Schumpel pursed his lips, as though nagged by uncertainty, and, again, stared at DeHaan. Yes, freighter captains could be scoundrels, smugglers, whoremasters — but, this captain? "May I see your passport?" he said.

DeHaan had it ready for him, from its drawer in the chartroom.

Schumpel took a long look at it, comparing DeHaan to the faded photograph taken years earlier. "I like the Dutch," he said. "Very upright and honorable people, as a rule. It pains me to encounter another sort."

A bad type, yes, how right you are. DeHaan looked down at his shoes and said nothing.

As for Schumpel, he snapped back to his former self, the bright smile back in place. Brighter than ever, now, because this was a great day, a glorious day. He had distinguished himself — the unmasking of this criminal ship, an enemy vessel, after all, in German waters, more or less, would shine on his record like a brilliant star.

A long, melancholy afternoon with, now, a slow, steady rain. The *Noordendam* dropped anchor, Schumpel returned to *M 56*, for consultation and a W/T report to headquarters, then came back to the ship and told DeHaan the freighter would be taken under guard to the naval base at Dragör on the Danish coast.

DeHaan remained in the wardroom as the ship was searched, waiting for them to find the weapons — the Browning automatic and the rifle — and wondering what they'd do to him when they were discovered. Of course he'd had some vague notion of retaking the ship, had lied instinctively — a foolish way to lie — and now regretted it. Still, what did it matter? They might beat him up a little, but not too much — he was, after all, a prize fish in their net. What else would they find? Not much. After all, you couldn't really search a ship like the *Noordendam* unless you had a week and fifty clever men with screwdrivers, it was nothing *but* hiding places.

They did, of course, using the ship's roster, find the officers, and the wardroom became a holding cell, guarded by a sailor with a rifle. First came Ratter, still barefoot, then Kees and Mr. Ali, followed by Poulsen. Kovacz did not appear, neither did Kolb. They'd evidently hidden themselves, for the time being, as had Shtern, who was brought to the wardroom with his hands tied behind his back and a swelling bruise under one eye. As for the German communists and Republican Spaniards, DeHaan could only speculate. Safe for the moment, he thought — there were no politics in seamen's papers — though investigation in Denmark might tell another story. As prisoners of the *Kriegsmarine* they had at least a chance of survival but, if the Gestapo chose to involve itself, they were finished. And, DeHaan had to admit to himself, once that happened, the station at Smygehuk was also finished. The crew of the *Noordendam* was brave but, under the Gestapo's methods of interrogation, the truth would be told.

It was Schumpel himself who escorted Maria Bromen to the wardroom, and his irritated glance at DeHaan said more than he realized. Had she worked on him? Maybe. As she came through the door their eyes met, for an instant, but not to say farewell. *It's not over,* she meant, even though, and they both knew it, once they were taken off the *Noordendam*, they would never see each other again.

1550 hours. Off Falsterbo headland.

DeHaan was led up to the bridge, in preparation for the voyage to Dragör, and it was there that Schumpel confronted him with a list of *Noordendam*'s sins. Item one: they'd found a pistol in the locker of the fireman Hemstra. If the Leutnant expected a reaction to this he was disappointed, because DeHaan was mystified and showed it. Hemstra? Plain, quiet, hardworking Hemstra? So, the Leutnant said, DeHaan had nothing to say? Very well, then item two: the chief engineer, Kovacz, was missing, as was the passenger S. Kolb. Any idea where they might be? Quite truthfully, DeHaan said he didn't know.

"We shall find them," Schumpel said. "Unless they've jumped into the sea. In which case, good riddance."

From here, Schumpel proceeded to item three. "We are unable to find your codebook," he said.

"I ordered it thrown overboard," DeHaan said. "As captain of an allied merchant vessel, that was my obligation."

"Ordered who, Captain, the radio officer?"

DeHaan did not speak.

"If you say nothing, we will assume that to be the case."

"I acted under the rules of war, Leutnant. A German officer would behave no differently."

That made Schumpel angry, the skin over his cheekbones turning pink — a captured codebook would have been the cherry on top of his triumph. But he could only say, "So, it's the radio officer. We'll let him know you told us." He had more to add, but one of the German sailors came to the bridge and handed him a message, saying, "The cutter brought it over, sir."

Schumpel read his message, then said to DeHaan, "You will remain on the bridge," and, to the ape, "Watch him carefully."

So, the two of them stood there, while Schumpel went off toward the gangway. And stood there. From the bridge, DeHaan could see the Leutnant, sitting at attention in the stern of the cutter as it made its way through the rain back to *M* 56. And, twenty minutes later, after the ape had rejected a very tentative attempt at conversation, DeHaan discovered how Kolb had managed to disappear.

With some admiration. Kolb, accompanied by a German guard, was walking along the deck, headed, perhaps, for the crew's quarters. Or, more likely, for the galley, because Kolb was wearing the filthiest cook's apron DeHaan had ever seen and, on his head, a freighter cook's traditional headgear — a paper bag with the rim folded up.

In rain, beneath overcast skies, the afternoon had turned to early dusk by the time

Schumpel returned. When he reached the bridge, DeHaan saw that he was virtually glowing with excitement. "We are going to Germany," he said.

It took some effort, but DeHaan showed no reaction.

"To the naval base at Warnemünde." *To heaven, to be serenaded by a chorus of angels.* "It turns out that this *Noordendam* is" — he paused, looking for the right words — "of interest," he said at last. "To certain people."

Again, DeHaan didn't answer, but Schumpel was observant.

"Don't like it, do you," he said. "If you would care to guess why, some reason for this interest, I will do for you one favor."

The bar in Algeciras, Hoek in his office, S. Kolb. "I don't know why," DeHaan said.

"This level of interest, is not usual."

"I can't help you, Leutnant."

Schumpel was disappointed. "Very well," he said. "I have ordered a helmsman sent to the bridge, and a crew to the engine room. Your course is south-southwest, compass bearing one nine zero. What is your best speed?"

"Eleven knots. In calm seas."

"You will go ten, my ship will escort us."

DeHaan calculated quickly. Under a

hundred nautical miles to the Baltic coast of Germany, ten hours. A lot could happen in ten hours. DeHaan looked at his watch, it was ten minutes after five.

The helmsman appeared a few minutes later, as DeHaan signaled to the engine room. "Hello, Scheldt," he said.

"Cap'n."

"We'll come about, then bear south-southwest at one nine zero." Outside, the sound of a winch engine, and the anchor being hauled in. "For Warnemünde, Scheldt."

"Aye-aye, sir."

Back to normal, life on the bridge of the *Noordendam*. Scheldt giving the wheel a quarter turn every few minutes in order to stay on course, the engine drumming away down below, DeHaan smoking one of his small cigars. *No ships sighted. All well on board.* Schumpel paced the bridge, making sure, now and again, that the compass bearing was as he'd ordered, then looking out at the *M 56*, black smoke streaming from her funnel as she chugged along in escort position, some three hundred yards off their stern quarter. The ape with the submachine gun leaned against the bulkhead, bored, with long hours of voyage ahead of him.

For DeHaan, the hours were even longer. He'd done his best, but the odds had caught up with them and what had begun in Tangier, two months earlier, was now finished. He said this to himself again and again, though he knew it meant surrender, true surrender, the end of hope. And he fought it — his imagination produced a coast watcher on Falsterbo, alerting the Royal Navy, who just then had a submarine beneath this Baltic sea-lane. *A sudden storm, an exploding boiler.* Or Ratter, and the officers in the wardroom, who rushed their guard, then retook the ship with the hidden weapons. That last was not beyond possibility, though, if it was somehow accomplished, they would soon enough be blown to pieces by the minesweeper's 105-millimeter cannon. But this was, at least, an honorable end, better than what awaited them in Germany. Interrogation, execution.

So his mind wandered, this way and that, from salvation to despair and back again. No point, really, except that it sometimes kept him from thinking about Maria Bromen, which, every time, brought with it a very bitter truth. Which was not that he had loved and lost her, but that he could not save her.

2035 hours. At sea.

"Where did you grow up, Captain?" Schumpel said.

"In Rotterdam."

"Oh? I have never been there."

"It's a port city, typical, like many others."

"Like Hamburg."

"Yes, or Le Havre."

"Perhaps you will see Rostock, where there is a central administration."

"I've put in there — up the estuary from Warnemünde."

"I suspect you won't go by ship, this time. Perhaps by automobile."

"Perhaps."

"Oh, I think you will."

He was quiet after that, pacing back and forth, looking at his watch, while, on the bridge, life went on as usual — the green glow of the binnacle light, the helmsman at the wheel, the mess boy bringing coffee.

But not the everyday service. Now that they had guests, Cornelius had brought up a full pot of coffee though, true to his Corneliusian soul, he had forgotten the lid, so the coffee steamed in the damp air. But, at least, for a change, hot coffee. And Cornelius was not alone — he was assisted by Xanos, the Greek stowaway from Crete, poor little man, who wore a grimy white steward's jacket and carried a tray of cups and saucers, and who was so nervous at this new job that his hands shook and the china rattled.

Schumpel was delighted. "Ah now, here you are more civilized than I thought."

"Coffee, sir?" Xanos said. For this important occasion, someone had taught him the German words.

"Yes, thank you, I'll have a cup."

Xanos held out the tray, Schumpel took a cup and saucer, then Cornelius filled it with coffee. The aroma was strong and delicious on the smoky bridge. Schumpel turned to DeHaan and said, "You will join me?"

DeHaan said he would, but Xanos's nerves got the best of him, and the tray slipped from his hands and the crockery went clattering to the deck. A startling event, to Schumpel, very startling, because he said, "Hah!" as though he'd been slapped on the back, and threw his cup and saucer in the air, the coffee splashing on his white shirt. But he didn't care so much about the shirt, because he turned his head and looked over his shoulder and, as Xanos leapt away, drew in a long breath through clenched teeth and twisted his head back the other way, his eyes wide with panic. Xanos stepped behind him and did something with his hand, then Schumpel said, "Ach," sank to his knees, tilted slowly, and toppled forward, with a loud thump as his forehead hit the deck.

On the other side of the bridge, the ape shouted, and DeHaan turned toward him. Head steaming, he howled and pressed his free hand to his eyes, while Cornelius stood gaping at him, the empty coffeepot dangling upside down from his fingers. Then the submachine gun swung toward him and he dropped the pot and grabbed the barrel with both hands and hung on for dear life, shoes sliding across the deck as he was spun around. The two of them circled twice before DeHaan and Scheldt got there. DeHaan drew his fist back but Scheldt shoved him aside and did it himself, three or four shots, bone on bone and loud. The last one worked, and as Cornelius fell backward with the gun clutched to his chest, the ape mumbled, "Leave me alone," and sat down.

Scheldt stood over him, shaking his hand and grimacing with pain. "Pardon, Cap'n," he said.

"Get the wheel," DeHaan said. If they drifted off course, the captain on *M* 56 would know something had gone wrong. DeHaan went over to Schumpel, who was still kneeling, his forehead resting on the deck, the hilt of a knife fixed between his shoulder blades. A kitchen knife? No, DeHaan saw that the handle was wrapped with tape, a killing weapon. "Thank you, Xanos," DeHaan said. "Also you, Cornelius."

"It was the little passenger," Cornelius said. "He drew it on a piece of paper. Just like you told him to."

"Where is he?"

"In the galley. He's peeling potatoes. For hours, Cap'n, pounds and pounds of 'em."

"Where are the other Germans, Cornelius, do you know?"

Cornelius's face knotted with concentration and he licked his lips. "He said to tell you, if the plan worked out, that there's one in the radio room." He thought for a moment, then said, "A signalman — he told me to tell you that. And I know there's two of them in the crew's quarters."

And one in the wardroom, and certainly two in the engine room. DeHaan looked aft. Out in the darkness, the lights of *M* 56 bobbed up and down in the swell, keeping station off their starboard quarter. DeHaan knelt beside Schumpel's body and slid his pistol, a heavy automatic with a short barrel, out of its holster. Xanos said a Greek word and pointed — the ape was trying to crawl out the door. DeHaan and Cornelius stopped him, then Cornelius got a length of line from the signal-flag rack and DeHaan tied his hands and feet, wrapping a signal flag around his head and knotting its cord in back. "If you move, we'll throw you overboard. Understood?"

"Yes," the man said, his voice muffled by the flag.

DeHaan put the pistol in his pocket, then picked up the submachine gun and handed it to Scheldt, who stood it on its stock by the helm. For DeHaan, there was a strong temptation to free the captives in the wardroom, but he couldn't take the chance. So far, there'd been no gunfire, which meant that the signalman in the radio room had not been alerted, so communication between the *Noordendam* and *M 56* was the next problem that had to be solved. And, eventually, they would have to deal with *M 56* itself, by force or by subterfuge. Board it? Ram it? *Somehow,* he told himself. "Stay sharp on one nine zero," he told Scheldt. "I'm leaving you and Xanos in charge of the prisoner, and the bridge. So, if any German shows up here, you can use that weapon. You better have a look at it."

Beckoning Cornelius to follow him, DeHaan left the bridge on the port wing — the side concealed from the view of the *M* 56. Quietly, they moved along the deck to the door of the radio office. It was closed. Locked? He wouldn't know until he tried. But, if he had to shoot the man inside, the wardroom guard would be alerted. DeHaan took the pistol from his pocket and examined it. *J. P. Sauer & Sohn, Suhl* was stamped on the barrel, then *CAL* 7,65, and it had a safety, operated by a thumb lever. He pushed the lever up, so the safety was off, then found a catch behind the trigger. What did it do? He didn't know. This didn't work like his Browning, but he assumed that with the safety off, the weapon would fire when he pulled the trigger. He detached the magazine, counted eight rounds in the clip, then snapped it back in place. "Stay behind me," he told Cornelius.

DeHaan approached the door, listened, then pressed his ear against the iron surface. Silence. He put two fingers on the metal lever that worked as a doorknob, steadied the automatic in his right hand, and held the barrel up. Slowly, he applied pressure to the lever. It gave. Then he took a breath, pushed down hard on the lever, aimed the pistol at the interior, and threw the door open.

The signalman was sitting tilted back in Mr. Ali's swivel chair with his feet up on the work desk and his hands clasped behind his head. He'd been staring at the ceiling, maybe dozing, but he was awake now. Eyes wide, he stared at the automatic aimed at his chest, then tried to sit upright, as the chair hung dangerously on its back wheel for an instant, then righted itself as he kicked his legs. He raised his hands in the air and said, "I surrender, understand? Surrender." He waved his hands so that DeHaan would see them.

"Did you call your ship?"

"No. I was just sitting here. Please."

"They call you?"

"An hour ago. I answered back, so they knew I was receiving, that's all."

"What's their call signal?"

"Seven-eight-zero, five-five-six. At six point nine megahertz."

DeHaan looked him over. In his early twenties, just somebody caught up in a war who'd joined the *Kriegsmarine*, then was lucky or clever enough to get duty on a minesweeper patrolling the Danish coast — *M* 56, scourge of the herring boats.

DeHaan checked the radio, found nothing to provoke his interest, then walked the signalman back up to the bridge. "So, that's two," Scheldt said. Then glanced at Schumpel's body and added, "Three, I mean." DeHaan sat the signalman down next to the other prisoner, and tied his hands and feet. "I'm going to the wardroom," he told Scheldt.

"Let me come with you, Cap'n. With the submachine gun."

DeHaan thought about it, then said, "No, I'll take Cornelius."

On the main deck, one level below the bridge, the wardroom was next to the officers' mess, down a passageway past the chartroom and the officers' cabins. DeHaan paused out on deck, in front of the heavy door. "Cornelius, I want you to go the wardroom. Look around, see what's going on in there, and where the guard is."

"Aye-aye, sir," Cornelius said. He was being brave, the fighting on the bridge had shaken him.

"You can do it," DeHaan said. "It's easy, just do what you always do, you don't have to be quiet, or clever. Take a walk down the passageway, tell the guard that Leutnant Schumpel sent you."

"Why did he send me, sir?"

"You're the mess boy — you're going to bring up something to eat. They haven't had any food for a long time, so you're there to, to count how many, and the cook is going to send up sandwiches and coffee."

Cornelius nodded. "Sandwiches."

"And coffee. Don't be scared."

"Aye, sir."

When Cornelius reached for the door lever, DeHaan realized that he had to know what happened in the wardroom — in case the guard didn't believe the story. He'd intended to wait for Cornelius on deck, but now realized he'd have to go inside. "I'll be right down the corridor," he said.

Cornelius hauled the door open and went inside. Behind him, DeHaan slammed it, and Cornelius, clomping down the passageway, made plenty of noise. He was halfway down the corridor, nearing the corner which led to the wardroom, when a German voice called out, "Who's that?"

"Mess boy!"

DeHaan went down on one knee, making himself a smaller target, and held the wrist of his gun hand to keep it steady. If the guard put his head around the corner . . .

Cornelius turned right and disappeared. Then, from the wardroom, voices, but very faint. DeHaan glanced at his watch — eight-fifty, the radio had been left unattended for fifteen minutes. More voices. What was there to talk about? *Come on, Cornelius, count heads and leave.*

Finally, footsteps. And a voice, just around the corner, where the guard would not lose sight of his captives. "Hey, mess boy."

"Yes?" Cornelius's voice was close to a squeak.

"Bring me two of them."

"Yes, sir."

"And hurry it up."

Cornelius did as he was told, trotting down the corridor. DeHaan followed him out on deck and slammed the door for effect.

"Well?" he said.

"He's got them lying down, on their stomachs, with their hands behind their heads."

"One guard?"

"Yes."

Undermanned. He realized Schumpel had made a mistake — this was a boarding crew, not a prize crew. "What does he look like?"

"A sailor, sir. With a mustache, like Hitler. He pointed his rifle at me the whole time I was there."

"Anybody say anything?"

"No, the guard asked if I'd talked to anybody, from the ship."

"What'd you tell him?"

"Just the German officer."

"Did he believe it?"

"He looked at me, Cap'n, scared me, the way he looked."

DeHaan didn't dare to send Cornelius to the galley — he needed someone to man the radio, and the mess boy's normal round trip never took less than half an hour. So he waited, standing on deck in the slow rain, with Cornelius beside him. Eight fifty-five, eight fifty-eight.

"Now we'll go back," he said, checking the automatic one last time.

"To ask again?"

"No," DeHaan said. "Just say who you are, as you go down the passageway, and run past the door. Quick. Understand?"

"Aye, sir. Are you going to kill him?"

"Yes."

DeHaan opened the door, and followed Cornelius down the corridor. Such familiar territory; the chartroom, his cabin, Ratter's cabin — strange and alien to him now.

In a whisper, DeHaan said, "Call out to him."

"Hello! It's the mess boy."

"Now what?"

"Mess boy."

They reached the corner, Cornelius hesitated, DeHaan let the guard have a look, then pushed him hard so that he went stumbling down the passageway. In three strides, DeHaan reached the open door of the wardroom, found the German sailor, pointed the pistol at him, and pulled the trigger. It was a double-action trigger so the shot didn't come immediately, and in that tenth of a second DeHaan realized the man wasn't who Cornelius said he was — yes he had a Hitler mustache but that was all. Tall and thin and nervous, he sat on the deck with the rifle resting across his lap. His mouth opened when he saw what DeHaan meant to do, then the automatic flared, and he yelped and threw the rifle out in front of him as blood poured down his face.

It was a mêlée after that, the officers struggling to their feet, Kees grabbing the rifle, Poulsen and Ratter grabbing the sailor — more because he'd held them captive than anything else, he was no threat to them now, breathing hard with his eyes closed. Dying, he thought. But he was wrong about that — DeHaan had aimed at his heart and clipped off a piece of his left ear.

2140 hours. At sea.

They now held the bridge and the top deck of the ship. Five and a half hours from Warnemünde, with the engine room and the crew's quarters still under the control of the four remaining sailors from *M* 56. DeHaan saw Maria Bromen only for a moment, in the wardroom, as she stamped her feet and rubbed her legs to get the circulation back. "You have the ship?" she said.

"Part of it."

"What will you do now?"

"Take the rest, then deal with the minesweeper. We may be shelled, it's likely, so I want you to stay in my cabin, and be ready to go to the lifeboats. On the first shot, go and wait there."

"You plan this?"

"It's one idea. In the darkness, one of the boats might get away, and make for Sweden."

"Better than going like sheep," she said.

Meanwhile, Shtern had torn the guard's undershirt into strips, and patched up his ear, then DeHaan told him to remain in the wardroom, with Poulsen, and walked the guard up to the bridge. When he was secured, DeHaan handed the automatic to Mr. Ali and told him to go to the radio room, accompanied by the German signalman. "He'll handle communication with the minesweeper," DeHaan said. "Shoot him if he betrays us."

"How would I know, Captain?"

"Cannon fire." He then translated into German for the signalman, and the two of them left the bridge. Now there was one job that remained to be done, and DeHaan and Ratter rolled Schumpel into a length of canvas, traditional sea coffin, tied the ends with rope, and dragged him out to the port side of the deck. They briefly considered sea burial, then and there, but the iron weights normally used for the ceremony were in the engine room, and they didn't want him floating past the *M* 56 lookouts. When they'd sent Xanos and Cornelius down to the wardroom, to join the reserve force, DeHaan, Ratter, and Kees remained on the bridge.

"Next is the engine room," DeHaan said. "Then the crew's quarters."

"Your pistol and the rifle are hidden in a duct," Ratter said. "Along with the minefield maps. Once I get them, we'll have a pistol, two rifles, and the submachine gun. Was the signalman armed?"

"No."

"Well, we better get moving. I was their prisoner for one afternoon, that was enough for me."

When he'd left, DeHaan said to Kees, "What can we do about the minesweeper? Board it? Ram it?"

"We'll never ram — she's too nimble. And we'd have a dozen shells in us in no time at all, with fighter planes here in twenty minutes. As for boarding, I don't see how we can get close enough, using the cutter. They have a searchlight, and machine guns. That's suicide, DeHaan."

Ten minutes later, Ratter arrived with the ship's armory. Kees took the Enfield rifle, Ratter the submachine gun, DeHaan his Browning automatic. "We'll give the guard's rifle to Poulsen," Ratter said.

DeHaan said, "Any ideas about them?"

He jerked his thumb back over his shoulder.

"Call on the radio, tell 'em thanks for everything, we're leaving."

"Tell them we're holding Schumpel and his men, and we'll shoot them if they fire on us," Kees said.

Ratter smiled a certain way — *not worth an answer.*

"That's for later," DeHaan said. "Now it's the engine room."

"Why not call them?" Ratter said. "See how they're doing."

Maybe not such a bad idea, DeHaan thought. He picked up the speaker tube and blew into it. When nobody answered, he used the whistle.

That produced a very hesitant "Yes? Who is it?"

"DeHaan, the captain. Feels like we're losing way, is everything working, down there?"

A count of ten, then, "All is in order."

"What about the engine? Working like it should?"

"Yes."

"You're sure?"

"Yes, I know these engines."

DeHaan hung the speaker tube back on its hook. "He knows these engines."

"Not so different than what they've got on the minesweeper," Kees said.

DeHaan held the Browning out in front of him, studied it for a moment, then worked the slide. "Time to go, gentlemen."

When they entered the wardroom, Cornelius's eyes glowed with admiration — his officers, armed and ready to fight. Ratter handed the German rifle to Poulsen. "Ever used one of these?"

"No. We shot at rabbits, when I was a boy, but we had a little shotgun." He hefted the rifle and said, "Bolt action — the last war, looks like. Simple enough."

Shtern rose to his feet, as though to join them.

DeHaan appreciated the gesture, but shook his head. "Better for you to stay here, I think."

"No, I'm coming with you."

"Sorry, but we can't have you shot — people may get hurt, later on."

"They'll get hurt now."

"Let him come, Eric," Ratter said.

Then Cornelius stood up, followed by Xanos. DeHaan waved them back down. "You've done your part," he said.

Single file, DeHaan leading, Shtern the

last in line, they stayed tight to the outside bulkhead, moving quickly along the slippery deck to the midship hatchway, then descending to the deck where the crew lived. Ghostly and silent, once they got there, nobody in sight, the crew apparently locked up in their sleeping quarters. A second hatch brought them to another ladderway, a steep one, then to a heavy sliding door. On the other side, a metal catwalk, which ran twenty feet high around the perimeter of the engine room. The beat of the engine had grown louder as they descended until, outside the sliding door, it became a giant drum, riding over the steady drone of the boiler furnaces.

DeHaan beckoned the others to come close — even so he had to raise his voice above the din below them. "You slide the door open," he said to Kees. "Just enough." Turning to Ratter and Poulsen, he said, "You stay behind me. If you hear a shot, go out there and return the fire. But don't hit the boilers." They all knew what live steam could do to anybody standing nearby. He looked at each of them, then said, "Ready?"

Ratter raised and lowered a flattened palm.

"You're right," DeHaan said. Better to

crawl, less of a target.

Kees slung the Enfield over his shoulder, took a tight grip on the steel handle, and slid the door open. DeHaan crouched, took a breath, then scuttled through the door onto the catwalk. He crawled a few feet, to where he could get a view of the engine room below, but he never saw a thing, because the instant his silhouette broke the plane of the catwalk, something hit the rim, inches from his face, and sang off over his head. DeHaan threw himself backward, into Ratter, as a hole was punched through the space where he'd knelt a second earlier.

DeHaan came up quickly, said, "Give me that goddamn thing," and snatched at the submachine gun. Ratter handed it over, just as the voice of Kovacz came roaring up from below. "You dumb fucking idiot! That was the fucking captain you just killed."

As DeHaan and the others climbed down the ladder to the engine room, Kovacz was waiting for them at the bottom rung, looking very relieved, his shirt and pants stained with black grease. "Where've *you* been?" DeHaan said.

Kovacz nodded toward a shadowed area

beyond the boilers, pipes, and rusted machinery abandoned during one of the ship's refittings. "Back there," he said. "For a long time. But I got tired of hiding, so . . ." He glanced at his crew, two oilers and a fireman, who had gathered behind him, and shrugged — *we did what we did.*

DeHaan saw what he meant — one of the German sailors was sitting propped up against a stanchion, his ankles bound with wire, while the other lay nearby, flat and lifeless, his cap at an odd angle.

To Shtern, Kovacz said, "Take a look at him, if you want."

Shtern walked over to the man and placed two fingers on his neck, where his pulse would have been.

"He turned around when I came out of there," Kovacz said. "And Boda hit him."

"I'll say he did." Shtern withdrew his fingers and stared down at the man, whose cap was now part of his head. "What with?"

Boda stepped forward. A massive fireman, wearing a flowered shirt with the sleeves torn off at the shoulders, he reached in his pocket and showed them a sock, stretched from the weight in its toe, which bulged with the round shapes of ball bearings. "The other one hid behind the workbench," Kovacz said. "He had a rifle, but we talked to him a little and he gave up. He's a Serb conscript. A *Volksdeutsch*, but he didn't want to die for Germany."

"Was that him, on the speaker tube?" DeHaan said.

Kovacz nodded. "I had him do it. When the signal came, I thought they still had the bridge."

"And who was the marksman?"

"I went to free a valve," Kovacz said, "so I gave the rifle to Flores."

Flores gave DeHaan a hesitant smile — part apology, part pride. He was one of the Spanish Republican fighters who'd come aboard with Amado.

"You were in the war, Flores?"

Flores held up three fingers. "Three *años,* sir. Río Ebro, Madrid."

A sharpshooter on board. He'd aimed and fired in a heartbeat, and come close.

"How'd you get free, up there?" Kovacz said.

DeHaan told him the story, then said, "It was Kolb who planned it. And I took the radio office, so that leaves two of them, guarding the crew."

"They can wait," Kovacz said. "For now, the patrol boat." He looked at his watch, thumbing the grease off its face — every few minutes they were a mile closer to the German coast.

"What would you do, Stas?"

"Back in there, that's all I thought about. And what I thought was, maybe we can run away. Walk away. The Serb was a storekeeper, but he says she does ten knots, which I think too. Of course if we put a weight on the safety valve and get thirteen, more maybe, they'll shell us when they figure it out. Not right away, their people are on board, so they'll use the W/T, loud-hailer, signal flags. It will take time, maybe too much time, because of the weather, visibility nothing, and because we have a trick."

"What's that?"

"Smoke."

Of course. "You mean, close the air flaps on the furnaces."

"They'll smoke like hell — a lot of it, thick and black."

Smoke had been an effective sea tactic all through the 1914 war — a destroyer with a smoke generator could lay down miles of it, then use it the way infantry used a wall; steam out to fire, then back in to hide.

Kovacz took a rag from his pocket and began to clean his hands. "So now we look at charts," he said.

2235 hours. At sea.

They moved the three German sailors to the wardroom, with Poulsen on guard, while the signalman remained in the radio office with Mr. Ali. DeHaan returned to the bridge, stopping at the chartroom on his way, with Kees, Ratter, and Kovacz. Scheldt stayed at the helm, holding steady on the one nine zero course.

DeHaan propped the Baltic charts on the binnacle, and used the end of a pencil as a pointer. "We're maybe here," he said. "Southwest of Bornholm." The Danish island held by Germany. "Johannes?"

"Close. The sea log says so, and we're about five hours from our last position."

"No stars to shoot."

"No moon either, Eric. It's black as a miner's ass, out there."

"They'll expect us to run north," DeHaan said. "To Sweden. We can't go west to Denmark or south to Germany. So then, it has to be east. To Lithuania." DeHaan spread his thumb and forefinger, marching east to the coast. "Oh, let's say, about two hundred and forty nautical miles."

"Seventeen hours, with safety valve down," Kovacz said.

"We'll blow the boilers," Kees said.

"Maybe not," Kovacz said. "But we can't go to Lithuania. See here? That's the German naval base, with minefields, at Klaipeda, or Memel, or whatever the hell they call it now. We'll have to head north of that."

"Liepaja."

"Yes. First port in Latvia."

"Soviet territory," Ratter said. "Won't they give us up to the Germans?"

"Not soon," Kovacz said. "They will lock us up, ask questions, call Moscow — you know, Russian time."

Ratter looked up from the chart and caught DeHaan's eye. "What about, the passengers?"

"They'll be all right," DeHaan said. "And we don't have a choice."

"Patrol planes at dawn, DeHaan," Kees said. "We'll be about here, by then." Not quite halfway.

"If they find us, we'll fly a white flag."

They waited, maybe somebody had a better idea, but nobody spoke. Finally, Ratter said, "What about the crew?"

"When the minesweeper fires at us, and they will, we'll signal *abandon ship*, bells and siren. That'll get the guards out of the crew quarters. So, you two" — he looked at Ratter and Kees — "with two men from

Stas's crew, will wait in the passageway, then take them as they come out. And, on your way down there, stop and tell Poulsen and Ali what's going on."

"When do we start?" Kees said.

"Now."

He gave Kovacz time to get down to the engine room and close the furnace flaps, then went out on the bridge wing and looked up at the smokestack, where the smoke was its usual dirty white color against the night sky. There was a slight wind, blowing from the southwest, but that wouldn't matter once they turned east. As he watched, the smoke grew a shadow, cleared, then turned gray. He walked to the end of the bridge house and looked aft at *M 56*, holding position, her running lights sharp yellow beams in the rain.

Back on the bridge, when he pushed the engine telegraph to *Full — Ahead,* Kovacz called from the engine room. "Safety valve off," he said. "We're trying for fourteen knots." DeHaan waited, watching the *M 56*, and checking the time. 10:48. Beneath his feet, the vibration increased in the deck plate and he could feel the engine working, straining, as the pressure rose in the boilers and the pistons were driven harder, and harder. 11:15. Was *M* 56 farther away? Lights dimmer? Maybe. No, they were.

From the radio room, Mr. Ali came on the speaker tube. "A W/T message from the minesweeper, Captain. They wish to know if everything is all right."

"Have the signalman send 'Yes.'"

A minute later, Ali was back. "Now they ask, 'Have you added speed?'"

"Tell them 'No.' Wait, cancel that, tell them 'I will find out.'"

11:35. "They are asking, 'Where are you?'"

"No answer, Mr. Ali. The signalman's gone up to the bridge."

11:45. DeHaan peered back at *M* 56 — lights dim now, pinpoints. She was well behind them and the smoke was obscuring her view. Ali returned. "They want to talk to Leutnant Schumpel. On the radio, immediately."

"Tell them Schumpel went down to the engine room. There's some sort of problem."

On the *M* 56, a searchlight went on and probed the smoky darkness, finally pinning *Noordendam* on her stern quarter. The powerful beam lit the smoke — a sluggish cloud, heavy, black and oily, drifting east in the wind, as the smell, burned oil, grew strong in the bridge house. Kovacz called from the engine room. "That's all she's got, Eric."

"They're falling behind," DeHaan said.

Well aft of them, DeHaan could hear the loud-hailer. "Leutnant Schumpel, Leutnant Schumpel. Come to the stern. Immediately. This is Kapitän Horst."

DeHaan thought about taking the role of Leutnant Schumpel, then called down to the radio room. "Tell them there's a fire, Mr. Ali."

"Is there, sir?"

"No, we're making smoke."

"Very well, sending your message."

A minute later, he was back. "They're sending 'Stand to.' Again and again, they're sending it."

"Acknowledge. Say you have to go up to the bridge to instruct the captain."

After thirty seconds, Mr. Ali said, "They're sending 'go immediately.' "

DeHaan looked back. The *Noordendam* was really pounding now, and the lights of the minesweeper winked out for a moment, then reappeared. DeHaan glanced at his watch — almost midnight. When he looked up, the lights were gone. Only the searchlight beam remained, faded and gray as it lit up the smoke. DeHaan called down to the radio room. "Send, 'Leutnant Schumpel acknowledges, ship standing to, he will call on the radio in ten minutes.' You have that?"

"I got it!" Ali's voice squeaked with excitement.

It took fifteen minutes. Which ended with a red flash from *M* 56, and a shell that whined over the ship and blew a spout of white water in the sea beyond their bow.

"Scheldt," DeHaan said. "Come sharp to north-northeast, bearing zero five zero."

DeHaan walked to the back wall of the bridge house and threw the switch that turned off the *Noordendam*'s running lights, then, as Scheldt swung the wheel over and the bow began to move, he heard a low drone in the sky. It grew louder and louder, passing far above them and headed northeast. These were heavy engines, bombers, dozens of them, no, more, many more, wave following wave. *What the hell is this?* It made no sense. *Flying northeast, to Russia? Why?*

DeHaan went back to the speaker tube. "Mr. Ali, tell them we're on fire, going to abandon ship."

"Yes, sir!"

"Send it a second time. Have the signalman stop in the middle."

"Sending, Captain. They're calling on the radio now, in clear. Shouting, sir, and rude."

"Send this, Ali: 'Sinking fast. Farewell to my family. Heil Hitler.'"

DeHaan looked at his watch, time had slowed to a crawl. Another flash from astern, the shell ripping the air and landing off their starboard beam. "Scheldt. Signal *abandon ship,* use the bells and the siren. I'll take the helm." They were at zero six eight now, almost on the new course. When DeHaan grasped the wooden spokes of the wheel, he could feel the driving pistons in his hands.

A third flash. *Noordendam* shivered and rocked forward as the shell tore into her stern.

As Scheldt took the wheel, DeHaan ran out to the bridge wing, heading for the stern, to get a look at the damage. *Just let it be above the waterline.* Then, from somewhere in the ship, gunfire, a series of muffled pops from down below. DeHaan froze — that was coming from the passageway outside the crew quarters. He listened hard, but all he heard was *M 56,* firing again. He had no idea where the shell went — somewhere in the smoke to their starboard he thought, where they would have been if they hadn't changed course. Far to the stern, he could just make out the searchlight, desperate now, sweeping back and forth, blinded by the smoke.

He made a decision and ran aft, lying on his belly and hanging out over the deck in order to see the ship's stern below him. Midway down the curve of the hull, he saw the hole, three feet across, smoke trickling from the ragged edge, gouts of water washing out as the ship rose and fell — the ballast in the aft hold. *Nothing vital.* The minesweeper fired again and again, he heard the reports, but couldn't see the flashes.

As he got back up to his feet, Ratter arrived. "What happened?" DeHaan said.

"It's done. But it wasn't clean. Kees was shot — in the leg, not bad but bad enough, Shtern is with him now. And Amado was hit, in the throat. He's unconscious."

"Will he live?"

Ratter shook his head. "Shtern did what he could."

M 56 fired once more, the shot far away and remote. Ratter stared back into the darkness. "Gone," he said. "Now we have until dawn."

Far above them, another flight of bombers headed east.

0230 hours. At sea.

Kovacz had readjusted the furnaces, so there was no smoke now. But they still ran hard, at fourteen knots, headed a few points north of east, to bypass the naval base at Memel and make port at Liepaja. Or Lipava — the merchant seaman's name for it. DeHaan had been in and out of there over the years; Latvia shipped wood and imported coal, and that meant tramp freighters. To the Germans it was Libau. They'd owned the country for centuries, calling themselves Brothers of the Sword — in the Baltic Crusade, Teutonic Knights, the Hanseatic League, then came 1918, independence, and the name changed. Then came 1940 and everything changed — in the Soviet Socialist Republic of Latvia.

Russia. Where Maria Bromen had better not go, maybe others on board as well, he wasn't sure. But then, there wasn't a harbor in the world where they weren't waiting to arrest *somebody*. Well, she wouldn't set foot on a pier as her true self,

419

he'd make sure of that. He'd found her, as Ratter walked him back to the bridge, waiting at the lifeboats as he'd asked. He'd told her where they were going, then sent her back to the cabin — they could scheme later, for now she might as well sleep. *God, I wish I could.* Not until 0400, when Ratter would relieve him. He yawned, raised his binoculars, and stared out into the empty darkness. He had a new helmsman now, Scheldt relieved and sent back to crew quarters. *Poor Amado.* They would bury him at sea at daybreak, along with the two Germans — if *Noordendam* was still afloat. Eight times, over the years, he'd led the burial service. The body in canvas laid on a bed of braced planks, which was held at the rail by six men, then tilted as the captain said, "One, two, three, in God's name."

"Captain DeHaan? Captain?" Mr. Ali, calling from the radio room.

"Yes?"

"BBC, Captain."

"Yes? Roosevelt speaks?"

"Germany invades Russia."

22 June, 0410 hours. At sea.
In the cabin, the lamp was on, and Maria Bromen sat cross-legged on the bed,

420

wearing only his denim shirt. "Is done," she said. He followed her eyes to the night table, and a small mound of blackened flakes in the ashtray. "Very sad," she said. "After all I did."

"And the photograph?"

"Yes, that too, because of the stamp." She almost smiled. "Such a photograph — this crazywoman is angry." Then she said, "Oh well, goodby. Should be, maybe, a ceremony for such things."

"Burning a passport?"

"Yes. Maybe the Jewish have it."

He sat next to her, rested a hand on her ankle.

"So, stateless person," she said.

"You'll need a name, a story."

"The name will be Natalya, I think. Natalya Pavlova, like a ballerina."

"And we met in Tangier?"

"Thanks God. Husband left, French husband. Good-for-nothing."

"You've made up the story."

"Oh yes, a long story. I am good at that, my love."

0715 hours. At sea.

No search planes. Only a flight of returning bombers, coming out of the rising sun — the men on deck shaded their eyes

421

and watched them fly over. At the tail of the formation, a straggler, flying low, smoke trailing from one of its engines, the propeller turning lazily in the wind.

Where were the search planes? By noon they still hadn't appeared. Maybe the captain of the minesweeper had reported that he sank the *Noordendam*, to save his own skin, maybe the search planes had other orders, once the invasion started. Or maybe they searched north. Much speculation on the bridge, but nobody showed up. So, DeHaan thought, we might just make it to Liepaja, and began to plan for that. "You better go burn the minefield maps," he told Ratter. "And get the officers to come to a wardroom meeting. In one hour."

Where they worked out a story, then went off to tell the crew. "We could be there for a long time," they said. "So watch what you say."

1740 hours. Off Liepaja.

They'd crossed the picket line of Russian patrol boats, but were still a long way out when they saw Liepaja. Not the port itself, but a column of brown smoke that climbed high into the air, a well-fed column, thick and sturdy. DeHaan radioed to the port office and a pair of Russian naval tugboats came out and took them under tow, docking the ship at the commercial harbor, on a stone quay lined with grain elevators and an enormous tractor plant. On its roof, soldiers had installed two antiaircraft guns and were busily stacking a wall of sandbags around them. And, passing the military harbor, they saw a small part of the Soviet Baltic Fleet — destroyers, minelayers, tenders, and one light cruiser, with steam up. "See the gun turrets?" Ratter said, standing by DeHaan on the bridge. "Facing inland."

As the gangway was lowered, the reception committee had already gathered — welcome to Liepaja! Two of them in stiff Russian suits, shirts buttoned at the neck, and three in naval uniform. An efficient committee; they looked down into the holds, checked the bridge and the ship's papers, had the German prisoners taken away, and made notes as DeHaan told them the story of *Noordendam*'s capture and escape. "Well done," one of the naval officers said. "Now let's go somewhere and have a talk."

He walked DeHaan down the gangway and along the quay, past a thirty-foot bomb crater, and up to an office in the port building. *Not the men in suits,* DeHaan thought. And not in a cellar. The office had only a bare desk and two chairs and a framed photograph of Stalin, hung from a nail that had broken the plaster when it was hammered in. "You may smoke if you like." The officer spoke German, and introduced himself as "Kapitän Leutnant Shalakov." A lieutenant commander. He was in his forties, with thinning hair, a broad nose — long ago broken, and lively green eyes. A Russian Jew? DeHaan thought he might be. "On the naval staff of the Baltic Fleet," he added. Which meant, to DeHaan, that he was in the same business as Leiden, and Hallowes.

DeHaan took him up on the invitation to smoke. "Care for one of these?" Shalakov peered at the box, declined — with some courtesy, lit one of his own, and threw the match on the floor.

"I am also a lieutenant commander," DeHaan said.

Shalakov was not all that surprised.

"In the Royal Dutch Navy."

"You are out of uniform, sir." Shalakov's eyes were amused. "And so's your ship." He stood, went to the window, and looked out over the port. "We've already had two air raids," he said. "Early this morning. They hit the air-force base, and the oil tanks at the port."

"We saw the smoke."

"How's your fuel?"

"Not bad."

"Because we can't give you any."

"Are we leaving?"

"Soviet heroes will stand and fight the fascist dogs, of course. Until Thursday, the way it looks now — should take them about four days to break in here. We can't hold it, we have one division facing Leeb's Army Group North, so you and your crew may have to do a little fighting, we shall see. But, for the moment, perhaps you'll tell me what you've been up to, sailing around the Baltic dressed as a Spaniard."

"A mission for the British navy."

"Our brave allies! We've always admired them — since midnight, anyhow. Care to tell me what and where?"

"You will understand, Kapitän Leutnant, that I can't."

Shalakov nodded — *yes, I do understand.* "Very honorable," he said. "And we'll grant you that luxury, for the time being. Now, had you shown up *yesterday* . . . But it isn't yesterday, it's today, and today everything is different, today you're a valued ally, and we can always use an extra cargo ship."

"Where would we go?"

"Maybe Riga, maybe — depends how fast the *Wehrmacht* move. More likely, the Liepaja elements of the Baltic Fleet will withdraw up to the naval base at Tallinn, in Estonia. We'll have to take equipment, personnel, some of the civilians — we'll save whatever we can, and that will be your job."

"We can do that," DeHaan said. "What about my crew?"

"They can stay as they are — we may interview your passengers, but, as for the crew, whatever you've got you can keep. But they'd better remain on board. As of this morning, the Latvian gangs are back in business — digging up their rifles in the chicken coops, and waiting eagerly for their German pals." Shalakov paused a moment, then said, "What was it, DeHaan? Agents? To Denmark? Not neutral Sweden, I hope. Dropping off agents, I would guess. Certainly not picking them up."

"Why not?"

"I admire the British navy, and I admire daring — as a quality in special operations, and I know the Germans are kicking the hell out of British merchant shipping, but there was no way under the sun that your ship was ever coming out of the Baltic."

After dusk, the bombers came again. From loudspeakers mounted on the streetlamps, a staticky voice called out, "Attention! Attention! Attention citizens of Liepaja, we are having an air raid. Prepare to take arms and fight the invaders!" In Russian first — Kovacz translated — and then in Lettish. DeHaan put the fire crews on alert, hoses reeled out, and had Van Dyck make sure of the pumps. Then the sirens whined, for a long time, it seemed, fifteen minutes, and then, from the south, the first bombs — muffled, deep-voiced *whumps* that marched north toward the city. As the antiaircraft started up, hammering away from the ships in the military harbor and the roofs of Liepaja, DeHaan looked out on the pier, at the foot of the gangway. It had been guarded since they docked, two soldiers with rifles, but they were no longer there.

As S. Kolb hurried across the quay, an incendiary hit the side of the tractor factory and a fiery river of green phosphorus came after him. He ran away from it, but

427

the bastards wouldn't leave him alone that night. Fallback from the antiaircraft fire came rattling down on the pavement, so Kolb held his briefcase over his head as he ran.

Nonetheless, he was gleeful, thanked his lucky stars that he was off and away from that accursed iron sea monster and her laconic Dutchmen. *Beans and canned fish,* the smell of oily steam up his nose as he ate, slept, read his book. Did he have it? Yes, he did, the history of Venice — three pounds of Doges, now just snuggle up to a building wall so it doesn't get skewered by some hot metal shard from heaven. Where the hell was he? The street signs were cut in stone on the corners of the buildings, so, here it was *Vitolu iela* — of course! Good old Vitolu iela, what happy times we had there! Had he ever in his life seen a street map of Liepaja? No. Who had? What sort of lunatic would ever come to such a place?

He heard the bomb whistle, his knees turned to water and he tucked his head down between his shoulders and scurried into a doorway. Sucked in his breath when the thing hit, a few blocks away. *Hah, missed!* He tried the knob on the door, but it was locked. A tarnished brass plate said the place was an art school, ichthyological illustration their specialty. *So that's what they do here, draw fish.* Above the plate, someone had printed *Closed* on a card tacked to the door.

Somewhere ahead of him, a building on fire. The flames threw flickering orange light on the street and, for a moment, a shadow moved. What was that? No policemen, please. Again it moved — a woman, out of one doorway and into another. He moved up two doorways, and waited. Not long. She was breathless and fat, carrying a huge bowl with a dish towel stretched over the top. Was that soup? Oh yes, by God it was. *Pea soup!* Nothing else smelled like that. "Good evening, madam," he said, in German.

She made a noise, a throttled scream, one hand rising to her throat.

Kolb lowered his briefcase and — the god of inspiration came to visit — tipped his hat.

The woman put her hand back on the bowl.

"Madam, can you tell me . . ." Two airplanes came roaring over the street, a hundred feet up, he couldn't hear himself think. Then they were gone. *"Madam,"* he said, raising his voice but keeping it gentle.

"*Can* you tell me where to find the railroad station?"

"*Vuss?*"

"Be calm, my dear, nothing can hurt you tonight."

She looked at him, then pointed.

"Railroad?"

She nodded.

"How far?"

"*Zwanzig minuten.*" Twenty minutes.

Again, Kolb tipped his hat. *Do you have, perhaps, a spoon?* "Good evening, madam," he said, and hurried away up the street.

Now train stations were a poor choice during air raids, but Kolb only needed to be close — any café or hallway would do — because the trains wouldn't run until the bombers got tired and went home. He had no Soviet papers, but bribery was a way of life in this empire and, with Adolf pounding on the city gates, he sensed it wouldn't be a problem.

Local or express, he'd be on a train tonight. A short run, up to enchanting Riga, "the Paris of hell," then a call at the British consulate. Where he'd look up the passport control officer, almost always connected to the spy people, if in fact he wasn't running the thing himself. Also at the consulate: secure W/T transmissions — or so they thought. *I say, Brown, dear boy, one of your chaps has turned up here — headed for Malmö, he says, but it seems he's gone a bit wide.*

So please advise.

And the loathsome Brown would surely have something in mind. Something dangerous, of course, unspeakably difficult and dreary.

Back in the street he'd just left, an explosion, then a façade fell off a building and came crashing down in a huge cloud of dust. Hadn't hit the woman, had it?

Bastards.

23 June, 0630 hours. Port of Liepaja.

DeHaan paced the bridge, standing a restless port watch. *Too far north,* he thought, every heart had its compass and his pointed far south of here. Here it was not summer — a cold early sky above the city and the marshland beyond, bending reeds, black ponds, pine forest. And some shadow of a future darkness that fell over him. He felt it.

Slowly, the *Noordendam* came back to life. Kees, hobbling with the aid of a stick, led Van Dyck and a crew of ABs in the repair of the stern hull — a length of sheet tin cut to fit, then welded on. It looked awful but it would keep the water out. There was coffee in the wardroom at 0800, and when DeHaan mentioned the absent Kolb, Shtern said that he'd left, during the air raid.

"Where the hell did he find to *go?*" Ratter said.

Shtern didn't know.

"He went back to work," Kovacz said.

"What will become of us now?" Mr. Ali said.

"First we get out of here," DeHaan said. "And then, part of the Soviet merchant fleet."

Many the silences that had descended over wardroom tables in DeHaan's years at sea, but this one had quite a heft to it. Certainly they'd foreseen this, individually. Now, however, it was said among them, and that made it worse. Because they'd all thought that somebody would have an idea, because somebody always did. But not now. Finally Kees said, "Maybe they'll send us to Britain."

"With what?" Kovacz said.

"Wheat, cattle."

"They can't feed their own," Maria Bromen said. "How to feed Britain?"

"And we can't get there," Ratter said.

"We can go north to Estonia, then Kronstadt, the naval base off Leningrad, but that's it. The Germans will mine the whole Baltic now — if they haven't already."

"They claim they have," Mr. Ali said. "In clear. On the radio."

"Trying to scare the Russian submarines," Poulsen said.

"What scares me," Shtern said, "is years. In Russia."

Cornelius came to the door and said, "Captain, sir? You are needed on the pier, sir."

"Now, Cornelius?"

"Yes, sir. I think you better come. Russian soldiers, sir."

DeHaan left, taking Kovacz with him as translator. At the foot of the gangway, an oiler and an AB stood sheepishly in the custody of a squad of Soviet marines. Called *black devils,* for their uniform caps, they wore striped sailor's jerseys beneath army blouses in honor of their service.

The sergeant stepped forward as DeHaan and Kovacz came down the gangway. He spoke briefly, then Kovacz said, " 'Here are your sailors,' he says. 'Out last night after the raid.' "

"Thank them," DeHaan said. "We're grateful."

Kovacz translated the answer as "Please to keep them where they belong, from now on."

"Tell him we will. And we mean it."

"One missing," Kovacz said.

"It's Xanos, sir," the AB said.

"What happened?"

"Press-ganged. We went looking for a bar and he wandered off, and they told us he'd been grabbed by seamen from one of the ships in port."

"Stas, ask them if they can find our sailor."

Kovacz tried. "They say they can't. Can't search all the ships. They regret."

The marines went off, and DeHaan sent the crewmen back to the quarters. "If you leave this ship again," he told them, "don't come back."

2040 hours. Port of Liepaja.

In the cabin, DeHaan and Maria Bromen waited. Tried to read, tried to talk, but they could hear the fighting now, south of the city, faint but steady, like a distant thunderstorm. A German reconnaissance plane flew high above the port and some of the gunners tried their luck but he was too far above the flak burst. Then the cruiser started up, with its heavy turret guns, the detonations echoing off the waterfront buildings.

"Who are they shooting at?" Maria Bromen said.

"Helping their army, trying to."

"How far, then, the battle?"

"Big guns like that? Maybe five miles."

"Not so far."

"No."

She rose from the bed and went to look out the porthole, at the dock and the city. "We are leaving soon, I think."

"We are?"

She beckoned him to the porthole. There was an army truck parked by the gangway. The canvas top was turned back and a few soldiers were wrestling with a bulky shape, pushing it toward the tailgate, while others waited on the pier to ease it to the ground. After a moment, DeHaan saw that what they were fighting with was a grand piano. Too heavy — when the weight shifted, the piano dropped the last two feet onto the stone quay. One of the soldiers in the truck picked up a piano bench, shouted something, and tossed it to the others.

With a sigh, DeHaan went up to the

deck, where Van Dyck and some of the crew had gathered to watch the show. "Where do you want it, Cap'n?" Van Dyck said.

"Forward hold. Get a sling on it, then cover it with canvas."

The soldiers had apparently intended to carry the piano up the gangway, but Van Dyck waved them off, pointed to the cargo derricks, and the soldiers smiled and nodded.

DeHaan went back to the cabin.

"So now," she said, "we go north."

"The Russian officer said Tallinn, the naval base."

"How far?"

"A day, twenty-four hours."

"Well," she said, "you warned me, in Lisbon."

"Are you sorry, that you didn't stay?"

She smoothed his hair. "No," she said. "No. It's better like this. Better to do what you want, and then what will happen will happen."

"It may not be so bad, up there."

"No, not too bad."

"They're at war now, and we are their allies."

She smiled, her fingers touching his face. "You don't know them," she said. "You want to think it's a good world." She stood, started to unbutton the shirt. "For me, a shower. I don't know what else to do." Looking out the porthole, she said, "And for you — out there."

On the pier a crowd, twenty or so, men and women, peering up at the ship and milling around their leader, a man with a dramatic beard, a fedora, a cape. Some of them carried suitcases, while others pushed wardrobe trunks on little wheels.

DeHaan grabbed his hat and said, "I'll be back."

By the time he reached the deck, the bearded man had already climbed the gangway. "Good evening," he said to DeHaan, in English. "Is this the *Noordenstadt*?"

"The *Noordendam*."

"It says *Santa Rosa*."

"Even so, it's the *Noordendam*."

"Ah, good. We're the Kiev."

"Which is what?"

"The *Kiev*. The Kiev Ballet, the touring company. We are expected, no?"

DeHaan started to laugh and raised his hands, meaning he didn't know a thing, and the bearded man relaxed. "Kherzhensky," he said, extending a hand. "The impresario. And you are?"

"DeHaan, I'm the captain. Was that your piano?"

"We don't have a piano, and the orchestra is on the *Burya*, the destroyer. Where do we go, Captain?"

"Anywhere you can find, Mr. Kherzhensky. Maybe the wardroom would be best, I'll show you."

Kherzhensky turned to the crowd of dancers and clapped his hands. "Come along now," he said. "We're going to a wardroom."

Twenty minutes later, two companies of marines showed up, singing as they climbed the gangway. Then came a truckload of office furniture, and a Grosser Mercedes automobile with a stove in the backseat, then three naval lieutenants with wives and children, two dogs and two cats. The deputy mayor of Liepaja brought his mother, her maid, and a commissar. A dozen trunks followed, their loading supervised by two mustached men in suits who carried submachine guns. A family of Jews, the men in skullcaps, arrived in a Liepaja taxi. The driver parked his taxi and followed them up the gangway. There followed a generator, then six railway conductors, and four wives, with children. "They are coming," one of the conductors said to DeHaan. He took off his hat, and wiped his brow with a handkerchief. It was one in the morning when Shalakov arrived, looking very harassed, with his tie loosened. He found DeHaan on the bridge.

"I see you've got steam up," he said.

"It seems we're leaving."

Shalakov looked around, the deck was full of wandering people, the mustached men sat on their trunks, smoking cigarettes and talking. "Did the messenger reach you?"

"No. Just, all this."

"It's a madhouse. We've had Latvian gangs in the city, and *Wehrmacht* commandos." He took a deep breath, then gave DeHaan a grim smile. "Will be a bad war," he said. "And long. Anyhow, here is a list of the ships in your convoy." A typed sheet of paper, the names of the ships transliterated into the Roman alphabet. "Communicate by radio, at six point five, don't worry about code — not tonight. We're going to the naval base at Tallinn, there's no point in trying for Riga now. You'll wait for the *Burya*, the lead destroyer, to sound her siren, and follow her. All ready to go?"

"Yes."

"I'm on the minelayer *Tsiklon* — cyclone. So then, good luck to you, and I'll see you in Tallinn."

0130. Scheldt at the helm, lookouts fore and aft and on the bridge wings, Van Dyck with the fire crews, Kovacz and Poulsen in the engine room, Ratter and Kees with DeHaan on the bridge. The bombing that night was to the south and the east, above Liepaja there was only a single plane in the sky, dropping clouds of leaflets, which fluttered in the breeze as they drifted down to the port. At 0142, a couple came running along the quay, the woman dressed for an evening at a nightclub. They shouted up to the freighter, pleading in several languages, and DeHaan had the gangway lowered and took them aboard. The woman, who had run with her shoes in her hand, had tears streaming down her face, and fell to her knees when she reached the deck. One of the dancers came over and put an arm around her shoulders. They were fighting in the city now, bursts of gunfire, then silence, and from the bridge they could see lines of red tracer, streaming from the top of a lighthouse and the steeple of a waterfront church. Good firing points, DeHaan knew, though they'd been built high for other reasons.

At 0220 hours, the siren.

DeHaan turned the engine-room telegraph to *Slow — Ahead,* and, without the aid of tugboats, they moved cautiously out of the harbor. They could see the *Burya,* a half mile ahead, and fell in between a motor torpedo boat and an icebreaker. On the last pier in the winter harbor, a crowd of people, standing amid bags and bundles and suitcases, yelled and waved at the ships as they steamed past.

Following the destroyer, *Noordendam* made a long, slow turn to the north and the land fell away behind them. By 0245 they were well out to sea; a stiff wind, a handful of stars among the clouds, a few whitecaps. DeHaan called for *Full — Ahead,* the engine-room bell rang, then he said, "Mr. Ratter?"

"Aye, sir?"

"Run up the Dutch flag, Mr. Ratter."

There were twenty ships, to begin with, strung out along the wake of the *Burya.* The working class of a naval fleet — supply tenders, tankers and minelayers, torpedo boats, minesweepers and icebreakers, a few old fishing trawlers made over into patrol boats, a small freighter. A little after three in the morning they lost the freighter, which broke down and had to drop anchor.

The passengers stood silently on the deck and watched the convoy as it went by. An hour later, the *Burya* began to maneuver, a long series of course changes. By then, Maria Bromen had joined Mr. Ali in the radio room, translating the orders as they came in. Bearing two six eight, bearing two six two. Scheldt spun the wheel as DeHaan called them out. "We're in a Russian minefield," Ratter said.

He was right. A few minutes later a submarine tanker made an error, swung wide, was blown in half, and sank immediately, with only a few survivors swimming away from the burning oil in the water. One of the torpedo boats stopped to pick them up, then reclaimed its position in the convoy. An hour after dawn, off Pavilosta, the torpedo boat itself broke down, and drifted helplessly as the crew tried to repair the engine.

On the *Noordendam*, daylight revealed a deck with passengers everywhere. Some of them seasick — a crowd of Kiev dancers at the stern rail; some of them going off to the galley to help with the food — stacks of onion-and-margarine sandwiches for everybody; and some who seemed to be in shock, listless, staring into space. There were two bad falls: a marine down a ladderway, and a young boy, running along the deck, who slipped on a patch of oil. Shtern was able to take care of both.

Also with daylight: a German patrol plane. Kees tracked it with his binoculars and said it was a Focke-Wulf Condor, a long-range reconnaissance bomber. The plane circled them, flew long loops as it tracked them, staying in contact with the convoy as it crawled along at ten knots.

"Not in any hurry, are they," Kees said.

"Back tonight," Ratter said. "With friends."

Night was still hours away. By ten o'clock on the morning of the twenty-fourth, they'd swung wide of the Gulf of Riga. "We're not taking the inside passage," DeHaan said, after orders repeated from the radio room. The inside passage, between the coast of Estonia and the islands of Hiiumaa and Saaremaa, was all shoals and shallows, marked by Estonian sailors with brooms mounted on buoys, a stretch of water avoided by merchant captains. So the officer on the *Burya*, or the fleet controllers at Tallinn, swung them to the west, into the open Baltic. By noon the Condor was back, well out of antiaircraft range, just making sure of their course and position before it flew home for lunch.

1930 hours. Off Hiiumaa island, Estonia.

Maria Bromen's voice on the speaker tube: "They say, 'Come to bearing zero one five degrees.' " This would lead them into the Gulf of Finland, then, in eight hours, to Tallinn. Safe passage, the first few miles, with air cover from the Russian naval base at Hangö, surrendered by the Finns in March of 1940 at the end of the Russo-Finnish war. Safe passage, and a long Baltic dusk, the light fading slowly to dark blue. They were all tired now, the crew and the passengers. When DeHaan went down to the wardroom for a ten-minute break, the impresario Kherzhensky was sprawled on the banquette, wrapped in his cape and snoring away.

By 2130 they were off the Estonian island of Osmussaar. From the radio room: "They say to proceed at five knots, and they have called for minesweepers to come ahead of *Burya*."

"German mines, now," Kees said. "Or Finnish."

"Could be anyone's," Ratter said. "They don't care."

After that, silence. Only the creak of the

derricks, and the sound of ships' engines nearby, running at dead slow, maneuvering themselves into line behind the two mine-sweepers. To port, DeHaan could see the minelayer *Tsiklon*, to starboard, a fishing trawler, its deck piled high with shipping crates. DeHaan kept looking at his watch. So, when the first ship hit a mine, some-where up ahead, he knew it was 10:05.

They saw it. No idea what it was — had been. It was sinking by the stern, bow high in the water, some of the crew paddling a life raft with their hands. From the radio room: "Aircraft is coming now."

They heard them, the rising drone, and the *Burya*'s searchlights went on, followed by those of the other ships, bright yellow beams stabbing at the sky. "Stand by the lifeboats," DeHaan said.

Kees swore and began to limp out to-ward the bridge wing. Ratter caught him by the arm. "I'll do it," he said.

"Hell you will." Kees shook free and limped away.

DeHaan called down to the engine room. "Stas, we're going to stand by life-boats. Maybe air attack on the way." Kovacz's normal duty was command of the second boat.

"Number three boiler is giving prob-

445

lems," Kovacz said. The run to Liepaja, DeHaan thought, had caught up with them.

"It has to be you, Stas." With passengers everywhere on deck there would be panic, chaos.

Kovacz grumbled, then said he would be up in a minute.

False alarm? Out on the bridge wing, an AB worked the *Noordendam*'s light, swinging it back and forth across an empty sky. Ratter was listening carefully to the distant drone, head cocked like a dog. "Are they circling us?"

DeHaan listened. Scheldt said, "That's it, sir."

At 10:20, Ratter said, "They've passed us by."

"Going to hit Kronstadt," DeHaan said. "Or Leningrad."

The others could hear it, their searchlights aimed forward of the *Burya*. "No," DeHaan said. The sound swelled, east of them, then grew loud. From the radio room: "Attack will be . . ."

The lead bomber came speeding through the lights, head on to the *Burya*, then flew over it. In the light, they could see a round ball, suspended from a parachute, as it floated down toward the destroyer. "Dorniers," Ratter said. "Parachute mines."

Behind the first, seven or eight more, flying abreast. As the explosions began at the front of the convoy, a silhouette flashed over the *Tsiklon* and a string of mines chained together plummeted to its deck. One breath, then a hot blast of air hit the bridge, as a second plane, wings tilted, roared over the *Noordendam*.

There were screams from the deck, tiny balls of yellow fire flashed through the bridge house, and a flight of chained mines spun through the air as the plane roared away. Then a hatch cover blew up, boards soaring into the sky, and a great peal of thunder rang deep inside the *Noordendam*, which made her heel over and shudder. It knocked DeHaan backward and, when he scrambled to his knees, Ratter was sitting next to him, looking puzzled. "Can't hear," he said. Then he reached for DeHaan's forehead and pulled out a triangle of broken glass. "Don't want this there, do you?"

DeHaan felt the blood running down his face. "I can do without it."

Ratter's face sparkled in the light and he began to brush at it with his fingertips.

Scheldt used the binnacle to haul himself upright, then took hold of the wheel. "Ahh the hell," he said. DeHaan stood up, wobbled, steadied himself, saw that Scheldt was staring at the compass. "Two eight two?" he said.

"Back to zero nine five, south of east," DeHaan said.

Scheldt shook his head, pulled down on one spoke of the wheel, which spun free until he stopped it. "Gone," he said.

DeHaan looked out through the shattered windows. The *Tsiklon* had vanished, and in the light of the burning trawler he could see smoke pouring from the forward hold, an orange shadow flickering at its center. "Johannes, are we making way?"

Ratter went out to the bridge wing and looked over the side. "Barely." From the radio room: "Are you alive, up there?"

"Yes."

"We are on fire."

"We are."

From their port beam, the blast of a foghorn, then another. It was an icebreaker, its searchlight playing over the deck of the *Noordendam*, then a voice shouted Russian over a loud-hailer. DeHaan went out on the bridge wing, where the AB was staring open-mouthed at the approaching bow of the icebreaker. Which now began to move right as the captain figured out that the *Noordendam*'s steering was gone. Some of the passengers were signaling with their hands, *go around us.* With a final angry blast on the horn, the icebreaker's bow passed the freighter's stern with ten feet to spare.

DeHaan turned to go back to the bridge, then saw Kovacz, staggering up the ladderway. "Damage report," he said. "The engine-room people are done for. That thing blew in the bulkhead, two of the boilers exploded, the third is still working. We have dead and wounded, one of the lifeboats is gone, and I can't find Kees."

"And we've lost our steering," DeHaan said. Up toward number three hold, he saw that Van Dyck had the fire crews working, which meant that steam from the remaining boiler was giving them pressure on the hoses.

What was left of the convoy was moving east. Searchlights on, antiaircraft firing as the Dorniers returned for a second attack. DeHaan looked down at his feet, money, bills he didn't recognize, was blowing all over the place. *The mustached men with the machine guns.* Who had built a small fortress of stacked trunks on the hatch cover of the forward hold.

Kovacz said, "I'm going back to the engine room, Eric. I'll get some help and do whatever I can. Is the rudder broken free?"

"Gear frozen in the steering tunnel," DeHaan said. "I'd bet that's what it is."

"Can't be fixed."

"No."

"So, we're going wherever we're pointed."

"Yes, a point or two west of north."

"Finland."

The battle moved east, slowly, ships and planes fighting hard, until there were only sudden flares of fire on the horizon, distant explosions, a few last searchlights in the sky, then darkness, and the *Noordendam* sailed alone. Opinion on the bridge had it that the small fleet was finished off, sunk, but they were not to know that. And there was a lot to be done. They were getting maybe two knots from the poor broken *Noordendam* but the one boiler, with Kovacz coaxing it along, kept them under way, helped by a following sea. Shtern worked hard, the passengers and crew helped — the dead were moved up to the afterdeck and decently covered, the wounded wrapped in blankets and sheltered from the wind. They searched everywhere for Kees, two missing ABs, and two passengers, but they'd apparently gone overboard during the Dornier attack and nobody had seen them after that.

Then it was quiet on the ship, and dark, because they were running with lights off. DeHaan ordered the scramble nets and gangway lowered and the lifeboats readied, then assigned crews to help the passengers — wounded first, then women and children. When that was done, the officers and crew began to gather their possessions.

0300 hours. At sea.

At DeHaan's direction, Mr. Ali made contact with some Finnish authority — at the port of Helsinki or a naval base, they never really discovered who it was. DeHaan got on the radio and told them they had dead and wounded aboard, and were headed for the islands west of Helsinki, on the south coast. There would be no question of resistance, the passengers and crew of the *Noordendam* would surrender peacefully.

And under what flag did they sail?

Under Dutch flag, as an allied merchant vessel of Britain.

Well then, he was told, the word wasn't precisely *surrender*. True, Finland was at war with Russia, despite their treaty, and true, that made her an ally of Germany. Technically. But, the fact was, Finland was not at war with Britain, and those who set foot on Finnish soil would have to be considered as survivors of maritime incident.

Was Finland, DeHaan wanted to know, at war with Holland?

This produced a longish silence, then the authority cleared its throat and confessed that it didn't know, it would have to look that up, but it didn't think so.

0520 hours. Off the coast of Finland.

In the watery light of the northern dawn, an island.

A dark shape that rose from the sea, low and flat, mostly forest, with quiet surf breaking white on the rocks. It was not unlike the other islands, some close, some distant, but this one lay dead ahead, a mile or so away, this was their island.

DeHaan moved the telegraph to *Done — With — Engines*, the bells acknowledged, and, a moment later, the slow, labored beat stopped, and left only silence. He picked up the speaker tube and said, "Come up to the bridge, Stas. We're going to beach on the rocks, so clear the engine room."

On the bridge, Scheldt was still on watch, standing before the dead helm. "Go and get your things together," DeHaan told him. That left Ratter, and Maria Bromen, who stood close by his side. DeHaan took the *Noordendam*'s log and made a final entry: date, time, and course. "Any idea what it's called?" he asked Ratter.

"Maybe Orslandet," Ratter said, looking at the chart. "But who knows."

"We'll call it that, then," DeHaan said. He wrote it in, added the phrase *Ran aground,* signed the entry, closed the log, and put it in his valise. With the engine off, the *Noordendam* was barely making way. Out on deck, the passengers and crew had gathered in the dawn light, standing amid their baggage, waiting. The *Noordendam,* very close now, caught on a sandbar, but, with the incoming tide, slid off it and headed for the island.

Maria Bromen's hand took his arm as they hit. The bow lifted, the hull scraped up over the rocks and then, with one long grinding note, iron on stone, the NV *Noordendam* canted over and came to rest, and all that remained was the sound of waves, lapping at the shore.

They searched for her, some time later, once the war in that part of the world had quieted down. She was, after all, worth something, there was always money to be made in rights of salvage, and all it would take was the filing of a claim. By that time it was full autumn, when the ice fog hung in the birch forests. There were two Swiss businessmen, a man of uncertain nationality who said he was a Russian émigré, several others, nobody knew who they were. They asked the people who lived along that rockbound coast, fishermen mostly, if they'd seen her, and some said they had, while others just shook their heads or shrugged. But, in the end, they found nothing, and she was never seen again.

ABOUT THE AUTHOR

Alan Furst is widely recognized as the master of the historical spy novel. He is the author of *Night Soldiers, Dark Star, The Polish Officer, The World at Night, Red Gold, Kingdom of Shadows,* and *Blood of Victory.* Born in New York, he has lived for long periods in France, especially Paris. He now lives on Long Island, New York.

Visit the author's website at www.alanfurst.net

Additional copyright information: